# The World's Best Short Stories

## Anthology & Criticism

Volume IX

## Cultures

# THE WORLD'S BEST SERIES

## The World's Best Short Stories

## The World's Best Poetry

Foundation Volumes I - X

## CoreFiche: *World's Best Drama*
Microfiche with companion reference

# The World's Best Short Stories

## Anthology & Criticism

Volume IX

# Cultures

Stories by Allen, Andreyev, Balzac, The Blackfoot, Du Bois, Fogazzaro, Graham, James, Kipling, Lagerlof, Lawson, Mansfield, Montague, Moore, Panchatantra, Tolstoy, Wells

Prepared by
The Editorial Board

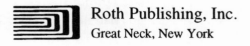 Roth Publishing, Inc.
Great Neck, New York

ISBN 0-89609-315-8
ISBN for 10 Volume Set 0-89609-400-6
Library of Congress Catalog Card Number 89-60440

Manufactured in the U.S.A.

# Contents

# Preface

**The World's Best Short Stories** is designed to give both the serious student and the general reader a large selection and broad range of stories from around the world. Its ten volumes organize the stories into seven reader-friendly groupings:

*Short Story Masters* (Volumes I and II)
*Famous Stories* (Volume III)
*Fables and Tales* (Volume IV)
*Mystery and Detection* (Volume V)
*Horror and Science Fiction* (Volume VI)
*Characters* (Volume VII)
*Places* (Volume VIII)
*Cultures* (Volume IX)

Volume X is a research and reference guide and includes a cumulative index to all the volumes.

The arrangement of the stories suggests the multiple approaches for using these volumes. *Short Story Masters* focuses on the author; it contains stories that demonstrate the development of the short story as a conscious art form. *Famous Stories* is the volume to go to for well-known stories by authors who may or may not themselves be well-known. *Fables and Tales* includes fairy tales and other short non-realistic literature, as well as tales that are ancestors of the short story form. Volumes V and VI contain genre fiction; they act as a kind of counterpart to *Short Story Masters*. Whereas *Masters* places the short story in the tradition of an evolving art, these genre-centered volumes put it at the disposal of the general reader and the popular imagination. *Mystery and Detection* makes the case for a genre that has been continuously popular and critically treated since Poe, while *Horror and Science Fiction* looks at two different styles of fantastic literature--one finding its elements in the supernatural, the other in the superscientific.

The later volumes contain stories that are remarkable for a salient feature. The stories in *Characters* are portrait studies: their primary function is to examine the character of the hero or heroine. *Places* compiles stories that evoke a setting in a way that is memorable and important to the being of the story. Finally, *Cultures* uses ethnicity as its backdrop. It carries stories that are informed by their cultural setting.

The organization, variety, and breadth of **The World's Best Short Stories** makes it a unique anthology collection that can be used for study or read for pleasure.

# Introduction

Included in this anthology are stories from the anonymous authors of ancient societies, closer in chronology to the oral roots of all fiction, and from the renowned literary figures of modern nations. The ancient tales are sometimes more descriptive than narrative, sometimes more bare-bones narrative with little concern for description. They are sometimes more didactic and informational than literary, and in general they do not exploit the conventions of plot and characterization familiar to readers of today's short fiction. The more recent selections are more similar in form to the 20th-century concept of the conventional short story--approximately ten thousand words long, character and tone-oriented rather than plot-heavy, and they possess a thematic, tonal, and structural unity.

Common to all the stories in this volume, however, is an emphasis on culture as represented in literature, on both exploring the universal and revealing the particular. Beliefs, customs, prejudices, traditions, technologies--of Eastern, Western, ancient, and modern peoples--are woven into the prose narratives of the authors represented in this international selection. The anthology is arranged in sections according to nation or geographical area. Beginning each section is a critical introduction to the works and personages of that particular culture's literature. Author biographical information immediately precedes each story.

*Critical and Biographical Material by Irena Spiegel*

# Egypt

Ancient Egypt contributed a number of tales to the cannon of short prose, some dating as early as 4000 B.C. One of the best known, attributed to the sons of King Cheops, is "The Shipwrecked Sailor." The sons, each taking a turn to narrate a tale for their father, conceived of these stories for his entertainment. The story selected for this volume is from the series entitled *The Adventures of Sanehat,* which chronicles Sanehat's flight from and eventual return to Egypt.

There is evidence in this tale that suggests several hypotheses concerning the culture of early Egypt. Sanehat's manner when addressing the King of Egypt, for example, is suggestive of the god-status afforded the ancient rulers by their subjects: "Thou, Good God, Lord of both Lands, Loved of Ra, Favorite of Mentu, the Lord of Thebes, and of Amen, lord of thrones of the lands." The descriptions of King Sehetepabra's death and the elaborate plans for Sanehat's burial attest to the presence of afterlife and divine creator concepts and provide details of how a person of rank and honor was properly put to rest.

## The Adventures Of Sanehat

**Anonymous Author of The Adventures of Sanehat:** The author of this tale remains anonymous. The story is part of a collection of Egyptian prose pieces known as the *The Tales of the Magicians.* The collection is estimated to have been written as early as 2700 B.C. Some scholars date it still earlier at circa 4000 B.C.

THE HEREDITARY PRINCE, royal seal-bearer, confidential friend, judge, keeper of the gate of the foreigners, true and beloved royal acquaintance, the royal follower Sanehat says:

I attended my lord as a follower of the King, of the house of the hereditary princess, the greatly favored, the royal wife, Ankhet-Usertesen, who shares the dwelling of the royal son Amenemhat in Kanefer.

In the thirtieth year, the month Paophi, the seventh day the god entered his horizon, the King Sehotepabra flew up to heaven and joined the sun's disk, the follower of the god met his maker. The palace was silenced, and in mourning, the great gates were closed, the courtiers crouching on the ground, the people in hushed mourning.

His Majesty had sent a great army with the nobles to the land of the Temehu (Lybia), his son and heir, the good god King Usertesen as their leader. Now he was returning, and had brought away living captives and all kinds of cattle without end. The councillors of the palace had sent to the West to let the King know the matter that had come to pass in the inner hall. The messenger was to meet him on the road, and reach him at the time of evening: the matter was urgent. "A hawk had soared with his followers." Thus said he, not to let the army know of it. Even if the royal sons who commanded in that army send a message, he was not to speak to a single one of them. But I was standing near, and heard his voice while he was speaking. I fled far away, my heart beating, my arms failing, trembling had fallen on all my limbs. I turned about in running to seek a place to hide me, and I threw myself between two bushes, to wait while they should pass by. Then I turned me toward the south, not from wishing to come into this place--for I knew not if war was declared--nor even thinking a wish to live after this sovereign, I turned my back to the sycamore, I reached Shi-Seneferu, and rested on the open field. In the morning I went on and overtook a man, who passed by the edge of the road. He asked of me mercy, for he feared me. By the evening I drew near to Kher-ahau (? old Cairo), and I crossed the river on a raft without a rudder. Carried over by the west wind, I passed over to the east to the quarries of Aku and the land of the goddess Herit, mistress of the red mountain (Gebel Ahmar). Then I fled on foot, northward, and reached the walls of the prince, built to repel the Sati. I crouched in a bush for fear of being seen by the guards, changed each day, who watch on the top of the fortress. I took my way by night, and at the lighting of the day I reached Peten, and turned me toward the valley of Kemur. Then thirst hasted me on; I dried up, and my throat narrowed, and I said, "This is the taste of death." When I lifted up my heart and gathered strength, I heard a voice and the lowing of cattle. I saw men of the Sati, and one of them---a friend unto Egypt--knew me. Behold he gave me water and boiled me milk, and I went with him to his camp; they did me good, and one tribe passed me on to another. I passed on to Sun, and reached the land of Adim (Edom).

When I had dwelt there half a year Amu-an-shi--who is the Prince of the Upper Tenu--sent for me and said: "Dwell thou with me that thou mayest hear the speech of Egypt." He said thus for that he knew of my excellence, and had heard tell of my worth, for men of Egypt who were there with him bore witness of me. Behold he said to me: "For what cause hast thou come hither? Has a matter come to pass in the palace? Has the King of the two lands, Sehetepabra, gone to heaven? That which has happened about this is not known." But I answered with concealment, and said: " When I came from the land of the Tamahu, and my desires were there changed in me, if I fled away it was not by reason of remorse that I took the way of a fugitive; I have not failed in my duty, my mouth has not said any bitter words, I have not heard any evil counsel, my name has not come into the mouth of a magistrate. I know not by what I have been led into this land." And Amu-an-shi said: "This is by the will of the god (King of Egypt); for what is a land like if it know not that excellent god, of whom the dread is upon the lands of strangers, as they dread Sekhet in a year of pestilence?" I spake to him, and replied: "Forgive me; his son now enters the palace, and has received the heritage of his father. He is a god who has none like him, and there is none before him. He is a master of wisdom, prudent in his designs, excellent in his decrees, with good-will to him who goes or who comes; he subdued the land of strangers while his father yet lived in his palace, and he rendered account of that which his father destined him to perform. He is a brave man, who verily strikes with his sword; a valiant one, who has not his equal; he springs upon the barbarians, and throws himself on the spoilers; he breaks the horns and weakens the hands, and those whom he smites cannot raise the buckler. He is fearless, and dashes the heads, and none can stand before him. He is swift of foot, to destroy him who flies; and none who flees from him reaches his home. His heart is strong in his time; he is a lion who strikes with the claw, and never has he turned his back. His heart is closed to pity; and when he sees multitudes, he leaves none to live behind him. He is a valiant one who springs in front when he sees resistance; he is a warrior who rejoices when he flies on the barbarians. He seizes the buckler, he rushes forward, he never needs to strike again, he slays and none can turn his lance; and when he takes the bow the barbarians flee from his arms like dogs; for the great goddess has given to him to strike those who know he's not; and if he reaches forth he spares none, and leaves naught behind. He is a friend of great sweetness, who knows how to gain love; his land loves him more than itself, and rejoices in him more than in its own god; men and women run to his call. A king, he has ruled from his birth; he, from his birth, has increased births, a sole being, a divine essence, by whom this land rejoices to be governed. He enlarges the borders of the South; but he covets not the lands of the North: he does not smite the Sati, nor crush the Nemau-shau. If he descends here, let him know thy name, by

4

the homage which thou wilt pay to his majesty. For he refuses not to bless the land which obeys him."

And he replied to me: "Egypt is indeed happy and well settled; behold thou art far from it, but whilst thou art with me I will do good unto thee." And he placed me before his children, he married his eldest daughter to me, and gave me the choice of all his land, even among the best of that which he had on the border of the next land. It is a goodly land, Iaa is its name. There are figs and grapes; there is wine commoner than water; abundant is the honey, many are its olives; and all fruits are upon its trees: there are barley and wheat, and cattle of kinds without end. This was truly a great thing that he granted me, when the prince came to invest me, and establish me as prince of a tribe in the best of his land. I had my continual portion of bread and of wine each day, of cooked meat, of roasted fowl, as well as the wild game which I took, or which was brought to me, beside what my dogs captured. They made me much butter, and prepared milk of all kinds. I passed many years, the children that I had became great, each ruling his tribe. When a messenger went or came to the palace, he turned aside from the way to come to me; for I helped every man. I gave water to the thirsty, I set on his way him who went astray, and I rescued the robbed. The Sati who went far, to strike and turn back the princes of other lands, I ordained their goings; for the Prince of the Tenu for many years appointed me to be general of his soldiers. In every land which I attacked I played the champion, I took the cattle, I led away the vassals, I carried off the slaves, I slew the people, by my sword, my bow, my marches and my good devices. I was excellent to the heart of my prince; he loved me when he knew my power, and set me over his children when he saw the strength of my arms.

A champion of the Tenu came to defy me in my tent: a bold man without equal, for he had vanquished the whole country. He said, "Let Sanehat fight with me "; for he desired to overthrow me; he thought to take my cattle for his tribe. The prince counselled with me. I said: "I know him not. I certainly am not of his degree, I hold me far from his place. Have I ever opened his door, or leaped over his fence? It is some envious jealousy from seeing me; does he think that I am like some steer among the cows, whom the bull overthrows? If this is a wretch who thinks to enrich himself at my cost, not a Bedawi and a Bedawi fit for fight, then let us put the matter to judgment. Verily a true bull loves battle, but a vainglorious bull turns his back for fear of contest; if he has a heart for combat, let him speak what he pleases. Will God forget what he has ordained, and how shall that be known?" I lay down; and when I had rested I strung my bow, I made ready my arrows, I loosened my poniard, I furbished my arms. At dawn the land of the Tenu came together; it had gathered its tribes and called all the neighboring people, it spake of nothing but the fight. Each heart burnt for me, men and women crying out; for each heart was troubled for me, and they said: "Is there another strong one who would fight with him? Behold the adversary has a buckler, a battle-axe, and an armful of javelins." Then I drew him to the attack; I turned aside his arrows, and they struck the ground in vain. One drew near to the other, and he fell on me, and then I shot him. My arrow fastened in his neck, he cried out, and fell on his face: I drove his lance into him, and raised my shout of victory on his back. While all the men of the land rejoiced, I, and his vassals whom he had oppressed, gave thanks unto Mentu. This prince Amu-an-shi, embraced me. Then I carried off his goods and took his cattle, that which he had wished to do to me, I did even so unto him; I seized that which was in his tent, I spoiled his dwelling. As time went on I increased the richness of my treasures and the number of my cattle.

## PETITION TO THE KING OF EGYPT

"Now behold what the god has done for me who trusted in him. Having once fled away, yet now there is a witness of me in the palace. Once having fled away, as a fugitive--now all in the palace give unto me a good name. After that I had been dying of hunger, now I give bread to those around. I had left my land naked, and now I am clothed in fine linen. After having been a wanderer without followers, now I possess many serfs. My house is fine, my land wide, my memory is established in the temple of all the gods. And let this flight obtain thy forgiveness; that I may be appointed in the place; that I may see the place where my heart dwells. How great a thing is it that my body should be embalmed in the land where I was born! To return there is happiness. I have made offering to God to grant me this thing. His heart suffers who has run away unto a strange land. Let him hear the prayer of him who is afar off, that he may revisit the palace of his birth, and the place from which he removed.

"May the King of Egypt be gracious to me that I may live of his favor. And I render my homage to the mistress of the land, who is in his palace; may I hear the news of her children. Thus will my limbs grow young again. Now old age comes, feebleness seizes me, my eyes are heavy, my arms are feeble, my legs will not move, my heart is slow. Death draws nigh to me, soon shall they lead me to the city of eternity. Let me follow the mistress of all (the queen, his former mistress); lo! let her tell me the excellencies of her children; may she bring eternity to me."

Then the majesty of King Kheper-ka-ra, the blessed, spake upon this my desire that I had made to him. His Majesty sent unto me with presents from the King, that he might enlarge the heart of his servant, like unto the province of any strange land; and the royal sons who are in the palace addressed themselves unto me.

## COPY OF THE DECREE WHICH WAS BROUGHT, TO ME WHO SPEAK TO YOU, TO LEAD ME BACK INTO EGYPT.

"The Horus, life of births, lord of the crowns, King of Upper and Lower Egypt, Kheper-ka-ra, son of the Sun, Amen-em-hat, ever living unto eternity. Order for the follower Sanehat. Behold this order of the King is sent to thee to instruct thee of his will.

"Now, although thou hast gone through strange lands from Adim to Tenu, and passed from one country to another at the wish of thy heart--behold, what hast thou done, or what has been done against thee, that is amiss? Moreover, thou reviledst not; but if thy word was denied, thou didst not speak again in the assembly of the nobles, even if thou wast desired. Now, therefore, that thou hast thought on this matter which has come to thy mind, let thy heart not change again; for this thy Heaven (queen), who is in the palace is fixed, she is flourishing, she is enjoying the best in the kingdom of the land, and her children are in the chambers of the palace.

"Leave all the riches that thou hast, and that are with thee, altogether. When thou shalt come into Egypt behold the palace, and when thou shalt enter the palace, bow thy face to the ground before the Great House; thou shalt be chief among the companions. And day by day behold thou growest old; thy vigor is lost, and thou thinkest on the day of burial. Thou shalt see thyself come to the blessed state, they shall give thee the bandages from the hand of Tait, the night of applying the oil of embalming. They shall follow thy funeral, and visit the tomb on the day of burial, which shall be in a gilded case, the head painted with blue, a canopy of cypress wood above thee, and oxen shall draw thee, the singers going before thee, and they shall dance the funeral dance. The weepers crouching at the door of thy tomb shall cry aloud the prayers for offerings: they shall slay victims for thee at the door of thy pit; and thy pyramid shall be carved in white stone, in the company of the royal children. Thus thou shalt not die in a strange land, nor be buried by the Amu; thou shall not be laid in a sheepskin when thou art buried; all people shall beat the earth, and lament on thy body when thou goest to the tomb."

When this order came to me, I was in the midst of my tribe. When it was read unto me, I threw me on the dust, I threw dust in my hair; I went around my tent rejoicing and saying: "How may it be that such a thing is done to the servant, who with a rebellious heart has fled to strange lands? Now with an excellent deliverance, and mercy delivering me from death, thou shalt cause me to end my days in the palace."

### COPY OF THE ANSWER TO THIS ORDER

"The follower Sanehat says: In excellent peace above everything consider of this flight that he made here in his ignorance; Thou, the Good God, Lord of both Lands, Loved of Ra, Favorite of Mentu, the Lord of Thebes, and of Amen, lord of thrones of the lands, of Sebek, Ra, Horus, Hathor, Atmu, and of his fellow-gods, of Sopdu, Neferbiu, Samsetu, Horus, lord of the east, and of the royal uraeus which rules on thy head, of the chief gods of the waters, of Min, Horus of the desert, Urrit, mistress of Punt, Nut, Harnekht , Ra, all the gods of the land of Egypt, and of the isles of the sea. May they give life and peace to thy nostril, may they load thee with their gifts, may they give to thee eternity without end, everlastingness without bound. May the fear of thee be doubled in the lands of the deserts. Mayest thou subdue the circuit of the sun's disk. This is the prayer to his master of the humble servant who is saved from a foreign land.

"O wise King, the wise words which are pronounced in the wisdom of the majesty of the sovereign, thy humble servant fears to tell. It is a great thing to repeat. O great God, like unto Ra in fulfilling that to which he has set his hand, what am I that he should take thought for me? Am I among those whom he regards, and for whom he arranges? Thy majesty is as Horus, and the strength of thy arms extends to all lands.

"Then let his Majesty bring Maki of Adma, Kenti-au-ush of Khenti-ke-shu, and Tenus from the two lands of the Fenkhu; these are the princes who bear witness of me as to all that has passed, out of love for thyself.

Does not Tenu believe that it belongs to thee like thy dogs? Behold this flight that I have made: I did not have it in my heart; it was like the leading of a dream, as a man of Adehi (Delta) sees himself in Abu (Elephantine), as a man of the plain of Egypt who sees himself in the deserts. There was no fear, there was no hastening after me, I did not listen to an evil plot, my name was not heard in the mouth of the magistrate; but my limbs went, my feet wandered, my heart drew me; my god commanded this flight, and drew me on; but I am not stiff-necked. Does a man fear when he sees his own land? Ra spread thy fear over the land, thy terrors in every strange land. Behold me now in the palace, behold me in this place; and lo ! thou art he who is over all the horizon; the sun rises at thy pleasure, the water in the rivers is drunk at thy will, the wind in heaven is breathed at thy saying.

"I who speak to thee shall leave my goods to the generations to follow in this land. And as to this messenger who is come even let thy majesty do as pleaseth him, for one lives by the breath that thou givest. O thou who art beloved of Ra, of Horus, and of Hathor; Mentu, lord of Thebes, desires that thy august nostril should live forever."

I made a feast in Iaa, to pass over my goods to my children. My eldest son was leading my tribe, all my goods passed to him, and I gave him my corn and all my cattle, my fruit, and all my pleasant trees. When I had taken my road to the south, and arrived at the roads of Horus, the officer who was over the garrison sent a messenger to the palace to give notice. His Majesty sent the good overseer of the peasants of the King's domains, and boats laden with presents from the King for the Sati who had come to conduct me to the roads of Horus. I spoke to each one by his name, and I gave the presents to each as was intended. I received and I returned the salutation, and I continued thus until I reached the city of Thetu.

When the land was brightened, and the new day began, four men came with a summons for me; and the four men went to lead me to the palace. I saluted with both my hands on the ground; the royal children stood at the courtyard to conduct me: the courtiers who were to lead me to the hall brought me on the way to the royal chamber.

I found his Majesty on the great throne in the hall of pale gold. Then I threw myself on my belly; this god, in whose presence I was, knew me not. He questioned me graciously, but I was as one seized with blindness, my spirit fainted, my limbs failed, my heart was no longer in my bosom, and I knew the difference between life and death. His Majesty said to one of the companions, "Lift him up, let him speak to me." And his Majesty said, "Behold thou hast come, thou hast trodden the deserts, thou hast played the wanderer. Decay falls on thee, old age has reached thee; it is no small thing that thy body should be embalmed, that the Pedtiu shall not bury thee. Do not, do not, be silent and speechless; tell thy name; is it fear that prevents thee?" I answered in reply, "I fear, what is it that my lord has said that I should answer it? I have not called on me the hand of God, but it is terror in my body, like that which brings sudden death. Now behold I am before thee; thou art life; let thy Majesty do what pleaseth him."

The royal children were brought in, and his Majesty said to the Queen, "Behold thou Sanehat has come as an Amu, whom the Sati have produced."

She cried aloud, and the royal children spake with one voice, saying, before his Majesty, "Verily it is not so, O king, my lord." Said his Majesty, "It is verily he." Then they brought their collars, and their wands, and their sistra in their hands, and displayed them before his Majesty; and they sang--

"May thy hands prosper, O King;

May the ornaments of the Lady of Heaven continue.

May the Goddess Nub give life to thy nostril;

May the mistress of the stars favor thee, when thou sailest south and north.

All wisdom is in the mouth of the Majesty;

Thy uraeus is on thy forehead, thou drivest away the miserable.

Thou art pacified, O Ra, lord of the lands;

They call on thee as on the mistress of all.

Strong is thy horn,

Thou lettest fly thine arrow.

Grant the breath to him who is without it;

Grant good things to this traveller, Samehit the Pedti, born in the land of Egypt,

Who fled away from fear of thee,

And fled this land from thy terrors.

Does not the face grow pale, of him who beholds thy countenance;

Does not the eye fear, which looks upon thee."

Said his Majesty, "Let him not fear, let him be freed from terror. He shall be a Royal Friend amongst the nobles; he shall be put within the circle of the courtiers. Go ye to the chamber of praise to seek wealth for him."

When I went out from the palace, the royal children offered their hands to me; we walked afterward to the Great Gates. I was placed in a house of a king's son, in which were delicate things, a place of coolness, fruits of the granary, treasures of the White House, clothes of the King's guardrobe, frankincense, the finest perfumes of the King and the nobles whom he loves, in every chamber. All the servitors were in their several offices.

Years were removed from my limbs: I was shaved, and polled my locks of hair; the foulness was cast to the desert with the garments of the Nemau-sha. I clothed me in fine linen, and anointed myself with the fine oil of Egypt; I laid me on a bed. I gave up the sand to those who lie on it; the oil of wood to him who would anoint himself therewith. There was given to me the mansion of a lord of serfs, which had belonged to a royal friend. There many excellent things were in its buildings; all its wood was renewed. There were brought to me portions from the palace, thrice and four times each day; beside the gifts of the royal children, always without ceasing. There was built for me a pyramid of stone among the pyramids. The overseer of the architects measured its ground; the chief treasurer wrote it; the sacred masons cut the well the chief of the laborers on the tombs brought the bricks; all things used to make a strong building were there used. There were given to me peasants; there were made for me a garden, and fields in it before my mansion, as is done for the chief royal friend. My statue was inlaid with gold, its girdle of pale gold; his majesty caused it to be made. Such is not done to a man of low degree.

May I be in the favor of the King until the day shall come of my death!

*(This is finished from beginning to end, as was found in the writing.)*

*Translator Unknown*

# India

Before many parts of the world developed a body of writing identifiable as a national or regional literature, India's literary culture thrived with poetry both religious and philosophical in theme. The selections from *The Hitopadesa* included here are illustrations of the eventual incorporation of these concerns into prose forms. These didactic tales' animal characters embody human characteristics, and through a carefully constructed, allegorical mode of presentation, a lesson on trust, friendship, greed or some such basic human concern is delivered to the reader. A work once used to teach the sons of kings proper social conduct, it continues to be popular in India for its instructive program. *The Hitopadesa* is also used in Britain as a text for teaching Sanskrit.

## HINDU TALES FROM THE BOOK OF GOOD COUNSELS:
## The Story of the Vulture, the Cat, and the Birds

**The Hitopadesa, or The Book Of Good Counsels:** The identity of *The Hitopadesa's* author is uncertain, as is its date of composition. It is approximated to have been written circa 1373 A.D. *The Hitopadesa,* also known as *The Book of Good Counsels, or Friendly Advice,* was first translated into English from the original Sanskrit in 1787 by Warren Hastings. It is based on an earlier work, *The Panchatantra,* in which twenty-five of the forty three fables are found. *The Panchatantra* has been traced to Buddhistic sources. Apparent from their earliest writings, the fable was a popular form among the ancient Buddhists. The tales were ascribed to Buddha and their sanctity increased by identifying the best character in each story with Buddha himself in a previous life.

*The Panchatantra* and *The Hitopadesa* were originally intended to serve the sons of kings as manuals of instruction in the principals of conduct. They were later used as guides for kings in domestic and foreign policy. They belong to a class of literature called niti-sastra, or "Science of Political Ethics."

"ON THE BANKS of the Ganges there is a cliff called Vulture-Crag, and thereupon grew a great fig-tree. It was hollow, and within its shelter lived an old Vulture, named Grey-pate, whose hard fortune it was to have lost both eyes and talons. The birds that roosted in the tree made subscriptions from their own store, out of sheer pity for the poor fellow, and by that means he managed to live. One day, when the old birds were gone, Long-ear, the Cat, came there to get a meal of the nestlings; and they, alarmed at perceiving him, set up a chirruping that roused Grey-pate.

'Who comes there?' croaked Grey-pate.

"Now Long-ear, on espying the Vulture, thought himself undone; but as flight was impossible, he resolved to trust his destiny and approach.

'My lord,' said he, 'I have the honor to salute thee.'

'Who is it?' said the Vulture.

'I am a Cat'

'Be off, Cat, or I shall slay thee,' said the Vulture.

'I am ready to die if I deserve death,' answered the Cat; 'but let what I have to say be heard.'

'Wherefore, then, comest thou?' said the Vulture.

'I live,' began Long-ear, 'on the Ganges, bathing, and eating no flesh, practising the moon-penance, like a Bramacharya. The birds that resort thither constantly praise your worship to me as one wholly given to the study of morality, and worthy of all trust; and so I came here to learn law from thee, Sir, who art so deep gone in learning and in years. Dost thou, then, so read the law of strangers as to be ready to slay a guest? What say the books about the householder?--

*'Bar thy door not to the stranger, be he friend or be he foe,*
For the tree will shade the woodman while his axe doth lay it low.'

And if means fail, what there is should be given with kind words, as--

*'Greeting fair, and room to rest in; fire, and water from the well--*
Simple gifts -- are given freely in the house where good men dwell,'--

and without respect of person--

*'Young, or bent with many winters; rich, or poor, whate'er thy guest,*
Honor him for thine own honor--better is he than the best.'

Else comes the rebuke--

*'Pity them that ask thy pity: who art thou to stint thy hoard,*
When the holy moon shines equal on the leper and the lord!'

And that other, too,

*'When thy gate is roughly fastened, and the asker turns away,*
Thence he bears thy good deeds with him, and his sins on thee doth lay

For verily,

*'In the house the husband ruleth, men the Brahmans "master" call;*
Agni is the Twice-born Master--but the guest is lord of all.'

"To these weighty words Grey-pate answered,
'Yes! but cats like meat, and there are young birds here, and therefore I said, go.'
'Sir,' said the Cat (and as he spoke he touched the ground, and then his two ears, and called on Krishna to witness to his words), 'I that have overcome passion, and practised the moon-penance, know the Scriptures; and howsoever they contend, in this primal duty of abstaining from injury they are unanimous. Which of them sayeth not--

*'He who does and thinks no wrong--*
He who suffers, being strong--
He whose harmlessness men know--
Unto Swerga such doth go.'

"And so, winning the old Vulture's confidence, Long-ear, the Cat, entered the hollow tree and lived there. And day after day he stole away some of the nestlings, and brought them down to the hollow to devour. Meantime the parent birds, whose little ones were being eaten, made an inquiry after them in all quarters; and the Cat, discovering this fact, slipped out from the hollow, and made his escape. Afterwards, when the birds came to look closely, they found the bones of their young ones in the hollow of the tree where Grey-pate lived; and the birds at once concluded that their nestlings had been killed and eaten by the old Vulture, whom they accordingly executed. That is my story, and why I warned you against unknown acquaintances."

"Sir," said the Jackal, with some warmth, "on the first day of your encountering the Deer you also were of unknown family and character: how is it, then, that your friendship with him grows daily greater? True, I am only Small-wit, the Jackal, but what says the saw?--

"*In the land where no wise men are, men of little wit are lords;*
And the castor-oil's a tree, where no tree else its shade affords."

The Deer is my friend; condescend, sir, to be my friend also."

'Oh!' broke in the Deer, 'why so much talking? We'll all live together, and be friendly and happy--

'*Foe is friend, and friend is foe,*
As our actions make them so.'

"Very good," said Sharp-sense; "as you will;" and in the morning each started early for his own feeding-ground (returning at night). One day the Jackal drew the Deer aside, and whispered, 'Deer, in one corner of this wood there is a field full of sweet young wheat; come and let me show you.' The Deer accompanied him, and found the field, and afterwards went every day there to eat the green corn, till at last the owner of the ground spied him and set a snare. The Deer came again very shortly, and was caught in it, and (after vainly struggling) exclaimed, 'I am fast in the net, and it will be a net of death to me if no friend comes to rescue me!' Presently Small-wit, the Jackal, who had been lurking near, made his appearance, and standing still, he said to himself, with a chuckle, 'O ho! my scheme bears fruit! When he is cut up, his bones, and gristle, and blood, will fall to my share and make me some beautiful dinners.' The Deer, here catching sight of him, exclaimed with rapture, 'Ah, friend, this is excellent! Do but gnaw these strings, and I shall be at liberty. How charming to realize the saying!--

*'That friend only is the true friend who is near when trouble comes;*
That man only is the brave man who can bear the battle-drums;
Words are wind; deed proveth promise: he who helps at need is kin;
And the leal wife is loving though the husband lose or win.'

And is it not written--

*'Friend and kinsman -- more their meaning than the idle-hearted mind.*
Many a friend can prove unfriendly, many a kinsman less than kind:
He who shares his comrade's portion, be he beggar, be he lord,
Comes as truly, comes as duly, to the battle as the board--
Stands before the king to succor, follows to the pile to sigh--
He is friend, and he is kinsman--less would make the name a lie.'

"Small-wit answered nothing, but betook himself to examining the snare very closely.

'This will certainly hold,' muttered he; then, turning to the Deer, he said, 'Good friend, these strings, you see, are made of sinew, and to-day is a fast-day, so that I cannot possibly bite them. To-morrow morning, if you still desire it, I shall be happy to serve you.'

When he was gone, the Crow, who had missed the Deer upon returning that evening, and had sought for him everywhere, discovered him; and seeing his sad plight, exclaimed--

'How came this about, my friend?'

'This came,' replied the Deer, 'through disregarding a friend's advice.'

'Where is that rascal Small-wit?' asked the Crow.

'He is waiting somewhere by,' said the Deer, 'to taste my flesh.'

'Well' sighed the Crow, 'I warned you; but it is as in the true verse--

*'Stars gleam, lamps flicker, friends foretell of fate;*

The fated sees, knows, hears them -- all too late.'

And then, with a deeper sigh, he exclaimed, 'Ah, traitor Jackal, what an ill deed hast thou done! Smooth-tongued knave -- alas! -- and in the face of the monition too--

*'Absent, flatterers' tongues are daggers--present, softer than the silk;*
Shun them! 'tis a jar of poison hidden under harmless milk;
Shun them when they promise little! Shun them when they promise much!
For, enkindled, charcoal burneth -- cold, it doth defile the touch.'

"When the day broke, the Crow (who was still there) saw the master of the field approaching with his club in his hand.

'Now, friend Deer,' said Sharp-sense on perceiving him, 'do thou cause thyself to seem like one dead: puff thy belly up with wind, stiffen thy legs out, and lie very still. I will make a show of pecking thine eyes out with my beak; and whensoever I utter a croak, then spring to thy feet and betake thee to flight.'

The Deer thereon placed himself exactly as the Crow suggested, and was very soon espied by the husbandman, whose eyes opened with joy at the sight.

'Aha!' said he, 'the fellow has died of himself, and so speaking, he released the Deer from the snare, and proceeded to gather and lay aside his nets. At that instant Sharp-sense uttered a loud croak, and the Deer sprang up and made off. And the club which the husbandman flung after him in a rage struck Small-wit, the Jackal (who was close by), and killed him. Is it not said, indeed?--

*'In years, or moons, or half-moons three,*
Or in three days -- suddenly,
Knaves are shent -- true men go free.'

"Thou seest, then," said Golden-skin, "there can be no friendship between food and feeder."

"I should hardly," replied the Crow, "get a large breakfast out of your worship; but as to that indeed you have nothing to fear from me. I am not often angry, and if I were, you know--

*'Anger comes to noble natures, but leaves there no strife or storm:*
Plunge a lighted torch beneath it, and the ocean grows not warm.'

"Then, also, thou art such a gad-about," objected the King.

"Maybe," answered Light o' Leap; "but I am bent on winning thy friendship, and I will die at thy door of fasting if thou grantest it not. Let us be friends! for

*'Noble hearts are golden vases--close the bond true metals make;*
Easily the smith may weld them, harder far it is to break.
Evil hearts are earthen vessels -- at a touch they crack a-twain,
And what craftsman's ready cunning can unite the shards again?'

And then, too,

*'Good men's friendships may be broken, yet abide they friends at heart;*
Snap the stem of Luxmee's lotus, and its fibres will not part.'

"Good sir," said the King of the Mice, "your conversation is as pleasing as pearl necklets or oil of sandal-wood in hot weather. Be it as you will" -- and thereon King Golden-skin made a treaty with the Crow, and after gratifying him with the best of his store reentered his hole. The Crow returned to his accustomed perch: -- and thenceforward the time passed in mutual presents of food, in polite inquiries, and the most unrestrained talk. One day Light o' Leap thus accosted Golden-skin:--

"This is a poor place, your Majesty, for a Crow to get a living in. I should like to leave it and go elsewhere."

"Whither wouldst thou go?" replied the King; they say,

*'One foot goes, and one foot stands,*
When the wise man leaves his lands'

"And they say, too," answered the Crow,

*'Over-love of home were weakness; wheresoe'er the hero come,*
Stalwart arm and steadfast spirit find or win for him a home.
Little recks the awless lion where his hunting jungles lie--
When he enters it be certain that a royal prey shall die.'

"I know an excellent jungle now."
"Which is that? " asked the Mouse-king.
"In the Nerbudda woods, by Camphor-water," replied the Crow. "There is an old and valued friend of mine lives there -- Slow-toes his name is, a very virtuous Tortoise; he will regale me with fish and good things."
"Why should I stay behind," said Golden-skin, "if thou goest? Take me also."

Accordingly, the two set forth together, enjoying charming converse upon the road. Slow-toes perceived Light o' Leap a long way off, and hastened to do him the guest-rites, extending them to the Mouse upon Light o' Leap's introduction.

"Good Slow-toes," said he, "this is Golden-skin, King of the Mice -- pay all honor to him -- he is burdened with virtues -- a very jewel-mine of kindnesses. I don't know if the Prince of all the Serpents, with his two thousand tongues, could rightly repeat them." So speaking, he told the story of Speckle-neck. Thereupon Slow-toes made a profound obeisance to Golden-skin, and said, "How came your Majesty, may I ask, to retire to an unfrequented forest?"

"I will tell you," said the King. "You must know that in the town of Champaka there is a college for the devotees. Unto this resorted daily a beggar-priest, named Chudakarna whose custom was to place his begging-dish upon the shelf, with such alms in it as he had not eaten, and go to sleep by it; and I, so soon as he slept, used to jump up, and devour the meal. One day a great friend of his, named Vinakarna, also a mendicant, came to visit him; and observed that while conversing, he kept striking the ground with a split cane, to frighten me. 'Why don't you listen?' said

Vinakarna. 'I am listening!' replied the other; 'but this plaguy mouse is always eating the meal out of my begging-dish.' Vinakarna looked at the shelf and remarked, 'However can a mouse jump as high as this? There must be a reason, though there seems none. I guess the cause -- the fellow is well off and fat.' With these words Vinakarna snatched up a shovel, discovered my retreat, and took away all my hoard of provisions. After that I lost strength daily, had scarcely energy enough to get my dinner, and, in fact, crept about so wretchedly, that when Chudakarna saw me he fell to quoting--

'Very feeble folk are poor folk; money lost takes wit away:--
All their doings fail like runnels, wasting through the summer day.'

"Yes!" I thought, "he is right, and so are the sayings--

'Wealth is friends, home, father, brother -- title to respect and fame;
Yea, and wealth is held for wisdom -- that it should be so is shame.'
'Home is empty to the childless; hearts to them who friends deplore:--
Earth unto the idle-minded; and the three worlds to the poor.'

'I can stay here no longer; and to tell my distress to another is out of the question -- altogether out of the question!--

'Say the sages, nine things name not: Age, domestic joys and woes,
Counsel, sickness, shame, alms, penance; neither Poverty disclose.
Better for the proud of spirit, death, than life with losses told;
Fire consents to be extinguished, but submits not to be cold.'

'Verily he was wise, methought also, who wrote--

'As Age doth banish beauty,
As moonlight dies in gloom,
As Slavery's menial duty

Is Honor's certain tomb;
As Hari's name and Hara's
Spoken, charm sin away,
So Poverty can surely
A hundred virtues slay.'

'And as to sustaining myself on another man's bread, that,' I mused, 'would be but a second door of death. Say not the books the same?--

*'Half-known knowledge, present pleasure purchased with a future woe,*
And to taste the salt of service -- greater griefs no man can know.'

'And herein, also--

*'All existence is not equal, and all living is not life;*
Sick men live; and he who, banished, pines for children, home, and wife;
And the craven-hearted eater of another's leavings lives,
And the wretched captive waiting for the word of doom survives;
But they bear an anguished body, and they draw a deadly breath,
And life cometh to them only on the happy day of death.'

Yet, after all these reflections, I was covetous enough to make one more attempt on Chudakarna's meal, and got a blow from the split cane for my pains. 'Just so,' I said to myself, 'the soul and organs of the discontented want keeping in subjection. I must be done with discontent:--

*'Golden gift, serene Contentment! have thou that, and all is had;*
Thrust thy slipper on, and think thee that the earth is leather-clad.'

'All is known, digested, tested; nothing new is left to learn
When the soul, serene, reliant, Hope's delusive dreams can spurn.'

And the sorry task of seeking favor is numbered in the miseries of life--

*'Hast thou never watched, a-waiting till the great man's door un-barred?*
Didst thou never linger parting, saying many a last sad word?
Spak'st thou never word of folly, one light thing thou wouldst recall?
Rare and noble hath thy life been! fair thy fortune did befall!'

'No!' exclaimed I, 'I will do none of these; but, by retiring into the quiet and untrodden forest, I will show my discernment of real good and ill. The holy Books counsel it--

*'True Religion! -- 'tis not blindly prating what the priest may prate,*
But to love, as God hath loved them, all things, be they small or great;
And true bliss is when a sane mind doth a healthy body fill;
And true knowledge is the knowing what is good and what is ill.'

"So came I to the forest, where, by good fortune and this good friend, I met much kindness; and by the same good fortune have encountered you, Sir, whose friendliness is as Heaven to me. Ah! Sir Tortoise,

*'Poisonous though the tree of life be, two fair blossoms grow thereon:*
One, the company of good men; and sweet songs of Poet's, one.'

"King!" said Slow-toes, "your error was getting too much, without giving. Give, says the sage--

*'Give, and it shall swell thy getting; give, and thou shalt safer keep:*
Pierce the tank-wall; or it yieldeth, when the water waxes deep.'

And he is very hard upon money-grubbing: as thus-

*'When the miser hides his treasure in the earth, he doeth well;*
For he opens up a passage that his soul may sink to hell.'

And thus--

*'He whose coins are kept for counting, not to barter nor to give,*
Breathe he like a blacksmith's bellows, yet in truth he doth not live.'

It hath been well written, indeed,

*'Gifts, bestowed with words of kindness, making giving doubly dear:--*
Wisdom, deep, complete, benignant, of all arrogancy clear;
Valor, never yet forgetful of sweet Mercy's pleading prayer;
Wealth, and scorn of wealth to spend it--oh! but these be virtues rare!'

"Frugal one may be," continued Slow-toes; "but not a niggard like the Jackal--

*'The Jackal-knave, that starved his spirit so,*
And died of saving, by a broken bow.'

"Did he, indeed," said Golden-skin; "and how was that?"
"I will tell you," answered Slow-toes:--

## The Story Of The Dead Game And The Jackal

"IN A TOWN called 'Well-to-Dwell' there lived a mighty hunter, whose name was 'Grim-face.' Feeling a desire one day for a little venison, he took his bow, and went into the woods; where he soon killed a deer. As he was carrying the deer home, he came upon a wild boar of prodigious proportions. Laying the deer upon the earth, he fixed and discharged an arrow and struck the boar, which instantly rushed upon him with a roar louder than the last thunder, and ripped the hunter up. He fell like a tree cut by the axe, and lay dead along with the boar, and a snake also, which had been crushed by the feet of the combatants. Not long afterwards, there came that way, in his prowl for food, a Jackal, named 'Howl o' Nights,' and cast eyes on the hunter, the deer, the boar, and the snake lying dead together. 'Aha!' said he, 'what luck! Here's a grand dinner got ready for me! Good fortune can come, I see, as well as ill fortune. Let me think: -- the man will be fine pickings for a month; the deer with the boar will last two more; the snake will do for to-morrow; and, as I am very particularly hungry, I will treat myself now to this bit of meat on the bow-horn.' So saying, he began to gnaw it asunder, and the bow-string slipping, the bow sprang back, and resolved Howl o' Nights into the five elements by death. That is my story," continued Slow-toes, "and its application is for the wise:

> 'Sentences of studied wisdom, nought avail they unapplied;
> Though the blind man hold a lantern, yet his footsteps stray aside.'

The secret of success, indeed, is a free, contented, and yet enterprising mind. How say the books thereon?--

> 'Wouldst thou know whose happy dwelling Fortune entereth unknown?
> His, who careless of her favor, standeth fearless in his own;
> His, who for the vague to-morrow barters not the sure to-day--
> Master of himself, and sternly steadfast to the rightful way:
> Very mindful of past service, valiant, faithful, true of heart--
> Unto such comes Lakshmi smiling -- comes, and will not lightly part.'

'What indeed,' continued Slow-toes, ' is wealth, that we should prize it, or grieve to lose it?--

> 'Be not haughty, being wealthy; droop not, having lost thine all;
> Fate doth play with mortal fortunes as a girl doth toss her ball.'

It is unstable by nature. We are told--

*'Worldly friendships, fair but fleeting, shadows of the clouds at noon*
Women, youth, new corn, and riches -- these be pleasures passing soon.'

And it is idle to be anxious; the Master of Life knows how to sustain it. Is it not written?--

*'For thy bread be not o'er thoughtful -- God for all hath taken thought:*
When the babe is born, the sweet milk to the mother's breast is brought.
He who gave the swan her silver, and the hawk her plumes of pride,
And his purples to the peacock -- He will verily provide.'

'Yes, verily,' said Slow-toes, 'wealth is bad to handle, and better left alone; there is no truer saying than this--

*'Though for good ends, waste not on wealth a minute;*
Mud may be wiped, but wise men plunge not in it.'

Hearing the wisdom of these monitions, Light o' Leap broke out, 'Good Slow-toes! thou art a wise protector of those that come to thee; thy learning comforts my enlightened friend, as elephants drag elephants from the mire.' And thus, on the best of terms, wandering where they pleased for food, the three lived there together.

One day it chanced that a Deer named Dapple-back, who had seen some cause of alarm in the forest, came suddenly upon the three in his flight. Thinking the danger imminent, Slow-toes dropped into the water, King Golden-skin slipped into his hole, and Light o' Leap flew up into the top of a high tree. Thence he looked all round to a great distance, but could discover nothing. So they all came back again, and sat down together. Slow-toes welcomed the Deer.

'Good Deer,' said he, 'may grass and water never fail thee at thy need. Gratify us by residing here, and consider this forest thine own.'

'Indeed,' answered Dapple-back, 'I came hither for your protection, flying from a hunter; and to live with you in friendship is my greatest desire.'

'Then the thing is settled,' observed Golden-skin.

'Yes! yes! ' said Light o' Leap, 'make yourself altogether at home!'

So the Deer, charmed at his reception, ate grass and drank water, and laid himself down in the shade of a Banyan-tree to talk. Who does not know?--

'*Brunettes, and the Banyan's shadow,*
Well-springs, and a brick-built wall,
Are all alike cool in the summer,
And warm in the winter -- all.'

'What made thee alarmed, friend Deer?' began Slow-toes. 'Do hunters ever come to this unfrequented forest?'

'I have heard,' replied Dapple-back, 'that the Prince of the Kalinga country, Rukmangada, is coming here. He is even now encamped on the Cheenab River, on his march to subjugate the borders; and the hunters have been heard to say that he will halt to-morrow by this very lake of "Camphor-water." Don't you think, as it is dangerous to stay, that we ought to resolve on something?'

'I shall certainly go to another pool,' exclaimed Slow-toes.

'It would be better,' answered the Crow and Deer together.

'Yes!' remarked the King of the Mice, after a minute's thought; 'but how is Slow-toes to get across the country in time? Animals like our amphibious host are best in the water; on land he might suffer from his own design, like the merchant's son--

'*The merchant's son laid plans for gains,*
And saw his wife kissed for his pains.'

'How came that about?' asked all.

"I'll tell you," answered Golden-skin.

*Translated by Sir Edwin Arnold*

## *Pre-Colonial America* ━━━━━━━━━━━

Native American written literature has its origin in a long-standing oral practice that held cadence and tone of voice as significant as form and plot. Tribal beliefs and customs are presented from a perspective distinct from that of writers of European descent who attempted to draw prose portraits of Native American life. This story, from the Blackfoot tribe, offers an explanation for the formation of Ursa Major in the shape of a bear. Nature, wildlife, and human culture are revealed as interactive agents rather than entities exclusive unto themselves.

## The Seven Stars

**The Blackfoot Native Americans:** This tale is believed to have been written before 1800. Just prior to this time the Blackfoot moved into the northern Great Plains area, acquired horses from southern tribes, and developed a nomadic plains culture that was largely dependent on the buffalo for survival.

In the early 19th century, the Blackfoot are known to have occupied a large range of land from the upper Missouri and North Saskatchewan rivers to the Rockies. Their name is derived from their moccasins, which they died black. The three main tribes comprising the Blackfoot were the Siksika, the Piegan, and the Kainah.

ONCE THERE WAS a young woman with many suitors; but she refused to marry. She had seven brothers and one little sister. Their mother had been dead many years and they had no relatives, but lived alone with their father. Every day the six brothers went out hunting with their father. It seems that the young woman had a bear for her lover, and, as she did not want any one to know this, she would meet him when she went out after wood. She always went after wood as soon as her father and brothers went out to hunt, leaving her little sister alone in the lodge. As soon as she was out of sight in the brush, she would run to the place where the bear lived.

As the little sister grew older, she began to be curious as to why her older sister spent so much time getting wood. So one day she followed her. She saw the young woman meet the bear and saw that they were lovers. When she found this out, she ran home as quickly as she could, and when her father returned she told him what she had seen. When he heard the story he said, "So, my elder daughter has a bear for a husband. Now I know why she does not want to marry." Then he went about the camp, telling all his people that they had a bear for a brother-in-law, and that he wished all the men to go out with him to kill this bear. So they went, found the bear, and killed him.

When the young woman found out what had been done, and that her little sister had told on her, she was very angry. She scolded her little sister vigorously, then ordered her to go out to the dead bear, and bring some flesh from his paws. The little sister began to cry, and said she was afraid to go out of the lodge, because a dog with young pups had tried to bite her. "Oh, do not be afraid!" said the young woman. "I will paint your face like that of a bear, with black marks across the eyes and at the corners of the mouth; then no one will touch you." So she went for the meat. Now the older sister was a powerful medicine-woman. She could tan hides in a new way. She could take up a hide, strike it four times with her skin-scraper and it would be tanned.

The little sister had a younger brother that she carried on her back. As their mother was dead, she took care of him. One day the little sister said to the older sister, "Now you be a bear and we will go out into the brush to play." The older sister agreed to this, but said, "Little sister, you must not touch me over my kidneys." So the big sister acted as a bear, and they played in the brush. While they were playing, the little sister forgot what she had been told, and touched her older sister in the wrong place. At once she turned into a real bear, ran into the camp, and killed many of the people. After she had killed a large number, she turned back into her former self. Now, when the little sister saw the older run away as a real bear, she became frightened, took up her little brother, and ran into their lodge. Here they waited; badly frightened, but were very glad to see their older sister return after a time as her true self.

Now the older brothers were out hunting, as usual. As the little sister was going down for water with her little brother on her back, she met her six brothers returning. The brothers noted how quiet and deserted the camp seemed to be. So they said to their little sister, "Where are all our people?" Then the little sister explained how she and her sister were playing, when the elder turned into a bear, ran through the camp, and killed many people. She told her brothers that they were in great danger, as their sister would surely kill them when they came home. So the six brothers decided to go into the brush. One of them had killed a jackrabbit. He said to the little sister, "You take this rabbit home with you. When it is dark, we will scatter prickly-pears all around the lodge, except in one place. When you come out, you must look for that place, and pass through."

When the little sister came back to the lodge, the elder sister said, "Where have you been all this time?" "Oh, my little brother mussed himself and I had to clean him," replied the little sister. "Where did you get that rabbit?" she asked. "I killed it with a sharp stick," said the little sister. "That is a lie. Let me see you do it," said the older sister. Then the little sister took up a stick lying near her, threw it at the rabbit, and it stuck in the wound in his body. "Well, all right," said the elder sister. Then the little sister dressed the rabbit and cooked it. She offered some of it to her older sister, but it was refused: so the little sister and her brother ate all of it. When the elder sister saw that the rabbit had all been eaten, she became very angry, and said, "Now I have a mind to kill you." So the little sister arose quickly, took her little brother on her back, and said, "I am going out to look for wood." As she went out, she followed the narrow trail through the prickly-pears and met her six brothers in the brush. Then they decided to leave the country, and started off as fast as they could go.

The older sister, being a powerful medicine-woman, knew at once what they were doing. She became very angry and turned herself into a bear to pursue them. Soon she was about to overtake them, when one of the boys tried his power. He took a little water in the hollow of his hand and sprinkled it around. At once it became a great lake between them and the bear. Then the children hurried on while the bear went around. After a while the bear caught up with them again, when another brother threw a porcupine-tail [a hairbrush] on the ground. This became a great thicket; but the bear forced its way through, and again overtook the children. This time they all climbed a high tree. The bear came to the foot of the tree, and, looking up at them, said, "Now I shall kill you all." So she took a stick from the ground, threw it into the tree and knocked down four of the brothers. While she was doing this, a little bird flew around the tree, calling out to the children, "Shoot her in the head! Shoot her in the head!" Then one of the boys shot an arrow into the head of the bear, and at once she fell dead. Then they came down from the tree.

Now the four brothers were dead. The little brother took an arrow, shot it straight up into the air, and when it fell one of the dead brothers came to life. This he repeated until all were alive again. Then they held a council, and said to each other, "Where shall we go? Our people have all been killed, and we are a long way from home. We have no relatives living in the world." Finally they decided that they preferred to live in the sky. Then the little brother said, "Shut your eyes." As they did so, they all went up. Now you can see them every night. The little brother is the North Star (?). The six brothers and the little sister are seen in the Great Dipper. The little sister and the eldest brother are in a line with the North Star, the little sister being nearest it because she used to carry her little brother on her back. The other brothers are arranged in order of their age, beginning with the eldest. This is how the seven stars [Ursa major] came to be.

*Translated by C. Wissler*

# *Japan*

The bulk of poetry and prose produced during centuries of Japanese isolation did not become accessible to American and European scholars until the 20th century. *The Tale of Genji,* from which the present excerpt was selected, is an epic of more than one thousand pages composed by Murasaki Shikibu, a courtesan of the Heian Period (794-1185). Lady Murasaki's position in the imperial court allowed her an observational access not available to those unaffiliated with the offices of royalty. She had immediate knowledge of the social dynamics at work among the Emperor and his wives and mistresses, the Emperor and his children, and among the wives and children themselves. These relationships are examined, as are the ideas of poetry as a mode of interpersonal communication, tradition, and honor, and the personal consequences of adhering too strictly to or rejecting too curtly long-established prescriptions for private and social behavior.

## The Chamber Of Kiri
### *Murasaki Shikibu*

**Murasaki Shikibu:** The exact birth and death dates of Murasaki Shikibu are unknown, though there is some indication that she may have died in 1014 at the age of 37. As an attendant to Empress Akiko, Lady Murasaki had access to the highest reaches of court society. Her diary provides some glimpses into her own life while *The Tale of Genji* examines the emotional intrigues of her courtly characters. Lady Murasaki's insights into her environment have been compared to Marcel Proust's observations on French society at the end of the 1800's.

IN THE REIGN of a certain Emperor, whose name is unknown to us, there was, among the Niogo and Koyi of the Imperial Court, one who, though she was not of high birth, enjoyed the full tide of Royal favor. Hence her superiors, each one of whom had always been thinking -- "I shall be the *one*," gazed upon her disdainfully with malignant eyes, and her equals and inferiors were more indignant still.

Such being the state of affairs, the anxiety which she had to endure was great and constant, and this was probably the reason why her health was at last so much affected, that she was often compelled to absent herself from Court, and to retire to the residence of her mother.

Her father, who was a Dainagon, was dead; but her mother, being a woman of good sense, gave her every possible guidance in the due performance of Court ceremony, so that in this respect she seemed but little different from those whose fathers and mothers were still alive to bring them before public notice, yet, nevertheless, her friendliness made her oftentimes feel very diffident from the want of any patron of influence.

These circumstances, however, only tended to make the favor shown to her by the Emperor wax warmer and warmer, and it was even shown to such an extent as to become a warning to after-generations. There had been instances in China in which favoritism such as this had caused national disturbance and disaster; and thus the matter became a subject of public animadversion, and it seemed not improbable that people would begin to allude even to the example of Yo-ki-hi.

In due course, and in consequence, we may suppose, of the divine blessing on the sincerity of their affection, a jewel of a little prince was born to her. The first prince who had been born to the Emperor was the child of Koki-den-Niogo, the daughter of the Udaijin (a great officer of State). Not only was he first in point of age, but his influence on his mother's side was so great that public opinion had almost unanimously fixed upon him as heir-apparent. Of this the Emperor was fully conscious, and he only regarded the new-born child with that affection which one lavishes on a domestic favorite. Nevertheless, the mother of the first prince had, not unnaturally, a foreboding that unless matters were managed adroitly her child might be superseded by the younger one. She, we may observe, had been established at Court before any other lady, and had more children than one. The Emperor, therefore, was obliged to treat her with due respect, and reproaches from her always affected him more keenly than those of any others.

To return to her rival. Her constitution was extremely delicate, as we have seen already, and she was surrounded by those who would fain lay bare, so to say, her hidden scars. Her apartments in the palace were Kiri-Tsubo (the chamber of Kiri); so called from the trees that were planted around. In visiting her there the Emperor had to pass before several other chambers, whose occupants universally chafed when they saw it. And again, when it was her turn to attend upon the Emperor, it often happened that they played off mischievous pranks upon her, at different points in the corridor, which leads to the Imperial quarters. Sometimes they would soil the skirts of her attendants, sometimes they would shut against her the door of the covered portico, where no other passage existed; and thus, in every possible way, they one and all combined to annoy her.

The Emperor at length became aware of this, and gave her, for her special chamber, another apartment, which was in the Kôrô-Den, and which was quite close to those in which he himself resided. It had been originally occupied by another lady who was now removed, and thus fresh resentment was aroused.

When the young Prince was three years old the Hakamagi took place. It was celebrated with a pomp scarcely inferior to that which adorned the investiture of the first Prince. In fact, all available treasures were exhausted on the occasion. And again the public manifested its disapprobation. In the summer of the same year the Kiri-Tsubo-Kôyi became ill, and wished to retire from the palace. The Emperor, however, who was accustomed to see her indisposed, strove to induce her to remain. But her illness increased day by day; and she had drooped and pined away until she was now but a shadow of her former self. She made scarcely any response to the affectionate words and expressions of tenderness which her Royal lover caressingly bestowed upon her. Her eyes were half-closed: she lay like a fading flower in the last stage of exhaustion, and she became so much enfeebled that her mother appeared before the Emperor and entreated with tears that she might be allowed to leave. Distracted by his vain endeavors to devise means to aid her, the Emperor at length ordered a Te-gruma to be in readiness to convey her to her own home, but even then he went to her apartment and cried despairingly: "Did not we vow that we would neither of us be either before or after the other even in travelling the last long journey of life? And can you find it in your heart to leave me now?" Sadly and tenderly looking up, she thus replied, with almost failing breath:--

*"Since my departure for this dark journey,*
Makes you so sad and lonely,
Fain would I stay though weak and weary,
And live for your sake only!"

"Had I but known this before----"

She appeared to have much more to say, but was too weak to continue. Overpowered with grief, the Emperor at one moment would fain accompany her himself, and at another moment would have her remain to the end where she then was.

At the last, her departure was hurried, because the exorcism for the sick had been appointed to take place on that evening at her home, and she went. The child Prince, however, had been left in the Palace, as his mother wished, even at that time, to make her withdrawal as privately as possible, so as to avoid any invidious observations on the part of her rivals. To the Emperor the night now became black with gloom. He sent messenger after messenger to make inquiries, and could not await their return with patience. Midnight came, and with it the sound of lamentation. The messenger, who could do nothing else, hurried back with the sad tidings of the truth. From that moment the mind of the Emperor was darkened, and he confined himself to his private apartments.

He would still have kept with himself the young Prince now motherless, but there was no precedent for this, and it was arranged that he should be sent to his grandmother for the mourning. The child, who understood nothing, looked with amazement at the sad countenances of the Emperor, and of those around him. All separations have their sting, but sharp indeed was the sting in a case like this.

Now the funeral took place. The weeping and wailing mother, who might have longed to mingle in the same flames, entered a carriage, accompanied by female mourners. The procession arrived at the cemetery of Otagi, and the solemn rites commenced. What were then the thoughts of the desolate mother? The image of her dead daughter was still vividly present to her -- still seemed animated with life. She must see her remains become ashes to convince herself that she was really dead. During the ceremony, an Imperial messenger came from the Palace, and invested the dead with the title of Sammi. The letters patent were read, and listened to in solemn silence. The Emperor conferred this title now in regret that during her lifetime he had not even promoted her position from a Kôyi to a Niogo, and wishing at this last moment to raise her title at least one step higher. Once more several tokens of disapprobation were manifested against the proceeding. But, in other respects, the beauty of the departed, and her gracious bearing, which had ever commanded admiration, made people begin to think of her with sympathy. It was the excess of the Emperor's favor which had created so many detractors during her lifetime; but now even rivals felt pity for her; and if any did not, it was in the

Koki-den. "When one is no more, the memory becomes so dear," may be an illustration of a case such as this.

Some days passed, and due requiem services were carefully performed. The Emperor was still plunged in thought, and no society had attractions for him. His constant consolation was to send messengers to the grandmother of the child, and to make inquiries after them. It was now autumn, and the evening winds blew chill and cold. The Emperor -- who, when he saw the first Prince, could not refrain from thinking of the younger one -- became more thoughtful than ever: and, on this evening, he sent Yugei-no Miôbu to repeat his inquiries. She went as the new moon just rose, and the Emperor stood and contemplated from his veranda the prospect spread before him. At such moments he had usually been surrounded by a few chosen friends, one of whom was almost invariably his lost love. Now she was no more. The thrilling notes of her music, the touching strains of her melodies, stole over him in his dark and dreary reverie.

The Miôbu arrived at her destination; and, as she drove in, a sense of sadness seized upon her.

The owner of the house had long been a widow; but the residence, in former times, had been made beautiful for the pleasure of her only daughter. Now, bereaved of this daughter, she dwelt alone; and the grounds were overgrown with weeds, which here and there lay prostrated by the violence of the winds; while over them, fair as elsewhere, gleamed the mild lustre of the impartial moon. The Miôbu entered, and was led into a front room in the southern part of the building. At first the hostess and the messenger were equally at a loss for words. At length the silence was broken by the hostess, who said:--

"Already have I felt that I have lived too long, but doubly do I feel it now that I am visited by such a messenger as you." Here she paused, and seemed unable to contend with her emotion.

"When Naishi-no-Ske returned from you," said the Miôbu, "she reported to the Emperor that when she saw you, face to face, her sympathy for you was irresistible. I, too, see now how true it is!" A moment's hesitation, and she proceeded to deliver the Imperial message:--

"The Emperor commanded me to say that for some time he had wandered in his fancy, and imagined he was but in a dream; and that, though he was now more tranquil, he could not find that it was only a dream. Again, that there is no one who can really sympathize with him;

and he hopes that you will come to the Palace, and talk with him. His Majesty said also that the absence of the Prince made him anxious, and that he is desirous that you should speedily make up your mind. In giving me this message, he did not speak with readiness. He seemed to fear to be considered unmanly, and strove to exercise reserve. I could not help experiencing sympathy with him, and hurried away here, almost fearing that, perhaps, I had not quite caught his full meaning."

So saying, she presented to her a letter from the Emperor. The lady's sight was dim and indistinct. Taking it, therefore, to the lamp, she said, "Perhaps the light will help me to decipher," and then read as follows, much in unison with the oral message: "I thought that time only would assuage my grief; but time only brings before me more vividly my recollection of the lost one. Yet, it is inevitable. How is my boy? Of him, too, I am always thinking. Time once was when we both hoped to bring him up together. May he still be to you a memento of his mother! "

Such was the brief outline of the letter, and it contained the following:--

*"The sound of the wind is dull and drear*
Across Miyagi's dewy lea,
And makes me mourn for the motherless deer
That sleeps beneath the Hagi tree."

She put gently the letter aside, and said, "Life and the world are irksome to me; and you can see, then, how reluctantly I should present myself at the Palace. I cannot go myself, though it is painful to me to seem to neglect the honored command. As for the little Prince, I know not why he thought of it, but he seems quite willing to go. This is very natural. Please to inform his Majesty that this is our position. Very possibly, when one remembers the birth of the young Prince, it would not be well for him to spend too much of his time as he does now."

Then she wrote quickly a short answer, and handed it to the Miôbu. At this time her grandson was sleeping soundly.

"I should like to see the boy awake, and to tell the Emperor all about him, but he will already be impatiently awaiting my return," said the messenger. And she prepared to depart.

"It would be a relief to me to tell you how a mother laments over her departed child. Visit me, then, sometimes, if you can, as a friend, when you are not engaged or pressed for time. Formerly, when you came here, your visit was ever glad and welcome; now I see in you the messenger of woe. More and more my life seems aimless to me. From the time of my child's birth, her father always looked forward to her being presented at Court, and when dying he repeatedly enjoined me to carry out that wish. You know that my daughter had no patron to watch over her, and I well knew how difficult would be her position among her fellow-maidens. Yet, I did not disobey her father's request, and she went to Court. There the Emperor showed her a kindness beyond our hopes. For the sake of that kindness she uncomplainingly endured all the cruel taunts of envious companions. But their envy ever deepening, and her troubles ever increasing, at last she passed away, worn out, as it were, with care. When I think of the matter in that light, the kindest favors seem to me fraught with misfortune. Ah! that the blind affection of a mother should make me talk in this way!"

"The thoughts of his Majesty may be even as your own," said the Miôbu. "Often when he alluded to his overpowering affection for her, he said that perhaps all this might have been because their love was destined not to last long. And that though he ever strove not to injure any subject, yet for Kiri-Tsubo, and for her alone he had sometimes caused the ill-will of others; that when all this has been done, she was no more! All this he told me in deep gloom, and added that it made him ponder on their previous existence."

The night was now far advanced, and again the Miôbu rose to take leave. The moon was sailing down westward and the cool breeze was waving the herbage to and fro, in which numerous *mushi* were plaintively singing. The messenger, being still somehow unready to start, hummed---

*"Fain would one weep the whole night long,*
As weeps the Sudu-Mushi's song,
Who chants her melancholy lay,
Till night and darkness pass away."

As she still lingered, the lady took up the refrain--

*"To the heath where the Sudu-Mushi sings,*
From beyond the clouds one comes from on high

And more dews on the grass around she flings,

And adds her own, to the night wind's sigh."

A Court dress and a set of beautiful ornamental hairpins, which had belonged to Kiri-Tsubo, were presented to the Miôbu by her hostess, who thought that these things, which her daughter had left to be available on such occasions, would be a more suitable gift, under present circumstances, than any other.

On the return of the Miôbu she found that the Emperor had not yet retired to rest. He was really awaiting her return, but was apparently engaged in admiring the Tsubo-Senzai -- or stands of flowers -- which were placed in front of the palaces, and in which the flowers were in full bloom. With him were four or five ladies, his intimate friends, with whom he was conversing. In these days his favorite topic of conversation was the "Long Regret." Nothing pleased him more than to gaze upon the picture of that poem, which had been painted by Prince Teishi-In, or to talk about the native poems on the same subject, which had been composed, at the Royal command, by Ise, the poetess, and by Tsurayuki, the poet. And it was in this way that he was engaged on this particular evening.

To him the Miôbu now went immediately, and she faithfully reported to him all that she had seen, and she gave to him also the answer to his letter. That letter stated that the mother of Kiri-Tsubo felt honored by his gracious inquiries, and that she was so truly grateful that she scarcely knew how to express herself. She proceeded to say that his condescension made her feel at liberty to offer to him the following:--

*"Since now no fostering love is found,*

And the Hagi tree is dead and sere,

The motherless deer lies on the ground,

Helpless and weak, no shelter near."

The Emperor strove in vain to repress his own emotion; and old memories, dating from the time when he first saw his favorite, rose up before him fast and thick. "How precious has been each moment to me, but yet what a long time has elapsed since then," thought he, and he said to the Miôbu, "How often have I, too, desired to see the daughter of the

Dainagon in such a position as her father would have desired to see her. 'Tis in vain to speak of that now!"

A pause, and he continued, "The child, however, may survive, and fortune may have some boon in store for him;  and his grandmother's prayer should rather be for long life."

The presents were then shown to him. "Ah," thought he, "could they be the souvenirs sent by the once lost love," as he murmured--

*"Oh, could I find some wizard sprite,*
To bear my words to her I love,
Beyond the shades of envious night,
To where she dwells in realms above!"

Now the picture of beautiful Yô-ki-hi, however skilful the painter may have been, is after all only a picture. It lacks life and animation. Her features may have been worthily compared to the lotus and to the willow of the Imperial gardens, but the style after all was Chinese, and to the Emperor his lost love was all in all, nor, in his eyes, was any other object comparable to her. Who doubts that they, too, had vowed to unite wings, and intertwine branches! But to what end? The murmur of winds, the music of insects, now only served to cause him melancholy.

In the meantime, in the Koki-Den was heard the sound of music. She who dwelt there, and who had not now for a long time been with the Emperor, was heedlessly protracting her strains until this late hour of the evening.

How painfully must these have sounded to the Emperor!

*"Moonlight is gone, and darkness reigns*
E'en in the realms 'above the clouds,'
Ah! how can light, or tranquil peace,
Shine o'er that lone and lowly home!"

Thus thought the Emperor, and he did not retire until "the lamps were trimmed to the end!" The sound of the night watch of the right guard was now heard. It was five o'clock in the morning. So, to avoid notice, he withdrew to his bedroom, but calm slumber hardly visited his eyes. This now became a common occurrence.

When he rose in the morning he would reflect on the time gone by when "they knew not even that the casement was bright." But now, too, he would neglect "Morning Court." His appetite failed him. The delicacies of the so-called "great table" had no temptation for him. Men pitied him much. "There must have been some divine mystery that predetermined the course of their love," said they, "for in matters in which she is concerned he is powerless to reason, and wisdom deserts him. The welfare of the State ceases to interest him." And now people actually began to quote instances that had occurred in a foreign Court.

Weeks and months had elapsed, and the son of Kiri-Tsubo was again at the Palace. In the spring of the following year the first Prince was proclaimed heir-apparent to the throne. Had the Emperor consulted his private feelings, he would have substituted the younger Prince for the elder one. But this was not possible, and, especially for this reason: -- There was no influential party to support him, and, moreover, public opinion would also have been strongly opposed to such measure, which, if effected by arbitrary power, would have become a source of danger. The Emperor, therefore, betrayed no such desire, and repressed all outward appearance of it. And now the public expressed its satisfaction at the self-restraint of the Emperor, and the mother of the first Prince felt at ease.

In this year, the mother of Kiri-Tsubo departed this life. She may not improbably have longed to follow her daughter at an earlier period; and the only regret to which she gave utterance, was that she was forced to leave her grandson, whom she had so tenderly loved.

From this time the young Prince took up his residence in the Imperial palace; and next year, at the age of seven, he began to learn to read and write under the personal superintendence of the Emperor. He now began to take him into the private apartments, among others, of the Koki-den, saying, "The mother is gone! now at least, let the child be received with better feeling." And if even stony-hearted warriors, or bitter enemies, if any such were, smiled when they saw the boy, the mother of the heir-apparent, too, could not entirely exclude him from her sympathies. This lady had two daughters, and they found in their half-brother a pleasant playmate. Every one was pleased to greet him, and there was already a winning coquetry in his manners, which amused people, and made them like to play with him. We need not allude to his studies in detail, but on musical instruments, such as the flute and the *koto*, he also showed great proficiency.

About this time there arrived an embassy from Corea, and among them was an excellent physiognomist. When the Emperor heard of this, he wished to have the Prince examined by him. It was, however, contrary to the warnings of the Emperor Wuda, to call in foreigners to the Palace. The Prince was, therefore, disguised as the son of one Udaiben, his instructor, with whom he was sent to the Kôro-Kwan, where foreign embassies are entertained.

When the physiognomist saw him, he was amazed, and, turning his own head from side to side, seemed at first to be unable to comprehend the lines of his features, and then said, "His physiognomy argues that he might ascend to the highest position in the State, but, in that case, his reign will be disturbed, and many misfortunes will ensue. If, however, his position should only be that of a great personage in the country, his fortune may be different."

This Udaiben was a clever scholar. He had with the Corean pleasant conversations, and they also interchanged with one another some Chinese poems, in one of which the Corean said what great pleasure it had given him to have seen before his departure, which was now imminent, a youth of such remarkable promise. The Coreans made some valuable presents to the Prince, who had also composed a few lines, and to them, too, many costly gifts were offered from the Imperial treasures.

In spite of all the precautions which were taken to keep all his rigidly secret, it did, somehow or other, become known to others, and among those to the Udaijin, who, not unnaturally, viewed it with suspicion, and began to entertain doubts of the Emperor's intentions. The latter, however, acted with great prudence. It must be remembered that, as yet, he had not even created the boy a Royal Prince. He now sent for a native physiognomist, who approved of his delay in doing so, and whose observations to this effect, the Emperor did not receive unfavorably. He wisely thought to be a Royal Prince, without having any influential support on the mother's side, would be of no real advantage to his son. Moreover, his own tenure of power seemed precarious, and he, therefore, thought it better for his own dynasty, as well as for the Prince, to keep him in a private station, and to constitute him an outside supporter of the Royal cause.

And now he took more and more pains with his education in different branches of learning; and the more the boy studied, the more talent did he evince -- talent almost too great for one destined to remain in a private station. Nevertheless, as we have said, suspicions would have been aroused had Royal rank been conferred upon him, and the astrologists, whom also the Emperor consulted, having expressed their disapproval of such a measure, the Emperor finally made up his mind to create a new family. To this family he assigned the name of Gen, and he made the young Prince the founder of it.

Some time had now elapsed since the death of the Emperor's favorite, but he was still often haunted by her image. Ladies were introduced into his presence, in order, if possible, to divert his attention, but without success.

There was, however, living at this time a young Princess, the fourth child of a late Emperor. She had great promise of beauty, and was guarded with jealous care by her mother, the Empress-Dowager. The Naishi-no-Ske, who had been at the Court from the time of the said Emperor, was intimately acquainted with the Empress and familiar with the Princess, her daughter, from her very childhood. This person now recommended the Emperor to see the Princess, because her features closely resembled those of Kiri-Tsubo.

"I have now fulfilled," she said, "the duties of my office under three reigns, and, as yet, I have seen but one person who resembles the departed. The daughter of the Empress-Dowager does resemble her, and she is singularly beautiful."

"There may be some truth in this," thought the Emperor, and he began to regard her with awakening interest.

This was related to the Empress-Dowager. She, however, gave no encouragement whatever to the idea. "How terrible!" she said. "Do we not remember the cruel harshness of the mother of the Heir-apparent, which hastened the fate of Kiri-Tsubo!"

While thus discountenancing any intimacy between her daughter and the Emperor, she too died, and the princess was left parentless. The Emperor acted with great kindness, and intimated his wish to regard her as his own daughter. In consequence of this her guardian, and her brother, Prince Hiob-Kio, considering that life at Court would be better for her and more attractive for her than the quiet of her own home, obtained for her an introduction there.

She was styled the Princess Fuji-Tsubo (of the Chamber of Wistaria), from the name of the chamber which was assigned to her.

There was, indeed, both in features and manners a strange resemblance between her and Kiri-Tsubo. The rivals of the latter constantly caused pain both to herself and to the Emperor; but the illustrious birth of the Princess prevented any one from ever daring to humiliate her, and she uniformly maintained the dignity of her position. And to her alas! the Emperor's thoughts were now gradually drawn, though he could not yet be said to have forgotten Kiri-Tsubo.

The young Prince, whom we now style Genji (the Gen), was still with the Emperor, and passed his time pleasantly enough in visiting the various apartments where the inmates of the palace resided. He found the companionship of all of them sufficiently agreeable; but beside the many who were now of maturer years, there was one who was still in the bloom of her youthful beauty, and who more particularly caught his fancy, the Princess Wistaria. He had no recollection of his mother, but he had been told by Naishi-no-Ske that this lady was exceedingly like her; and for this reason he often yearned to see her and to be with her.

The Emperor showed equal affection to both of them, and he sometimes told her that he hoped she would not treat the boy with coldness or think him forward. He said that his affection for the one made him feel the same for the other too, and that the mutual resemblance of her own and of his mother's face easily accounted for Genji's partiality to her. And thus as a result of this generous feeling on the part of the Emperor, a warmer tinge was gradually imparted both to the boyish humor and to the awakening sentiment of the young Prince.

The mother of the Heir-apparent was not unnaturally averse to the Princess, and this revived her old antipathy to Genji also. The beauty of her son, the Heir-apparent, though remarkable, could not be compared to his, and so bright and radiant was his face that Genji was called by the public Hikal-Genji-no-Kimi (the shining Prince Gen).

When he attained the age of twelve the ceremony of Gembuk (or crowning) took place. This was also performed with all possible magnificence. Various *fêtes*, which were to take place in public, were arranged by special order by responsible officers of the Household. The Royal chair was placed in the Eastern wing of the Seiriô-Den, where the Emperor dwells, and in front of it were the seats of the hero of the ceremony and of the Sadaijin, who was to crown him and to regulate the ceremonial.

About ten o'clock in the forenoon Genji appeared on the scene. The boyish style of his hair and dress excellently became his features; and it almost seemed matter for regret that it should be altered. The Okura-Kiô-Kurahito, whose office it was to rearrange the hair of Genji, faltered as he did so. As to the Emperor, a sudden thought stole into his mind. "Ah! could his mother but have lived to have seen him now!" This thought, however, he at once suppressed. After he had been crowned the Prince withdrew to a dressing-room, where he attired himself in the full robes of manhood. Then descending to the Court-yard he performed a measured dance in grateful acknowledgment. This he did with so much grace and skill that all present were filled with admiration; and his beauty, which some feared might be lessened, seemed only more remarkable from the change. And the Emperor, who had before tried to resist them, now found old memories irresistible.

Sadaijin had by his wife, who was a Royal Princess, an only daughter. The Heir-apparent had taken some notice of her, but her father did not encourage him. He had, on the other hand, some idea of Genji, and had sounded the Emperor on the subject. He regarded the idea with favor, and especially on the ground that such a union would be of advantage to Genji, who had not yet any influential supporters.

Now all the Court and the distinguished visitors were assembled in the palace, where a great festival was held; Genji occupied a seat next to that of the Royal Princess. During the entertainment Sadaijin whispered something several times into his ear, but he was too young and diffident to make any answer.

Sadaijin was now summoned before the dais of the Emperor, and, according to custom, an Imperial gift, a white O-Uchiki (grand robe), and a suit of silk vestments were presented to him by a lady. Then proffering his own wine-cup, the Emperor addressed him thus:--

*"In the first hair-knot of youth,*
Let love that lasts for age be bound!"

This evidently implied an idea of matrimony. Sadaijin feigned surprise and responded:--

*"Aye! if the purple of the cord,*
I bound so anxiously, endure!"

He then descended into the Court-yard, and gave expression to his thanks in the same manner in which Genji had previously done. A horse from the Imperial stables and a falcon from the Kurand-Dokoro were on view in the yard, and were now presented to him. The princes and nobles were all gathered together in front of the grand staircase, and appropriate gifts were also presented to each one of them. Among the crowd baskets and trays of fruits and delicacies were distributed by the Emperor's order, under the direction of Udaiben; and more rice-cakes and other things were given away now than at the Gembuk of the Heir-apparent.

In the evening the young Prince went to the mansion of the Sadaijin, where the espousal with the young daughter of the latter was celebrated with much splendor. The youthfulness of the beautiful boy was well pleasing to Sadaijin; but the bride, who was some years older than he was, and who considered the disparity in their age to be unsuitable, blushed when he thought of it.

Not only was this Sadaijin himself a distinguished personage in the State, but his wife was also the sister of the Emperor by the same mother, the late Empress; and her rank therefore was unequivocal. When to this we add the union of their daughter with Genji, it was easy to understand that the influence of Udaijin, the grandfather of the Heir-apparent, and who therefore seemed likely to attain great power, was not after all of very much moment.

Sadaijin had several children. One of them, who was the issue of his Royal wife, was the Kurand Shioshio.

Udaijin was not, for political reasons, on good terms with this family; but nevertheless he did not wish to estrange the youthful Kurand. On the contrary, he endeavored to establish friendly relations with him, as was indeed desirable, and he went so far as to introduce him to his fourth daughter, the younger sister of the Koki-Den.

Genji still resided in the palace, where his society was a source of much pleasure to the Emperor, and he did not take up his abode in a private house. Indeed, his bride, Lady Aoi (Lady Hollyhock), though her position insured her every attention from others, had few charms for him, and the Princess Wistaria much more frequently occupied his thoughts. "How pleasant her society, and how few like her!" he was always thinking; and a hidden bitterness blended with his constant reveries.

The years rolled on, and Genji being now older was no longer allowed to continue his visits to the private rooms of the Princess as before. But the pleasure of overhearing her sweet voice, as its strains flowed occasionally through the curtained casement, and blended with the music of the flute and *koto*, made him still glad to reside in the Palace. Under these circumstances he seldom visited the home of his bride, sometimes only for a day or two after an absence of five or six at Court.

His father-in-law, however, did not attach much importance to this, on account of his youth; and whenever they did receive a visit from him, pleasant companions were invited to meet him, and various games likely to suit his taste were provided for his entertainment.

In the Palace, Shigeisa, his late mother's quarters, was allotted to him, and those who had waited on her waited on him. The private house, where his grandmother had resided, was beautifully repaired for him by the Shuri Takmi -- the Imperial Repairing Committee -- in obedience to the wishes of the Emperor. In addition to the original loveliness of the landscape and the noble forest ranges, the basin of the lake was now enlarged, and similar improvements were effected throughout with the greatest pains. "Oh, how delightful would it not be to be in a place like that which such an one as one might choose!" thought Genji within himself.

We may here also note that the name Hikal Genji is said to have been originated by the Corean who examined his physiognomy.

*Translated by Suyematz Kenchio*

# Russia

The work of Russian writers Pushkin and Gogol was integral to the development of the short story form as it is conceptualized today. Pushkin, though noted primarily as an accomplished poet for *Eugene Onegin*, employed an unadorned prose style that identified him with the Russian Realist movement. This movement demanded attention to the minute details of environment and appearance, as well as to the psychological realities of character behavior and interaction. Only fiction that culled its subjects and situations from the writer's immediate cultural context and presented these elements in a form that made meaningful commentary on the social issues of the time was considered to be significant fiction of the Realist school.

Tolstoy adopts these techniques in "Where Love Is, There God Is Also," a retelling of the Biblical story of the Good Samaritan. His diction is plain, his study of character detailed. Martin Avdyeeich, his protagonist, is a cobbler living a simple life that, though uncomplicated, is not untroubled by a general disillusionment with God. Martin's eventual return to faith comes not by acceptance of the tenets of organized religion, but by the exertion of his own good will. He achieves happiness not through supplication, but through acts of charity. Tolstoy presents an idea of kindness and humanity in religion that has its origin outside the religious establishment. This is a revelation appropriate to Martin, who exists himself outside the establisments of the intelligentsia, the arts, and science.

Tolstoy was an innovator among the Realists in that he did introduce elements of disease and death into a literary movement some considered too prudish, too concerned with the more delicate and moral aspects of existence. Gorky and Andreyev, however, pushed further by depicting in their fiction what they considered truths yet uglier and more horrific. Andreyev, with his obsessive contemplation of terror, idolized the tales of Edgar Allan Poe. Still, his fiction is not a superficial imitation of Poe's-- Andreyev moves beyond a flat depiction of horror and death into a philosophical realm where human weakness and vulnerability are foregrounded, nihilism is the operative doctrine, and the end of existence is its sole reality.

# Where Love Is, There God Is Also
## Leo Tolstoy

**Leo Tolstoy 1828-1910:**  Tolstoy's masterpieces include *War and Peace* (1869) and *Anna Karenina* (1877). Tolstoy was born at Yasnaya Polyana, his family's estate near Tula. His parents died when he was a child and he was sent to live with relatives. His elementary education was given by tutors, and in 1844 he entered the University of Kazan. He became bored, however, and did not earn a degree. He then returned to the estate and devoted himself to independent study. The three semi-autobiographical novels that deal with his coming up are *Childhood* (1852), *Boyhood* (1854), and *Youth* (1857).

As a young man, Tolstoy spent time among the socialites of Moscow and St. Petersburg. Finding no satisfaction in social pursuits, however, he volunteered for the Russian Army. He served during the Crimean War (1853-1856) and was honored for bravery at the Battle of Sevastopol. He wrote several sketches of Sevastopol for magazines that depicted a bloody reality that contradicted the long-held romantic notions of the glory of war. He also wrote a short novel, *The Cossacks* (1863), that was also based on his battle experience.

After his 1856 retirement from military service, Tolstoy traveled to Europe. It was there that he became interested in educational methodologies. When he returned to his estate he opened a school for peasant children. His teachings followed the guiding principle that each lesson should be customized for the individual student.

Then, in 1862, he married Sonya Behrs. It was during this time that he wrote his two best-known works, *War and Peace* and *Anna Karenina*. In approximately 1882, Tolstoy experienced a spiritual upheaval. He conceived his own form of Christianity as he rejected the dogma of the Russian Orthodox Church, accepting instead the idea that insight and understanding of oneself could affirm each person's good. He went through a period in which he felt that literature should help to morally instruct and improve the populace. He also proposed that literature should be for everyone and not just for the highly educated. He denounced his earlier works, labelling them "aristocratic art," as not being accessible to the masses, but it is those works, not his religious and moralistic compositions, that are judged most successful by today's critics.


IN A CERTAIN CITY dwelt Martin Avdyeeich, the cobbler. He lived in a cellar, a wretched little hole with a single window. The window looked up towards the street, and through it Martin could just see the passers by. It is true that he could see little more than their boots, but Martin Avdyeeich could read a man's character by his boots; so he needed no more. Martin Avdyeeich had lived long in that one place, and had many acquaintances. Few indeed were the boots in that neighborhood which had not passed through his hands at some time or other. On some he would fasten new soles, to others he would give side-pieces, others again he would stitch all round, and even give them new uppers if need be. And often he saw his own handiwork through the window. There was always lots of work for him, for Avdyeeich's hand was cunning and his leather good; nor did he overcharge, and always kept his word. He always engaged to do a job by a fixed time if he could; but if he could not, he said so at once, and deceived no man. So every one knew Avdyeeich, and he had no lack of work. Avdyeeich had always been a pretty good man, but as he grew old he began to think more about his soul, and draw nearer to his God. While Martin was still a journeyman his wife had died; but his wife had left him a little boy -- three years old. Their other children had not lived. All the eldest had died early. Martin wished at first to send his little child into the country to his sister, but afterwards he thought better of it. "My Kapitoshka," thought he, "will feel miserable in a strange household. He shall stay here with me." And so Avdyeeich left his master, and took to living in lodgings alone with his little son. But God did not give Avdyeeich happiness in his children. No sooner had the little one begun to grow up and be a help and a joy to his father's heart, than a sickness fell upon Kapitoshka; the little one took to his bed, lay there in a raging fever for a week, and then died. Martin buried his son in despair -- so desperate was he that he began to murmur against God. Such disgust of life overcame him that he more than once begged God that he might die; and he reproached God for taking not him, an old man, but his darling, his only son, instead. And after that Avdyeeich left off going to church.

And, lo! one day there came to Avdyeeich from the Troitsa Monastery an aged peasant-pilgrim -- it was already the eighth year of his pilgrimage. Avdyeeich fell a-talking with him, and began to complain of his great sorrow. "As for living any longer, thou man of God," said he, "I desire it not. Would only that I might die! That is my sole prayer to God. I am now a man who has no hope."

And the old man said to him: "Thy speech, Martin, is not good. How shall we judge the doings of God? God's judgments are not our thoughts. God willed that thy son shouldst die, but that thou shouldst live. Therefore 'twas the best thing both for him and for thee. It is because thou wouldst fain have lived for thy own delight that thou dost now despair."

"But what then *is* a man to live for?" asked Avdyeeich.

And the old man answered: "For God, Martin! He gave thee life, and for Him therefore must thou live. When thou dost begin to live for Him, thou wilt grieve about nothing more, and all things will come easy to thee."

Martin was silent for a moment, and then he said: "And how must one live for God?"

"Christ hath shown us the way. Thou knowest thy letters. Buy the Gospels and read; there thou wilt find out how to live for God. There everything is explained."

These words made the heart of Avdyeeich burn within him, and he went the same day and bought for himself a New Testament printed in very large type, and began to read.

Avdyeeich set out with the determination to read it only on holidays; but as he read, it did his heart so much good that he took to reading it every day. And the second time he read until all the kerosene in the lamp had burnt itself out, and for all that he could not tear himself away from the book. And so it was every evening. And the more he read, the more clearly he understood what God wanted of him, and how it behooved him to live for God; and his heart grew lighter and lighter continually. Formerly, whenever he lay down to sleep he would only sigh and groan, and think of nothing but Kapitoshka, but now he would only say to himself: "Glory to Thee! Glory to Thee, O Lord! Thy will be done!"

Henceforth the whole life of Avdyeeich was changed. Formerly, whenever he had a holiday, he would go to the tavern to drink tea, nor would he say "no" to a drop of brandy now and again. He would tipple with his comrades, and though not actually drunk, would, for all that, leave the inn a bit merry, babbling nonsense and talking loudly and censoriously. He had done with all that now. His life became quiet and joyful. With the morning light he sat down to his work, worked out his time, then took down his lamp from the hook, placed it on the table, took down his book from the shelf, bent over it, and sat him down to read. And the more he read the more he understood, and his heart grew brighter and happier.

It happened once that Martin was up reading till very late. He was reading St. Luke's Gospel. He was reading the sixth chapter, and as he read he came to the words: "And to him that smiteth thee on the one cheek, offer also the other." This passage he read several times, and presently he came to that place where the Lord says: "And why call ye me Lord, Lord, and do not the things which I say? Whosoever cometh to Me, and heareth My sayings, and doeth them, I will show you whom he is like. He is like a man which built an house, and dug deep, and laid the foundations on a rock. And when the flood arose, the storm beat vehemently upon that house, and could not shake it, for it was founded upon a rock. But he that heareth and doeth not, is like a man that without a foundation built an house upon the sand, against which the storm did beat vehemently, and immediately it fell, and the ruin of that house was great."

Avdyeeich read these words through and through, and his heart was glad. He took off his glasses, laid them on the book, rested his elbow on the table, and fell a-thinking. And he began to measure his own life by these words. And he thought to himself, "Is my house built on the rock or on the sand? How good to be as on a rock! How easy it all seems to thee sitting alone here! It seems as if thou wert doing God's will to the full, and so thou takest no heed and fallest away again. And yet thou wouldst go on striving, for so it is good for thee. O Lord, help me!" Thus thought he, and would have laid him down, but it was a grief to tear himself away from the book. And so he began reading the seventh chapter. He read all about the Centurion, he read all about the Widow's Son, he read all about the answer to the disciples of St. John; and so he came to that place where the rich Pharisee invited our Lord to be his guest. And he read all about how the woman who was a sinner anointed His feet and washed them with her tears, and how He justified her. And so he came at last to the forty-fourth verse, and there he read these words, "And He turned to the woman and said to Simon, Seest thou this woman? I entered into thine house, thou gavest Me no water for My feet; but she has washed My feet with tears and wiped them with the hairs of her head. Thou gavest Me no kiss, but this woman, since the time I came in, hath not ceased to kiss My feet. Mine head with oil thou didst not anoint." And again Avdyeeich took off his glasses, and laid them on the book, and fell a-thinking.

"So it is quite plain that I, too, have something of the Pharisee about me. Am I not always thinking of myself? Am I not always thinking of drinking tea, and keeping myself as warm and cosy as possible, without thinking at all about the guest? Simon thought about himself, but did not give the slightest thought to his guest. But who was his guest? The Lord Himself. And suppose He were to come to me, should I treat Him as the Pharisee did?"

And Avdyeeich leaned both his elbows on the table and, without perceiving it, fell a-dozing.

"Martin!" -- It was as the voice of someone close to his ear.

Martin started up from his nap. "Who's there?"

He turned round, he gazed at the door, but there was no one. Again he dozed off. Suddenly he heard quite plainly,

"Martin, Martin, I say! Look tomorrow into the street. I am coming."

Martin awoke, rose from his chair, and began to rub his eyes. And he did not know himself whether he had heard these words asleep or awake. He turned down the lamp and laid him down to rest.

At dawn next day Avdyeeich arose, prayed to God, lit his stove, got ready his gruel and cabbage soup, filled his samovar, put on his apron, and sat him down by his window to work. There Avdyeeich sits and works, and thinks of nothing but the things of yesternight. His thoughts were divided. He thought at one time that he must have gone off dozing, and then again he thought he really must have heard that voice. It might have been so, thought he.

Martin sits at the window and looks as much at his window as at his work, and whenever a strange pair of boots passes by, he bends forward and looks out of the window, so as to see the face as well as the feet of the passers-by. The house porter passed by in new felt boots, the water-carrier passed by, and after that there passed close to the window an old soldier, one of Nicholas's veterans, in tattered old boots, with a shovel in his hands. Avdyeeich knew him by his boots. The old fellow was called Stepanuich, and lived with the neighboring shopkeeper, who harbored him of his charity. His duty was to help the porter. Stepanuich stopped before Avdyeeich's window to sweep away the snow. Avdyeeich cast a glance at him, and then went on working as before.

"I'm not growing sager as I grow older," thought Avdyeeich, with some self-contempt. "I make up my mind that Christ is coming to me and, lo! 'tis only Stepanuich clearing away the snow. Thou simpleton, thou! thou art wool-gathering!" Then Avdyeeich made ten more stitches, and then he stretched his head once more towards the window. He looked through the window again, and there he saw that Stepanuich had placed the shovel against the wall, and was warming himself and taking breath a bit.

"The old man is very much broken," thought Avdyeeich to himself. "It is quite plain that he has scarcely strength enough to scrape away the snow. Suppose I make him drink a little tea! the samovar, too, is just on the boil." Avdyeeich put down his awl, got up, placed the samovar on the table, put some tea in it, and tapped on the window with his fingers.

Stepanuich turned round and came to the window. Avdyeeich beckoned to him, and then went and opened the door.

"Come in and warm yourself a bit," cried he. "You're a bit chilled, eh?"

"Christ requite you! Yes, and all my bones ache, too," said Stepanuich. Stepanuich came in, shook off the snow, and began to wipe his feet so as not to soil the floor, but he tottered sadly.

"Don't trouble about wiping your feet. I'll rub it off myself. It's all in the day's work. Come in and sit down," said Avdyeeich. "Here, take a cup of tea."

And Avdyeeich filled two cups, and gave one to his guest, and he poured his own tea out into the saucer and began to blow it.

Stepanuich drank his cup, turned it upside down, put a gnawed crust on the top of it, and said, "Thank you." But it was quite plain that he wanted to be asked to have some more.

"Have a drop more. Do!" said Avdyeeich, and poured out fresh cups for his guest and himself, and as Avdyeeich drank his cup, he could not help glancing at the window from time to time.

"Dost thou expect anyone?" asked his guest.

"Do I expect anyone? Well, honestly, I hardly know. I am expecting, and I am not expecting, and there's a word which has burnt itself right into my heart. Whether it was a vision or no, I know not. Look now, my brother! I was reading yesterday about our little Father Christ, how He suffered, how He came on earth. Hast thou heard of Him, eh?"

"I have heard, I have heard," replied Stepanuich, "but we poor ignorant ones know not our letters."

"Anyhow, I was reading about this very thing -- how He came down upon earth. I was reading how He went to the Pharisee, and how the Pharisee did not receive Him at all. Thus I thought, and so, about yest-ernight, little brother mine, I read that very thing, and bethought me how the Honorable did not receive our little Father Christ honorably. But suppose, I thought, if He came to one like me -- would I receive Him? Simon at any rate did not receive Him at all. Thus I thought, and so thinking, fell asleep. I fell asleep, I say, little brother mine, and I heard my name called. I started up. A voice was whispering at my very ear. 'Look out tomorrow!' it said, 'I am coming.' And so it befell twice. Now look! wouldst thou believe it? the idea stuck to me -- I scold myself for my folly, and yet I look for Him, our little Father Christ!"

Stepanuich shook his head and said nothing, but he drank his cup dry and put it aside. Then Avdyeeich took up the cup and filled it again.

"Drink some more. 'Twill do thee good. Now it seems to me that when our little Father went about on earth, He despised no one, but sought unto the simple folk most of all. He was always among the simple folk. Those disciples of His, too, he chose most of them from amongst our brother-laborers, sinners like unto us. He that exalteth himself, He says, shall be abased, and he that abaseth himself shall be exalted. Ye, says He, call me Lord, and I, says He, wash your feet. He who would be the first among you, He says, let him become the servant of all. And therefore it is that He says, Blessed are the lowly, the peacemakers, the humble, and the long-suffering."

Stepanuich forgot his tea. He was an old man, soft-hearted, and tearful. He sat and listened, and the tears rolled down his cheeks.

"Come, drink a little more," said Avdyeeich. But Stepanuich crossed himself, expressed his thanks, pushed away his cup, and got up.

"I thank thee, Martin Avdyeeich," said he. "I have fared well at thy hands, and thou hast refreshed me both in body and soul."

"Thou wilt show me a kindness by coming again. I am very glad to have a guest," said Avdyeeich. Stepanuich departed, and Martin poured out the last drop of tea, drank it, washed up, and again sat down by the window to work -- he had some back-stitching to do. He stitched and stitched, and now and then cast glances at the window -- he was looking for Christ, and could think of nothing but Him and His works. And the divers sayings of Christ were in his head all the time.

Two soldiers passed by, one in regimental boots, the other in boots of his own making; after that, the owner of the next house passed by in nicely brushed goloshes. A baker with a basket also passed by. All these passed by in turn, and then there came alongside the window a woman in worsted stockings and rustic shoes, and as she was passing by she stopped short in front of the partition wall. Avdyeeich looked up at her from his window, and he saw that the woman was a stranger and poorly clad, and that she had a little child with her. She was leaning up against the wall with her back to the wind, and tried to wrap the child up, but she had nothing to wrap it up with. The woman wore summer clothes, and thin enough they were. And from out of his corner Avdyeeich heard the child crying and the woman trying to comfort it, but she could not. Then Avdyeeich got up, went out of the door and on to the steps, and cried, "My good woman! my good woman!"

The woman heard him and turned round.

"Why dost thou stand out in the cold there with the child? Come inside! In the warm room thou wilt be better able to tend him. This way!"

The woman was amazed. What she saw was an old fellow in an apron and with glasses on his nose, calling to her. She came towards him.

They went down the steps together -- they went into the room. The old man led the woman to the bed. "There," said he, "sit down, gossip, nearer to the stove, and warm and feed thy little one. . . ."

He went to the table, got some bread and a dish, opened the oven door, put some cabbage soup into the dish, took out a pot of gruel, but it was not quite ready, so he put some cabbage soup only into the dish, and placed it on the table. Then he fetched bread, took down the cloth from the hook, and spread it on the table.

"Sit down and have something to eat, gossip," said he, "and I will sit down a little with the youngster. I have had children of my own, and know how to manage them."

The woman crossed herself, sat down at the table, and began to eat, and Avdyeeich sat down on the bed with the child. Avdyeeich smacked his lips at him again and again, but his lack of teeth made it a clumsy joke at best. And all the time the child never left off shrieking. Then Avdyeeich hit upon the idea of shaking his finger at him, so he snapped his fingers up and down, backwards and forwards, right in front of the child's mouth, because his finger was black and sticky with cobbler's wax. And the child stared at the finger and was silent, and presently it began to laugh. And Avdyeeich was delighted. But the woman went on eating, and told him who she was and whence she came.

"I am a soldier's wife," she said: "my eight months' husband they drove right away from me, and nothing has been heard of him since. I took a cook's place till I became a mother. They could not keep me and the child. It is now three months since I have been drifting about without any fixed resting-place. I have eaten away my all. I wanted to be a wet-nurse, but people wouldn't have me: 'Thou art too thin,' they said. I have just been to the merchant's wife where our grandmother lives, and there they promised to take me in. I thought it was all right, but she told me to come again in a week. But she lives a long way off. I am chilled to death, and he is quite tired out. But, God be praised! our landlady has compassion on us, and gives us shelter for Christ's sake. But for that I don't know how we could live through it all."

Avdyeeich sighed, and said, "And have you no warm clothes?"

"Ah, kind friend! this is indeed warm-clothes time, but yesterday I pawned away my last shawl for two *grivenki*."

The woman went to the bed and took up the child, but Avdyeeich stood up, went to the wall cupboard, rummaged about a bit, and then brought back with him an old jacket.

"Look!" said he, "'Tis a shabby thing, 'tis true, but it will do to wrap up in."

The woman looked at the old jacket, then she gazed at the old man, and, taking the jacket, fell a-weeping. Avdyeeich also turned away, crept under the bed, drew out a trunk, and seemed to be very busy about it, whereupon he again sat down opposite the woman.

Then the woman said: "Christ requite thee, dear little father! It is plain that it was He who sent me by thy window. When I first came out it was warm, and now it has turned very cold. And He it was, little father, who made thee look out of the window and have compassion on wretched me."

Avdyeeich smiled slightly, and said: "Yes, He must have done it, for I looked not out of the window in vain, dear gossip!"

And Avdyeeich told his dream to the soldier's wife also, and how he had heard a voice promising that the Lord should come to him that day.

"All things are possible," said the woman. Then she rose up, put on the jacket, wrapped it round her little one, and then began to curtsy and thank Avdyeeich once more.

"Take this for Christ's sake," said Avdyeeich, giving her a two-*givenka* piece, "and redeem your shawl." The woman crossed herself, Avdyeeich crossed himself, and then he led the woman to the door.

The woman went away. Avdyeeich ate up the remainder of the cabbage soup, washed up, and again sat down to work. He worked on and on, but he did not forget the window, and whenever the window was darkened, he immediately looked up to see who was passing. Acquaintances passed, strangers passed, but there was no one in particular.

But now Avdyeeich sees how, right in front of his window, an old woman, a huckster, has taken her stand. She carries a basket of apples. Not many now remained; she had evidently sold them nearly all. Across her shoulder she carried a sack full of shavings. She must have picked them up near some new building, and was taking them home with her. It was plain that the sack was straining her shoulder. She wanted to shift it on to the other shoulder, so she rested the sack on the pavement, placed the apple-basket on a small post, and set about shaking down the shavings in the sack. Now while she was shaking down the sack, an urchin in a ragged cap suddenly turned up, goodness knows from whence, grabbed at one of the apples in the basket, and would have made off with it, but the wary old woman turned quickly round and gripped the youth by the sleeve. The lad fought and tried to tear himself loose, but the old woman seized him with both hands, knocked his hat off, and tugged hard at his hair. The lad howled, and the old woman reviled him. Avdyeeich ran out into the street.

The old woman was tugging at the lad's hair and wanted to drag him off to the police, while the boy fought and kicked.

"I didn't take it," said he. "What are you whacking me for? Let me go!"

Avdyeeich came up and tried to part them. He seized the lad by the arm and said: "Let him go, little mother! Forgive him for Christ's sake!"

"I'll forgive him so that he sha'n't forget the taste of fresh birchrods. I mean to take the rascal to the police station."

Avdyeeich began to entreat with the old woman.

"Let him go, little mother; he will not do so any more. Let him go for Christ's sake."

The old woman let him go. The lad would have bolted, but Avdyeeich held him fast.

"Beg the little mother's pardon," said he, "and don't do such things any more. I saw thee take them."

Then the lad began to cry and beg pardon.

"Well, that's all right! And now, there's an apple for thee." And Avdyeeich took one out of the basket and gave it to the boy. "I'll pay thee for it, little mother," he said to the old woman.

"Thou wilt ruin them that way, the blackguards," said the old woman. "If I had the rewarding of him, he should not be able to sit down for a week."

"Oh, little mother, little mother!" cried Avdyeeich, "that is our way of looking at things, but it is not God's way. If he ought to be whipped so for the sake of one apple, what do we deserve for our sins?"

The old woman was silent.

And Avdyeeich told the old woman about the parable of the master who forgave his servant a very great debt, and how that servant immediately went out and caught his fellow-servant by the throat because he was his debtor. The old woman listened to the end, and the lad listened, too.

"God bade us forgive," said Avdyeeich, "otherwise He will not forgive us. We must forgive everyone, especially the thoughtless."

The old woman shook her head and sighed.

"That's all very well," she said, "but they are spoiled enough already."

"Then it is for us old people to teach them better," said Avdyeeich.

"So say I," replied the old woman. "I had seven of them at one time and now I have but a single daughter left." And the old woman began telling him where and how she lived with her daughter, and how many grandchildren she had. "I'm not what I was," she said, "but I work all I can. I am sorry for my grandchildren, and good children they are, too. No one is so glad to see me as they are. Little Aksyutka will go to none but me. 'Grandma dear! darling grandma!'" and the old woman was melted to tears. "As for him," she added, pointing to the lad, "boys will be boys, I suppose. Well, God be with him!"

Now just as the old woman was about to hoist the sack on to her shoulder, the lad rushed forward and said:

"Give it here and I'll carry it for thee, granny! It is all in my way."

The old woman shook her head, but she did put the sack on the lad's shoulder.

And so they trudged down the street together side by side. And the old woman forgot to ask Avdyeeich for the money for the apple. Avdyeeich kept standing and looking after them, and heard how they talked to each other, as they went, about all sorts of things.

Avdyeeich followed them with his eyes till they were out of sight; then he turned homewards and found his glasses on the steps (they were not broken), picked up his awl, and sat down to work again. He worked away for a little while, but soon he was scarcely able to distinguish the stitches, and saw the lamplighter going round to light the lamps. "I see it is time to light up," thought he; so he trimmed his little lamp, lighted it, and again sat down to work. He finished one boot completely, turned it round and inspected it. "Good!" he cried. He put away his tools, swept up the cuttings, removed the brushes and tips, put away the awl, took down the lamp, placed it on the table, and took down the Gospels from the shelf. He wanted to find the passage where he had last evening placed a strip of morocco leather by way of marker, but he lit upon another place. And just as Avdyeeich opened the Gospel, he recollected his dream of yesterday evening. And no sooner did he call it to mind than it seemed to him as if some persons were moving about and shuffling with their feet behind him. Avdyeeich glanced round and saw that somebody was indeed standing in the dark corner -- yes, someone was really there, but who he could not exactly make out. Then a voice whispered in his ear:

"Martin! Martin! dost thou not know me?"

"Who art thou?" cried Avdyeeich.

"'Tis I," cried the voice, "lo, 'tis I!" And forth from the dark corner stepped Stepanuich. He smiled, and it was as though a little cloud were breaking, and he was gone.

"It is I!" cried the voice, and forth from the corner stepped a woman with a little child; and the woman smiled and the child laughed, and they also disappeared.

"And it is I!" cried the voice, and the old woman and the lad with the apple stepped forth, and both of them smiled, and they also disappeared.

And the heart of Avdyeeich was glad. He crossed himself, put on his glasses, and began to read the Gospels at the place where he had opened them. And at the top of the page he read these words: "And I was an hungered and thirsty, and ye gave Me to drink. I was a stranger, and ye took Me in."

And at the bottom of the page he read this: "Inasmuch as ye have done it to the least of these My brethren, ye have done it unto Me."

And Avdyeeich understood that his dream had not deceived him, and that the Savior had really come to him that day, and he had really received Him.

*Translator Unknown*

# The Seven That Were Hanged
## *Leonid Andreyev*

**Leonid Nicolaievich Andreyev 1871-1919:** Andreyev's family belonged to the small provincial intelligentsia. Leonid learned to read at the age of six. He favored such authors as Jules Verne, James Fenimore Cooper, Edgar Allan Poe, and Charles Dickens. Despite his father's death which left the family in poverty, Leonid did receive a middle class education at the Gymnasium of Orel and eventually attended the University of Petersburg. After a failed romance, while still at the University, he attempted suicide. He then went home and spent his time in idleness. Not moved by Revolutionary ideas, he filled his life with drunken bauchus. When he finally returned to the University he received his degree in law and was admitted to the bar in 1897.

Andreyev had been determined to become a writer since age seventeen. Henceforth he developed his technique by imitating the published authors he admired. In 1895 he published an article and two stories in the *Orlovskiy vestnik.* He was then able to secure steadier copy-writing positions that allowed him the income and time to pursue his literary goals. After his short-lived legal career he attracted the attention of Maksim Gorky with his story, "Bargamot and Garaska." Gorky introduced Andreyev to a group of writers, known as the Wednesday Circle, who gathered to read and comment upon stories the attendees had written. Andreyev, however, was too shy to read his story "Silence" aloud -- so Gorky read it for him.

Andreyev became one of the most controversial authors in Russia. This was due in large part to the publication of *The Abyss* and *In the Fog.* Both presented sexual issues with an audacity that pushed beyond the boundaries of standard realistic practice. Although there was a tone of moralism in these works, they nevertheless offended Countess S. A. Tolstoy, who wrote a letter to the press expressing her outrage that such filth could find its way into print. Despite this and the press' discourteous treatment, Andreyev achieved great success with the public, a success that permitted him overall a rather ostentatious lifestyle.

Andreyev's work has been criticized as unyieldingly pessimistic, but he achieved a combination of realism and symbolism that favorable critics agree accurately reflects the mood of early 20th-century Russia. He is noted for the following works: *The Abyss, In the Fog, The Red Laugh,* and his most successful play, *The Life of Man.*

60   Leonid Andreyev

## I: "AT ONE O'CLOCK IN THE AFTERNOON, YOUR EXCELLENCY!"

AS THE MINISTER was a very fat man, predisposed to apoplexy, and as it was necessary therefore to spare him every dangerous emotion, they took the minutest precautions in warning him that a serious attempt upon his life had been planned. When they saw that he received the news calmly, they gave him the details: the attempt was to be made the next day, at the moment when His Excellency was to leave the house to go to make his report. A few terrorists, armed with revolvers and bombs, whom a police spy had betrayed and who were now being watched by the police, were to meet near the steps at one o'clock in the afternoon and await the Minister's exit. There the criminals would be arrested.

"Pardon me," interrupted the Minister in surprise. "How do they know that I am to go to present my report at one o'clock in the afternoon, when I learned it myself only two days ago?"

The commander of the body-guard made a vague gesture signifying ignorance.

"At one o'clock in the afternoon, Your Excellency!"

Astonished, and at the same time satisfied with the police who had managed the affair so well, the Minister shook his head; a disdainful smile appeared on his thick red lips; quickly he made all the necessary preparations to pass the night in another palace; in no way did he wish to embarrass the police. His wife and children also were removed from the dangerous premises.

As long as the lights gleamed in this new residence, and while his familiars bustled about him expressing their indignation, the Minister felt a sensation of agreeable excitement. It seemed to him that he had just received, or was about to receive, a great and unexpected reward. But the friends went away, and the lights were put out. The intermittent and fantastic glare of the arc-lights in the street fell upon the ceiling and the walls, penetrating through the high windows, symbolizing, as it were, the fragility of all bolts and walls, the vanity of all supervision. Then, in the silence and the solitude of a strange chamber, the dignitary was seized with an unspeakable terror.

He was afflicted with a kidney trouble. Every violent emotion caused his face, feet, and hands to swell, and made him appear heavier, more massive. Now, like a heap of bloated flesh that made the bed-springs bend, massive. Now, like a heap of bloated flesh that made the bed-springs bend, he suffered the anguish of the sick as he felt his face puff up and become, as it were, something foreign to his body. His thought recurred obstinately to the cruel fate that his enemies were preparing for him. He evoked one after the other all the horrible attempts of recent date, in which bombs had been thrown against persons as noble as himself and bearing even higher titles, tearing their bodies into a thousand shreds, hurling their brains against foul brick walls, and knocking their teeth from their jaws. And, at these recollections, it seemed to him that his diseased body was another man's body suffering from the fiery shock of the explosion. He pictured to himself his arms detached from his shoulders, his teeth broken, his brain crushed. His legs, stretched out in the bed, grew numb and motion-less, the feet pointing upward, like those of a dead man. He breathed noisily, coughing occasionally, to avoid all resemblance to a corpse: he moved about, that he might hear the sound of the metallic springs, the rustling of the silk coverlet. And, to prove that he was really alive, he exclaimed in a loud and clear voice:

"Brave fellows! Brave fellows!"

These words of praise were for the police, the gendarmes, the soldiers, all those who protected his life and had prevented the assassination. But in vain did he stir about, lavish his praise, and smile at the discomfiture of the terrorists; he could not yet believe that he was saved. It seemed to him that the death evoked for him by the anarchists, and which existed in their thought, was already there and would remain there, refusing to go away until the assassins should be seized, deprived of their bombs, and lodged safely in prison. There it stood, in the corner yonder, declining to leave, and unable to leave, like an obedient soldier placed on guard by an unknown will.

"At one o'clock in the afternoon, Your Excellency!" This phrase came back to him continually, uttered in all tones, now joyously and ironically, now irritably, now obstinately and stupidly. One would have said that a hundred phonographs had been placed in the chamber, and were crying one after the other, with the idiotic persistence of machines:

"At one o'clock in the afternoon, Your Excellency!"

And this "one o'clock in the afternoon" of the next day, which so short a time before was in no way to be distinguished from other hours, had taken on a menacing importance; it had stepped out of the clock-dial, and was beginning to live a distinct life, stretching itself like an immense black curtain, to divide life into two parts. Before it and after it no other hour existed; it alone, presumptuous and obsessing, was entitled to a special life.

Grinding his teeth, the Minister raised himself in his bed to a sitting posture. It was positively impossible for him to sleep.

Pressing his bloated hands against his face, he pictured to himself with terrifying clearness how he would have risen on the morrow if he had been left in ignorance; he would have taken his coffee, and dressed. And neither he, or the Swiss who would have helped him on with his fur coat, or the valet who would have served his coffee, would have understood the uselessness of breakfasting and dressing, when a few moments later everything would be annihilated by the explosion. . . . The Swiss opens the door. . . . And it is he, this good and thoughtful Swiss, with the blue eyes, and the open countenance, and the numerous military decorations -- he it is who opens the terrible door with his own hands. . . .

"Ah!" suddenly exclaimed the Minister aloud; slowly he removed his hands from his face. Gazing far before him into the darkness with a fixed and attentive look, he stretched out his hand to turn on the light. Then he arose, and in his bare feet walked around the strange chamber so unfamiliar to him; finding another light, he turned that on also. The room became bright and agreeable; there was only the disordered bed and the fallen coverlet to indicate a terror that had not yet completely disappeared.

Clad in a night-shirt, his beard in a tangle, a look of irritation on his face, the Minister resembled those old people who are tormented by asthma and insomnia. One would have said that the death prepared for him by others had stripped him bare, had torn him from the luxury with which he was surrounded. Without dressing he threw himself into an arm-chair, his eyes wandered to the ceiling.

"Imbeciles!" he cried in a contemptuous tone of conviction.

"Imbeciles!" And he was speaking of the policemen whom but a few moments before he had called "brave fellows," and who, through excess of zeal, had told him all the details of the attack that had been planned.

"Evidently," he thought with lucidity, "I am afraid now because I have been warned and because I know. But, if I had been left in ignorance, I should have taken my coffee quietly. And then, evidently, this death. . . . But am I then so afraid of death? I have a kidney trouble; some day I must die of it, and yet I am not afraid, because I don't know when. And these imbeciles say to me: 'At one o'clock in the afternoon, Your Excellency!'"

They thought that I would be glad to know about it! . . . Instead of that, death has placed himself in the corner yonder, and does not go away! He does not go away, because I have that fixed idea! To die is not so terrible; the terrible thing is to know that one is going to die. It would be quite impossible for a man to live if he knew the hour and day of his death with absolute certainty. And yet these idiots warn me: 'At one o'clock in the afternoon, Your Excellency!'"

Recently he had been ill, and the doctors had told him that he was going to die and should make his final arrangements. He had refused to believe them; and, in fact, he did not die. Once, in his youth, it had happened to him to get beyond his depth; he had decided to put an end to his existence; he had loaded his revolver, written some letters, and even fixed the hour of his suicide; then, at the last moment, he had reconsidered. And always, at the supreme moment, something unexpected may happen; consequently no man can know when he will die.

"At one o'clock in the afternoon, Your Excellency!" these amiable idiots had said to him. They had informed him only because his death had been plotted; and yet he was terrified simply to learn the hour when it might have occurred. He admitted that they would kill him some day or other, but it would not be the next day. . . . it would not be the next day, and he could sleep quietly, like an immortal being. . . The imbeciles! They did not know what a gulf they had dug in saying, with stupid amiability: "At one o'clock in the afternoon, Your Excellency!"

From the bitter anguish that shot through his heart, the Minister understood that he would know neither sleep, nor rest, nor joy, until this black and accursed hour, thus detached from the course of time, had passed. It was enough in itself to annihilate the light and enwrap the man in the opaque darkness of fear. Now that he was awake, the fear of death permeated his entire body, filtered into his bones, exuded from every pore.

Already the Minister had ceased to think of the assassins of the morrow: they had disappeared, forgotten in the multitude of inauspicious things that surrounded his life. He feared the unexpected, the inevitable: an attack of apoplexy, a laceration of the heart, the rupture of a little artery suddenly made powerless to resist the flow of blood and splitting like a glove on swollen hands.

His thick, short neck frightened him; he dared not look at his swollen fingers, full of some fatal fluid. And though, just before, in the darkness, he had been compelled to stir in order to avoid resemblance to a corpse, now, under this bright, cold, hostile, frightful light, it seemed to him horrible, impossible, to move even to light a cigarette or ring for a servant. His nerves were at a tension. With red and upturned eyes and burning head, he stifled.

Suddenly, in the darkness of the sleeping house, the electric bell just under the ceiling, among the dust and spiders' webs, became animate. Its little metallic tongue beat hurriedly against its sonorous edge. It stopped for a moment, and then began to ring again in a continuous and terrifying fashion.

People came running. Here and there lamps were lighted on the walls and chandeliers -- too few of them for intense illumination, but enough to create shadows. On every hand appeared these shadows: they arose in the corners and stretched out upon the ceiling, fastening upon all projections and running along the walls. It was difficult to understand where all these taciturn, monstrous, and innumerable shadows could have kept themselves before -- mute souls of mute things.

A thick and trembling voice said something indistinguishable. Then they telephoned to the doctor: the Minister was ill. His Excellency's wife was summoned also.

## II:  SENTENCED TO BE HANGED

The predictions of the police were realized. Four terrorists, three men and one woman, carrying bombs, revolvers, and infernal machines, were taken in front of the steps of the residence; a fifth accomplice was arrested at her dwelling, where the implements had been manufactured and the conspiracy planned. A large quantity of dynamite and many weapons were found there. All five were very young: the eldest of the men was twenty-eight, the younger of the women nineteen. They were tried in the fortress where they had been imprisoned after their arrest; they were tried quickly and secretly, as was the custom at that merciless epoch.

Before the court all five were calm, but serious and thoughtful; their contempt for the judges was so great that they did not care to emphasize their fearlessness by a useless smile or a pretence of gaiety. They were just tranquil enough to protect their souls and the deep gloom of their agony from the malevolent gaze of strangers. Some questions they refused to answer, some they answered simply, briefly, precisely, as if they were speaking, not to judges, but to statisticians desirous of completing tables of figures. Three of them, one woman and two men, gave their real names; two refused to disclose their identity, which remained unknown to the court. In everything that happened they manifested that distant and attenuated curiosity peculiar to people seriously ill or possessed by a single all-powerful idea. They cast swift glances, seized upon an interesting word in its flight, and went back to their thoughts, resuming them at the exact point where they had dropped them.

The accused placed nearest the judges had given his name as Sergey Golovin, a former officer, son of a retired colonel. He was very young, with broad shoulders, and so robust that neither the prison nor the expectation of certain death had been able to dim the color of his cheeks or the expression of happy innocence in his blue eyes. Throughout the trial he twisted his thick blond beard, to which he had not yet become accustomed, and gazed steadily at the window, knitting his brows.

It was the latter part of winter, that period into which, among snow-storms and gray, cold days, the approaching spring projects sometimes, as a forerunner, a warm and luminous day, or even a single hour, so passionately young and sparkling that the sparrows in the street become mad with joy and men seem intoxicated. Now, through the upper window, still covered with the dust of the previous summer, a very odd and beautiful sky was to be seen; at the first glance it seemed a thick and milky gray; then, upon a second examination, it appeared to be covered with azure stains, of an ever-deepening blue, a blue pure and infinite. And because it did not strip itself suddenly, but modestly draped itself in the transparent veil of clouds, it became charming, like one's fiancée. Sergey Golovin looked at the sky, pulled at his mustache, winked now one and now the other of his eyes behind the long, heavy eyelashes, and reflected profoundly on nobody knows what. Once, even, his fingers moved rapidly, and an expression of naive joy appeared upon his face; but he looked around him, and his joy was extinguished like a live coal upon which one steps. Almost instantaneously, almost without transition, the redness of his cheeks gave place to a corpse-like pallor; a fine hair painfully pulled out was pressed as in a vice between his bloodless finger-ends. But the joy of life and of the spring was still stronger. A few minutes later the young face resumed its naive expression and sought again the sky of spring.

Toward the sky also looked an unknown young girl, surnamed Musya. She was younger than Golovin, but seemed his elder because of the severity, the gravity, of her proud and loyal eyes. The delicate neck and slender arms alone revealed that intangible something which is youth itself, and which sounded so distinctly in the pure harmonious voice that resembled a costly instrument in perfect tune. Musya was very pale, of that passionate pallor peculiar to those who burn with an inner, radiant, and powerful fire. She scarcely stirred; from time to time only, with a gesture that was hardly visible, she felt for a deep trace in the third finger of her right hand -- the trace of a ring recently removed. She looked at the sky with calmness and indifference; she looked at it simply because everything in this commonplace and dirty hall was hostile to her and seemed to scrutinize her face. This bit of blue sky was the only pure and true thing upon which she could look with confidence.

The judges pitied Sergey Golovin and hated Musya.

Musya's neighbor, motionless also, with hands folded between his knees and somewhat of affectation in his pose, was an unknown surnamed Werner. If one can bolt a face as one bolts a heavy door, the unknown had bolted his as if it were a door of iron. He gazed steadily at the floor, and it was impossible to tell whether he was calm or deeply moved, whether he was thinking of something or listening to the testimony of the policemen. He was rather short of stature; his features were fine and noble. He gave the impression of an immense and calm force, of a cold and audacious valor. The very politeness with which he uttered his clear and curt replies seemed dangerous on his lips. On the backs of the other prisoners the customary cloak seemed a ridiculous costume; on him it was not even noticeable, so foreign was the garment to the man. Although Werner had been armed only with a poor revolver, while the others carried bombs and infernal machines, the judges looked upon him, as the leader, and treated him with a certain respect, with the same brevity which he employed toward them.

In his neighbor, Vasily Kashirin, a frightful moral struggle was going on between the intolerable terror of death and the desperate desire to subdue this fear and conceal it from the judges. Ever since the prisoners had been taken to court in the morning, he had been stifling under the hurried beating of his heart. Drops of sweat appeared continually on his brow; his hands were moist and cold; his damp and icy shirt, sticking to his body, hindered his movements. By a superhuman effort of the will he kept his fingers from trembling, and maintained the firmness and moderation of his voice and the tranquillity of his gaze. He saw nothing around him; the sound of the voice that he heard seemed to reach him through a fog, and it was in a fog also that he stiffened himself in a desperate effort to answer firmly and aloud. But, as soon as he had spoken, he forgot the questions, as well as his own phrases; the silent and terrible struggle began again. And upon his person death was so in evidence that the judges turned their eyes away from him. It was as difficult to determine his age as that of a rotting corpse. According to his papers he was only twenty-three. Once or twice Werner touched him gently on the knee, and each time he answered briefly:

"It's nothing."

His hardest moment was when he suddenly felt an irresistible desire to utter inarticulate cries, like a hunted beast. Then he gave Werner a slight push; without raising his eyes, the latter answered in a low voice:

"It's nothing, Vasya. It will soon be over!"

Consumed by anxiety, Tanya Kovalchuk, the fifth terrorist, sheltered her comrades with a maternal look. She was still very young; her cheeks seemed as highly colored as those of Sergey Golovin; and yet she seemed to be the mother of all the accused, so full of tender anxiety and infinite love were her looks, her smile, her fear. The progress of the trial did not interest her. She listened to her comrades simply to see if their voices trembled, if they were afraid, if they needed water.

But she could not look at Vasya; his anguish was too intense; she contented herself with cracking her plump fingers. At Musya and Werner she gazed with proud and respectful admiration, her face then wearing a grave and serious expression. As for Sergey Golovin, she continually tried to attract his attention by her smile.

"The dear comrade, he is looking at the sky. Look, look!" thought she, as she observed the direction of his eyes.

"And Vasya? My God! My God! . . . What can be done to comfort him? If I speak to him, perhaps it will make matters worse; suppose he should begin to weep?"

Like a peaceful pool reflecting every wandering cloud, her amiable and clear countenance showed all the feeling and all the thoughts, however fleeting, of her four comrades. She forgot that she was on trial too and would be hanged; her indifference to this was absolute. It was in her dwelling that the bombs and dynamite had been found; strange as it may seem, she had received the police with pistol shots, and had wounded one of them in the head.

The trial ended toward eight o'clock, just as the day was drawing to its close. Little by little, in the eyes of Sergey and Musya, the blue sky disappeared; without reddening, without smiling, it grew dim gently as on a summer evening, becoming grayish, and suddenly cold and wintry. Golovin heaved a sigh, stretched himself, and raised his eyes toward the window, where the chilly darkness of the night was already making itself manifest; still pulling his beard, he began to examine the judges, the soldiers, and their weapons, exchanging a smile with Tanya Kovalchuk. As for Musya, when the sun had set completely, she did not lower her gaze to the ground, but directed it toward a corner where a spider's web was swaying gently in the invisible current of warm air from the stove; and thus she remained until the sentence had been pronounced.

After the verdict, the condemned said their farewells to their lawyers, avoiding their disconcerted, pitying, and confused looks; then they grouped themselves for a moment near the door, and exchanged short phrases.

"It's nothing, Vasya! All will soon be over!" said Werner.

"But there is nothing the matter with me, brother!" answered Kashirin, in a strong, quiet, and almost joyous voice. In fact, his face had taken on a slight color, no longer resembling that of a corpse.

"The devil take them! They have hanged us all just the same!" swore Golovin naively.

"It was to have been expected," answered Werner, without agitation.

"Tomorrow the final judgment will be rendered, and they will put us all in the same cell," said Tanya, to console her comrades. "We shall remain together until the execution."

Silently, and with a resolute air, Musya started off.

### III: "I MUST NOT BE HANGED"

A fortnight before the affair of the terrorists, in the same court, but before other judges, Ivan Yanson, a peasant, had been tried and sentenced to be hanged.

Ivan Yanson had been hired as a farm-hand by a well-to-do farmer, and was distinguished in no way from the other poor devils of his class. He was a native of Wesenberg, in Esthonia; for some years he had been advancing gradually toward the capital, passing from one farm to another.

He had very little knowledge of Russian. As there were none of his countrymen living in the neighborhood, and as his employer was a Russian, named Lazaref, Yanson remained silent for almost two years. He said hardly a word to either man or beast. He led the horse to water and harnessed it without speaking to it, walking about it lazily, with short hesitating steps. When the horse began to run, Yanson did not say a word, but beat it cruelly with his enormous whip. Drink transformed his cold and wicked obstinacy into fury. The hissing of the lash and the regular and painful sound of his wooden shoes on the floor of the shed could be heard even at the farmhouse. To punish him for torturing the horse the farmer at first beat Yanson, but, not succeeding in correcting him, he gave it up.

Once or twice a month Yanson got drunk, especially when he took his master to the station. His employer once on board the train, Yanson drove a short distance away, and waited until the train had started.

Then he returned to the station, and got drunk at the buffet. He came back to the farm on the gallop, a distance of seven miles, beating the unfortunate beast unmercifully, giving it its head, and singing and shouting incomprehensible phrases in Esthonian. Sometimes silent, with set teeth, impelled by a whirlwind of indescribable fury, suffering, and enthusiasm, he was like a blind man in his mad career; he did not see the passers-by, he did not insult them, uphill and down he maintained his furious gait.

His master would have discharged him, but Yanson did not demand high wages, and his comrades were no better than he.

One day he received a letter written in Esthonian; but, as he did not know how to read or write, and as no one about him knew this language, Yanson threw it into the muck-heap with savage indifference, as if he did not understand that it brought him news from his native country. Probably needing a woman, he tried also to pay court to the girl employed on the farm. She repulsed him, for he was short and puny, and covered with hideous freckles; after that, he let her alone.

But, though he spoke little, Yanson listened continually. He listened to the desolate snow-covered fields, containing hillocks of frozen manure that resembled a series of little tombs heaped up by the snow; he listened to the bluish and limpid distance, the sonorous telegraph-poles. He alone knew what the fields and telegraph-poles were saying. He listened also to the conversations of men, the stories of murder, pillage, fire.

One night, in the village, the little church-bell began to ring in a feeble and lamentable way; flames appeared. Malefactors from nobody knew where were pillaging the neighboring farm. They killed the owner and his wife, and set fire to the house. This caused a feeling of anxiety on the farm where Yanson lived: day and night the dogs were loose; the master kept a gun within reach of his bed. He wished also to give an old weapon to Yanson, but the latter, after examining it, shook his head and refused it. The farmer did not understand that Yanson had more confidence in the efficacy of his Finnish knife than in this rusty old machine.

"It would kill me myself!" said he.

"You are only an imbecile, Ivan!"

And one winter evening, when the other farm-hand had gone to the station, this same Ivan Yanson, who was afraid of a gun, committed robbery and murder, and made an attempt at rape. He did it with an astonishing simplicity. After shutting the servant in the kitchen, lazily, like a man almost dead with sleep, he approached his master from behind, and stabbed him several times in the back. The master fell unconscious; his wife began to cry and to run about the chamber. Showing his teeth, and holding his knife in his hand, Yanson began to ransack trunks and drawers. He found the money; then, as if he had just seen the master's wife for the first time, he threw himself upon her to rape her, without the slightest premeditation. But he happened to drop his knife; and, as the woman was the stronger, she not only resisted Yanson, but half strangled him. At this moment the farmer recovered his senses, and the servant broke in the kitchen-door and came in. Yanson fled. They took him an hour later, squatting in the corner of the shed, and scratching matches which continually went out. He was trying to set fire to the farm.

A few days later the farmer died. Yanson was tried and sentenced to death. In the court one would have said that he did not understand what was going on; he viewed the large imposing hall without curiosity, and explored his nose with a shrunken finger that nothing disgusted. Only those who had seen him at church on Sunday could have guessed that he had done something in the way of making a toilet; he wore a knitted cravat of dirty red; in spots his hair was smooth and dark; in others it consisted of light thin locks, like wisps of straw on an uncultivated and devastated field.

When the sentence of death by hanging was pronounced, Yanson suddenly showed emotion. He turned scarlet, and began to untie and tie his cravat, as if it were choking him. Then he waved his arms without knowing why, and declared to the presiding judge, who had read the sentence:

"She has said that I must be hanged."

"'She'? Who?" asked the presiding judge, in a deep bass voice.

Yanson pointed at the presiding judge with his finger, and, looking at him furtively, answered angrily:

"You!"

"Well?"

Again Yanson turned his eyes toward one of the judges, in whom he divined a friend, and repeated:

"She has said that I must be hanged. I must not be hanged."

"Take away the accused."

But Yanson still had time to repeat, in a grave tone of conviction:

"I must not be hanged."

And with his outstretched finger and irritated face, to which he tried in vain to give an air of gravity, he seemed so stupid that the guard, in violation of orders, said to him in an undertone as he led him away:

"Well, you are a famous imbecile, you are!"

"I must not be hanged!" repeated Yanson, obstinately.

They shut him up again in the cell in which he had passed a month, and to which he had become accustomed, as he had become accustomed to everything: to blows, to brandy, to the desolate and snow-covered country sown with rounded hillocks resembling tombs. It even gave him pleasure to see his bed again, and his grated window, and to eat what they gave him; he had taken nothing since morning. The disagreeable thing was what had happened in court, about which he knew not what to think. He had no idea at all of what death by hanging was like.

The guard said to him, in a tone of remonstrance:

"Well, brother, there you are, hanged!"

"And when will they hang me?" asked Yanson, in a tone of incredulity. The guard reflected.

"Ah! wait, brother; you must have companions; they do not disturb themselves for a single individual, and especially for a little fellow like you."

"Then, when?" insisted Yanson.

He was not offended that they did not want to take the trouble to hang him all alone; he did not believe in this excuse, and thought they simply wanted to put off the execution, and then pardon him.

"When? When?" resumed the guard. "It is not a question of hanging a dog, which one takes behind a shed and dispatches with a single blow! Is that what you would like, imbecile?"

"Why, no, I would not like it!" said Yanson suddenly, with a joyous grimace. "'Twas she that said I must be hanged, but I, I do not want to be hanged!"

And, for the first time in his life perhaps, he began to laugh -- a grinning and stupid laugh, but terribly gay. He seemed like a goose beginning to quack. The guard looked at Yanson in astonishment, and then knitted his brows: this stupid gaiety on the part of a man who was to be executed insulted the prison, the gallows itself, and made them ridiculous. And suddenly it seemed to the old guard, who had passed all his life in prison and considered the laws of the gaol as those of nature, that the prison and all of life were a sort of mad-house in which he, the guard, was the chief madman.

"The devil take you!" said he, spitting on the ground. "Why do you show your teeth? This is no wine-shop!"

"And I, I do not want to be hanged! Ha! ha! ha!"

Yanson laughed always.

"Satan!" replied the guard, crossing himself.

All the evening Yanson was calm, and even joyous. He repeated the phrase that he had uttered: "I must not be hanged," and so convincing, so irrefutable was it that he had no occasion for anxiety. He had long since forgotten his crime; sometimes he simply regretted that he had not succeeded in raping the woman. Soon he thought no more about the matter.

Every morning Yanson asked when he would be hanged, and every morning the guard answered him angrily:

"You have time enough." And he went out quickly, before Yanson began to laugh.

Thanks to this invariable exchange of words, Yanson persuaded himself that the execution would never take place; for whole days he lay upon his bed, dreaming vaguely of the desolate and snow-covered fields, of the buffet at the railway station, and also of things farther away and more luminous. He was well fed in prison, he took on flesh.

"She would love me now," he said to himself, thinking of his master's wife. "Now I am as big as her husband."

He had only one desire -- to drink brandy and course madly over the roads with his horse at full gallop.

When the terrorists were arrested, the whole prison learned of it. One day, when Yanson put his customary question, the guard answered him abruptly, in an irritated voice:

"It will be soon. In a week, I think."

Yanson turned pale; the gaze of his glassy eyes became so thick that he seemed as if asleep.

"You are joking?" he asked.

"Formerly you could not await the time, today you say that I am joking. No jokes are tolerated here. It is you who like jokes, but we do not tolerate them," replied the guard with dignity; then he went out.

When evening came, Yanson had grown thin. His skin, which had become smooth again for a few days, was contracted into a thousand little wrinkles. He took no notice of anything; his movements were made slowly, as if every toss of the head, every gesture of the arm, every step, were a difficult undertaking, that must first be deeply studied. During the night Yanson lay on his camp-bed, but his eyes did not close; they remained open until morning.

"Ah!" exclaimed the guard, on seeing him the next day.

With the satisfaction of the *savant* who has made a new and a successful experiment, he examined the condemned man attentively and without haste; now everything was proceeding in the usual fashion. Satan was covered with shame; the sanctity of the prison and of the gallows was re-established. Indulgent, and even full of sincere pity, the old man asked:

"Do you want to see someone?"

"Why?"

"To say good-bye, of course . . . to your mother, for instance, or to your brother."

"I must not be hanged," said Yanson in a low voice, casting a glance sidewise at the gaoler. "I do not want to be hanged."

The guard looked at him, without saying a word.

Yanson was a little calmer in the evening. The day was so ordinary, the
cloudy winter sky shone in so usual a fashion, so familiar was the sound
of steps and conversations in the corridor, that he ceased to believe in the
execution. Formerly the night had been to him simply the moment of
darkness, the time for sleep. But now he was conscious of its mysterious
and menacing essence. To disbelieve in death one must see and hear about
one the customary course of life: steps, voices, light. And now everything
seemed extraordinary to him; this silence, these shades, that seemed to be
already the shades of death; already he felt the approach of inevitable
death; in bewilderment he climbed the first steps of the gibbet.

The day, the night, brought him alternations of hope and fear; and so
things went until the evening when he felt, or understood, that the
inevitable death would come three day later, at sunrise.

He had never thought of death; for him it had no shape. But now he felt
plainly that it had entered his cell, and was groping about in search of him.
To escape it he began to run.

The room was so small that the corners seemed to push him back
toward the centre. He could not hide himself anywhere. Several times he
struck the walls with his body; once he hurled himself against the door.
He staggered and fell, with his face upon the ground; he felt the grasp of
death upon him. Glued to the floor, his face touching the dirty black
asphalt, Yanson screamed with terror until help came . When they had
lifted him up, seated him on his bed, and sprinkled him with cold water,
he did not dare to open both eyes. He half opened one, perceived an empty
and luminous corner of his cell, and began again to scream.

But the cold water had its effect. The guard, moreover, always the same
old man, slapped Yanson several times on the head in a fatherly fashion.
This sensation of life drove out the thought of death. Yanson slept deeply
the rest of the night. He lay on his back, with mouth open, snoring loud
and long. Between his half-closed eyelids appeared a whitish, flat, and
dead eye, without a pupil.

Then day, night, voices, steps, the cabbage soup, everything became
for him one continuous horror that plunged him into a state of wild
astonishment. His weak mind could not reconcile the monstrous contradiction between, on the one hand, the bright light and the odor of the
cabbage, and, on the other, the fact that two days later he must die. He
thought of nothing; he did not even count the hours; he was simply the
prey of a dumb terror in the presence of this contradiction that bewildered

his brain: today life, tomorrow death. He ate nothing, he slept no more; he sat timidly all night long on a stool, with his legs crossed under him, or else he walked up and down his cell with furtive steps. He appeared to be in a state of open-mouthed astonishment; before taking the most commonplace article into his hands he would examine it suspiciously.

The gaolers ceased to pay attention to him. His was the ordinary condition of the condemned man, resembling, according to his gaoler who had not experienced it himself, that of an ox felled by a club.

"He is stunned; now he will feel nothing more until the moment of death," said the guard, examining him with his experienced eye. "Ivan, do you hear? Ho there, Ivan!"

"I must not be hanged!" answered Yanson, in a colorless voice; his lower jaw had dropped.

"If you had not killed, they would not hang you," reproachfully said the chief gaoler, a highly important young man, wearing a decoration. "To steal, you have killed, and you do not want to be hanged!"

"I do not want to be hanged!" replied Yanson.

"Well, you don't have to want to; that's your affair. But, instead of talking nonsense, you would do better to dispose of your possessions. You surely must have something."

"He has nothing at all! A shirt and a pair of pantaloons! And a fur cap!"

Thus time passed until Thursday. And Thursday, at midnight, a large number of people entered Yanson's cell; a man with cloth epaulets said to him:

"Get ready! it is time to start."

Always with the same slowness and the same indolence Yanson dressed himself in all that he possessed, and tied his dirty shawl around his neck. While watching him dress, the man with the epaulets, who was smoking a cigarette, said to one of the assistants:

"How warm it is today! It is spring!"

Yanson's eyes closed; he was in a complete drowse. The guard shouted:

"Come, come! Make haste! You are going to sleep!"

Suddenly Yanson ceased to move.

"I must not be hanged," said he, with indolence.

He began to walk submissively, shrugging his shoulders. In the court-yard the moist spring air had a sudden effect upon him; his nose began to run; it was thawing; close by, drops of water were falling with a joyous sound. While the gendarmes were getting into the unlighted vehicle, bending over and rattling their swords, Yanson lazy passed his finger under his running nose, or arranged his badly-tied shawl.

## IV: WE OF OREL

The court that had tried Yanson sentenced to death at the same session Michael Goloubetz, known as Michka the Tzigane, a peasant of the department of Orel, district of Eletz. The last crime of which they accused him, with evidence in support of the charge, was robbery, followed by the assassination of three persons. As for his past, it was unknown. There were vague indications to warrant the belief that the Tzigane had taken part in a whole series of other murders. With absolute sincerity and frankness he termed himself a brigand, and overwhelmed with his irony those who, to follow the fashion, pompously styled themselves "expropriators"; his last crime he described willingly in all its details. But, at the slightest reference to the past, he answered:

"Go ask the wind that blows over the fields!"

And, if they persisted in questioning him, the Tzigane assumed a dignified and serious air.

"We of Orel are all hot-heads, the fathers of all the robbers of the world," said he, in a sedate and judicial tone.

They had nicknamed him Tzigane because of his physiognomy and his thieving habits. He was thin and strangely dark; yellow spots outlined themselves upon his cheek-bones which were as prominent as those of a Tartar. He had a way of rolling the whites of his eyes, that reminded one of a horse. His gaze was quick and keen, full of curiosity, terrifying. The things over which his swift glance passed seemed to lose something or other, and to become transformed by surrendering to him part of themselves. One hesitated to take a cigarette that he had looked at, as if it had already been in his mouth. His extraordinarily mobile nature made him seem now to coil and concentrate himself like a twisted handkerchief, now to scatter himself like a sheaf of sparks. He drank water almost by the pailful, like a horse.

When the judges questioned him, he raised his head quickly, and answered without hesitation, even with satisfaction:

"It is true!"

Sometimes, to lend emphasis, he rolled his "r's" vigorously.

Suddenly he jumped to his feet, and said to the presiding judge:

"Permit me to whistle?"

"Why?" exclaimed the judge, in astonishment.

"The witnesses say that I gave the signal to my comrades; I will show you how I did it. It is very interesting."

A little disconcerted, the judge granted the desired permission. The Tzigane quickly placed four fingers in his mouth, two of each hand; he rolled his eyes furiously. And the inanimate air of the court-room was rent by a truly savage whistle. There was everything in the piercing sound, partly human, partly animal; the mortal anguish of the victim, and the savage joy of the assassin; a threat, a call, and the tragic solitude, the darkness, of a rainy autumn night.

The judge shook his head; with docility the Tzigane stopped. Like an artist who has just played a difficult air with assured success, he sat down, wiped his wet fingers on his cloak, and looked at the spectators with a satisfied air.

"What a brigand!" exclaimed one of the judges, rubbing his ear. But another, who had Tartar eyes, like the Tzigane's, was looking dreamily into the distance, over the brigand's head; he smiled, and replied:

"It was really interesting."

Without remorse, the judges sentenced the Tzigane to death.

"It is just!" said the Tzigane, when the sentence had been pronounced.

And, turning to a soldier of the guard, he added with an air of bravado:

"Well, let us be off, imbecile! And keep a good hold of your gun, lest I snatch it from you!"

The soldier looked at him seriously and timidly; he exchanged a glance with his comrade, and tested his weapon to see if it was in working order. The other did the same. And all the way to the prison it seemed to the soldiers that they did not walk, but flew; they were so absorbed by the condemned man that they were unconscious of the route, of the weather, and of themselves.

Like Yanson, Michka the Tzigane remained seventeen days in prison before being executed. And the seventeen days passed as rapidly as a single day, filled with a single thought, that of flight, of liberty, of life. The turbulent and incoercible spirit of the Tzigane, stifled by the walls, the gratings, and the opaque window through which nothing could be seen, employed all its force in setting Michka's brain on fire. As in a vapor of intoxication, bright but incomplete images whirled, clashed, and mingled in his head; they passed with a blinding and irresistible rapidity, and they all tended to the same end: flight, liberty, life. For entire hours, with nostils distended like those of a horse, the Tzigane sniffed the air; it seemed to him that he inhaled the odor of hemp and flame, of dense smoke. Or else he turned in his cell like a top, examining the walls, feeling them with his fingers, measuring them, piercing the ceiling with his gaze, sawing the bars in his mind. His agitation was a source of torture to the soldier who watched him through the window; several times he threatened to fire on him.

During the night the Tzigane slept deeply, almost without stirring, in an invariable but living immobility, like a temporarily inactive spring. But, as soon as he jumped to his feet, he began again to plan, to grope, to study. His hands were always dry and hot. Sometimes his heart suddenly congealed, as if they had placed in his breast a new block of ice which did not melt, and which caused a continuous shiver to run over his skin. At these times his naturally dark complexion became darker still, taking on the blue-black shade of bronze. Then a queer tic seized him; he constantly licked his lips, as if he had eaten a dish that was much too sweet; then, with a hiss, and with set teeth, he spat upon the ground the saliva that had thus accumulated in his mouth. He left his words unfinished; his thoughts ran so fast that his tongue could no longer keep up with them.

One day the chief of the guards entered his cell, accompanied by a soldier. He squinted at the spittle with which the ground was spattered, and said rudely:

"See how he has dirtied his cell!"

The Tzigane replied quickly:

"And you, you ugly mug, you have soiled the whole earth, and I haven't said a word to you. Why do you annoy me?"

With the same rudeness the chief of the guards offered him the post of hangman. The Tzigane showed his teeth, and began to laugh:

"So they can find none! That's not bad! Go on, then, hanging people! Ah! Ah! There are necks and ropes, and nobody to do the hanging! My God, that's not bad."

"They will give your life as a reward!"

I should say so: I could hardly play the hangman after I am dead!"

"Well, what do you say, yes or no?"

"And how do they hang here? They probably choke people secretly."

"No, they hang them to music!" retorted the chief.

"Imbecile! Of course there must be music . . . like this. . . ."

And he began to sing a captivating air.

"You have gone completely mad, my friend!" said the guard. "Come, speak seriously, what is your decision?"

The Tzigane showed his teeth.

"Are you in a hurry? Come back later, and I will tell you!"

And to the chaos of unfinished images which overwhelmed the Tzigane was added a new idea: how agreeable it would be to be the headsman! He clearly pictured to himself the square black with people, and the scaffold on which he, the Tzigane, walked back and forth, in a red shirt, with axe in hand. The sun illuminates the heads, plays gaily on the axe blade; everything is so joyous, so sumptuous, that even he whose head is to be cut off smiles. Behind the crowd are to be seen the carts and the noses of the horses; the peasants have come to town for the occasion. Still farther away fields. The Tzigane licked his lips, and spat upon the ground. Suddenly it seemed to him that his fur cap had just been pulled down over his mouth; everything became dark; he gasped for breath; and his heart changed into a block of ice, while little shivers ran through his body.

Twice more the chief came back; the Tzigane, showing his teeth again, answered:

"What a hurry you are in! Come back another time!"

Finally, one day, the gaoler cried to him, as he was passing by the window:

"You have lost your chance, my ill-favored raven. They have found another."

"The devil take you! Go, be the hangman yourself!" replied the Tzigane. And he ceased to dream of the splendors of his trade.

But toward the end, the nearer drew the day of execution, the more intolerable became the impetuosity of the torn images. The Tzigane would have liked to wait, to halt, but the furious torrent carried him on, giving him no chance to get a hold on anything; for everything was in a whirl. And his sleep became agitated; he had new and shapeless visions, as badly squared as painted blocks, and even more impetuous than his thoughts had been. It was no longer a torrent, but a continual fall from an infinite height, a whirling flight through the whole world of colors. Formerly the Tzigane had worn only a mustache tolerably well cared for; in prison he had been obliged to grow his beard, which was short, black, and stubbly; giving him a crazy look. There were moments, in fact, when the Tzigane lost his mind. He turned about in his cell all unconscious of his movements, continuing to feel for the rough and uneven walls. And he always drank great quantities of water, like a horse.

One evening, when they were lighting the lamps, the Tzigane dropped on all fours in the middle of his cell, and began to howl like a wolf. He did this very seriously, as if performing an indispensable and important act. He filled his lungs with air, and then expelled it slowly in a prolonged and trembling howl. With knit brows, he listened to himself attentively. The very trembling of the voice seemed a little affected; he did not shout indistinctly; he made each note in this wild beast's cry sound separately, full of unspeakable suffering and terror.

Suddenly he stopped, and remained silent for a few minutes, without getting up. He began to whisper, as if speaking to the ground:

"Dear friends, good friends . . . dear friends . . . good friends . . . have pit . . . friends! My friends!"

He said a word, and listened to it.

He jumped to his feet, and for a whole hour poured forth a steady stream of the worst curses.

"Go to the devil, you scoundrels!" he screamed, rolling his bloodshot eyes. "If I must be hanged, hang me, instead of . . . Ah, you blackguards!"

The soldier on guard, as white as chalk, wept with anguish and fear; he pounded the door with the muzzle of his gun, and cried in a lamentable voice:

"I will shoot you! By God, do you hear? I will shoot you!"

But he did not dare to fire; they never fire on prisoners sentenced to death, except in case of revolt. And the Tzigane ground his teeth, swore, and spat. His brain, placed on the narrow frontier that separates life from death, crumbled like a lump of dried clay.

When they came, during the night, to take him to the gallows, he regained a little of his animation. His cheeks took on some color; in his eyes the usual strategy, a little savage, sparkled again, and he asked of one of the functionaries:

"Who will hang us? The new one? Is he accustomed to it yet?"

"You needn't disturb yourself about that," answered the personage thus appealed to.

"What? Not disturb myself! It is not Your Highness that is going to be hanged, but I! At least don't spare the soap on the slip-noose; the State pays for it!"

"I beg you to hold your tongue!"

"This fellow, you see, consumes all the soap in the prison; see how his face shines," continued the Tzigane, pointing to the chief of the guards.

"Silence!"

"Don't spare the soap!"

Suddenly he began to laugh, and his legs became numb. Yet, when he arrived in the courtyard, he could still cry:

"Say, there! you fellows yonder, come forward with my carriage!"

## V: "KISS HIM AND BE SILENT"

The verdict against the five terrorists was pronounced in its final form and confirmed the same day. The condemned were not notified of the day of execution. But they foresaw that they would be hanged, according to custom, the same night, or, at the latest, the night following. When they were offered the opportunity of seeing their families the next day, they understood that the execution was fixed for Friday at daybreak.

Tanya Kovalchuk had no near relatives. She knew only of some distant relatives living in Little Russia, who probably knew nothing of the trial or the verdict. Musya and Werner, not having revealed their identity, did not insist on seeing any of their people. Only Sergey Golovin and Vasily Kashirin were to see their families. The thought of this approaching interview was frightful to both of them, but they could not make up their minds to refuse a final conversation, a last kiss.

Sergey Golovin thought sadly of this visit. He was fond of his father and mother; he had seen them very recently, and he was filled with terror at the thought of what was going to happen. The hanging itself, in all its monstrosity, in its disconcerting madness, outlined itself more readily in his imagination than these few short, incomprehensible minutes that seemed apart from time, apart from life. What to do? What to say? The most simple and customary gestures -- to shake hands, embrace, and say, "How do you do, father?" -- seemed to him frightful in their monstrous, inhuman, insane insignificance.

After the verdict they did not put the condemned in the same cell, as Tanya expected them to do. All the morning, up to the time when he received his parents, Sergey Golovin walked back and forth in his cell, twisting his short beard, his features pitiably contracted. Sometimes he stopped suddenly, filled his lungs with air, and puffed like a swimmer who has remained too long under water. But, as he was in good health, and as his young life was solidly implanted within him, even in these minutes of atrocious suffering, the blood coursed under his skin, coloring his cheeks; his blue eyes preserved their usual brilliancy.

Everything went off better than Sergey expected; his father, Nicolas Sergiévitch Golovin, a retired colonel, was the first to enter the room where the visitors were received. Everything about him was white and of the same whiteness: face, hair, beard, hands. His old and well-brushed garment smelt of benzine; his epaulets seemed new. He entered with a firm and measured step, straightening himself up. Extending his dry, white hand, he said aloud:

"How do you do, Sergey?"

Behind him came the mother, with short steps; she wore a strange smile. But she too shook hands with her son, and repeated aloud:

"How do you do, my little Sergey?"

She kissed him and sat down without saying a word. She did not throw herself upon her son, she did not begin to weep or cry as Sergey expected her to do. She kissed him and sat down without speaking. With a trembling hand she even smoothed the wrinkles in her black silk gown.

Sergey did not know that the colonel had spent the entire previous night in rehearsing this interview. "We must lighten the last moments of our son's life, and not make them more painful for him," the colonel had decided; and he had carefully weighed each phrase, each gesture, of the morrow's visit. But sometimes, in the course of the rehearsal, he became confused, he forgot what he had prepared himself to say, and he wept bitterly, sunk in the corner of his sofa. The next morning he had explained to his wife what she was to do.

"Above all, kiss him and be silent," he repeated. "You will be a able to speak later, a little later; but, after kissing him, be silent. Do not speak immediately after kissing him, do you understand? Otherwise you will say what you should not."

"I understand, Nicolas Sergiévitch!" answered the mother, with tears.

"And do not weep! May God keep you from that! Do not weep! You will kill him if you weep, mother!"

"And why do you weep yourself?"

"Why should one not weep here with the rest of you? You must not weep, do you hear?"

"All right, Nicolas Sergiévitch."

They got into a cab and started off, silent, bent, old; they were plunged in their thoughts amid the gay roar of the city; it was the carnival season, and the streets were filled with a noisy crowd.

They sat down. The colonel assumed a suitable attitude, his right hand thrust in the front of his frock-coat. Sergey remained seated a moment; his look met his mother's wrinkled face; he rose suddenly.

"Sit down, my little Sergey! " begged the mother.

"Sit down, Sergey!" repeated the father.

They kept silence. The mother wore a strange smile.

"How many moves we have made in your behalf, Sergey! Your father . . ."

"It was useless, my little mother!"

The colonel said, firmly:

"We were in duty bound to do it that you might not think that your parents had abandoned you."

Again they became silent. They were afraid to utter a syllable, as if each word of the language had lost its proper meaning and now meant but one thing: death. Sergey looked at the neat little frock-coat smelling of benzine, and thought: "He has no orderly now; then he must have cleaned his coat himself. How is it that I have never seen him clean his coat? Probably he does it in the morning." Suddenly he asked:

"And my sister? Is she well?"

"Ninotchka knows nothing!" answered the mother, quickly.

But the colonel sternly interrupted her:

"What is the use of lying? She has read the newspaper . . . let Sergey know that . . . all . . . his own . . . have thought . . . and . . ."

Unable to continue, he stopped. Suddenly the mother's face contracted, her features became confused and wild. Her colorless eyes were madly distended; more and more she panted for breath.

"Se . . . Ser. . . Ser. . . Ser. . ." she repeated, without moving her lips; "Ser. . ."

"My little mother!"

The colonel took a step; trembling all over, without knowing how frightful he was in his corpse-like pallor, in his desperate and forced firmness, he said to his wife:

"Be silent! Do not torture him! Do not torture him! Do not torture him! He must die! Do not torture him!"

Frightened, she was silent already, and he continued to repeat, with his trembling hands pressed against his breast:

"Do not torture him!"

Then he took a step backward, and again thrust his hand into the front of his frock-coat; wearing an expression of forced calmness, he asked aloud, with pallid lips:

"When?"

"Tomorrow morning," answered Sergey.

The mother looked at the ground, biting her lips, as if she heard nothing. And she seemed to continue to bite her lips as she let fall these simple words:

"Ninotchka told me to kiss you, my little Sergey!"

"Kiss her for me!" said the condemned man.

"Good! The Chvostofs send their salutations. . . ."

"Who are they? Ah! yes. . . ."

The colonel interrupted him:

"Well, we must start. Rise, mother, it is necessary!"

The two men lifted the swooning woman.

"Bid him farewell!" ordered the colonel. "Give him your blessing!"

She did everything that she was told. But, while giving her son a short kiss and making on his person the sign of the cross, she shook her head and repeated distractedly:

"No, it is not that! No, it is not that!"

"Adieu, Sergey!" said the father. They shook hands, and exchanged a short, but earnest, kiss.

"You . . ." began Sergey.

"Well?" asked the father, spasmodically.

"No, not like that. No, no! What shall I say?" repeated the mother, shaking her head.

She had sat down again, and was tottering.

"You . . ." resumed Sergey. Suddenly his face took on a lamentable expression, and he grimaced like a child, tears filling his eyes. Through their sparkling facets he saw beside him the pale face of his father, who was weeping also.

"Father, you are a strong man!"

"What do you say? What do you say?" said the bewildered colonel. Suddenly, as if completely broken, he fell, with his head on his son's shoulder. And the two covered each other with ardent kisses, the father receiving them on his light hair, the prisoner on his cloak.

"And I?" asked suddenly a hoarse voice.

They looked: the mother was on her feet again, and, with her head thrown back, was watching them wrathfully, almost hatefully.

"What is the matter with you, mother?" cried the colonel.

"And I?" she repeated, shaking her head with an insane energy. "You embrace each other, and I? You are men, are you not? And I? And I?. . ."

"Mother!" and Sergey threw himself into her arms.

The last words of the colonel were:

"My blessing for your death, Sergey! Die with courage, like an officer!"

And they went away. . . . On returning to his cell Sergey lay upon his camp-bed, with face turned toward the wall that the soldiers might not see him, and wept a long time.

Vasily Kashirin's mother came alone to visit him. The father, a rich merchant, had refused to accompany her. When the old woman entered, Vasily was walking in his cell. In spite of the heat, he was trembling with cold. The conversation was short and painful.

"You ought not to have come, mother. Why should we two torment each other?"

"Why all this, Vasya? Why have you done this, my son? God! God!"

The old woman began to weep, drying her tears with her black silk neckerchief.

Accustomed as they were, his brothers and he, to treat their mother roughly, she being a simple woman who did not understand them, he stopped, and, in the midst of his shivering, said to her, harshly:

"That's it, I knew how it would be. You understand nothing, mama, nothing!"

Very well, my son. What is the matter with you? Are you cold?"

I am cold," answered Vasily, and he began to walk again, looking sidewise now and then at the old woman with the same air of irritation.

"You are cold, my son . . ."

"Ah! You speak of cold, but soon . . ." He made a gesture of desperation.

Again the mother began to sob.

"I said to your father: 'Go to see him, he is your son, your flesh; give him a last farewell.' He would not."

"The devil take him! He is not a father. All his life he has been a scoundrel. He remains one!"

"Yet, Vasya, he is your father. . . ."

And the old woman shook her head reproachfully.

It was ridiculous and terrible. This paltry and useless conversation engaged them when face to face with death. While almost weeping, so sad was the situation, Vasily cried out:

"Understand then, mother. They are going to hang me, to hang me! Do you understand, yes or no?"

"And why did you kill?" she cried.

"My God! What are you saying? Even the beasts have feelings. Am I your son or not?"

He sat down and wept. His mother wept also; but, in their incapability of communicating in the same affection in order to face the terror of the approaching death, they wept cold tears that did not warm the heart.

"You ask me if I am your mother? You heap reproaches on me; and yet I have turned completely white these last few days."

"All right, all right, forgive me. Adieu! Embrace my brothers for me."

"Am I not your mother? Do I not suffer for you?"

At last she departed. She was weeping so that she could not see her way. And, the farther she got from the prison, the more abundant became her tears. She retraced her steps, losing herself in this city in which she was born, in which she had grown up, in which she had grown old. She entered a little abandoned garden, and sat down on a damp bench.

And suddenly she understood: tomorrow they would hang her son! She sprang to her feet, and tried to shout and run, but suddenly her head turned, and she sank to the earth. The path, white with frost, was wet and slippery; the old woman could not rise again. She rested her weight on her wrists, and then fell back again. The black neckerchief slipped from her head, uncovering her dirty gray hair. It seemed to her that she was celebrating her son's wedding. Yes, they had just married him, and she had drunk a little wine; she was slightly intoxicated.

"I cannot help myself! My God, I cannot help myself!"

And, with swinging head, she said to herself that she had drunk too much, and was crawling around on the wet ground, . . . but they gave her wine to drink and wine again, and still more wine. And from her heart arose the laugh of the drunkard and the desire to abandon herself to a wild dance; . . . but they kept on lifting cups to her lips, one after another, one after another.

## VI: "THE HOURS FLY"

In the fortress where the condemned terrorists were confined there was a steeple with an old clock. Every hour, every half-hour, every quarter of an hour, this clock struck in a tone of infinite sadness, like the distant and plaintive cry of birds of passage. In the daytime this odd and desolate music was lost in the noise of the city, of the broad and animated street that passed the fortress. The tramways rumbled, the shoes of the horses rattled, the trembling automobiles sounded their hoarse horns far into the distance. As the carnival was approaching, the peasants of the suburbs had come to town to earn some money as cab drivers; the bells of the little Russian horses tinkled noisily. The conversations were gay, and had a flavor of intoxication, real holiday conversations. The weather harmonized with the occasion; the spring had brought a thaw, and the road was wet with dirty puddles. The trees on the squares had suddenly darkened. A slightly warm wind was blowing from the sea in copious moist puffs -- a light, fresh air that seemed to have started on a joyous flight toward the infinite.

By night the street was silent under the brilliancy of the large electric suns. The immense fortress with its smooth walls was plunged in darkness and silence; a barrier of calm and shadow separated it from the ever-living city. Then they heard the striking of the hours, the slow, sad birth and death of a strange melody, foreign to the land. Like big drops of transparent glass, the hours and the minutes fell from an immeasurable height into a metallic basin that was vibrating gently. Sometimes they were like birds that passed.

Into the cells came, day and night, this single sound. It penetrated through the roof, through the thick stone walls; it alone broke the silence. Sometimes they forgot it, or did not hear it. Sometimes they awaited it with despair; they lived only by and for this sound, having learned to be distrustful of silence. The prison was reserved for criminals of note; its special, rigorous regulations were as rigid and sharp as the corners of the walls. If there is nobility in cruelty, then the solemn, deaf, dead silence that caught up every breath and every rustle was noble.

In this silence, penetrated by the desolate striking of the flying minutes, three men and two women, separated from the world, were awaiting the coming of the night, of the dawn, and of the execution; and each was preparing for it in his own fashion.

Throughout her life Tanya Kovalchuk had thought only of others, and now also it was for her comrades that she underwent suffering and torture. She pictured death to herself only because it threatened Sergey Golovin, Musya, and the others; but her thoughts did not dwell on the fact that she too would be executed.

As if to reward herself for the artificial firmness that she had shown before the judges, she wept for hours altogether. This is characteristic of old women, who have suffered much. When it occurred to her that Sergey might be unprovided with tobacco, or that Werner possibly was deprived of the tea of which he was so fond -- and this at the moment when they were about to die -- she suffered perhaps as much as at the idea of the execution. The execution was something inevitable, even incidental, not worthy of consideration; but that an imprisoned man should be without tobacco on the very eve of his execution was an idea absolutely intolerable. Evoking the pleasant memories of their common life, she lamented over the interview between Sergey and his parents.

For Musya she felt a special pity. For a long time it had seemed to her, mistakenly, however, that Musya was in love with Werner; she had beautiful and luminous dreams for their future. Before her arrest Musya wore a silver ring on which was engraved a skull and crossbones surrounded with a crown of thorns. Often Tanya Kovalchuk had looked at this ring sorrowfully, viewing it as a symbol of renunciation; half serious, half joking, she had asked Musya to take it off.

"No, Tanya, I will not give it to you. You will soon have another on your finger!"

Her comrades always thought that she would soon be married, which much offended her. She wanted no husband. And, as she recalled these conversations with Musya and reflected that Musya was indeed sacrificed, Tanya, full of motherly pity, felt the tears choking her. Every time the clock struck, she lifted her face, covered with tears, and listened, wondering how this plaintive and persistent summons of death was being received in the other cells.

## VII: "THERE IS NO DEATH"

And Musya was happy!

With arms folded behind her back, dressed in a prisoner's gown that was too large for her and that made her look like a youth wearing a borrowed costume, she walked back and forth in her cell, at a regular pace, never wearying. She had tucked up the long sleeves of her gown, and her thin and emaciated arms, the arms of a child, emerged from the flaring breadths like flower-stems from a coarse and unclean pitcher. The roughness of the stuff irritated the skin of her white and slender neck; sometimes, with her two hands, she released her throat, and felt cautiously for the spot where her skin was burning.

Musya walked with a long stride, and tried blushingly to justify to herself the fact that the finest of deaths, reserved hitherto for martyrs, had been assigned to her, so young, so humble, and who had done so little. It seemed to her that, in dying upon the scaffold, she was making a pretentious show that was in bad taste.

At her last interview with her lawyer she had asked him to procure poison for her, but immediately had given up the idea: would not people think that she was actuated by fear or by ostentation? Instead of dying modestly and unnoticed, would she not cause still further scandal? And she had added, quickly:

"No, no, it is useless!"

Now her sole desire was to explain, to prove, that she was not a heroine, that it was not a frightful thing to die, and that no one need pity her or worry on her account.

Musya sought excuses, pretexts of such a nature as to exalt her sacrifice and give it a real value, as if it had actually been called in question.

"In fact," she said to herself, "I am young; I might have lived for a long time. But . . ."

Just as the gleam of a candle is effaced by the radiance of the rising sun, youth and life seem to her dull and sombre beside the magnificent and luminous halo that is about to crown her modest person.

"Is it possible?" Musya asks herself, in great confusion. "Is it possible that I am worth anybody's tears?"

And she is seized with an unspeakable joy. There is no more doubt; she has been taken into the pale. She has a right to figure among the heroes who from all countries go to heaven through flames and executions. What serene peace, what infinite happiness! An immaterial being, she believes herself hovering in a divine light.

Of what else was Musya thinking? Of many things, since for her the thread of life was not severed by death but continued to unroll in a calm and regular fashion. She was thinking of her comrades, of those who at a distance were filled with anguish at the idea of her approaching execution, of those who nearer at hand would go with her to the gallows. She was astonished that Vasily should be a prey to terror, he who had always been brave. On Tuesday morning, when they had prepared themselves to kill, and then to die themselves, Tanya Kovalchuk had trembled with emotion; they had been obliged to send her away, whereas Vasily joked and laughed and moved about amid the bombs with so little caution that Werner had said to him severely:

One should not play with death!"

Why, then, was Vasily afraid now? And this incomprehensible terror was so foreign to Musya's soul that she soon ceased to think about it and to inquire into its cause. Suddenly she felt a mad desire to see Sergey Golovin and laugh with him.

Perhaps too her thought was unwilling to dwell long on the same subject, resembling therein a light bird that hovers before infinite horizons, all space, the caressing and tender azure, being accessible to it. The hours continued to strike. Thoughts blended in this harmonious and distant symphony; fleeting images became a sort of music. It seemed to Musya that she was travelling on a broad and easy road in a quiet night; the carriage rode easily on its springs. All care had vanished; the tired body was dissolved in the darkness; joyous and weary, the thought peacefully created vivid images, and became intoxicated on their beauty. Musya recalled three comrades who had been hanged lately; their faces were illuminated and near, nearer than those of the living. . . . So in the morning one thinks gaily of the hospitable friends who will receive you in the evening with smiles on their lips.

At last Musya became weary from walking. She lay down cautiously on the camp-bed, and continued to dream, with half-closed eyes.

"Is this really death? My God, how beautiful it is! Or is it life? I do not know, I do not know! I am going to see and hear. . . ."

From the first days of her imprisonment she had been a prey to hallucinations. She had a very musical ear; her sense of hearing, sharpened by the silence, gathered in the slightest echoes of life; the footsteps of the sentinels in the corridor, the striking of the clock, the whispering of the wind over the zinc roof, the creaking of a lantern, all blended for her in a vast and mysterious symphony. At first the hallucinations frightened Musya, and she drove them away as morbid manifestations; then, perceiving that she was in good health and had no pathological symptoms, she ceased to resist.

But now she hears very plainly the sound of the military band. She opens her eyes in astonishment, and raises her head. Through the windows she sees the night; the clock strikes. "Again!" she thought, as she closed her eyes without disturbing herself. Again the music begins. Musya clearly distinguishes the steps of the soldiers as they turn the corner of the prison; a whole regiment is passing before her windows. The boots keep time to the music on the frozen ground; one! two! one! two! Sometimes a boot squeaks; a foot slips and then recovers itself. The music draws nearer; it is playing a noisy and stirring triumphal march which Musya does not know. There is probably some festival in the fortress.

The soldiers are under her windows, and the cell is filled with joyous, regular, and harmonious sounds. A big brass trumpet emits false notes: it is not in time; now it is in advance, now it lags behind in a ridiculous fashion. Musya pictures to herself a little soldier playing this trumpet assiduously, and she laughs.

The regiment has passed; the sound of the footsteps grows fainter and fainter; one! two! one! two! In the distance the music becomes gayer and more beautiful. Several times more the trumpet sounds out of time, with its metallic, sonorous, and gay voice, and then all is quiet. Again the clock in the steeple strikes the hours.

New forms come and lean over her, surrounding her with transparent clouds and lifting her to a great height, where birds of prey are hovering. At left and right, above and below, everywhere birds are crying like heralds; they call, they warn. They spread their wings, and immensity sustains them. And on their inflated breasts that split the air is reflected the sparkling azure. The beating of Musya's heart becomes more and more regular, her respiration more and more calm and peaceful. She sleeps; her face is pale; her features are drawn; there are dark rings around her eyes. On her lips a smile. Tomorrow, when the sun shall rise, this intelligent and fine face will be deformed by a grimace in which no trace of the human will be left; the brain will be inundated with thick blood; the glassy eyes will protrude from their orbits. But today Musya sleeps quietly, and smiles in her immortality.

Musya sleeps.

And the prison continues to live its special, blind, vigilant life, a sort of perpetual anxiety. They walk. They whisper. A gun rings out. It seems as if someone cries out. Is this reality or hallucination?

The grating in the door lowers noiselessly. In the dark opening appears a sinister bearded face. For a long time the widely-opened eyes view with astonishment the sleeping Musya; then the face disappears as quietly as it came.

The bells in the steeple ring and sing interminably. One would say that the weary hours were climbing a high mountain toward midnight. The ascent grows more and more painful. They slip, fall back with a groan, and begin again to toil painfully toward the black summit.

There is a sound of footsteps. Whispering voices are heard. Already they are harnessing the horses to the sombre, unlighted vehicle.

## VIII  "DEATH EXISTS, AND LIFE ALSO"

Sergey Golovin never thought of death. It seemed to him something incidental and foreign. He was robust, endowed with that serenity in the joy of living which causes all evil thoughts, all thoughts fatal to life, to disappear rapidly, leaving the organism intact. Just as, with him, physical wounds healed quickly, so all injuries to his soul were immediately nullified. He brought into all his acts, into his pleasures and into his preparations for crime, the same happy and tranquil gravity: everything in life was gay, everything was important, worthy of being well done.

And he did everything well; he sailed a boat admirably, he was an excellent marksman. He was as faithful in friendship as in love, and had an unshakeable confidence in the "word of honor." His comrades declared laughingly that, if one who had been proved a spy should swear to Sergey that he was not a spy, Sergey would believe him and shake hands with him. A single fault: he thought himself a good singer, whereas he sang atrociously false, even in the case of revolutionary hymns. He got angry when they laughed at him.

"Either you are all asses, or else I am an ass! " he said in a serious and offended tone. And, after a moment's reflection, the comrades declared, in a tone quite as serious:

"It is you who are an ass. You show it in your voice!"

And, as is sometimes the case with worthy people, they loved him perhaps more for his eccentricities than for his virtues.

He thought so little of death, he feared it so little, that on the fatal morning, before leaving the dwelling of Tanya Kovalchuk, he alone had breakfasted with appetite, as usual. He had taken two glasses of tea, and eaten a whole two-cent loaf. Then, looking with sadness at Werner's untouched bread, he said to him:

"Why don't you eat? Eat; it is necessary to get strength!"

"I am not hungry."

"Well, I will eat your bread! Shall I?"

"What an appetite you have, Sergey!"

By way of reply, Sergey, with his mouth full, began to sing, in a false and hollow voice:

*"A hostile wind is blowing o'er our heads."*

After the arrest Sergey had a moment of sadness; the plot had been badly planned. But he said to himself: "Now there is something else that must be done well: to die." And his gaiety returned. On his second day in the fortress he began gymnastic exercises, according to the extremely rational system of a German named Müller, which interested him much. He undressed himself completely; and, to the amazement of the anxious sentinel, he went carefully through the eighteen prescribed exercises.

As a propagandist of the Müller system, it gave him much satisfaction to see the soldier follow his movements. Although he knew that he would get no answer, he said to the eye that appeared at the grating:

"That is the kind of thing that does you good, brother; that gives you strength! That is what they ought to make you do in the regiment," he added, in a gentle and persuasive voice, that he might not frighten the soldier, not suspecting that his guardian took him for a madman.

The fear of death showed itself in him progressively, seemingly by shocks: it seemed to him that someone was thumping him violently in the heart from below. Then the sensation disappeared, but came back a few hours later, each time more intense and prolonged. It was beginning already to take on the vague outlines of an unendurable anguish.

"Is it possible that I am afraid?" thought Sergey, in astonishment. "How stupid!"

It was not he who was afraid; it was his young, robust, and vigorous body, which neither the gymnastics of Müller or the cold shower-baths could deceive. The stronger and fresher he became after his cold-water ablutions, the more acute and unendurable was his sensation of temporary fear. And it was in the morning, after his deep sleep and physical exercises, that this atrocious fear like something foreign appeared -- exactly at the moment when formerly he had been particularly conscious of his strength and his joy in living. He noticed this, and said to himself:

"You are stupid, my friend. In order that the body may die more easily, it should be weakened, not fortified."

From that time he gave up his gymnastics and his massage. And, to explain this right-about-face, he cried to the soldier:

"Brother, the method is a good one. It is only for those who are going to be hanged that it is good for nothing."

In fact, he felt a sort of relief. He tried also to eat less in order to weaken himself, but, in spite of the lack of air and exercise, his appetite remained excellent. Sergey could not resist it, and ate everything that they brought him. Then he resorted to a subterfuge; before sitting down to table, he poured half of his soup into his bucket. And this method succeeded; a great weariness, a vague numbness, took possession of him."

"I will teach you!" he said, threatening his body; and he caressed his softening muscles sadly.

But soon the body became accustomed to this regime and the fear of death appeared again, not in so acute a form, but as a vague sensation of nausea, still harder to bear. "It is because this lasts so long," thought Sergey. "If only I could sleep all the time until the day of execution!" He tried to sleep as much as possible. His first efforts were not altogether fruitless; then insomnia set in, accompanied with obsessing thoughts and, with these, a regret that he must part with life.

"Am I, then, afraid of it?" he asked himself, thinking of death. "It is the loss of life that I regret. Life is an admirable thing, whatever the pessimists may say. What would a pessimist say if they were to hang him? Ah! I regret to lose my life, I regret it much."

When he clearly understood that for him all was over, that he had before him only a few hours of empty waiting and then death, he had a queer feeling. It seemed to him that they had stripped him naked in an extraordinary fashion. Not only had they taken away his clothes, but also sun, air, sound and light, speech and the power of action. Death had not yet arrived, and yet life seemed already absent; he felt a strange sensation, sometimes incomprehensible, sometimes intelligible, but very subtle and mysterious.

"What is it, then?" wondered Sergey, in his torment. "And I, where am I? I . . . What I?"

He examined himself attentively, with interest, beginning with his loose slippers, such as the prisoners wore, and stopping with his belly, over which hung his ample cloak. He began to walk back and forth in his cell, with arms apart, and continued to look at himself as a woman does when trying on a gown that is too long. He tried to turn his head: it turned. And what seemed to him a little terrifying was he himself, Sergey Golovin, who soon would be no more!

Everything became strange.

He tried to walk, and it seemed queer to him to walk. He tried to sit down, and he was surprised that he could do so. He tried to drink water, and it seemed queer to him to drink, to swallow, to hold the goblet, to see his fingers, his trembling fingers. He began to cough, and thought: "How curious it is! I cough."

"What is the matter? Am I going mad?" he asked himself. "That would be the last straw, indeed!"

He wiped his brow, and this gesture seemed to him equally surprising. Then he fixed himself in a motionless posture, without breathing -- for entire hours, it seemed to him, extinguishing all thought, holding his breath, avoiding all motion; for every thought was madness, every gesture an aberration. Time disappeared as if transformed into space, into a transparent space in which there was no air, into an immense place containing everything -- land and life and men. And one could take in everything at a glance, to the very extremity, to the edge of the unknown gulf, to death. And it was not because he saw death that Sergey suffered, but because he saw life and death at the same time. A sacrilegious hand had lifted the curtain which from all eternity had hidden the mystery of life and the mystery of death; they had ceased to be mysteries, but they were no more comprehensible than truth written in a foreign language.

"And here we are back to Müller again!" he suddenly declared aloud, in a voice of deep conviction. He shook his head, and began to laugh gaily, sincerely:

"Ah, my good Müller! My dear Müller! My worthy German! You are right, after all, Müller; as for me, brother Müller, I am only an ass!"

He quickly made the round of his cell; and, to the great astonishment of the soldier who was watching him through the grating, he entirely undressed and went through the eighteen exercises with scrupulous exactness. He bent and straightened up his young body, which had grown a little thin; he stooped, inhaling and exhaling the air; he raised himself on tiptoe, and moved his arms and legs.

"Yes, but, you know, Müller," reasoned Sergey, throwing out his chest, his ribs outlining themselves plainly under his thin, distended skin -- "you know, Müller, there is still a nineteenth exercise -- suspension by the neck in a fixed position. And that is called hanging. Do you understand, Müller? They take a living man, Sergey Golovin, for example; they wrap him up like a doll, and they hang him by the neck until he is dead. It is stupid, Müller, but that is the way it is; one must be resigned!"

He leaned on his right side, and repeated:

"One must be resigned, Müller!"

## IX: "THE HORRIBLE SOLITUDE"

Under the same roof and to the same melodious chant of the indifferent hours, separated from Sergey and from Musya by a few empty cells, but as isolated as if he alone had existed in the whole universe, the unhappy Vasily Kashirin was finishing his life in anguish and terror.

Covered with sweat, his shirt adhering to his body, his formerly curly hair now falling in straight locks, he went back and forth in his cell with the jerky and lamentable gait of one suffering atrociously with the toothache. He sat down for a moment, and then began to run again; then he rested his forehead against the wall, stopped, and looked about as if in search of a remedy. He had so changed that one might think that he possessed two different faces, one of which, the younger, had gone nobody knows where, to give place to the second, a terrible face, that seemed to have come from darkness.

Fear had shown itself suddenly to him, and had seized upon his person as an exclusive and sovereign mistress. On the fatal morning, when he was marching to certain death, he had played with it; but that evening, confined in his cell, he had been carried away and lashed by a wave of mad terror. As long as he had gone freely forward to meet danger and death, as long as he had held his fate in his own hands, however terrible it might be, he had appeared tranquil and even joyous, the small amount of shameful and decrepit fear that he had felt having disappeared in a consciousness of infinite liberty, in the firm and audacious affirmation of his intrepid will, leaving no trace behind. With an infernal machine strapped around his waist, he had transformed himself into an instrument of death, he had borrowed from the dynamite its cruel reason and its flashing and homicidal power. In the street, among the busy people preoccupied with their affairs and quickly dodging the tramcars and the cabs, it seemed to him as if he came from another and an unknown world, where there was no such thing as death or fear.

Suddenly a brutal, bewildering change had taken place. Vasily no longer went where he wanted to go, but was led where others wanted him to go. He no longer chose his place; they placed him in a stone cage and locked him in, as if he were a thing. He could no longer choose between life and death; they led him to death, certainly and inevitably. He who had been for a moment the incarnation of will, of life, and of force, had become a lamentable specimen of impotence; he was nothing but an animal destined for the slaughter. Whatever he might say, they would not listen; if he started to cry out, they would stuff a rag in his mouth; and, if he even tried to walk, they would take him away and hang him. If he resisted, if he struggled, if he lay down on the ground, they would be stronger than he; they would pick him up, they would tie him, and thus they would carry him to the gallows. And his imagination gave to the men charged with his execution, men like himself, the new, extraordinary, and terrifying aspect of unthinking automata, whom nothing in the world could stop, and who seized a man, overpowered him, hanged him, pulled him by the feet, cut the rope, put the body in a coffin, carried it way, and buried it.

From the first day of his imprisonment, people and life had transformed themselves for him into an unspeakably frightful world filled with mechanical dolls. Almost mad with fear, he tried to fancy to himself that these people had tongues and spoke, but he did not succeed. Their mouths opened, something like a sound came from them; then they separated with movements of their legs, and all was over. He was in the situation of a man who, left alone in a house at night, should see all things become animate, move, and assume over him an unlimited power; suddenly the wardrobe, the chair, the sofa, the writing-table would sit in judgment upon him. He would cry out, call for help, beg, and rove from room to room; and the things would speak to each other in their own tongue; and then the wardrobe, the chair, the sofa, and the writing-table would start to hang him, the other things looking on.

In the eyes of Vasily Kashirin, sentenced to be hanged, everything took on a puerile aspect; the cell, the grated door, the striking apparatus of the clock, the fortress with its carefully modelled ceilings, and, above, the mechanical doll equipped with a musket, who walked up and down in the corridor, and the other dolls who frightened him by looking through the grating and handing him his food without a word.

A man had disappeared from the world.

In court the presence of the comrades had brought Kashirin back to himself. Again for a moment he saw people; they were there, judging him, speaking the language of men, listening, and seeming to understand. But, when he saw his mother, he felt clearly, with the terror of a man who is going mad and he knows it, that this old woman in a black neckerchief was a simple mechanical doll. He was astonished at not having suspected it before, and at having awaited this visit as something infinitely sorrowful in its distressing gentleness. While forcing himself to speak, he thought with a shudder:

"My God! But it is a doll! A doll-mother! And yonder is a doll-soldier; at home there is a doll-father, and this is the doll Vasily Kashirin."

When the mother began to weep, Vasily again saw something human in her, but this disappeared with the first words that she uttered. With curiosity and terror he watched the tears flow from the doll's eyes.

When his fear became intolerable, Vasily Kashirin tried to pray. There remained with him only a bitter, detestable, and enervating rancor against all the religious principles upon which his youth had been nourished, in the house of his father, a large merchant. He had no faith. But one day, in his childhood, he had heard some words that had made an impression upon him and that remained surrounded forever with a gentle poesy: These words were:

"Joy of all the afflicted!"

Sometimes, in painful moments, he whispered, without praying, without even accounting to himself for what he was doing: "Joy of all the afflicted!" And then he suddenly felt relieved; he had a desire to approach someone who was dear to him and complain gently:

"Our life! . . . but is it really a life? Say, my dear, is it really a life?"

And then suddenly he felt himself ridiculous; he would have liked to bare his breast and ask someone to beat it.

He had spoken to no one, not even to his best comrades, of his "Joy of all the afflicted!" He seemed to know nothing of it himself, so deeply hidden was it in his soul. And he evoked it rarely, with precaution.

Now that the fear of the unfathomable mystery which was rising before him completely covered him, as the water covers the plants on the bank when the tide is rising, he had a desire to pray. He wanted to fall upon his knees, but was seized with shame before the sentinel; so, with hands clasped upon his breast, he murmured in a low voice:

"Joy of all the afflicted!"

And he repeated with anxiety, in a tone of supplication:

"Joy of all the afflicted, descend into me, sustain me!"

Something moved softly. It seemed to him that a sorrowful and gentle force hovered in the distance and then vanished, without illuminating the shades of the agony. In the steeple the hour struck. The soldier yawned long and repeatedly.

"Joy of all the afflicted! You are silent! And you will say nothing to Vasily Kashirin!"

He wore an imploring smile, and waited. But in his soul there was the same void as around him. Useless and tormenting thoughts came to him; again he saw the lighted candles, the priest in his robe, the holy image painted on the wall, his father bending and straightening up again, praying and kneeling, casting furtive glances at Vasily to see if he too was praying or was simply amusing himself. And Kashirin was in still deeper anguish than before.

Everything disappeared.

His consciousness went out like the dying embers that one scatters on the hearth; it froze, like the body of a man just dead in which the heart is still warm while the hands and feet are already cold.

Vasily had a moment of wild terror when they came into his cell to get him. He did not even suspect that the hour of the execution had arrived; he simply saw the people and took fright, almost like a child.

"I will not do it again! I will not do it again!" he whispered , without being heard; and his lips became icy as he recoiled slowly toward the rear of his cell, just as in childhood he had tried to escape the punishments of his father.

"You will have to go . . ."

They talked, they walked around him, they gave him he knew not what. He closed his eyes, staggered, and began to prepare himself painfully. Undoubtedly he had recovered consciousness; he suddenly asked a cigarette of one of the officials, who amiably extended his cigarette-case.

## X: "THE WALLS CRUMBLE"

The unknown, surnamed Werner, was a man fatigued by struggle. He had loved life, the theatre, society, art, literature, passionately. Endowed with an excellent memory, he spoke several languages perfectly. He was fond of dress, and had excellent manners. Of the whole group of terrorists he was the only one who was able to appear in society without risk of recognition.

For a long time already, and without his comrades having noticed it, he had entertained a profound contempt for men. More of a mathematician than a poet, ecstasy and inspiration had remained so far things unknown to him; at times he would look upon himself as a madman seeking to square the circle in seas of human blood. The enemy against which he daily struggled could not inspire him with respect; it was nothing but a compact network of stupidities, treasons, falsehoods, base deceits. The thing that had finally destroyed in him forever, it seemed to him, the desire to live, was his execution of a police-spy in obedience to the order of his party. He had killed him tranquilly, but at sight of this human countenance, inanimate, calm, but still false, pitiable in spite of everything, he suddenly lost his esteem for himself and his work. He considered himself as the most indifferent, the least interesting, of beings. Being a man of will, he did not leave his party; apparently he remained the same; but from that time there was something cold and terrifying in his eyes. He said nothing to anyone.

He possessed also a very rare quality: he knew not fear. He pitied those of his comrades who had this feeling, especially Vasily Kashirin. But his pity was cold, almost official.

Werner understood that the execution was not simply death, but also something more. In any case, he was determined to meet it calmly, to live until the end as if nothing had happened or would happen. Only in this way could he express the profoundest contempt for the execution and preserve his liberty of mind. In the courtroom -- his comrades, although knowing well his cold and haughty intrepidity, perhaps would not have believed it themselves -- he thought not of life or of death: he played in his mind a difficult game of chess, giving it his deepest and quietest attention. An excellent player, he had begun this game on the very day of his imprisonment, and he kept it up continually. And the verdict that condemned him did not displace a single piece on the invisible board.

The idea that he probably would not finish the game did not stop Werner. On the morning of the last day he began by correcting a plan that had failed the night before. With hands pressed between his knees he sat

a long time motionless; then he arose, and began to walk, reflecting. He
had a gait of his own; the upper part of his body inclined a little forward,
and he brought down his heels forcibly; even when the ground was dry,
he left clear foot-prints behind him. He whistled softly a rather simple
Italian melody, which helped him to reflect.

But now he was shrugging his shoulders and feeling his pulse. His
heart beat fast, but tranquilly and regularly, with a sonorous force. Like a
novice thrown into prison for the first time, he examined attentively the
cell, the bolts, the chair screwed to the wall, and said to himself:

"Why have I such a sensation of joy, of liberty? Yes, of liberty; I think
of tomorrow's execution, and it seems to me that it does not exist. I look
at the walls, and they seem to me not to exist either. And I feel as free as
if instead of being in prison, I had just come out of another cell in which
I had been confined all my life."

Werner's hands began to tremble, a thing unknown to him. His
thoughts became more and more vibrant. It seemed to him that tongues of
fire were moving in his head, trying to escape from his brain to lighten the
still obscure distance. Finally the flame darted forth, and the horizon was
brilliantly illuminated.

The vague lassitude that had tortured Werner during the last two years
had disappeared at the sight of death; his beautiful youth came back as he
played. It was even something more than beautiful youth. With the
astonishing clearness of mind that sometimes lifts man to the supreme
heights of meditation, Werner saw suddenly both life and death; and the
majesty of this new spectacle struck him. He seemed to be following a
path as narrow as the edge of a blade, on the crest of the loftiest mountain.
On one side he saw life, and on the other he saw death; and they were like
two deep seas, sparkling and beautiful, melting into each other at the
horizon in a single infinite extension.

"What is this, then? What a divine spectacle!" said he slowly.

He arose involuntarily and straightened up, as if in the presence of the
Supreme Being. And, annihilating the walls, annihilating space and time,
by the force of his all-penetrating look, he cast his eyes into the depths of
the life that he had quitted.

And life took on a new aspect. He no longer tried, as of old, to translate
into words what he was; moreover, in the whole range of human language,
still so poor and miserly, he found no words adequate. The paltry, dirty,
and evil things that suggested to him contempt and sometimes even

disgust at the sight of men had completely disappeared, just as, to people rising in a balloon, the mud and filth of the narrow streets become invisible, and ugliness changes into beauty.

With an unconscious movement Werner walked toward the table and leaned upon it with his right arm. Haughty and authoritarian by nature, he had never been seen in a prouder, freer, and more imperious attitude; never had his face worn such a look, never had he so lifted up his head, for at no previous time had he been as free and powerful as now, in this prison, on the eve of execution, at the threshold of death.

In his illuminated eyes men wore a new aspect, an unknown beauty and charm. He hovered above time, and never had this humanity, which only the night before was howling like a wild beast in the forests, appeared to him so young. What had heretofore seemed to him terrible, unpardonable, and base became suddenly touching and naïve, just as we cherish in the child the awkwardness of its behavior, the incoherent stammerings in which its unconscious genius glimmers, its laughable errors and blunders, its cruel bruises.

"My dear friends!"

Werner smiled suddenly, and his attitude lost its haughty and imposing force. Again he became the prisoner suffering in his narrow cell, weary of seeing a curious eye steadily fixed upon him through the door. He sat down, but not in his usual stiff position, and looked at the walls and the gratings with a weak and gentle smile such as his face had never worn. And something happened which had never happened to him before: he wept.

"My dear comrades!" he whispered, shedding bitter tears. "My dear comrades!"

What mysterious path had he followed to pass from a feeling of unlimited and haughty liberty to this passionate and moving pity? He did not know. Did he really pity his comrades, or did his tears hide something more passionate, something really greater? His heart, which had suddenly revived and reblossomed, could not tell him. Werner wept, and whispered:

"My dear comrades! My dear comrades!"

And in this man who wept, and who smiled through his tears, no one -- not the judges, or his comrades, or himself -- would have recognized the cold and haughty Werner, sceptical and insolent.

## XI:  ON THE WAY TO THE GALLOWS

Before getting into the vehicles, all five of the condemned were gathered in a large cold room with an arched ceiling, resembling an abandoned office or an unused reception-room. They were permitted to talk with each other.

Only Tanya Kovalchuk took immediate advantage of the permission. The others pressed in silence hands as cold as ice or as hot as fire; dumb, trying to avoid each other's gaze, they formed a confused and distracted group. Now that they were reunited, they seemed to be ashamed of what they had felt individually in the solitude. They were afraid to look at each other, afraid to show the new, special, somewhat embarrassing thing that they felt or suspected in each other.

Nevertheless, they did look, and, after a smile or two, all found themselves at ease, as before; no change revealed itself, or, if something had happened, all had taken an equal share in it, so that nothing special was noticeable in any one of them. All talked and moved in a queer and jerky fashion, impulsively, either too slowly or too quickly. Sometimes one of them quickly repeated the same words, or else failed to finish a phrase that he had begun or thought he had already spoken. But nothing of all this did they notice. All blinkingly examined the familiar objects without recognizing them, like people who have suddenly taken off their glasses. They often turned around quickly, as if someone were calling them from the rear. But they did not notice this. The cheeks and ears of Musya and Tanya were burning. At first Sergey was a little pale; he soon recovered, and appeared as usual.

Vasily alone attracted attention. Even in such a group he was extraordinary and dreadful. Werner was moved, and said in a low voice to Musya, with deep anxiety:

"What is the matter with him, Musya? Is it possible that he has. . .? Really, we must speak to him."

Vasily looked at Werner from a distance, as if he had not recognized him; then he lowered his eyes.

"But, Vasily, what is the matter with your hair? What is the matter with you? It is nothing, brother, it will soon be over! We must control ourselves! We really must!"

Vasily did not break the silence. But, when they had already concluded that he would say absolutely nothing, there came a hollow, tardy, terribly distant reply, such as the grave might give up after a long appeal:

"But there is nothing the matter with me. I am in control of myself!"

He repeated:

"I am in control of myself!"

Werner was delighted.

"Good, good! You are a brave fellow! All is well!" But, when his eyes met the dark and heavy gaze of Vasily, he felt a momentary anguish, asking himself: "But whence does he look? whence does he speak?" In a tone of deep tenderness, he said:

"Vasily, do you hear? I love you much!"

"And I too, I love you much!" replied a tongue that moved painfully.

Suddenly Musya seized Werner by the arm, and, expressing her astonishment forcibly, like an actress on the stage, she said:

"Werner, what is the matter with you? You said: 'I love you'? You never said that to anyone before. And why is your face so sparkling and your voice so tender? What is it? What is it?"

And Werner, also in the manner of an actor dwelling upon his words, answered, as he pressed the young girl's hand:

"Yes, I love, now! Do not tell the others. I am ashamed of it, but I love my brothers passionately!"

Their eyes met and burst into flame: everything about them became extinct, just as all other lights pale in the fugitive flash of the lightning.

"Yes!" said Musya. "Yes, Werner!"

"Yes!" he answered. "Yes, Musya, yes!"

They had understood something and ratified it forever. With sparkling eyes and quick steps Werner moved on again in the direction of Sergey.

"Sergey!"

But it was Tanya Kovalchuk that answered. Full of joy, almost weeping with maternal pride, she pulled Sergey violently by the sleeve.

"Just listen, Werner! I weep on his account. I torment myself, and he, he does gymnastics!"

"The Muller system?" asked Werner, with a smile.

Sergey, somewhat confused, knit his brows.

"You do wrong to laugh, Werner! I have absolutely convinced myself . . ."

Everybody began to laugh. Gaining strength and firmness from their mutual communion, they gradually became again what they used to be; they did not notice it, and thought that they were always the same. Suddenly Werner stopped laughing; with perfect gravity he said to Sergey:

"You are right, Sergey! You are perfectly right!"

"Understand this, then!" rejoined Sergey, satisfied. "Of course we . . . "

Just then they were asked to get into the vehicles. The officials even had the amiability to allow them to place themselves in their own fashion, in pairs. In general, they were very amiable with them, even too much so; were they trying to give evidence of a little humanity, or to show that they were not responsible for what was taking place and that everything was happening of itself? It is impossible to say, but all those taking part were pale.

"Go with him, Musya!" said Werner, pointing the young girl to Vasily, who stood motionless.

"I understand!" she answered, nodding her head. "And you?"

"I? Tanya will go with Sergey, you with Vasily. As for me, I shall be alone! What matters it? I can stand it, you know!"

When they had reached the courtyard, the damp and slightly warm air fell softly upon their faces and eyes, cut their breathing, and penetrated their shivering bodies, purifying them. It was hard to believe that this stimulant was simply the wind, a spring wind, gentle and moist.

The astonishing spring night had a flavor of melted snow, of infinite space; it made the stones resound. Brisk and busy little drops of water fell rapidly, one after another, making a sonorous song. But, if one of them delayed a little or fell too soon, the song changed into a joyous splash, an animated confusion. Then a big drop fell heavily, and again the spring-like song began, rhythmical and sonorous. Above the city, higher than the walls of the fortress, was the pale halo formed by the electric lights.

Sergey Golovin heaved a deep sigh, and then held his breath, as if regretting to expel from his lungs air so pure and fresh.

"Have we had this fine weather long?" Werner inquired. "It is spring!"

"Only since yesterday!" they answered politely and promptly. "There have been many cold days."

One after another the black vehicles came up, took in two persons, and went away in the darkness, toward the spot where a lantern was swinging in the gateway. Around each vehicle were moving the gray outlines of soldiers; their horses' shoes resounded loudly; often the beasts slipped on the wet snow.

When Werner bent to get into the vehicle, a gendarme said to him, in a vague way:

"There is another in there who *goes* with you!"

Werner was astonished.

"Who *goes* where? Ah! Yes! Another one! Who is it?"

The soldier said nothing. In a dark corner something small and motionless, but alive, lay rolled up: an open eye shone under an oblique ray of the lantern. As he sat down, Werner brushed against a knee with his foot.

"Pardon me, comrade!"

There was no answer. Not until the vehicle had started did the man ask hesitatingly, in bad Russian:

"Who are you?"

"My name is Werner, sentenced to be hanged for an attempt upon the life of XX. And you?"

"I am Yanson. . . . I must not be hanged. . . ."

In two hours they would be face to face with the great mystery as yet unsolved; in two hours they would leave life for death; thither both were going, and yet they became acquainted. Life and death were marching simultaneously on two different planes, and to the very end, even in the most laughable and most stupid details, life remained life.

"What did you do, Yanson?"

"I stuck a knife into my boss. I stole money."

From the sound of his voice it seemed as if Yanson were asleep. Werner found his limp hand in the darkness, and pressed it. Yanson lazily withdrew it.

"You are afraid?" asked Werner.

"I do not want to be hanged."

They became silent. Again Werner found the Esthonian's hand, and pressed it tightly between his dry and burning palms. It remained motionless, but Yanson did not try again to release it.

They stifled in the cramped vehicle, whose musty smell mingled with the odors of the soldiers' uniforms, of the muck-heap, and of wet leather. The breath of a young gendarme, redolent of garlic and bad tobacco, streamed continually into the face of Werner, who sat opposite. But the keen fresh air came in at the windows, and thanks to this the presence of spring was felt in the little moving box even more plainly than outside. The vehicle turned now to the right, now to the left; sometimes it seemed to turn around and go back. There were moments when it appeared to the prisoners as if they had been going in a circle for hours. At first the bluish electric light came in between the heavy lowered curtains; then suddenly, after a turn, darkness set in; it was from this that the travellers gathered that they had reached the suburbs and were approaching the station of S----. Sometimes, at a sudden turn, Werner's bent and living knee brushed in a friendly way against the bent and living knee of the gendarme, and it was hard to believe in the approaching execution.

"Where are we going?" asked Yanson, suddenly. The continuous and prolonged shaking of the sombre vehicle gave him vertigo and a little nausea.

Werner answered, and pressed the Esthonian's hand more tightly than before. He would have liked to say specially friendly and kind words to this little sleeping man, whom already he loved more than anyone in the world.

"Dear friend! I think that you are in an uncomfortable position! Draw nearer to me!"

At first Yanson said nothing, but after a moment he replied:

"Thank you! I am comfortable! And you, they are going to hang you too?"

"Yes!" replied Werner, with an unlooked-for gaiety, almost laughing. He made a free-and-easy gesture, as if they were speaking of some futile and stupid prank that a band of affectionate practical jokers were trying to play upon them.

"You have a wife?" asked Yanson.

"No! A wife! I! No, I am alone!"

"So am I! I am alone."

Werner, too, was beginning to feel the vertigo. At times it seemed to him that he was on his way to some festivity. A queer thing; almost all those who were going to the execution had the same feeling; although a prey to fear and anguish, they rejoiced vaguely in the extraordinary thing that was about to happen. Reality became intoxicated on madness, and death, coupling with life, gave birth to phantoms.

"Here we are at last!" said Werner, gay and curious, when the vehicle stopped; and he leaped lightly to the ground. Not so with Yanson, who resisted, without saying a word, very lazily it seemed, and who refused to descend. He clung to the handle of the door; the gendarme loosened his weak fingers, and grasped his arm. Ivan caught at the corner, at the door, at the high wheel, but yielded at every intervention of the gendarme. He adhered to things rather than gripped them. And it was not necessary to use much force to loosen his grasp. In short, they prevailed over him.

As always at night, the station was dark, deserted, and inanimate. The passenger trains had already passed, and for the train that was waiting on the track for the prisoners there was no need of light or activity. Werner was seized with ennui. He was not afraid, he was not in distress, buy he was bored; an immense, heavy, fatiguing ennui filled him with a desire to go away no matter where, lie down, and close his eyes. He stretched himself, and yawned repeatedly.

"If only they did these things more quickly!" said he, wearily.

Yanson said nothing, and shuddered.

When the condemned passed over the deserted platform surrounded with soldiers, on their way to the poorly-lighted railway carriages, Werner found himself placed beside Sergey Golovin. The latter designated something with his hand, and began to speak; his neighbor clearly understood only the word "lamp"; the rest of the phrase was lost in a weary and prolonged yawn.

"What did you say?" asked Werner, yawning also.

"The reflector . . . the lamp of the reflector is smoking," said Sergey.

Werner turned around. It was true; the glass shades were already black.

"Yes, it is smoking!"

Suddenly he thought: "What matters it to me whether the lamp is smoking, when. . .?" Sergey undoubtedly had the same idea. He threw a quick glance at Werner, and turned away his head. But both stopped yawning.

All walked to the train without difficulty; Yanson alone had to be led. At first he stiffened his legs, and glued the soles of his feet to the platform; then he bent his knees. The entire weight of his body fell upon the arms of the policemen; his legs dragged like those of a drunken man; and the toes of his boots ground against the wooden platform. With a thousand difficulties, but in silence, they lifted him into the railway carriage.

Vasily Kashirin himself walked unsupported; unconsciously he imitated the movements of his comrades. After mounting the steps of the carriage, he drew back; a policeman took him by the elbow to sustain him. Then Vasily began to tremble violently and uttered a piercing cry, pushing away the policeman!

"Aie!"

"Vasily, what is the matter with you?" asked Werner, rushing toward him.

Vasily kept silence, shivering the while. The policeman, vexed and even chagrined, explained:

"I wanted to sustain him, and he -- he . . ."

"Come, Vasily, I will sustain you," said Werner.

He tried to take his comrade's arm. But the latter repulsed him, and cried louder than ever.

"Vasily, it is I, Werner!"

"I know! Don't touch me! I want to walk alone!"

And, still trembling, he entered the carriage and sat down in a corner. Werner leaned toward Musya, and asked in a low voice, designating Vasily with his eyes:

"Well, how are things with him?"

"Badly!" answered Musya, in a whisper. "He is already dead. Tell me, Werner, does death really exist?"

"I don't know, Musya; but I think not!" answered Werner is a serious and thoughtful tone.

"That is what I thought! And he? I suffered on his account during the whole ride; it seemed to me that I was travelling beside a dead man.

"I don't know, Musya. Perhaps death still exists for some. Later it will not exist at all. For me, for instance, death has existed, but now it exists no more."

The slightly pallid cheeks of Musya reddened.

"It has existed for you, Werner? For you?"

"Yes, but no more. As for you!"

They heard a sound at the door of the railway carriage; Michka the Tzigane entered spitting, breathing noisily, and making a racket with his boot-heels. He glanced about him, and stopped short.

"There is no room left, officer!" he declared to the fatigued and irritated policeman. "See to it that I travel comfortably, otherwise I will not go with you! Rather hang me right here, to the lamp-post! Oh, the scoundrels, what a carriage they have given me! Do you call this a carriage? The devil's guts, yes, but not a carriage!"

But suddenly he lowered his head, stretched out his neck, and advanced towards the other prisoners. From the frame of his bushy hair and beard his black eyes shot a savage, sharp, and rather crazy look.

"Oh, my God!" he cried; "so this is where we are! How do you do, sir!"

He sat down opposite Werner, holding out his hand; then, with a wink, he leaned over and swiftly passed his hand across his companion's neck:

"You too? Eh?"

"Yes!" smiled Werner.

"All?"

"All!"

"Oh! oh!" said the Tzigane, showing his teeth. He examined the other prisoners with a swift glance, which nevertheless dwelt longest on Musya and Yanson.

"On account of the Minister?"

"Yes. And you?"

"Oh, sir, my case is quite another story. I am not so distinguished! I, sir, am a brigand, an assassin. That makes no difference, sir; move up a little to make room for me; it is not my fault that they have put me in your company! In the other world there will be room for all."

He took the measure of all the prisoners with a watchful, distrustful, and savage gaze. But they looked at him without a word, seriously and even with evident compassion. Again he showed his teeth, and slapped Werner several times on the knee.

"So that is how it is, sir! As they say in the song:

*"'Take care to make no sound, O forest of green oaks!'"*

"Why do you call me sir, when all of us . . . "

"You are right!" acquiesced the Tzigane, with satisfaction. "Why should you be sir, since you are to be hanged beside me? There sits the real sir!"

He pointed his finger at the silent policeman.

"And your comrade yonder, he doesn't seem to be enjoying himself hugely!" he added, looking at Vasily. "Say there, you are afraid?"

"No!" answered a tongue that moved with difficulty.

"Well, then, don't be so disturbed; there is nothing to be ashamed of. It is only dogs that wag their tails and show their teeth when they are going to be hanged; you are a man. And this marionette, who is he? He certainly is not one of your crowd?"

His eyes danced incessantly; constantly, with a hissing sound, he spat out his abundant and sweetish saliva. Yanson, doubled up motionless in a corner, slightly shook the ears of his bald fur cap, but said nothing. Werner answered for him.

"He killed his employer."

"My God!" exclaimed the Tzigane, in astonishment. "How is it that they permit such birds as that to kill people?"

For a moment he looked at Musya stealthily; then suddenly he turned, and fixed his straight and piercing gaze upon her.

"Miss! Say there, Miss! what is the matter with you? Your cheeks are pink, and you are laughing! Look, she is really laughing! Look! Look!" And he seized Werner's knee with his hooked fingers.

Blushing and somewhat confused, Musya squarely returned the gaze of the attentive and savage eyes that questioned her. All kept silence.

The little cars bounced speedily along the narrow track. At every turn or grade-crossing the whistle blew, the engineer being afraid of crushing somebody. Was it not atrocious to think that so much care and effort, in short all human activity, was being expended in taking men to be hanged? The maddest thing in the world was being done with an air of simplicity and reasonableness. Cars were running; people were sitting in them as usual, travelling as people ordinarily travel. Then there would be a halt as usual: "Five minutes' stop."

And then would come death -- eternity -- the great mystery.

## XII: THE ARRIVAL

The train advanced rapidly.

Sergey Golovin remembered to have spent the summer, some years before, in a little country-house along this very line. He had often travelled the road by day and by night, and knew it well. Closing his eyes, he could fancy himself returning by the last train, after staying out late at night with friends.

"I shall arrive soon," thought he, straightening up: and his eyes met the dark grated window. Around him nothing stirred. Only the Tzigane kept on spitting, and his eyes ran the length of the car, seeming to touch the doors and the soldiers.

"It is cold," said Vasily Kashirin between his thin lips, which seemed frozen.

Tanya Kovalchuk bestirred herself in a maternal fashion:

"Here's a very warm kerchief to wrap around your . . ."

"Neck?" asked Sergey, and he was frightened by his own question.

"What matters it, Vasya? Take it."

"Wrap yourself up. You will be warmer," added Werner.

He turned to Yanson, and asked him tenderly:

"And aren't you cold, too?"

"Werner, perhaps he wants to smoke. Comrade, do you want to smoke?" asked Musya. "We have some tobacco."

"Yes, I want to."

"Give him a cigarette, Sergey," said Werner.

But Sergey was already holding out his cigarette-case.

And all began to watch tenderly Yanson's clumsy fingers as they took the cigarette and struck the match, and the little curl of bluish smoke that issued from his mouth.

"Thank you," said Yanson. "It is good."

"How queer it is," said Sergey.

"How queer what is?" asked Werner.

"The cigarette," answered Sergey, unwilling to say all that he thought.

Yanson held the cigarette between his pale and living fingers. With astonishment he looked at it. And all fixed their gaze on this tiny bit of paper, on this little curl of smoke rising from the gray ashes.

The cigarette went out.

"It is out," said Tanya.

"Yes, it is out."

"The devil take it!" said Werner, looking anxiously at Yanson, whose hand, holding the cigarette, hung as if dead. Suddenly the Tzigane turned, placed his face close to Werner's, and, looking into the whites of his eyes, whispered:

"Suppose, sir, we were to attack the soldiers of the convoy? What do you think about it?"

"No," answered Werner.

"Why? It is better to die fighting. I will strike a blow, they strike back, and I shall die without noticing it."

"No, it is not necessary," said Werner. And he turned to Yanson:

"Why don't you smoke?"

Yanson's dried-up face wrinkled pitifully, as if someone had pulled the threads that moved the creases in his face. As in a nightmare, Yanson sobbed in a colorless voice, shedding no tears:

"I can't smoke. Ah! Ah! Ah! I must not be hanged. Ah! Ah! Ah!"

Everybody turned toward him. Tanya, weeping copiously, stroked his arms and readjusted his fur cap.

"My dear, my friend, don't cry, my friend! My poor friend!"

Suddenly the cars bumped into one another and began to slow up. The prisoners rose, but immediately sat down again.

"Here we are," said Sergey.

It was as if all the air had suddenly been pumped out of the car. It became difficult to breathe. Their swollen hearts became heavy in their breasts, rose to their throats, beat desperately and their blood, in its terror, seemed to revolt. Their eyes looked at the trembling floor, their ears listened to the slowly-turning wheels, which began to turn more slowly still, and gently stopped.

The train halted.

The prisoners were plunged into a strange stupor. They did not suffer. They seemed to live an unconscious life. Their corporeal being was absent; only its phantom moved about, voiceless but speaking, silent but walking. They went out. They arranged themselves in pairs, breathing in the fresh air of the woods. Like one in a dream, Yanson struggled awkwardly: they dragged him from the car.

"Are we to go on foot?" asked someone, almost gaily.

"It isn't far," answered a careless voice.

Without a word they advanced into the forest, along a damp and muddy road. Their feet slipped and sank into the snow, and their hands sometimes clung involuntarily to those of their comrade. Breathing with difficulty the soldiers marched in single file, on either side of the prisoners. An irritated voice complained:

"Could they not have cleared the road? It is difficult to advance."

A deferential voice answered:

"It was cleaned, Your Honor, but it is thawing. There is nothing to be done."

The prisoners began to recover their consciousness. Now they seemed to grasp the idea: "It is true, they could not clean the roads"; now it became obscured again, and there remained only the sense of smell, which perceived with singular keenness the strong and healthy odor of the forest; and now again all became very clear and comprehensible, the forest, and the night, and the road . . . and the certainty that very soon, in a minute, implacable death would lay its hands upon them. And little by little a whispering began:

"It is almost four o'clock."

"I told you so. We started too early."

"The sun rises at five."

"That's right, at five: we should have waited."

They halted in the twilight. Near by, behind the trees, whose huge shadows were waving on the ground, swung silently two lanterns. There the gallows had been erected.

"I have lost one of my rubbers," said Sergey.

"Well?" asked Werner, not understanding.

"I have lost it. I am cold."

"Where is Vasily?"

"I don't know. There he is."

Vasily was standing close by them, gloomy and motionless.

"Where is Musya?"

"Here I am. Is that you, Werner?"

They looked at each other, their eyes avoiding the silent and terrible significant swaying of the lanterns. At the left the thin forest seemed to be growing lighter. And beyond, something vast and gray and flat appeared, whence came a moist breeze.

"That is the sea," said Sergey, sucking in the damp air. "That is the sea."

Musya answered by a line from the song:

*"My love as broad as is the sea."*

"What did you say, Musya?"

*"The shores of life cannot contain*

My love as broad as is the sea."

"'My love as broad as is the sea,'" repeated Sergey, pensively.

"'My love as broad as is the sea,'" echoed Werner. And suddenly he exclaimed in astonishment:

"Musya, my little Musya, how young you still are!"

Just then, close to Werner's ear, sounded the breathless and passionate voice of the Tzigane:

"Sir, sir, look at the forest. My God! What is all that? And yonder! The lanterns! My God, is that the scaffold?"

Werner looked at him. The convulsed features of the unfortunate man were frightful to see.

"We must say our farewells," said Tanya.

"Wait! They still have to read the sentence. Where is Yanson?"

Yanson lay stretched in the snow, surrounded by people. A strong smell of ammonia filled the air around him.

"Well, doctor, will you soon be through?" asked someone, impatiently.

"It's nothing. A fainting fit. Rub his ears with snow. He is better already. You can read."

The light of a dark lantern fell upon the paper and the ungloved white hands. Both paper and hands trembled. The voice also.

"Gentlemen, perhaps it is better not to read. You all know the sentence."

"Do not read!" answered Werner for all: and the light immediately went out.

The condemned refused also the services of the priest. Said the Tzigane:

"No nonsense, father; you will forgive me, they will hang me."

The broad dark silhouette of the priest took a few steps backward and disappeared. The day was breaking. The snow became whiter, the faces of the condemned darker, and the forest barer and sadder.

"Gentlemen, you will go in pairs, choosing your companion. But I beg you to make haste."

Werner pointed to Yanson, who now was standing again, sustained by two soldiers.

"I will go with him. You, Sergey, take Vasily. You go first."

"All right."

"I am going with you, Musya," said Tanya. "Come, let us kiss each other!"

Quickly they kissed all round. The Tzigane kissed forcibly; they felt his teeth. Yanson kissed gently and softly, with mouth half open. He did not seem to understand what he was doing. When Sergey and Kashirin had taken a few steps, the latter stopped suddenly, and in a loud voice, which seemed strange and unfamiliar, shouted:

"Good-bye, comrades."

"Good-bye, comrade," they answered him.

The two started off again. All was quiet. The lanterns behind the trees became motionless. They expected to hear a cry, a voice, some sound or other, but there as here all was calm.

"Oh! My God!" exclaimed someone, hoarsely.

They turned around: it was the Tzigane, crying desperately:

"They are going to hang us."

He struggled, clutching the air with his hands, and cried again:

"God! Am I to be hanged alone? My God!"

His convulsive hands gripped the hand of Werner, and he continued:

"Sir, my dear sir, my good sir. You will come with me, won't you?"

Werner, his face drawn with sorrow, answered:

"I cannot; I am with Yanson."

"Oh! My God! then I shall be alone. Why? Why?"

Musya took a step toward him, and said softly:

"I will go with you."

The Tzigane drew back, and fixed his big swollen eyes upon her:

"Will you?"

"Yes."

"But you are so little! You are not afraid of me? No, I don't want you to. I will go alone."

"But I am not afraid of you."

The Tzigane grinned.

"Don't you know that I am a brigand? And you are willing to go with me? Think a moment. I shall not be angry if you refuse."

Musya was silent. And in the faint light of the dawn her face seemed to take on a luminous and mystic pallor. Suddenly she advanced rapidly toward the Tzigane, and, taking his head in her hands, kissed him vigorously. He took her by the shoulders, put her away a little, and then kissed her loudly on her cheeks and eyes.

The soldier nearest them stopped, opened his hands, and let his gun fall. But he did not stoop to pick it up. He stood still for a moment, then turned suddenly, and began to walk into the forest.

"Where are you going?" shouted his comrade, in a frightened voice. "Stay!"

But the other painfully endeavored to advance. Suddenly he clutched the air with his hands, and fell, face downward.

"Milksop, pick up your gun, or I will pick it up for you" cried the Tzigane, firmly. "You don't know your duty. Have you never seen a man die?"

Again the lantern swung. The turn of Werner and Yanson had come.

"Good-bye, sir!" said the Tzigane, in a loud voice. "We shall meet again in the other world. When you see me there, don't turn away from me."

"Good-bye!"

"I must not be hanged," said Yanson again, in a faint voice.

But Werner grasped his hand, and Yanson took a few steps. Then he was seen to sink into the snow. They bent over him, lifted him up, and carried him, while he weakly struggled in the soldiers' arms.

And again the yellow lanterns became motionless.

"And I, Musya? Am I then to go alone?" said Tanya, sadly. "We have lived together, and now . . ."

"Tanya, my good Tanya!"

The Tzigane hotly interrupted, holding Musya as if he feared that they might tear her from him.

"Miss," he cried, "you are able to go alone. You have a pure soul. You can go alone where you like. But I cannot. I am a bandit. I cannot go alone. 'Where are you going?' they will say to me, 'you who have killed, you who have stolen?' For I have stolen horses, too Miss. And with her I shall be as if I were with an innocent child. Do you understand?"

"Yes, I understand. Go on, then! Let me kiss you once more Musya."

"Kiss each other! Kiss each other!" said the Tzigane. "You are women. You must say good-bye to each other."

Then came the turn of Musya and the Tzigane. The woman walked carefully, her feet slipping, lifting her skirts by force of habit. Holding her with a strong hand, and feeling the ground with his foot, the man accompanied her to death. The lights became motionless. Around Tanya all was tranquil again, and solitary. The soldiers, gray in the dawn's pale light, were silent.

"I am left alone," said Tanya. And she sighed. "Sergey is dead, Werner and Vasily are dead. And Musya is dying. I am alone. Soldiers, my little soldiers, you see, I am alone, alone . . ."

The sun appeared above the sea. . . .

They placed the bodies in boxes, and started off with them. With elongated necks, bulging eyes, and blue tongues protruding, from their mouths, the dead retraced the road by which, living, they had come.

And the snow was still soft, and the air of the forest was still pure and balmy.

On the white road lay the black rubber that Sergey had lost. . . .

Thus it was that men greeted the rising sun.

*Translator Unknown*

# United States

The individualist character of American literature gained recognition as an organically American element in the work of such 19th-century American authors as Washington Irving and James Fenimore Cooper. Irving created a New England folklore that depicted the essence of life in the Northeast as effectively as Cooper's work captured the romance and danger of life on the frontier.

Though aggressively individualist in posture, American writers have certainly been involved in movements, such as Romanticism, Gothicism, and Realism, that correspond to similar literary ideologies in Europe and the rest of the world. Edgar Allan Poe, for example, constructed heavily-plotted short stories in the Gothic tradition, while Herman Melville's *Billy Budd* and *Moby Dick* and Nathaniel Hawthorne's *The Scarlett Letter* and "The Birthmark" (See Volume I) were crafted in a more symbolic mode concerned to a greater extent with exploring character than with developing plot.

American Realism sought to reveal with minute detail the hardships of the lower social classes, the tedium of a bourgeois existence, and the hypocrisy of the affluent in the age of social Darwinism. Henry James' story "An International Episode" presents the particulars of 19th-century American and English socialite interaction. Both the American and the English characters harbor negative preconceptions about their foreign counterparts: "I thought you Americans were always dancing," Lambeth says to Bessie, who replies, "I am sure that we don't have so many balls as you have in England." Issues of pride and personal dignity arise as Bessie, the quintessential Jamesian American--naive, outspoken, and unacquainted with the intricacies of the English class system--remains undaunted by various attempts to discourage her interest in the aristocratic Lambeth. The eventual conclusion of this "International Episode" exhibits a kind of American individualism that functions outside oppressive social mores while maintaining a focus on what the character believes to be the true principal of the matter.

Margaret Montague's "England to America" also explores relationships between Americans and the English. Her study focuses primarily upon Skipworth, whose preconceptions about the "English personality" prevent him from perceiving the benevolent motives behind the seemingly standoffish behavior of his hosts.

James Lane Allen's "Two Men of Kentucky" and W. E. B. Du Bois' "On Being Crazy" present an America entirely removed from the landscape of "The International Episode." Allen plots the courses of two lives, Colonel Field and his former slave, Peter Cotton, in the post-Civil War South. The two men must cope not only with physical aging but with the radically disrupted Southern culture as well. In 1907's "Crazy" we see an African American man still struggling to lead a free life only to find himself despised for wanting equality.

# England To America
## *Margaret Prescott Montague*

**Margaret Prescott Montague 1878-20th Century:** Margaret Montague was born in Sulphur Springs, West Virginia, in 1878. She lived there most of her life, but eventually moved to Richmond, Virginia. The story presented here was chosen as the O. Henry Memorial Prize Story in 1920. Her stories include "Of Water and the Spirit," Uncle Sam of Freedom Ridge," "Deep Chanel," and "Up Eel River." "England to America" was first published in the *Atlantic Monthly* in September, 1919.

LORD, but English people are funny!

This was the perplexed mental ejaculation that young Lieutenant Skipworth Cary, of Virginia, found his thoughts constantly reiterating during his stay in Devonshire. Had he been, he wondered, a confiding fool, to accept so trustingly Chev Sherwood's suggestion that he spend a part of his leave, at least, at Bishopsthorpe, where Chev's people lived? But why should he have anticipated any difficulty here, in this very corner of England which had bred his own ancestors, when he had always hit it off so splendidly with his English comrades at the Front? Here, however, though they were all awfully kind -- at least, he was sure they meant to be kind -- something was always bringing him up short; something that he could not lay hold of, but which made him feel like a blind man groping in a strange place, or worse, like a bull in a china-shop. He was prepared enough to find differences in the American and English points of view. But this thing that baffled him did not seem to have to do with that; it was something deeper, something very definite, he was sure -- and yet, what was it? The worst of it was that he had a curious feeling as if they were all -- that is, Lady Sherwood and Gerald; not Sir Charles so much -- protecting him from himself -- keeping him from making breaks, as he phrased it. That hurt and annoyed him, and piqued his vanity. Was he a social blunderer, and weren't a Virginia gentleman's manners to be trusted in England without leading-strings?

He had been at the Front for several months with the Royal Flying Corps; and when his leave came, his Flight Commander, Captain Cheviot Sherwood, discovering that he meant to spend it in England where he hardly knew a soul, had said his people down in Devonshire would be jolly glad to have him stop with them; and Skipworth Cary, knowing that, if the circumstances had been reversed, his people down in Virginia would indeed have been jolly glad to entertain Captain Sherwood, had accepted unhesitatingly. The invitation had been seconded by a letter from Lady Sherwood, -- Chev's mother, -- and after a few days' sight-seeing in London, he had come down to Bishopsthorpe, very eager to know his friend's family, feeling as he did about Chev himself." He's the finest man that ever went up in the air," he had written home; and to his own family's disgust, his letters had been far more full of Chev Sherwood than they had been of Skipworth Cary.

And now here he was, and he almost wished himself away -- wished almost that he was back again at the Front, carrying on under Chev. There, at least, you knew what you were up against. The job might be hard enough, but it wasn't baffling and queer, with hidden undercurrents that you couldn't chart. It seemed to him that this baffling feeling of constraint had rushed to meet him on the very threshold of the drawing-room, when he made his first appearance.

As he entered, he had a sudden sensation that they had been awaiting him in a strained expectancy, and that, as he appeared, they adjusted unseen masks and began to play-act at something. " But English people don't play-act very well," he commented to himself, reviewing the scene afterwards.

Lady Sherwood had come forward and greeted him in a manner which would have been pleasant enough, if he had not, with quick sensitiveness, felt it to be forced. But perhaps that was English stiffness.

Then she had turned to her husband, who was standing staring into the fireplace, although, as it was June, there was no fire there to stare at.

"Charles," she said, "here is Lieutenant Cary"; and her voice had a certain note in it which at home Cary and his sister Nancy were in the habit of designating "mother-making-dad-mind-his-manners."

At her words the old man -- and Cary was startled to see how old and broken he was -- turned round and held out his hand. "How d'you do?" he said jerkily, "how d' you do?" and then turned abruptly back again to the fireplace.

"Hello! What's up? The old boy doesn't like me!" was Cary's quick, startled comment to himself.

He was so surprised by the look the other bent upon him, that he involuntarily glanced across to a long mirror to see if there was anything wrong with his uniform. But no, that appeared to be all right. It was himself, then -- or his country; perhaps the old sport didn't fall for Americans.

"And here is Gerald," Lady Sherwood went on in her low remote voice, which somehow made the Virginian feel very far away.

It was with genuine pleasure, though with some surprise, that he turned to greet Gerald Sherwood, Chev's younger brother, who had been, tradition in the corps said, as gallant and daring a flyer as Chev himself, until he got his in the face five months ago.

"I'm mighty glad to meet you," he said eagerly, in his pleasant, muffled Southern voice, grasping the hand the other stretched out, and looking with deep respect at the scarred face and sightless eyes.

Gerald laughed a little, but it was a pleasant laugh, and his hand-clasp was friendly.

"That's real American, isn't it?" he said. "I ought to have remembered and said it first. Sorry."

Skipworth laughed too. "Well," he conceded, "we generally are glad to meet people in my country, and we don't care who says it first. But," he added, "I didn't think I'd have the luck to find you here."

He remembered that Chev had regretted that he probably wouldn't see Gerald, as the latter was at St. Dunstan's, where they were reeducating the blinded soldiers.

The other hesitated a moment, and then said rather awkwardly, "Oh, I'm just home for a little while; I only got here this morning, in fact."

Skipworth noted the hesitation. Did the old people get panicky at the thought of entertaining a wild man from Virginia, and send an S O S for Gerald, he wondered.

"We are so glad you could come to us," Lady Sherwood said rather hastily just then. And again he could not fail to note that she was prompting her husband.

The latter reluctantly turned around, and said, "Yes, yes, quite so. Welcome to Bishopsthorpe, my boy," as if his wife had pulled a string, and he responded mechanically, without quite knowing what he said. Then, as his eyes rested a moment on his guest, he looked as if he would like to bolt out of the room. He controlled himself, however, and, jerking round again to the fireplace, went on murmuring, "Yes, yes, yes," vaguely -- just like the dormouse at the Mad Tea-Party, who went to sleep, saying, "Twinkle, twinkle, twinkle," Cary could not help thinking to himself.

But after all, it wasn't really funny; it was pathetic. Gosh, how doddering the poor old boy was! Skipworth wondered, with a sudden twist at his heart, if the war was playing the deuce with his home people, too. Was his own father going to pieces like this, and had his mother's gay vivacity fallen into that still remoteness of Lady Sherwood's? But of course not! The Carys hadn't suffered as the poor Sherwoods had, with their youngest son, Curtin, killed early in the war, and now Gerald knocked out so tragically. Lord, he thought, how they must all bank on Chev! And of course they would want to hear at once about him. "I left Chev as fit as anything, and he sent all sorts of messages," he reported thinking it more discreet to deliver Chev's messages thus vaguely than to repeat his actual care-free remark, which had been, "Oh, tell 'em I'm jolly as a tick."

But evidently there was something wrong with the words as they were, for instantly he was aware of that curious sense of withdrawal on their part. Hastily reviewing them, he decided that they had sounded too familiar from a stranger and a younger man like himself. He supposed he ought not to have spoken of Chev by his first name. Gee, what sticklers they were! Wouldn't his family -- dad and mother and Nancy -- have fairly lapped up any messages from him, even if they had been delivered a bit awkwardly? However, he added, as a concession to their point of view, "But of course you'll have had later news of Captain Sherwood."

To which, after a pause, Lady Sherwood responded, "Oh, yes," in that remote and colorless voice which might have meant anything or nothing.

At this point dinner was announced.

Lady Sherwood drew her husband away from the empty fireplace, and Gerald slipped his arm through the Virginian's, saying pleasantly, "I'm learning to carry on fairly well at St. Dunstan's, but I confess I still like to have a pilot."

To look at the tall young fellow beside him, whose scarred face was so reminiscent of Chev's untouched good looks, who had known all the immense freedom of the air, but who was now learning to carry on in the dark, moved Skipworth Cary to generous homage.

"You know my saying I'm glad to meet you isn't just American," he said half shyly, but warmly. "It's plain English, and the straight truth. I've wanted to meet you awfully. The oldsters are always holding up your glorious exploits to us newcomers. Withers never gets tired telling about that fight of yours with the four enemy planes. And besides," he rushed on eagerly, "I'm glad to have a chance to tell Chev's brother -- Captain Sherwood's brother, I mean -- what I think of him. Only as a matter of fact, I can't," he broke off with a laugh. "I can't put it exactly into words, but I tell you I'd follow that man straight into hell and out the other side -- or go there alone if he told me to. He is the finest chap that ever flew."

And then he felt as if a cold douche had been flung in his face, for after a moment's pause, the other returned, "That's awfully good of you," in a voice so distant and formal that the Virginian could have kicked himself. What an ass he was to be so darned enthusiastic with an Englishman! He supposed it was bad form to show any pleasure over praise of a member of your family. Lord, if Chev got the V. C., he reckoned it would be awful to speak of it. Still, you would have thought Gerald might have stood for a little praise of him. But then, glancing sideways at his companion, he surprised on his face a look so strange and suffering that it came to him almost violently what it must be never to fly again; to be on the threshold of life, with endless days of blackness ahead. Good God! How cruel he had been to flaunt Chev in his face! In remorseful and hasty reparation he stumbled on, "But the old fellows are always having great discussions as to which was the best -- you or your brother. Withers always maintains you were."

"Withers lies, then!" the other retorted. "I never touched Chev -- never came within a mile of him, and never could have."

They reached the dinner-table with that, and young Cary found himself bewildered and uncomfortable. If Gerald hadn't liked praise of Chev, he had liked praise of himself even less, it seemed.

Dinner was not a success. The Virginian found that, if there was to be conversation, the burden of carrying it on was upon him, and gosh! they don't mind silences in this man's island, do they? he commented desperately to himself, thinking how different it was from America. Why, there they acted as if silence was an egg that had just been laid, and everyone had to cackle at once to cover it up. But here the talk constantly fell to the ground, and nobody but himself seemed concerned to pick it up. His attempt to praise Chev had not been successful, and he could understand their not wanting to hear about flying and the war before Gerald.

So at last, in desperation, he wandered off into descriptions of America, finding to his relief that he had struck the right note at last. They were glad to hear about the States, and Lady Sherwood inquired politely if the Indians still gave them much trouble; and when he assured her that in Virginia, except for the Pocahontas tribe, they were all pretty well subdued, she accepted his statement with complete innocency. And he was so delighted to find at last a subject to which they were evidently cordial, that he was quite carried away, and wound up by inviting them all to visit his family in Richmond, as soon as the war was over.

Gerald accepted at once, with enthusiasm; Lady Sherwood made polite murmurs, smiling at him in quite a warm and almost, indeed, maternal manner. Even Sir Charles, who had been staring at the food on his plate as if he did not quite know what to make of it, came to the surface long enough to mumble, "Yes, yes, very good idea. Countries must carry on together -- What?"

But that was the only hit of the whole evening, and when the Virginian retired to his room, as he made an excuse to do early, he was so confused and depressed that he fell into an acute attack of homesickness.

Heavens, he thought, as he tumbled into bed, just suppose now, this was little old Richmond, Virginia, U.S.A., instead of being Bishopthorpe, Avery Cross near Wick, and all the rest of it! And at that, he grinned to himself. England wasn't such an all-fired big country that you'd think they'd have to ticket themselves with addresses a yard long, for fear they'd get lost -- now, would you? Well, anyway, suppose it was Richmond, and his train just pulling into the Byrd Street Station. He stretched out luxuriously, and let his mind picture the whole familiar scene. The wind was blowing right, so there was the mellow, homely smell of the tobacco in the streets, and plenty of people all along the way to hail him with outstretched hands and shouts of "Hey, Skip Cary, when did you get back?" "Welcome home, my boy!" "Well, will you look what the cat dragged in! "And so he came to his own front door-step, and walking straight in, surprised the whole family at breakfast; and yes -- doggone it! if it wasn't Sunday, and they having waffles! And after that his obliging fancy bore him up Franklin Street, through Monroe Park, and so to Miss Sallie Berkeley's door. He was sound asleep before he reached it, but in his dreams, light as a little bird, she came flying down the broad stairway to meet him, and--

But when he waked next morning, he did not find himself in Virginia, but in Devonshire, where, to his unbounded embarrassment, a white housemaid was putting up his curtains and whispering something about his bath. And though he pretended profound slumber, he was well aware that people do not turn brick-red in their sleep. And the problem of what was the matter with the Sherwood family was still before him.

"They're playing a game," he told himself after a few days. "That is, Lady Sherwood and Gerald are -- poor old Sir Charles can't make much of a stab at it. The game is to make me think they are awfully glad to have me, when in reality there's something about me, or something I do, that gets them on the raw."

"He almost decided to make some excuse and get away; but after all, that was not easy. In English novels, he remembered, they always had a wire calling them to London; but darn it all! the Sherwoods knew mighty well there wasn't anyone in London who cared a hoot about him.

The thing that got his goat most, he told himself, was that they apparently didn't like his friendship with Chev. Anyway they didn't seem to want him to talk about him; and whenever he tried to express his warm appreciation for all that the older man had done for him, he was instantly aware of a wall of reserve on their part, a holding of themselves aloof from him. That puzzled and hurt him, and put him on his dignity. He concluded that they thought it was cheeky of a youngster like him to think that a man like Chev could be his friend; and if that was the way they felt, he reckoned he'd jolly well better shut up about it.

But whatever it was that they didn't like about him, they most certainly did want him to have a good time. He and his pleasure appeared to be for the time being their chief consideration. And after the first day or so he began indeed to enjoy himself extremely. For one thing, he came to love the atmosphere of the old place and of the surrounding country, which he and Gerald explored together. He liked to think that ancestors of his own had been inheritors of these green lanes, and pleasant mellow stretches. Then, too, after the first few days, he could not help seeing that they really began to like him, which of course was reassuring, and tapped his own warm friendliness, which was always ready enough to be released. And, besides, he got by accident what he took to be a hint as to the trouble. He was passing the half-open door of Lady Sherwood's morning-room, when he heard Sir Charles' voice break out, "Good God, Elizabeth, I don't see how you stand it! When I see him so straight and fine-looking, and so untouched, beside our poor lad, and think -- and think--"

Skipworth hurried out of earshot, but now he understood that look of aversion in the old man's eyes which had so startled him at first. Of course the poor old boy might easily hate the sight of him beside Gerald. With Gerald himself he really got along famously. He was a most delightful companion, full of anecdotes and history of the countryside, every foot of which he had apparently explored in the old days with Chev and the younger brother, Curtin. Yet even with Gerald, Cary sometimes felt that aloofness and reserve, and that older protective air that they all showed him. Take, for instance, that afternoon when they were lolling together on the grass in the park. The Virginian, running on in his usual eager manner, had plunged without thinking into an account of a particularly daring bit of flying on Chev's part, when suddenly he realized that Gerald had rolled over on the grass and buried his face in his arms, and interrupted himself awkwardly. "But of course," he said "he must have written home about it himself."

"No, or if he did, I didn't hear of it. Go on," Gerald said in a muffled voice.

A great rush of compassion and remorse overwhelmed the Virginian, and he burst out penitently, "What a brute I am! I'm always forgetting and running on about flying, when I know it must hurt like the very devil!"

The other drew a difficult breath. "Yes," he admitted, "what you say does hurt in a way -- in a way you can't understand. But all the same I like to hear you. Go on about Chev."

So Skipworth went on and finished his account, winding up. "I don't believe there's another man in the service who could have pulled it off -- but I tell you your brother's one in a million."

"Good God, don't I know it!" the other burst out. "We were all three the jolliest pals together," he got out presently in a choked voice, "Chev and the young un and I; and now--"

He did not finish, but Cary guessed his meaning. Now the young un, Curtin, was dead, and Gerald himself knocked out. But, heavens! the Virginian thought, did Gerald think Chev would go back on him now on account of his blindness? Well, you could everlastingly bet he wouldn't!

"Chev thinks the world and all of you!" he cried in eager defense of his friend's loyalty. "Lots of times when we're all awfully jolly together, he makes some excuse and goes off by himself; and Withers told me it was because he was so frightfully cut up about you. Withers said he told him once that he'd a lot rather have got it himself--so you can everlastingly bank on him!"

Gerald gave a terrible little gasp. "I -- I knew he'd feel like that," he got out. "We've always cared such a lot for each other." And then he pressed his face harder than ever into the grass, and his long body quivered all over. But not for long. In a moment he took fierce hold on himself, muttering. "Well, one must carry on, whatever happens," and apologized disjointedly. "What a fearful fool you must think me! And -- and this isn't very pippy for you, old chap." Presently, after that, he sat up, and said, brushing it all aside, "We're facing the old moat, aren't we? There's an interesting bit of tradition about it that I must tell you."

And there you were, Cary thought: no matter how much Gerald might be suffering from his misfortune, he must carry on just the same, and see that his visitor had a pleasant time. It made the Virginian feel like an outsider and very young, as if he were not old enough for them to show him their real feelings.

Another thing that he noticed was that they did not seem to want him to meet people. They never took him anywhere to call, and if visitors came to the house, they showed an almost panicky desire to get him out of the way. That again hurt his pride. What in heaven's name was the matter with him anyway!

However, on the last afternoon of his stay at Bishopsthorpe he told himself with a rather rueful grin, that his manners must have improved a little, for they took him to tea at the rectory.

He was particularly glad to go there because, from certain jokes of Withers's who had known the Sherwoods since boyhood, he gathered that Chev and the rector's daughter were engaged. And just as he would have liked Chev to meet Sallie Berkeley, so he wanted to meet Miss Sybil Gaylord.

He had little hope of having a *tête-a-tête* with her, but as it fell out he did. They were all in the rectory garden, together, Gerald and the rector a little behind Miss Gaylord and himself, as they strolled down a long walk with high hedges bordering it. On the other side of the hedge Lady Sherwood and her hostess still sat at the tea-table, and then it was that Cary heard Mrs. Gaylord say distinctly, "I'm afraid the strain has been too much for you -- you should have let us have him."

To which Lady Sherwood returned quickly, "Oh, no, that would have been impossible with--"

"Come -- come this way -- I must show you the view from the arbor," Miss Gaylord broke in breathlessly; and laying a hand on his arm, she turned him abruptly into a side path.

Glancing down at her, the Southerner could not but note that the overheard words referred to him, and he was so bewildered by the whole situation, that he burst out impulsively, "I say, what is the matter with me? Why do they find me so hard to put up with? Is it something I do -- or don't they like Americans? Honestly, I wish you'd tell me."

She stood still at that, looking at him, her blue eyes full of distress and concern.

"Oh, I am so sorry," she cried. "They would be so sorry to have you think anything like that."

"But what is it?" he persisted. "Don't they like Americans?"

"Oh, no, it isn't that -- Oh, quite the contrary!" she returned eagerly.

"Then it's something about me they don't like?"

"Oh, no, no! Least of all, that -- don't think that!" she begged.

"But what am I to think then?"

"Don't think anything just yet," she pleaded. "Wait a little, and you will understand."

She was so evidently distressed, that he could not press her further; and fearing she might think him unappreciative, he said "Well, whatever it is, it hasn't prevented me from having a ripping good time. They've seen to that, and just done everything for my pleasure."

She looked up quickly, and to his relief he saw that for once he had said the right thing.

"You have enjoyed it, then?" she questioned eagerly.

"Most awfully," he assured her warmly. "I shall always remember what a happy leave they gave me."

She gave a little sigh of satisfaction. "I am so glad," she said "They wanted you to have a good time -- that was what we all wanted."

He looked at her gratefully, thinking how sweet she was in her fair English beauty, and how good to care that he should have enjoyed his leave. How different she was too from Sallie Berkeley -- why she would have made two of his little girl! And how quiet! Sallie Berkeley, with her quick glancing vivacity, would have been all around her and off again like a humming-bird before she would have uttered two words. And yet he was sure that they would have been friends, just as he and Chev were. Perhaps they all would be, after the war. And then he began to talk about Chev, being sure that, had the circumstances been reversed, Sallie Berkeley would have wanted news of him. Instantly he was aware of a tense listening stillness on her part. That pleased him. Well, she did care for the old fellow all right, he thought; and though she made no response, averting her face, and plucking nervously at the leaves of the hedge as they passed slowly along, he went on pouring out his eager admiration for his friend.

At last they came to a seat in an arbor, from which one looked out upon a green beneficent landscape. It was an intimate, secluded little spot -- and oh, if Sallie Berkeley were only there to sit beside him! And as he thought of this, it came to him whimsically that in all probability she must be longing for Chev, just as he was for Sallie.

Dropping down on the bench beside her, he leaned over, and said with a friendly, almost brotherly, grin of understanding, "I reckon you're wishing Captain Sherwood was sitting here, instead of Lieutenant Cary."

The minute the impulsive words were out of his mouth, he knew he had blundered, been awkward, and inexcusably intimate. She gave a little choked gasp, and her blue eyes stared up at him, wide and startled. Good heavens, what a break he had made! No wonder the Sherwoods couldn't trust him in company! There seemed no apology that he could offer in words, but at least, he thought, he would show her that he would not have intruded on her secret without being willing to share his with her. With awkward haste he put his hand into his breast-pocket, and dragged forth the picture of Sallie Berkeley he always carried there.

"This is the little girl I'm thinking about," he said, turning very red, yet boyishly determined to make amends, and also proudly confident of Sallie Berkeley's charms. "I'd like mighty well for you two to know one another."

She took the picture in silence, and for a long moment stared down at the soft little face, so fearless, so confident and gay, that smiled appealingly back at her. Then she did something astonishing, -- something which seemed to him wholly un-English, -- and yet he thought it the sweetest thing he had ever seen. Cupping her strong hands about the picture with a quick protectiveness, she suddenly raised it to her lips, and kissed it lightly. "O little girl! " she cried, "I hope you will be very happy!"

The little involuntary act, so tender, so sisterly and spontaneous, touched the Virginian extremely.

"Thanks awfully," he said unsteadily. "She'll think a lot of that, just as I do -- and I know she'd wish you the same."

She made no reply to that, and as she handed the picture back to him, he saw that her hands were trembling, and he had a sudden conviction that, if she had been Sallie Berkeley, her eyes would have been full of tears. As she was Sybil Gaylord, however, there were no tears there, only a look that he never forgot. The look of one much older, protective, maternal almost, and as if she were gazing back at Sallie Berkeley and himself from a long way ahead on the road of life. He supposed it was the way most English people felt nowadays. He had surprised it so often on all their faces, that he could not help speaking of it.

"You all think we Americans are awfully young and raw, don't you?" he questioned.

"Oh, no, not that," she deprecated. "Young perhaps for these days, yes -- but it is more that you -- that your country is so -- so unsuffered. And we don't want you to suffer!" she added quickly.

Yes, that was it! He understood now, and, heavens, how fine it was! Old England was wounded deep -- deep. What she suffered herself she was too proud to show; but out of it she wrought a great maternal care for the newcomer. Yes, it was fine -- he hoped his country would understand.

Miss Gaylord rose. "There are Gerald and father looking for you," she said, "and I must go now." She held out her hand. "Thank you for letting me see her picture, and for everything you said about Captain Sherwood -- for everything, remember -- I want you to remember."

With a light pressure of her fingers she was gone, slipping away through the shrubbery, and he did not see her again.

So he came to his last morning at Bishopsthorpe; and as he dressed, he wished it could have been different; that he were not still conscious of that baffling wall of reserve between himself and Chev's people, for whom, despite all, he had come to have a real affection.

In the breakfast-room he found them all assembled, and his last meal there seemed to him as constrained and difficult as any that had preceded it. It was over finally, however, and in a few minutes he would be leaving.

"I can never thank you enough for the splendid time I've had here," he said as he rose. "I'll be seeing Chev tomorrow, and I'll tell him all about everything."

Then he stopped dead. With a smothered exclamation, old Sir Charles had stumbled to his feet, knocking over his chair, and hurried blindly out of the room; and Gerald said, "Mother!" in a choked appeal.

As if it were a signal between them, Lady Sherwood pushed her chair back a little from the table, her long delicate fingers dropped together loosely in her lap; she gave a faint sign as if a restraining mantle slipped from her shoulders, and looking up at the youth before her, her fine pale face lighted with a kind of glory, she said, "No, dear lad, no. You can never tell Chev, for he is gone."

"Gone!" he cried.

"Yes," she nodded back at him just above a whisper; and now her face quivered, and the tears began to rush down her cheeks.

"Not dead!" he cried. "Not Chev -- not that! O my God, Gerald, not that!"

"Yes," Gerald said. "They got him two days after you left."

It was so overwhelming, so unexpected and shocking, above all so terrible, that the friend he had so greatly loved and admired was gone out of his life forever, that young Cary stumbled back into his seat, and crumpling over, buried his face in his hands, making great uncouth gasps as he strove to choke back his grief.

Gerald groped hastily around the table, and flung an arm about his shoulders.

"Steady on, dear fellow, steady," he said, though his own voice broke.

"When did you hear?" Cary got out at last.

"We got the official notice just the way before you came -- and Withers has written us particulars since."

"And you let me come in spite of it! And stay on, when every word I said about him must have -- have fairly crucified each one of you! Oh, forgive me! forgive me!" he cried distractedly. He saw it all now; he understood at last. It was not on Gerald's account that they could not talk of flying and of Chev, it was because -- because their hearts were broken over Chev himself. "Oh, forgive me!" he gasped again.

"Dear lad, there is nothing to forgive," Lady Sherwood returned. "How could we help loving your generous praise of our poor darling? We loved it, and you for it; we wanted to hear it, but we were afraid. We were afraid we might break down, and that you would find out."

The tears were still running down her cheeks. She did not brush them away now; she seemed glad to have them there at last.

Sinking down on his knees, he caught her hands. "Why did you let me do such a horrible thing?" he cried. "Couldn't you have trusted me to understand? Couldn't you see I loved him just as you did -- No, no!" he broke down humbly, "Of course I couldn't love him as his own people did. But you must have see how I felt about him -- how I admired him, and would have followed him anywhere -- and of course if I had known, I should have gone away at once."

"Ah, but that was just what we were afraid of," she said quickly. "We were afraid you would go away and have a lonely leave somewhere. And in these days a boy's leave is so precious a thing that nothing must spoil it -- nothing," she reiterated; and her tears fell upon his hands like a benediction. "But we didn't do it very well, I'm afraid," she went on presently, with gentle contrition. "You were too quick and understanding; you guessed there was something wrong. We were sorry not to manage better," she apologized.

"Oh, you wonderful, wonderful people!" he gasped. "Doing everything for my happiness, when all the time -- all the time--"

His voice went out sharply, as his mind flashed back to scene after scene: to Gerald's long body lying quivering on the grass; to Sybil Gaylord wishing Sallie Berkeley happiness out of her own tragedy; and to the high look on Lady Sherwood's face. They seemed to him themselves, and yet more than themselves -- shining bits in the mosaic of a great nation. Disjointedly there passed through his mind familiar words--

"these are they who have washed their garments -- having come out of great tribulation." No wonder they seemed older.

"We -- we couldn't have done it in America," he said humbly.

He had a desperate desire to get away to himself; to hide his face in his arms and give vent to the tears that were stifling him; to weep for his lost friend, and for this great heartbreaking heroism of theirs.

"But why did you do it?" he persisted. "Was it because I was his friend?"

"Oh, it was much more than that," Gerald said quickly. "It was a matter of the two countries. Of course, we jolly well knew you didn't belong to us, and didn't want to, but for the life of us we couldn't help a sort of feeling that you did. And when America was in at last, and you fellows began to come, you seemed like our very own come back after many years, and," he added, a throb in his voice, "we were most awfully glad to see you -- we wanted a chance to show you how England felt."

Skipworth Cary rose to his feet. The tears for his friend were still wet upon his lashes. Stooping, he took Lady Sherwood's hands in his and raised them to his lips. "As long as I live, I shall never forget," he said. "And others of us have seen it too in other ways -- be sure America will never forget, either."

She looked up at his untouched youth out of her beautiful sad eyes, the exalted light still shining through her tears. "Yes," she said, "you see it was -- I don't know exactly how to put it -- but it was England to America."

# An International Episode
## Henry James

**Henry James 1843-1916:** He was born in New York City in 1843, the brother of the well known psychologist and philosopher William James. Henry was influenced by his father's interest in philosophy, theology, and the cultural life of New York and cities abroad. James received his early education in England, Switzerland, France and Germany. He briefly studied painting and at nineteen he began studying law at Harvard. Two years later he began the intense work on his writings that produced the portrayals of conflict between American and European cultures and the experimentation with those psychological devices in the depiction of character that influenced such writers as D. H. Lawrence, James Joyce, Joseph Conrad, Edith Wharton, Virginia Woolf, Willa Cather, and T.S. Eliot.

In 1875 he published his first collection of stories, *A Passionate Pilgrim and Other Tales*. In this early part of his career he spent a great deal of time in Paris, where he befriended Flaubert and Turgenev. These naturalists influenced his style, as evidenced by his adoption of the idea that the writer is a researcher into life. He did not, however, accept the notion that humans are left to the whim of chance. It was this sense of determinism that distinguished him from his naturalist counterparts.

His works include *The American, The Portrait of a Lady , Daisy Miller*, and such short pieces as "The Beast in the Jungle" and "The Turn of the Screw".

## PART I

Four years ago -- in 1874 -- two young Englishmen had occasion to go to the United States. They crossed the ocean at midsummer, and, arriving in New York on the first day of August, were much struck with the fervid temperature of that city. Disembarking upon the wharf, they climbed into one of those huge high-hung coaches which convey passengers to the hotels, and with a great deal of bouncing and bumping, took their course through Broadway. The midsummer aspect of New York is not, perhaps, the most favorable one; still, it is not without its picturesque and even brilliant side. Nothing could well resemble less a typical English street than the interminable avenue, rich in incongruities, through which our two travelers advanced -- looking out on each side of them at the comfortable animation of the sidewalks, the high-colored, heterogeneous architecture, the huge white marble facades glittering in the strong, crude light, and bedizened with gilded lettering, the multifarious awnings, banners, and streamers, the extraordinary number of omnibuses, horse cars, and other democratic vehicles, the vendors of cooling fluids, the white trousers and big straw hats of the policemen, the tripping gait of the modish young persons on the pavement, the general brightness, newness, juvenility, both of people and things. The young men had exchanged few observations; but in crossing Union Square, in front of the monument to Washington -- in the very shadow, indeed, projected by the image of the *pater, patrioe* -- one of them remarked to the other, "It seems a rum-looking place."

"Ah, very odd, very odd," said the other, who was the clever man of the two.

"Pity it's so beastly hot," resumed the first speaker after a pause.

"You know we are in a low latitude," said his friend.

"I daresay," remarked the other.

"I wonder," said the second speaker presently, "if they can give one a bath?"

"I daresay not," rejoined the other.

"Oh, I say!" cried his comrade.

This animated discussion was checked by their arrival at the hotel, which had been recommended to them by an American gentleman whose acquaintance they made -- with whom, indeed, they became very intimate -- on the steamer, and who had proposed to accompany them to the inn and introduce them, in a friendly way, to the proprietor. This plan, however, had been defeated by their friend's finding that his "partner" was awaiting him on the wharf and that his commercial associate desired him instantly to come and give his attention to certain telegrams received from St. Louis. But the two Englishmen, with nothing but their national prestige and personal graces to recommend them, were very well received at the hotel, which had an air of capacious hospitality. They found that a bath was not unattainable, and were indeed struck with the facilities for prolonged and reiterated immersion with which their apartment was supplied. After bathing a good deal -- more, indeed, than they had ever done before on a single occasion -- they made their way into the dining room of the hotel, which was a spacious restaurant, with a fountain in the middle, a great many tall plants in ornamental tubs, and an array of French waiters. The first dinner on land, after a sea voyage, is, under any circumstances, a delightful occasion, and there was something particularly agreeable in the circumstances in which our young Englishmen found themselves. They were extremely good natured young men; they were more observant than they appeared; in a sort of inarticulate, accidentally dissimulative fashion, they were highly appreciative. This was perhaps, especially the case with the elder, who was also as I have said, the man of talent. They sat down at a little table, which was a very different affair from the great clattering seesaw in the saloon of the steamer. The wide doors and windows of the restaurant stood open, beneath large awnings, to a wide pavement, where there were other plants in tubs, and rows of spreading trees, and beyond which there was a large shady square, without any palings, and with marble-paved walks. And above the vivid verdure rose other facades of white marble and of pale chocolate-colored stone, squaring themselves against the deep blue sky. Here, outside, in the light and the shade and the heat, there was a great tinkling of the bells of innumerable street-cars, and a constant strolling and shuffling and rustling of many pedestrians, a large proportion of whom were young women in Pompadour-looking dresses. Within, the place was cool and vaguely lighted, with the plash of water, the odor of flowers, and the flitting of French waiters, as I have said, upon soundless carpets.

"It's rather like Paris, you know," said the younger of our two travelers.

"It's like Paris -- only more so," his companion rejoined.

"I suppose it's the French waiters," said the first speaker. "Why don't they have French waiters in London?"

"Fancy a French waiter at a club," said his friend.

The young Englishman stared a little, as if he could not fancy it. "In Paris I'm very apt to dine at a place where there's an English waiter. Don't you know what's-his-name's, close to the thingumbob? They always set an English waiter at me. I suppose they think I can't speak French."

"Well, you can't." And the elder of the young Englishmen unfolded his napkin.

His companion took no notice whatever of this declaration. "I say," he resumed in a moment, "I suppose we must learn to speak American. I suppose we must take lessons."

"I can't understand them," said the clever man.

"What the deuce is he saying?" asked his comrade, appealing from the French waiter.

"He is recommending some soft-shell crabs," said the clever man.

And so, in desultory observation of the idiosyncrasies of the new society in which they found themselves, the young Englishmen proceeded to dine -- going in largely, as the phrase is, for cooling draughts and dishes, of which their attendant offered them a very long list. After dinner they went out and slowly walked about the neighboring streets. The early dusk of waning summer was coming on, but the heat was still very great. The pavements were hot even to the stout boot soles of the British travelers, and the trees along the curbstone emitted strange exotic odors. The young men wandered through the adjoining square -- that queer place without palings, and with marble walls arranged in black and white lozenges. There were a great many benches, crowded with shabby-looking people, and the travelers remarked, very justly, that was not much like Belgrave Square. On one side was an enormous hotel, lifting up into the hot darkness an immense array of open, brightly lighted windows. At the base of this populous structure was an eternal jangle of horsecars, and all around it, in the upper dusk, was a sinister hum of mosquitoes. The ground floor of the hotel seemed to be a huge transparent cage, flinging a wide glare of gaslight into the street, of which it formed a sort of public adjunct, absorbing and emitting the passersby promiscuously. The young Englishmen went in with everyone else, from curiosity, and saw a couple of hundred men sitting on divans along a great marble-paved corridor, with their legs stretched out, together with several dozen more standing in a queue, as at the ticket office of a railway station, before a brilliantly illuminated counter of vast extent. These latter persons, who carried portmanteaus in their hands, had a dejected, exhausted look; their garments were not very fresh, and they seemed to be rendering some mysterious tribute to a magnificent young man with a waxed mustache, and a shirtfront adorned with diamond buttons, who every now and then dropped an absent glance over their multitudinous patience. They were American citizens doing homage to a hotel clerk.

"I'm glad he didn't tell us to go there," said one of our Englishmen, alluding to their friend on the steamer, who had told them so many things. They walked up the Fifth Avenue, where, for instance, he had told them that all the first families lived. But the first families were out of town, and our young travellers had only the satisfaction of seeing some of the second -- or perhaps even the third -- taking the evening air upon balconies and high flights of doorsteps, in the streets which radiate from the more ornamental thoroughfare. They went a little way down one of these side streets, and they saw young ladies in white dresses -- charming-looking persons -- seated in graceful attitudes on the chocolate-colored steps. In one or two places these young ladies were conversing across the street with other young ladies seated in similar postures and costumes in front of the opposite houses, and in the warm night air their colloquial tones sounded strange in the ears of the young Englishmen. One of our friends, nevertheless -- the younger one -- intimated that he felt a disposition to interrupt a few of these soft familiarities; but his companion observed, pertinently enough, that he had better be careful. "We must not begin with making mistakes," said his companion.

"But he told us you know -- he told us," urged the young man, alluding again to the friend on the steamer.

"Never mind what he told us!" answered his comrade, who, if he had greater talents, was also apparently more of a moralist.

By bedtime -- in their impatience to taste of a terrestrial couch again our seafarers went to bed early -- it was still insufferably hot, and the buzz of the mosquitoes at the open windows might have passed for an audible crepitation of the temperature. "We can't stand this, you know," the young Englishmen said to each other; and they tossed about all night more boisterously than they had tossed upon the Atlantic billows. On the morrow, their first thought was that they would re-embark that day for England; and then it occurred to them that they might find an asylum nearer at hand. The cave of Aeolus became their ideal of comfort, and they wondered where the Americans went when they wished to cool off. They had not the least idea, and they determined to apply for information to Mr. J. L. Westgate. This was the name inscribed in a bold hand on the back of a letter carefully preserved in the pocketbook of our junior traveler. Beneath the address, in the left-hand corner of the envelope, were the words, "Introducing Lord Lambeth and Percy Beaumont, Esq." The letter had been given to the two Englishmen by a good friend of theirs in London, who had been in America two years previously, and had singled out Mr. J. L. Westgate from the many friends had left there as the consignee, as it were, of his compatriots. "He is a capital fellow," the Englishman in London had said, "and he has got an awfully pretty wife. He's tremendously hospitable -- he will do everything in the world for you and as he knows everyone over there, it is quite needless I should give you any other introduction. He will make you see everyone; trust to him for putting you into circulation. He has got a tremendously pretty wife." It was natural that in the hour of tribulation Lord Lambeth and Mr. Percy Beaumont should have bethought themselves of a gentleman whose attractions had been thus vividly depicted; all the more so that he lived in the Fifth Avenue, and that the Fifth Avenue, as they had ascertained the night before, was contiguous to their hotel. "Ten to one he'll be out of town," said Percy Beaumont; "but we can at least find out where he has gone, and we can immediately start in pursuit. He can't possibly have gone to a hotter place, you know."

"Oh, there's only one hotter place," said Lord Lambeth, "and I hope he hasn't gone there."

They strolled along the shady side of the street to the number indicated upon the precious letter. The house presented an imposing chocolate-colored expanse, relieved by facings and window cornices of florid sculpture, and by a couple of dusty rose trees which clambered over the balconies and the portico. This last-mentioned feature was approached by a monumental flight of steps.

"Rather better than a London house," said Lord Lambeth, looking down from this altitude, after they had rung the bell.

"It depends upon what London house you mean," replied his companion. "You have a tremendous chance to get wet between the house door and your carriage."

"Well," said Lord Lambeth, glancing at the burning heavens, "I 'guess' it doesn't rain so much here!"

The door was opened by a long Negro in a white jacket, who grinned familiarly when Lord Lambeth asked for Mr. Westgate.

"He ain't at home, sah; he's downtown at his o'fice."

"Oh, at his office?" said the visitors. "And when will he be at home?"

"Well, sah, when he goes out dis way in de mo'ning, he ain't liable to come home all day."

This was discouraging; but the address of Mr. Westgate's office was freely imparted by the intelligent black and was taken down by Percy Beaumont in his pocketbook. The two gentlemen then returned, languidly, to their hotel, and sent for a hackney coach, and in this commodious vehicle they rolled comfortably downtown. They measured the whole length of Broadway again and found it a path of fire; and then, deflecting to the left, they were deposited by their conductor before a fresh, light, ornamental structure, ten stories high, in a street crowded with keen-faced, light-limbed young men, who were running about very quickly and stopping each other eagerly at corners and in doorways. Passing into this brilliant building, they were introduced by one of the keen faced young men -- he was a charming fellow, in wonderful cream-colored garments and a hat with a blue ribbon, who had evidently perceived them to be aliens and helpless -- to a very snug hydraulic elevator, in which they took their place with many other persons, and which, shooting upward in its vertical socket, presently projected them into the seventh horizontal compartments of the edifice. Here, after brief delay, they found themselves face to face with the friend of their friend in London. His office was composed of several different rooms, and they waited very silently in one of them after they had sent in their letter and their cards. The letter was not one which it would take Mr. Westgate very long to read, but he came out to speak to them more instantly than they could have expected; he had evidently jumped up from his work. He was a tall, lean personage and was dressed all in fresh white linen; he had a thin, sharp, familiar face, with an expression that was at one and the same time sociable and businesslike, a quick, intelligent eye, and a large brown mustache, which concealed his mouth and made his chin, beneath it, look small. Lord Lambeth thought he looked tremendously clever.

"How do you do, Lord Lambeth -- how do you do, sir?" he said, holding the open letter in his hand. "I'm very glad to see you; I hope you're very well. You had better come in here; I think it's cooler," and he led the way into another room, where there were law books and papers, and windows wide open beneath striped awning. Just opposite one of the windows, on a line with his eyes, Lord Lambeth observed the weather-vane of a church steeple. The uproar of the street sounded infinitely far below, and Lord Lambeth felt very high in the air. "I say it's cooler," pursued their host, "but everything is relative. How do you stand the heat?"

"I can't say we like it," said Lord Lambeth; "but Beaumont likes it better than I."

"Well, it won't last," Mr. Westgate very cheerfully declared; "nothing unpleasant lasts over here. It was very hot when Captain Littledale was here; he did nothing but drink sherry cobblers. He expressed some doubt in his letter whether I will remember him -- as if I didn't remember making six sherry cobblers for him one day in about twenty minutes. I hope you left him well, two years having elapsed since then."

"Oh, yes, he's all right," said Lord Lambeth.

"I am always very glad to see your countrymen," Mr. Westgate pursued. "I thought it would be time some of you should be coming along. A friend of mine was saying to me only a day or two ago, 'It's time for the watermelons and the Englishmen.'"

"The Englishmen and the watermelons just now are about the same thing," Percy Beaumont observed, wiping his dripping forehead.

"Ah, well, we'll put you on ice, as we do the melons. You must go down to Newport."

"We'll go anywhere," said Lord Lambeth.

"Yes, you want to go to Newport; that's what you want to do," Mr. Westgate affirmed. "But let's see -- when did you get here?"

"Only yesterday," said Percy Beaumont.

"Ah, yes, by the *Russia*. Where are you staying?"

"At the Hanover, I think they call it."

"Pretty comfortable?" inquired Mr. Westgate.

"It seems a capital place, but I can't say we like the gnats," said Lord Lambeth.

Mr. Westgate stared and laughed. "Oh, no, of course you don't like the gnats. We shall expect you to like a good many things over here, but we shan't insist upon your liking the gnats; though certainly you'll admit that, as gnats, they are fine, eh? But you oughtn't to remain in the city."

"So we think," said Lord Lambeth. "If you would kindly suggest something-----"

"Suggest something, my dear sir?" and Mr. Westgate looked at him, narrowing his eyelids. "Open your mouth and shut your eyes! Leave it to me, and I'll put you through. It's a matter of national pride with me that all Englishmen should have a good time; and as I have had considerable practice, I have learned to minister to their wants. I find they generally want the right thing. So just please to consider yourselves my property; and if anyone should try to appropriate you, please to say 'Hands off; too late for the market.' But let's see," continued the American, in his slow, humorous voice, with a distinctness of utterance which appeared to his visitors to be part of a humorous intention -- a strangely leisurely speculative voice for a man evidently so busy and, as they felt, so professional -- "let's see; are you going to make something of a stay, Lord Lambeth?"

"Oh, dear, no," said the young Englishman; "my cousin was coming over on some business, so I just came across, at an hour's notice, for the lark."

"Is it your first visit to the United States?"

"Oh, dear, yes."

"I was obliged to come on some business," said Percy Beaumont, "and I brought Lambeth along."

"And *you* have been here before, sir?"

"Never--never."

"I thought, from your referring to business-----" said Mr. Westgate.

"Oh, you see I'm by way of being a barrister," Percy Beaumont answered. "I know some people that think of bringing a suit against one of your railways, and they asked me to come over and take measures accordingly."

Mr. Westgate gave one of his slow, keen looks again. "What's your railroad?" he asked.

"The Tennessee Central."

The American tilted back his chair a little and poised it an instant. "Well, I'm sorry you want to attack one of our institutions," he said, smiling. "But I guess you had better enjoy yourself *first!*"

"I'm certainly rather afraid I can't work in this weather," the young barrister confessed.

"Leave that to the natives," said Mr. Westgate. "Leave the Tennessee Central to me, Mr. Beaumont. Some day we'll talk it over, and I guess I can make it square. But didn't know you Englishmen ever did any work, in the upper classes."

"Oh, we do a lot of work; don't we, Lambeth?" asked Percy Beaumont.

"I must certainly be at home by the 19th of September said the younger Englishman, irrelevantly but gently.

"For the shooting, eh? or is it-the hunting, or the fishing?" inquired his entertainer.

"Oh, I must be in Scotland," said Lord Lambeth, blushing a little.

"Well, then," rejoined Mr. Westgate, "you had better amuse yourself first, also. You must go down and see Mrs. Westgate."

"We should be so happy, if you would kindly tell us the train," said Percy Beaumont.

"It isn't a train -- it's a boat."

"Oh, I see. And what is the name of--a--the--a--town?"

"It isn't a town," said Mr. Westgate, laughing. "It's a -- well what shall I call it? It's a watering place. In short, it's Newport. You'll see what it is. It's cool; that's the principal thing. You will greatly oblige me by going down there and putting yourself into the hands of Mrs. Westgate. It isn't perhaps for me to say it, but you couldn't be in better hands. Also in those of her sister, who is staying with her. She is very fond of Englishmen. She thinks there is nothing like them."

"Mrs. Westgate or a--her sister?" asked Percy Beaumont modestly, yet in the tone of an inquiring traveler.

"Oh, I mean my wife," said Mr. Westgate. "I don't suppose my sister-in-law knows much about them. She has always led a very quiet life; she has lived in Boston."

Percy Beaumont listened with interest. "That, I believe," he said, "is the most--a--intellectual town?"

"I believe it is very intellectual. I don't go there much," responded his host.

"I say, we ought to go there," said Lord Lambeth to his companion.

"Oh, Lord Lambeth, wait till the great heat is over," Mr. Westgate interposed. "Boston in this weather would be very trying; it's not the temperature for intellectual exertion. At Boston, you know, you have to pass an examination at the city limits; and when you come away they give you a kind of degree."

Lord Lambeth stared, blushing a little; and Percy Beaumont stared a little also -- but only with his fine natural complexion -- glancing aside after a moment to see that his companion was not looking too credulous, for he had heard a great deal of American humor. "I daresay it is very jolly," said the younger gentleman.

"I daresay it is," said Mr. Westgate. "Only I must impress upon you that at present -- tomorrow morning, at an early hour -- you will be expected at Newport. We have a house there; half the people in New York go there for the summer. I am not sure that at this very moment my wife can take you in; she has got a lot of people staying with her; I don't know who they all are; only she may have no room. But you can begin with the hotel, and meanwhile you can live at my house. In that way -- simply sleeping at the hotel -- you will find it tolerable. For the rest, you must make yourself at home at my place. You mustn't be shy, you know; if you are only here for a month that will be a great waste of time. Mrs. Westgate won't neglect you, and you had better not try to resist her. I know something about that. I expect you'll find some pretty girls on the premises. I shall write to my wife by this afternoon's mail, and tomorrow morning she and Miss Alden will look out for you. Just walk right in and make yourself comfortable. Your steamer leaves from this part of the city, and I will immediately send out and get you a cabin. Then, at half past four o'clock, just call for me here, and I will go with you and put you on board. It's a big boat; you might get lost. A few days hence, at the end of the week, I will come down to Newport and see how you are getting on."

The two young Englishmen inaugurated the policy of not resisting Mrs. Westgate by submitting, with great docility and thankfulness, to her husband. He was evidently a very good fellow, and he made an impression upon his visitors; his hospitality seemed to recommend itself consciously -- with a friendly wink, as it were -- as if it hinted, judicially, that you could not possibly make a better bargain. Lord Lambeth and his cousin left their entertainer to his labors and returned to their hotel, where they spent three or four hours in their respective shower baths. Percy Beaumont had suggested that they ought to see something of the town; but "Oh, damn the town!" his noble kinsman had rejoined. They returned to Mr. Westgate's office in a carriage, with their luggage, very punctually; but it must be reluctantly recorded that, this time, he kept them waiting so long that they felt themselves missing the steamer, and were deterred only by an amiable modesty from dispensing with his attendance and starting on a hasty scramble to the wharf. But when at last he appeared, and the carriage plunged into the purlieus of Broadway, they jolted and jostled to such good purpose that they reached the huge white vessel while the bell for departure was still ringing and the absorption of passengers still active. It was indeed, as Mr. Westgate had said, a big boat, and his leadership in the innumerable and interminable corridors and cabins, with which he seemed perfectly acquainted, and of which anyone and everyone appeared to have the entree, was very grateful to the slightly bewildered voyagers. He showed them their stateroom -- a spacious apartment, embellished with gas lamps, mirrors *en pied*, and sculptured furniture -- and then, long after they had been intimately convinced that the steamer was in motion and launched upon the unknown stream that they were about to navigate, he bade them a sociable farewell.

"Well, goodbye , Lord Lambeth," he said; "goodbye, Mr. Percy Beaumont. I hope you'll have a good time. Just let them do what they want with you. I'll come down by-and-by and look after you."

The young Englishmen emerged from their cabin and amused themselves with wandering about the immense labyrinthine steamer, which struck them as an extraordinary mixture of a ship and a hotel. It was densely crowded with passengers, the larger number of whom appeared to be ladies and very young children; and in the big saloons, ornamented in white and gold, which followed each other in surprising succession, beneath the swinging gaslight, and among the small side passages where the Negro domestics of both sexes assembled with an air of philosophic leisure, everyone was moving to and fro and exchanging loud and familiar observations. Eventually, at the instance of a discriminating black, our young men went and had some "supper" in a wonderful place arranged like a theater, where, in a gilded gallery, upon which little boxes appeared to open, a large orchestra was playing operatic selections, and, below, people were handing about bills of fare, as if they had been programs. All this was sufficiently curious; but the agreeable thing, later, was to sit out on one of the great white decks of the steamer, in the warm breezy darkness, and, in the vague starlight, to make out the line of low, mysterious coast. The young Englishmen tried American cigars -- those of Mr. Westgate -- and talked together as they usually talked, with many odd silences, lapses of logic, and incongruities of transition; like people who have grown old together and learned to supply each other's missing phrases; or, more especially, like people thoroughly conscious of a common point of view, so that a style of conversation superficially lacking in finish might suffice for reference to fund of associations the light of which everything was all right.

"We really seem to be going out to sea," Percy Beaumont observed. "Upon my word, we are going back to England. He has shipped us off again. I call that 'real mean.'"

"I suppose it's all right," said Lord Lambeth. "I want see those pretty girls at Newport. You know, he told us the place was an island; and aren't all islands in the sea?"

"Well," resumed the elder traveler after a while, "if his house is as good as his cigars, we shall do very well."

"He seems a very good fellow," said Lord Lambeth, as if this idea had just occurred to him.

"I say, we had better remain at the inn," rejoined his companion presently. "I don't think I like the way he spoke of his house. I don't like stopping in the house with such a tremendous lot of women."

"Oh, I don't mind," said Lord Lambeth. And then they smoked a while in silence. "Fancy his thinking we do not work in England!" the young man resumed.

"I daresay he didn't really think so," said Percy Beaumont.

"Well, I guess they don't know much about England over here!" declared Lord Lambeth humorously. And then there was another long pause. "He was devilish civil," observed the young nobleman.

"Nothing, certainly, could have been more civil," rejoined his companion.

"Littledale said his wife was great fun," said Lord Lambeth.

"Whose wife -- Littledale's?"

"This American's -- Mrs. Westgate. What's his name? J. L."

Beaumont was silent a moment. "What was fun to Littledale," he said at last, rather sententiously, "may be death to us."

"What do you mean by that?" asked his kinsman. "I am as good a man as Littledale."

"My dear boy, I hope you won't begin to flirt," said Percy Beaumont.

"I don't care. I daresay I shan't begin."

"With a married woman, if she's bent upon it, it's all very well," Beaumont expounded. "But our friend mentioned a young lady -- a sister, a sister-in-law. For God's sake, don't get entangled with her!"

"How do you mean entangled?"

"Depend upon it she will try to hook you."

"Oh, bother!" said Lord Lambeth.

"American girls are very clever," urged his companion.

"So much the better," the young man declared.

"I fancy they are always up to some game of that sort," Beaumont continued.

"They can't be worse than they are in England," said Lord Lambeth judicially.

"Ah, but in England," replied Beaumont, "you have got your natural protectors. You have got your mother and sisters."

"My mother and sisters" began the young nobleman with a certain energy. But he stopped in time, puffing at his cigar.

"Your mother spoke to me about it, with tears in her eyes," said Percy Beaumont. "She said she felt very nervous. I promised to keep you out of mischief."

"You had better take care of yourself," said the object of maternal and ducal solicitude.

"Ah," rejoined the young barrister, "I haven't the expectation of a hundred thousand a year, not to mention other attractions."

"Well," said Lord Lambeth, "don't cry out before you're hurt!"

It was certainly very much cooler at Newport, where our travelers found themselves assigned to a couple of diminutive bedrooms in a faraway angle of an immense hotel. They had gone ashore in the early summer twilight and had very promptly put themselves to bed; thanks to which circumstance and to their having, during the previous hours, in their commodious cabin, slept the sleep of youth and health they began to feel, toward eleven o'clock, very alert and inquisitive. They looked out of their windows across a row of small green fields, bordered with low stone walls of rude construction, and saw a deep blue ocean lying beneath a deep blue sky, and flecked now and then with scintillating patches of foam. A strong, fresh breeze came in through the curtainless casements and prompted our young men to observe, generally, that it didn't seem half a bad climate. They made other observations after they had emerged from their rooms in pursuit of breakfast -- a meal of which they partook in a huge bare hall, where a hundred Negroes, in white jackets, were shuffling about upon an uncarpeted floor; where the flies were superabundant, and the tables covered over with a strange, voluminous integument of coarse blue gauze; and where several little boys and girls, who had risen late, were seated in fastidious solitude at the morning repast. These young persons had not the morning paper before them, but they were engaged in languid perusal of the bill of fare.

This latter document was a great puzzle to our friends who, on reflecting that its bewildering categories had relation to breakfast alone, had an uneasy prevision of an encyclopedic dinner list. They found a great deal of entertainment at the hotel, an enormous wooden structure, for the erection of which it seemed to them that the virgin forests of the West must have been terribly deflowered. It was perforated from end to end with immense bare corridors, through which a strong draught was blowing -- bearing along wonderful figures of ladies in white morning dresses and clouds of Valenciennes lace, who seemed, to float down the long vistas with expanded furbelows, like angels spreading their wings. In front was a gigantic veranda, upon which an army might have encamped -- a vast wooden terrace, with a roof as lofty as the nave of a cathedral. Here our young Englishmen enjoyed, as they supposed, a glimpse of American society, which was distributed over the measureless expanse in a variety of sedentary attitudes, and appeared to consist largely of pretty young girls, dressed as if for a *fête champêtre*, swaying to and fro in rocking chairs, fanning themselves with large straw fans, and enjoying an enviable exemption from social cares. Lord Lambeth had a theory, which it might be interesting to trace to its origin, that it would be not only agreeable, but easily possible, to enter into relations with one of the young ladies; and his companion (as he had done a couple of days before) found occasion to check the young nobleman's colloquial impulses.

"You had better take care," said Percy Beaumont, "or you will have an offended father or brother pulling out a bowie knife."

"I assure you it is all right," Lord Lambeth replied. "You know the Americans come to these big hotels to make acquaintances."

"I know nothing about it, and neither do you," said his kinsman, who, like a clever man, had begun to perceive that the observation of American society demanded a readjustment of one's standard.

"Hang it, then, let's find out!" cried Lord Lambeth with some impatience. "You know I don't want to miss anything."

"We will find out," said Percy Beaumont very reasonably. "We will go and see Mrs. Westgate and make all proper inquiries."

And so the two inquiring Englishmen, who had this lady's address inscribed in her husband's hand upon a card, descended from the veranda of the big hotel and took their way, according to direction, along a large straight road, past a series of fresh-looking villas embosomed in shrubs and flowers and enclosed in an ingenious variety of wooden palings. The morning was brilliant and cool, the villas were smart and snug, and the walk of the young travelers was very entertaining. Everything looked as if it had received a coat of fresh paint the day before -- the red roofs, the green shutters, the clean, bright browns and buffs of the housefronts. The flower beds on the little lawns seemed to sparkle in the radiant air, and the gravel in the short carriage sweeps to flash and twinkle. Along the road came a hundred little basket phaetons, in which, almost always, a couple of ladies were sitting -- ladies in white dresses and long white gloves, holding the reins and looking at the two Englishmen, whose nationality was not elusive, through thick blue veils tied tightly about their faces as if to guard their complexions. At last the young men came within sight of the sea again, and then, having interrogated a gardener over the paling of a villa, they turned into an open gate. Here they found themselves face to face with the ocean and with a very picturesque structure, resembling a magnified chalet, which was perched upon a green embankment just above it. The house had a veranda of extraordinary width all around it and a great many doors and windows standing open to the veranda. These various apertures had, in common, such an accessible, hospitable air, such a breezy flutter within of light curtains, such expansive thresholds and reassuring interiors, that our friends hardly knew which was the regular entrance, and, after hesitating a moment, presented themselves at one of the windows. The room within was dark, but in a moment a graceful figure vaguely shaped itself in the rich-looking gloom, and a lady came to meet them. Then they saw that she had been seated at a table writing, and that she had heard that and had got up. She stepped out into the light; she wore a frank, charming smile, with which she held out her hand to Percy Beaumont.

"Oh, you must be Lord Lambeth and Mr. Beaumont." she said. "I have heard from my husband that you would come. I am extremely glad to see you." And she shook hands with each of her visitors. Her visitors were a little shy, but they had very good manners; they responded with smiles and exclamations, and they apologized for not knowing the front door. The lady rejoined, with vivacity, that when she wanted to see people very much she did not insist upon those distinctions, and that Mr. Westgate had written to her of his English friends in terms that made her really anxious. "He said you were so terribly prostrated," said Mrs. Westgate.

"Oh, you mean by the heat?" replied Percy Beaumont. "We were rather knocked up, but we feel wonderfully better. We had such a jolly--a--voyage down here. It's so very good of you to mind."

"Yes, it's so very kind of you," murmured Lord Lambeth.

Mrs. Westgate stood smiling; she was extremely pretty. "Well, I did mind," she said; "and I thought of sending for you this morning to the Ocean House. I am very glad you are better, and I am charmed you have arrived. You must come round to the other side of the piazza." And she led the way with a light, smooth step, looking back at the young men and smiling.

The other side of the piazza was, as Lord Lambeth presently remarked, a very jolly place. It was of the most liberal proportions, and with its awnings, its fanciful chairs, its cushions and rugs, its view of the ocean, close at hand, tumbling along the base of the low cliffs whose level tops intervened in lawnlike smoothness, it formed a charming complement to the drawing room. As such it was in course of use at the present moment; it was occupied by a social circle. There were several ladies and two or three gentlemen, to whom Mrs. Westgate proceeded to introduce the distinguished strangers. She mentioned a great many names very freely and distinctly; the young Englishmen, shuffling about and bowing, were rather bewildered. But at last they were provided with chairs -- low, wicker chairs, gilded, and tied with a great many ribbons -- and one of the ladies (a very young person, with a little snub nose and several dimples) offered Percy Beaumont a fan. The fan was also adorned with pink love knots; but Percy Beaumont declined it, although he was very hot. Presently, however, it became cooler; the breeze from the sea was delicious, the view was charming, and the people sitting there looked exceedingly fresh and comfortable. Several of the ladies seemed to be young girls, and the gentlemen were slim, fair youths, such as our friends had seen the day before in New York. The ladies were working upon bands of tapestry, and one of the young men had an open book in his lap. Beaumont afterward learned from one of the ladies that this young man had been reading aloud, that he was from Boston and was very fond of reading aloud. Beaumont said it was a great pity that they had interrupted him; he should like so much (from all he had heard) to hear a Bostonian read. Couldn't the young man be induced to go on?

"Oh no," said his informant very freely; "he wouldn't be able to get the young ladies to attend to him now."

There was something very friendly, Beaumont perceived, in the attitude of the company; they looked at the young Englishmen with an air of animated sympathy and interest; they smiled, brightly and unanimously, at everything either of the visitors said. Lord Lambeth and his companion felt that they were being made very welcome. Mrs. Westgate seated herself between them, and, talking a great deal to each, they had occasion to observe that she was as pretty as their friend Littledale had promised. She was thirty years old, with the eyes and the smile of a girl of seventeen, and she was extremely light and graceful, elegant, exquisite. Mrs. Westgate was extremely spontaneous. She was very frank and demonstrative and appeared always -- while she looked at you delightedly with her beautiful young eyes to be making sudden confessions and concessions, after momentary hesitations.

"We shall expect to see a great deal of you," she said to Lord Lambeth with a kind of joyous earnestness. We are very fond of Englishmen here; that is, there are a great many we have been fond of. After a day or two you must come and stay with us; we hope you will stay a long time. Newport's a very nice place when you come really to know it, when you know plenty of people. Of course you and Mr. Beaumont will have no difficulty about that. Englishmen are very well received here; they are almost always two or three of them about. I think they always like it, and I must say I should think they would. They receive ever so much attention. I must say I think they sometimes get spoiled; but I am sure you and Mr. Beaumont are proof against that. My husband tells me you are a friend of Captain Littledale; he was such a charming man. He made himself most agreeable here, and I am sure I wonder he didn't stay. It couldn't have been pleasanter for him in his own country, though, I suppose, it is very pleasant in England, for English people. I don't know myself; I have been there very little. I have been a great deal abroad, but I am always on the Continent. I must say I'm extremely fond of Paris; you know we Americans always are; we go there when we die. Did you ever hear that before? That was said by a great wit, I mean the good Americans; but we are all good; you'll see that for yourself. All I know of England is London, and all I know of London is that place on the little corner, you know, where you buy jackets -- jackets with that coarse braid and those big buttons. They make very good jackets in London, I will do you the justice to say that. And some people like the hats; but about the hats I was always a heretic; I always got my hats in Paris. You can't wear an English hat -- at least I never could -- unless you dress your hair *á l'Anglaise*; and I must say that is a talent I have never possessed. In Paris they will make things to suit your peculiarities; but in England I think you like much more to have -- how shall I say it? -- one thing for everybody. I mean as regards dress. I don't know about other things; but I have always supposed that in other things everything was different. I mean according to the people -- according to the classes, and all that. I am afraid you will think that I don't take a very favorable view; but you know you can't take a very favorable view in Dover Street in the month of November. That has always been my fate. Do you know Jones's Hotel in Dover Street? That's all I know of

England. O course everyone admits that the English hotels are your weak point. There was always the most frightful fog; I couldn't see to try my things on. When I got over to America -- into the light -- I usually found they were twice too big. The next time I mean to go in the season; I think I shall go next year. I want very much to take my sister; she has never been to England. I don't know whether you know what I mean by saying that the Englishmen who come here sometimes get spoiled. I mean that they take things as a matter of course -- things that are done for them. Now, naturally, they are only a matter of course when the Englishmen are very nice. But, of course, they are almost always very nice. Of course this isn't nearly such an interesting country as England; there are not nearly so many things to see, and we haven't your country life. I have never seen anything of your country life; when I am in Europe I am always on the Continent. But I have heard a great deal about it; I know that when you are among yourselves in the country you have the most beautiful time. Of course we have nothing of that sort, we have nothing on that scale. I don't apologize, Lord Lambeth; some Americans are always apologizing; you must have noticed that. We have the reputation of always boasting and bragging and waving the American flag; but I must say that what strikes me is that we are perpetually making excuses and trying to smooth things over. The American flag has quite gone out of fashion; it's very carefully folded up, like an old tablecloth. Why should we apologize? The English never apologize -- do they? No; I must say I never apologized. You must take us as we come -- with all our imperfections on our heads. Of course we haven't your country life, and your old ruins, and your great estates, and your leisure class, and all that. But if we haven't, I should I think you might find it a pleasant change -- I think any country is pleasant where they have pleasant manners. Captain Littledale told me he had never seen such pleasant manners as at Newport, and he had been a great deal in European society. Hadn't he been in the diplomatic service? He told me the dream of his life was to get appointed to a diplomatic post Washington. But he doesn't seem to have succeeded. I suppose that in England promotion -- and all that sort of thing -- is fearfully slow. With us, you know, it's a great deal too fast. You see, I admit our drawbacks. But I must confess I think Newport is an ideal place. I don't know anything like it anywhere. Captain Littledale told me he didn't know anything like it anywhere. It's entirely different from most watering places; it's a most charming life. I must say I think that when one goes to a foreign country one ought to enjoy the differences. Of course there are differences, otherwise what did one come abroad for? Look for your pleasure in the differences, Lord Lambeth; that's the way to do it; and then I am sure you will find American society -- at least Newport society -- most charming and most interesting. I wish very much my husband were here; but he's dreadfully confined to New York. I suppose you think that is very strange--for gentleman. But you see we haven't any leisure class."

Mrs. Westgate's discourse, delivered in a soft, sweet voice, flowed on like a miniature torrent, and was interrupted by a hundred little smiles, glances, and gestures, which might have figured the irregularities and abstractions of such a stream. Lord Lambeth listened to her with, it must be confessed, a rather ineffectual attention, although he indulged in a good many little murmurs and ejaculations of assent and deprecation. He had no great faculty for apprehending generalizations. There were some three or four indeed which, in the play of his own intelligence, he had originated, and which had seem convenient at the moment; but at the present time he could hardly have been said to follow Mrs. Westgate as she darted gracefully about in the sea of speculation. Fortunately she asked for no especial rejoinder, for she looked about at the rest of the company as well, and smiled at Percy Beaumont, on the other side of her, as if he too must understand her and agree with her. He was rather more successful than his companion; for besides being, as we know, cleverer, his attention was not vaguely distracted by close vicinity to a remarkably interesting young girl, with dark hair and blue eyes. This was the case with Lord Lambeth, to whom it occurred after a while that the young girl with blue eyes and dark hair was the pretty sister of whom Mrs. Westgate had spoken. She presently turned to him with a remark which established her identity.

"It's a great pity you couldn't have brought my brother-in-law with you. It's a great shame he should be in New York in these days."

"Oh, yes; it's so very hot," said Lord Lambeth.

"It must be dreadful," said the young girl.

"I daresay he is very busy," Lord Lambeth observed.

"The gentlemen in America work too much," the young girl went on.

"Oh, do they? I daresay they like it," said her interlocutor.

"I don't like it. One never sees them."

"Don't you, really?" asked Lord Lambeth. "I shouldn't have fancied that."

"Have you come to study American manners?" asked the young girl.

"Oh, I don't know. I just came over for a lark. I haven't got long." Here there was a pause, and Lord Lambeth began again. "But Mr. Westgate will come down here, will not he?"

"I certainly hope he will. He must help to entertain you and Mr. Beaumont."

Lord Lambeth looked at her a little with his handsome brown eyes. "Do you suppose he would have come down with us if we had urged him?"

Mr. Westgate's sister-in-law was silent a moment, and then, "I daresay he would," she answered.

"Really!" said the young Englishman. "He was immensely civil to Beaumont and me," he added.

"He is a dear good fellow," the young lady rejoined, "and he is a perfect husband. But all Americans are that," she continued, smiling.

"Really!" Lord Lambeth exclaimed again and wondered whether all American ladies had such a passion for generalizing as these two.

He sat there a good while: there was great deal of talk; it was all very friendly and lively and jolly. Everyone present, sooner or later, said something to him, and seemed to make a particular point of addressing him by name. Two or three other persons came in, and there was a shifting of seats and changing of places; the gentlemen all entered into intimate conversation with the two Englishmen, made them urgent offers of hospitality, and hoped they might frequently be of service to them. They were afraid Lord Lambeth and Mr. Beaumont were not very comfortable at their hotel; that it was not, as one of them said, "so private as those dear little English inns of yours." This last gentleman went on to say that unfortunately, as yet, perhaps, privacy was not quite so easily obtained in America as might be desired; still, he continued, you could generally get it by paying for it; in fact, you could get everything in America nowadays by paying for it. American life was certainly growing a great deal more private; it was growing very much like England. Everything at Newport, for instance, was thoroughly private; Lord Lambeth would probably be struck with that. It was also represented to the strangers that it mattered very little whether their hotel was agreeable, as everyone would want them to make visits; they would stay with other people, and, in any case, they would be a great deal at Mrs. Westgate's. They would find that very charming; it was the pleasantest house in Newport. It was a pity Mr. Westgate was always away; he was a man of the highest ability -- very acute, very acute. He worked like a horse, and he left his wife -- well, to do about as she liked. He liked her to enjoy herself, and she seemed to know how. She was extremely brilliant and a splendid talker. Some people preferred her sister; but Miss Alden was very different; she was in a different style altogether. Some people even thought her prettier, and, certainly, she was not so sharp. She was more in the Boston style; she had lived a great deal in Boston, and she was very highly educated. Boston girls, it was propounded, were more like English young ladies.

Lord Lambeth had presently a chance to test the truth of this proposition, for on the company rising in compliance with a suggestion from their hostess that they should walk down to the rocks and look at the sea, the young Englishman again found himself, as they strolled across the grass, in proximity to Mrs. Westgate's sister. Though she was but a girl of twenty, she appeared to feel the obligation to exert an active hospitality; and this was, perhaps, the more to be noticed as she seemed by nature a reserved and retiring person, and had little of her sister's fraternizing quality. She was perhaps rather too thin, and she was a little pale; but as she moved slowly over the grass, with her arms hanging at her sides, looking gravely for a moment at the sea and then brightly, for all her gravity, at him, Lord Lambeth thought her at least as pretty as Mrs. Westgate, and reflected that if this was the Boston style the Boston style was very charming. He thought she looked very clever; he could imagine that she was highly educated; but at the same time she seemed gentle and graceful. For all her cleverness, however, he felt that she had to think a little what to say; she didn't say the first thing that came into her head; he had come from a different part of the world and from a different society, and she was trying to adapt her conversation. The others were scattering themselves near the rocks; Mrs. Westgate had charge of Percy Beaumont.

"Very jolly place, isn't it?" said Lord Lambeth. "It's a very jolly place to sit."

"Very charming," said the young girl. "I often sit here; there are all kinds of cozy corners -- as if they had been made on purpose."

"Ah! I suppose you have had some of them made," said the young man.

Miss Alden looked at him a moment. "Oh no, we have had nothing made. It's pure nature."

"I should think you would have a few little benches -- rustic seats and that sort of thing. It might be so jolly to sit here, you know," Lord Lambeth went on.

"I am afraid we haven't so many of those things as you," said the young girl thoughtfully.

"I daresay you go in for pure nature, as you were saying. Nature over here must be so grand, you know." And Lord Lambeth looked about him.

The little coast line hereabouts was very pretty, but it was not at all grand, and Miss Alden appeared to rise to a perception of this fact. "I am afraid it seems to you very rough," she said. "It's not like the coast scenery in Kingsley's novels."

"Ah, the novels always overdo it, you know," Lord Lambeth rejoined "You must not go by the novels."

They were wandering about a little on the rocks, and they stopped and looked down into a narrow chasm where the rising tide made a curious bellowing sound. It was loud enough to prevent their hearing each other, and they stood there for some moments in silence. The young girl looked at her companion, observing him attentively, but covertly, as women, even when very young, know how to do. Lord Lambeth repaid observation; tall, straight, and strong, he was handsome as certain young Englishmen, and certain young Englishmen almost alone, are handsome; with a perfect finish of feature and a look of intellectual repose and gentle good temper which seemed somehow to be consequent upon his well-cut nose and chin. And to speak of Lord Lambeth's expression of intellectual repose is not simply a civil way of saying that he looked stupid. He was evidently not a young man of an irritable imagination; he was not, as he would himself have said, tremendously clever; but though there was a kind of appealing dullness in his eye, he looked thoroughly reasonable and competent, and his appearance proclaimed that to be a nobleman, an athlete, and an excellent fellow was a sufficiently brilliant combination of qualities. The young girl beside him, it may be attested without further delay, thought him the handsomest young man she had ever seen; and Bessie Alden's imagination, unlike that of her companion, was irritable. He, however, was also making up his mind that she was uncommonly pretty.

"I daresay it's very gay here, that you have lots of balls and parties," he said; for, if he was not tremendously clever, he rather prided himself on having, with women, a sufficiency of conversation.

"Oh, yes, there is a great deal going on," Bessie Alden replied. "There are not so many balls, but there are a good many other things. You will see for yourself; we live rather in the midst of it."

"It's very kind of you to say that. But I thought you Americans were always dancing."

"I suppose we dance a good deal; but I have never seen much of it. We don't do it much, at any rate, in summer. And I am sure," said Bessie Alden, "that we don't have so many balls as you have in England."

"Really!" exclaimed Lord Lambeth. "Ah, in England it all depends, you know."

"You will not think much of our gaieties," said the young girl, looking at him with a little mixture of interrogation and decision which was peculiar to her. The interrogation seemed earnest and the decision seemed arch; but the mixture, at any rate, was charming. "Those things, with us, are much less splendid than in England."

"I fancy you don't mean that," said Lord Lambeth, laughing.

"I assure you I mean everything I say," the young girl declared. "Certainly, from what I have read about English society, it is very different."

"Ah well, you know," said her companion, "those things are often described by fellows who know nothing about them. You mustn't mind what you read."

"Oh, I *shall* mind what I read!" Bessie Alden rejoined. "When I read Thackeray and George Eliot, how can I help minding them?"

"Ah well, Thackeray, and George Eliot," said the young nobleman; "I haven't read much of them."

"Don't you suppose they know about society?" asked Bessie Alden.

"Oh, I daresay they know; they were so very clever. But these fashionable novels," said Lord Lambeth, "they are awful rot, you know."

His companion looked at him a moment with her dark blue eyes, and then she looked down in the chasm where the water was tumbling about. "Do you mean Mrs. Gore, for instance?" she said presently, raising her eyes.

"I am afraid I haven't read that, either," was the young man's rejoinder, laughing a little and blushing. "I am afraid you'll think I am not very intellectual."

"Reading Mrs. Gore is no proof of intellect. But I like reading everything about English life -- even poor books. I am so curious about it."

"Aren't ladies always curious?" asked the young man jestingly.

But Bessie Alden appeared to desire to answer his question seriously. "I don't think so -- I don't think we are enough so -- that we care about many things. So it's all the more of a compliment," she added, "that I should want to know so much about England."

The logic here seemed a little close;·but Lord Lambeth, made conscious of a compliment, found his natural modesty just at hand. "I am sure you know a great deal more than I do."

"I really think I know a great deal -- for a person who has never been there."

"Have you really never been there?" cried Lord Lambeth. "Fancy!"

"Never -- except in imagination," said the young girl.

"Fancy!" repeated her companion. "But I daresay you'll go soon, won't you?"

"It's the dream of my life!" declared Bessie Alden, smiling.

"But your sister seems to know a tremendous lot about London," Lord Lambeth went on.

The young girl was silent a moment. "My sister and I are two very different persons," she presently said. "She has been a great deal in Europe. She has been in England several times. She has known a great many English people."

"But you must have known some, too," said Lord Lambeth.

"I don't think that I have ever spoken to one before. You are the first Englishman that -- to my knowledge -- I have ever talked with."

Bessie Alden made this statement with a certain gravity -- almost, as it seemed to Lord Lambeth, an impressiveness. Attempts at impressiveness always made him feel awkward, and he now began to laugh and swing his stick. "Ah, you would have been sure to know!" he said. And then he added, after an instant, "I'm sorry I am not a better specimen."

The young girl looked away; but she smiled, laying aside her impressiveness. "You must remember that you are only a beginning," she said. Then she retraced her steps, leading the way back to the lawn, where they saw Mrs. Westgate come toward them with Percy Beaumont still at her side. "Perhaps I shall go to England next year," Miss Alden continued; "I want to, immensely. My sister is going to Europe, and she has asked me to go with her. If we go, I shall make her stay as long as possible in London."

"Ah, you must come in July," said Lord Lambeth. "That's the time when there is most going on."

"I don't think I can wait till July," the young girl rejoined. "By the first of May I shall be very impatient." They had gone further, and Mrs. Westgate and her companion were near them. "Kitty," said Miss Alden, "I have given out that we are going to London next May. So please to conduct yourself accordingly."

Percy Beaumont wore a somewhat animated -- even a slightly irritated -- air. He was by no means so handsome a man as his cousin, although in his cousin's absence he might have passed for a striking specimen of the tall, muscular, fair-bearded, clear-eyed Englishman. Just now Beaumont's clear eyes, which were small and of a pale gray color, had a rather troubled light, and, after glancing at Bessie Alden while she spoke, he rested them upon his kinsman. Mrs. Westgate meanwhile, with her superfluously pretty gaze, looked at everyone alike.

"You had better wait till the time comes," she said to her sister. "Perhaps next May you won't care so much about London. Mr Beaumont and I," she went on, smiling at her companion, "have had a tremendous discussion. We don't agree about anything. It's perfectly delightful."

"Oh, I say, Percy!" exclaimed Lord Lambeth.

"I disagree," said Beaumont, stroking down his back hair, "even to the point of not thinking it delightful."

"Oh, I say!" cried Lord Lambeth again.

"I don't see anything delightful in my disagreeing with Mrs. Westgate," said Percy Beaumont.

"Well, I do!" Mrs Westgate declared; and she turned to her sister. "You know you have to go to town. The phaeton is there. You had better take Lord Lambeth."

At this point Percy Beaumont certainly looked straight at his kinsman; he tried to catch his eye. But Lord Lambeth would not look at him; his own eyes were better occupied. "I shall be very happy," cried Bessie Alden. "I am only going to some shops. But I will drive you about and show you the place."

"An American woman who respects herself," said Mrs. Westgate, turning to Beaumont with her bright expository air, "must buy something every day of her life. If she can not do it herself, she must send out some member of her family for the purpose. So Bessie goes forth to fulfill my mission."

The young girl had walked away, with Lord Lambeth by her side, to whom she was talking still; and Percy Beaumont watched them as they passed toward the house. "She fulfills her own mission," he presently said; "that of being a very attractive young lady."

"I don't know that I should say very attractive," Mrs. Westgate rejoined. "She is not so much that as she is charming when you really know her. She is very shy."

"Oh, indeed!" said Percy Beaumont.

"Extremely shy," Mrs. Westgate repeated. "But she is a dear good girl; she is a charming species of girl. She is not in the least a flirt; that isn't at all her line; she doesn't know the alphabet of that sort of thing. She is very simple, very serious. She has lived a great deal in Boston, with another sister of mine -- the eldest of us -- who married a Bostonian. She is very cultivated, not at all like me; I am not in the least cultivated. She has studied immensely and read everything; she is what they call in Boston 'thoughtful.'"

"A rum sort of girl for Lambeth to get hold of!" his lordship's kinsman privately reflected.

"I really believe," Mrs. Westgate continued, "that the most charming girl in the world is a Boston superstructure upon a New York *fonds*; or perhaps a New York superstructure upon a Boston *fonds*. At any rate, it's the mixture," said Mrs. Westgate, who continued to give Percy Beaumont a great deal of information.

Lord Lambeth got into a little basket phaeton with Bessie Alden, and she drove him down the long avenue, whose extent he had measured on foot a couple of hours before, into the ancient town, as it was called in that part of the world, of Newport. The ancient town was a curious affair -- a collection of fresh-looking little wooden houses, painted white, scattered over a hillside and clustered about a long straight street paved with enormous cobblestones. There were plenty of shops -- a large proportion of which appeared to be those of fruit vendors, with piles of huge watermelons and pumpkins stacked in front of them; and, drawn up before the shops, or bumping about on the cobblestones, were innumerable other basket phaetons freighted with ladies of high fashion, who greeted each other from vehicle to vehicle and conversed on the edge of the pavement

in a manner that struck Lord Lambeth as demonstrative, with a great many
"Oh, my dears," and little quick exclamations and caresses. His companion went into seventeen shops -- he amused himself with counting them
-- and accumulated at the bottom of the phaeton a pile of bundles that
hardly left the young Englishman a place for his feet. As she had no groom
nor footman, he sat in the phaeton to hold the ponies, where, although he
was not a particularly acute observer, he saw much to entertain him --
especially the ladies just mentioned, who wandered up and down with the
appearance of a kind of aimless intentness, as if they were looking for
something to buy, and who, tripping in and out of their vehicles, displayed
remarkably pretty feet. It all seemed to Lord Lambeth very odd, and
bright, and gay. Of course, before they got back to the villa, he had had a
great deal of desultory conversation with Bessie Alden.

The young Englishmen spent the whole of that day and the whole of
many successive days in what the French call the *intimité* of their new
friends. They agreed that it was extremely jolly, that they had never known
anything more agreeable. It is not proposed to narrate minutely the
incidents of their sojourn on this charming shore; though if it were
convenient I might present a record of impressions nonetheless delectable
that they were not exhaustively analyzed. Many of them still linger in the
minds of our travelers, attended by a train of harmonious images -- images
of brilliant mornings on lawns and piazzas that overlooked the sea; of
innumerable pretty girls; of infinite lounging and talking and laughing
and flirting and lunching and dining; of universal friendliness and frankness; of occasions on which they knew everyone and everything and had
an extraordinary sense of ease; of drives and rides in the late afternoon
over gleaming beaches, on long sea roads, beneath a sky lighted up by
marvelous sunsets; of suppers, on the return, informal, irregular, agreeable; of evenings at open windows or on the perpetual verandas, in the
summer starlight, above the warm Atlantic. The young Englishmen were
introduced to everybody, entertained by everybody, intimate with everybody. At the end of three days they had removed their luggage from the
hotel and had gone to stay with Mrs. Westgate -- a step to which Percy
Beaumont at first offered some conscientious opposition. I call his opposition conscientious, because it was founded upon some talk that he had
had, on the second day, with Bessie Alden. He had indeed had a good deal
of talk with her, for she was not literally always in conversation with Lord
Lambeth. He had meditated upon Mrs. Westgate's account of her sister,
and discovered for himself that the young lady was clever, and appeared

to have read a great deal. She seemed very nice, though he could not make out that, as Mrs. Westgate had did, she was shy. If she was shy, she carried it off very well.

"Mr. Beaumont," she had said, "please tell me something about Lord Lambeth's family. How would you say it in England -- his position?"

"His position" Percy Beaumont repeated.

"His rank, or whatever you call it. Unfortunately we haven't got a *Peerage*, like the people in Thackeray."

"That's a great pity," said Beaumont. "You would find it all set forth there so much better than I can do it."

"He is a peer, then?"

"Oh, yes, he is a peer."

"And has he any other title than Lord Lambeth?"

"His title is the Marquis of Lambeth," said Beaumont; and then he was silent. Bessie Alden appeared to be looking at him with interest. "He is the son of the Duke of Bayswater," he added presently.

"The eldest son?"

"The only son."

"And are his parents living?"

"Oh yes; if his father were not living he would be a duke."

"So that when his father dies," pursued Bessie Alden with more simplicity than might have been expected in a clever girl, "he will become Duke of Bayswater?"

"Of course," said Percy Beaumont. "But his father is in excellent health."

"And his mother?"

Beaumont smiled a little. "The duchess is uncommonly robust."

"And has he any sisters?"

"Yes, there are two."

"And what are they called?"

"One of them is married. She is the Countess of Pimlico."

"And the other?"

"The other is unmarried; she is plain Lady Julia."

Bessie Alden looked at him a moment. "Is she very plain?"

Beaumont began to laugh again. "You would not find her so handsome as her brother," he said; and it was after this that he attempted to dissuade the heir of the Duke of Bayswater from accepting Mrs. Westgate's invitation. "Depend upon it," he said, "that girl means to try for you."

"It seems to me you are doing your best to make a fool of me," the modest young nobleman answered.

"She has been asking me," said Beaumont, "all about your people and your possessions."

"I am sure it is very good of her!" Lord Lambeth rejoined.

"Well, then," observed his companion, "if you go, you go with your eyes open."

"Damn my eyes!" exclaimed Lord Lambeth. "If one is to be a dozen times a day at the house, it is a great deal more convenient to sleep there. I am sick of traveling up and down this beastly avenue."

Since he had determined to go, Percy Beaumont would, of course, have been very sorry to allow him to go alone; he was a man of conscience, and he remembered his promise to the duchess. It was obviously the memory of this promise that made him say to his companion a couple of days later that he rather wondered he should be so fond of that girl.

"In the first place , how do you know how fond I am of her?" asked Lord Lambeth. "And, in the second place, why shouldn't I be fond of her?"

"I shouldn't think she would be in your line."

"What do you call my 'line'? You don't set her down as 'fast'?"

"Exactly so. Mrs. Westgate tells me that there is no such thing as the 'fast girl' in America; that it's an English invention, and that the term has no meaning here."

"All the better. It's an animal I detest."

"You prefer a bluestocking."

"Is that what you call Miss Alden?"

"Her sister tells me," said Percy Beaumont, "that she is tremendously literary."

"I don't know anything about that. She is certainly very clever."

"Well," said Beaumont, "I should have supposed you would have found that sort of thing awfully slow."

"In point of fact," Lord Lambeth rejoined, "I find it uncommonly lively."

After this, Percy Beaumont held his tongue; but on the 10th of August he wrote to the Duchess of Bayswater. He was, as I have said, a man of conscience, and he had a strong, incorruptible sense of the proprieties of life. His kinsman, meanwhile, was having a great deal of talk with Bessie Alden -- on the red sea rocks beyond the lawn; in the course of long island rides, with a slow return in the glowing twilight; on the deep veranda late in the evening. Lord Lambeth, who had stayed at many houses, had never stayed at a house in which it was possible for a young man to converse so frequently with a young lady. This young lady no longer applied to Percy Beaumont for information concerning his lordship. She addressed herself directly to the young nobleman. She asked him a great many questions, some of which bored him a little; for he took no pleasure in talking about himself.

"Lord Lambeth," said Bessie Alden, "are you a hereditary legislator?"

"Oh, I say!" cried Lord Lambeth, "don't make me call myself such names as that."

"But you are a member of Parliament," said the young girl.

"I don't like the sound of that, either."

"Don't you sit in the House of Lords?" Bessie Alden went on.

"Very seldom," said Lord Lambeth.

"Is it an important position?" she asked.

"Oh, dear, no," said Lord Lambeth.

"I should think it would be very grand," said Bessie Alden, "to possess, simply by an accident of birth, the right to make laws for a great nation."

"Ah, but one doesn't make laws. It's a great humbug."

"I don't believe that," the young girl declared. "It must be a great privilege, and I should think that if one thought of it in the right way -- from a high point of view -- it would be very inspiring."

"The less one thinks of it, the better," Lord Lambeth affirmed.

"I think it's tremendous," said Bessie Alden; and on another occasion she asked him if he had any tenantry. Hereupon it was that, as I have said, he was a little bored.

"Do you want to buy up their leases?" he asked.

"Well, have you got any livings?" she demanded.

"Oh, I say!" he cried. "Have you got a clergy man that is looking out?" But she made him tell her that he had a castle; he confessed to but one. It was the place in which he had been born and brought up, and, as he had an old-time liking for it, he was beguiled into describing it a little and saying it was really very jolly. Bessie Alden listened with great interest and declared that she would give the world to see such a place. Whereupon -- "It would be awfully kind of you to come and stay there," said Lord Lambeth. He took a vague satisfaction in the circumstance that Percy Beaumont had not heard him make the remark I have just recorded.

Mr. Westgate all this time had not, as they said at Newport, "come on." His wife more than once announced that she expected him on the morrow; but on the morrow   she wandered about a little, with a telegram in her jeweled fingers, declaring it was very tiresome that his business detained him in New York; that he could only hope the Englishmen were having a good time. "I must say," said Mrs. Westgate, "that it is no thanks to him if you are." And she went on to explain, while she continued that slow-paced promenade which enabled her well-adjusted skirts to display themselves so advantageously, that unfortunately in America there was no leisure class. It was Lord Lambeth's theory, freely propounded when the young men were together, that Percy Beaumont was having a very good time with Mrs. Westgate, and that, under the pretext of meeting for the purpose of animated discussion, they were indulging in practices that imparted a shade of hypocrisy to the lady's regret for her husband's absence.

"I assure you we are always discussing and differing," said Percy Beaumont. "She is awfully argumentative. American ladies certainly don't mind contradicting you. Upon my word I don't think I was ever treated so by a woman before. She's so devilish positive."

Mrs. Westgate's positive quality, however, evidently had its attractions, for Beaumont was constantly at his hostess's side. He detached himself one day to the extent of going to New York to talk over the Tennessee Central with Mr. Westgate; but he was absent only forty-eight hours, during which, with Mr. Westgate's assistance, he completely settled this piece of business. "They certainly do things quickly in New York," he observed to his cousin; and he added that Mr. Westgate had seemed very uneasy lest his wife should miss her visitor -- he had been in such an awful hurry to send him back to her. "I'm afraid you'll never come up to an American husband, if that's what the wives expect," he said to Lord Lambeth.

Mrs. Westgate, however, was not to enjoy much longer the entertainment with which an indulgent husband had desired to keep her provided. On the 21st of August Lord Lambeth received a telegram from his mother, requesting him to return immediately to England; his father had been taken ill, and it was his filial duty to come to him.

The young Englishman was visibly annoyed. "What the deuce does it mean?" he asked of his kinsman. "What am I to do?"

Percy Beaumont was annoyed as well; he had deemed it his duty, as I have narrated, to write to the duchess, but he had not expected that this distinguished woman would act so promptly upon his hint. "It means," he said, "that your father is laid up. I don't suppose it's anything serious; but you have no option. Take the first steamer; but don't be alarmed."

Lord Lambeth made his farewells; but the few last words that he exchanged with Bessie Alden are the only ones that have a place in our record. "Of course I needn't assure you," he said, "that if you should come to England next year, I expect to be the first person that you inform of it."

Bessie Alden looked at him a little, and she smiled. "Oh, if we come to London," she answered, "I should think you would hear of it."

Percy Beaumont returned with his cousin, and his sense of duty compelled him, one windless afternoon, in mid-Atlantic, to say to Lord Lambeth that he suspected that the duchess's telegram was in part the result of something he himself had written to her. "I wrote to her -- as I explicitly notified you I had promised to do -- that you were extremely interested in a little American girl."

Lord Lambeth was extremely angry, and he indulged for some moments in the simple language of indignation. But I have said that he was a reasonable young man, and I can give no better proof of it than the fact that he remarked to his companion at the end of half an hour, "You were quite right, after all. I am very much interested in her. Only, to be far," he added, "you should have told my mother also that she is not -- seriously -- interested in me."

Percy Beaumont gave a little laugh. "There is nothing so charming as modesty in a young man in your position. That speech is a capital proof that you are sweet on her."

"She is not interested -- she is not!" Lord Lambeth repeated.

"My dear fellow," said his companion, "you are very far gone."

## PART II

In point of fact, as Percy Beaumont would have said, Mrs. Westgate disembarked on the 18th of May on the British coast. She was accompanied by her sister, but she was not attended by any other member of her family. To the deprivation of her husband's society Mrs. Westgate was, however, habituated; she had made half a dozen journeys to Europe without him, and she now accounted for his absence, to interrogative friends on this side of the Atlantic, by allusion to the regrettable but conspicuous fact that in America there was no leisure class. The two ladies came up to London and alighted at Jones's Hotel, where Mrs. Westgate, who had made on former occasions the most agreeable impression at this establishment, received an obsequious greeting. Bessie Alden had felt much excited about coming to England; she had expected the "associations" would be very charming, that it would be an infinite pleasure to rest her eyes upon the things she had read about in the poets and historians. She was very fond of the poets and historians, of the picturesque, of the past, of retrospect, of mementos and reverberations of greatness; so that on coming into the great English world, where strangeness and familiarity would go hand in hand, she was prepared for a multitude of fresh emotions. They began very promptly -- these tender, fluttering sensations; they began with the sight of the beautiful English landscape, whose dark richness was quickened and brightened by the season; with the carpeted fields and flowering hedgerows, as she looked at them from the window of the train; with the spires of the rural churches peeping above the rook-haunted treetops; with the oak-studded parks, the ancient homes, the cloudy light, the speech, the manners, the thousand differences. Mrs. Westgate's impressions had, of course, much less novelty and keenness, and she gave but a wandering attention to her sister's ejaculations and rhapsodies.

"You know my enjoyment of England is not so intellectual as Bessie's," she said to several of her friends in the course of her visit to this country. "And yet if it is not intellectual, I can't say it is physical. I don't think I can quite say what it is, my enjoyment of England." When once it was settled that the two ladies should come abroad and should spend a few weeks in England on their way to the Continent, they of course exchanged a good many allusions to their London acquaintance.

"It will certainly be much nicer having friends there," Bessie Alden had said one day as she sat on the sunny deck of the steamer at her sister's feet on a large blue rug.

"Whom do you mean by friends?" Mrs. Westgate asked.

"All those English gentlemen whom you have known and entertained. Captain Littledale, for instance. And Lord Lambeth and Mr. Beaumont," added Bessie Alden.

"Do you expect them to give us a very grand reception?"

Bessie reflected a moment; she was addicted, as we know, to reflection. "Well, yes."

"My poor, sweet child," murmured her sister.

"What have I said that is so silly?" asked Bessie.

"You are a little too simple; just a little. It is very becoming, but it pleases people at your expense."

I am certainly too simple to understand you," said Bessie.

"Shall I tell you a story?" asked her sister.

"If you would be so good. That is what they do to amuse simple people."

Mrs. Westgate consulted her memory, while her companion sat gazing at the shining sea. "Did you ever hear of the Duke of Green-Erin?"

"I think not," said Bessie.

"Well, it's no matter," her sister went on.

"It's a proof of my simplicity."

"My story is meant to illustrate that of some other people," said Mrs. Westgate. "The Duke of Green-Erin is what they call in England a great swell, and some five years ago he came to America. He spent most of his time in New York, and in New York he spent his days and his nights at the Butterworths'. You have heard, at least, of the Butterworths. *Bien.* They did everything in the world for him -- they turned themselves inside out. They gave him a dozen dinner parties and balls and were the means of his being invited to fifty more. At-first he used to come into Mrs. Butterworth's box at the opera in a tweed traveling suit; but someone stopped that. At any rate, he had a beautiful time, and they parted the best friends in the world. Two years elapse, and the Butterworths come abroad and go to London. The first thing they see in all the papers -- in England those things are in the most prominent place -- is that the Duke of Green-Erin has arrived in town for the Season. They wait a little, and then Mr. Butterworth -- as polite as ever -- goes and leaves a card. They wait a little more; the visit is not returned; they wait three weeks -- *silence de mort* -- the Duke gives no sign. The Butterworths see a lot of other people, put down the Duke of Green-Erin as a rude, ungrateful man, and forget all about him. One fine day they go to Ascot Races, and there they meet him face to face. He stares a moment and then comes up to Mr. Butterworth, taking something from his pocketbook -- something which proves to be a banknote. 'I'm glad to see you, Mr. Butterworth,' he says, 'so that I can pay you that ten pounds I lost to you in New York. I saw the other day you remembered our bet; here are the ten pounds, Mr. Butterworth. Goodbye, Mr. Butterworth.' And off he goes, and that's the last they see of the Duke of Green-Erin."

"Is that your story?" asked Bessie Alden.

"Don't you think it's interesting?" her sister replied.

"I don't believe it," said the young girl.

"Ah," cried Mrs. Westgate, "you are not so simple after all! Believe it or not, as you please; there is no smoke without fire."

"Is that the way," asked Bessie after a-moment, "that you expect your friends to treat you?"

"I defy them to treat me very ill, because I shall not give them the opportunity. With the best will in the world, in that case they can't be very offensive."

Bessie Alden was silent a moment. "I don't see what makes you talk that way," she said. "The English are a great people."

"Exactly; and that is just the way they have grown great -- by dropping you when you have ceased to be useful. People say they are not clever; but I think they are very clever."

"You know you have liked them -- all the Englishmen you have seen," said Bessie.

"They have liked me," her sister rejoined; "it would be more correct to say that. And, of course, one likes that."

Bessie Alden resumed for some moments her studies in sea green. "Well," she said, "whether they like me or not, I mean to like them. And happily," she added, "Lord Lambeth does not owe me ten pounds."

During the first few days after their arrival at Jones's Hotel our charming Americans were much occupied with what they would have called looking about them. They found occasion to make a large number of purchases, and their opportunities for conversation were such only as were offered by the deferential London shopmen. Bessie Alden, even in driving from the station, took an immense fancy to the British metropolis, and at the risk of exhibiting her as a young woman of vulgar tastes it must be recorded that for a considerable period she desired no higher pleasure than to drive about the crowded streets in a hansom cab. To her attentive eyes they were full of a strange picturesque life, and it is at least beneath the dignity of our historic muse to enumerate the trivial objects and incidents which this simple young lady from Boston found so entertaining. It may be freely mentioned, however, that whenever, after a round of visits in Bond Street and Regent Street, she was about to return with her sister to Jones's Hotel, she made an earnest request that they should be driven home by way of Westminster Abbey. She had begun by asking whether it would not be possible to take the Tower on the way to their lodgings; but it happened that at a more primitive stage of her culture Mrs. Westgate had paid a visit to this venerable monument, which she spoke of ever afterward vaguely as a dreadful disappointment; so that she expressed the liveliest disapproval of any attempt to combine historical researches with the purchase of hairbrushes and notepaper. The most she would consent to do in this line was to spend half an hour at Madame Tussaud's, where she saw several dusty wax effigies of members of the royal family. She told Bessie that if she wished to go to the Tower she must get someone else to take her. Bessie expressed hereupon an earnest disposition to go alone but upon this proposal as well Mrs. Westgate sprinkled cold water.

"Remember," she said, "that you are not in your innocent little Boston. It is not a question of walking up and down Beacon Street." Then she went on to explain that there were two classes of American girls in Europe -- those that walked about alone and those that did not. "You happen to belong, my dear," she said to her sister, "to the class that does not."

"It is only," answered Bessie, laughing, "because you happen to prevent me." And she devoted much private meditation to this question of effecting a visit to the Tower of London.

Suddenly it seemed as if the problem might be solved; the two ladies at Jones's Hotel received a visit from Willie Woodley. Such was the social appellation of a young American who had sailed from New York a few days after their own departure, and who, having the privilege of intimacy with them in that city, had lost no time, on his arrival in London, in coming to pay them his respects. He had, in fact, gone to see them directly after going to see his tailor, than which there can be no greater exhibition of promptitude on the part of a young American who has just alighted at the Charing Cross Hotel. He was a slim, pale youth, of the most amiable disposition, famous for the skill with which he led the "German" in New York. Indeed, by the young ladies who habitually figured in this Terpsichorean revel he was believed to be "the best dancer in the world"; it was in these terms that he was always spoken of, and that his identity was indicated. He was the gentlest, softest young man it was possible to meet; he was beautifully dressed -- "in the English style" -- and he knew an immense deal about London. He had been at Newport during the previous summer, at the time our young Englishmen's visit, and he took extreme pleasure in the society of Bessie Alden, whom he always addressed as "Miss Bessie." She immediately arranged with him, in the presence of her sister, that he should conduct her to the scene of Anne Boleyn's execution.

"You may do as you please," said Mrs. Westgate. "Only -- if you desire the information -- it is not the custom here for young ladies to knock about London with young men."

"Miss Bessie has waltzed with me so often," observed Willie Woodley; "she can surely go out with me in a hansom."

"I consider waltzing," said Mrs. Westgate, "the most innocent pleasure of our time."

"It's a compliment to our time!" exclaimed the young man with a little laugh, in spite of himself.

"I don't see why I should regard what is done here," said Bessie Alden. "Why should I suffer the restrictions of a society of which I enjoy none of the privileges?"

"That's very good -- very good," murmured Willie Woodley.

"Oh, go to the Tower, and feel the ax, if you like," said Mrs. Westgate. "I consent to your going with Mr. Woodley; but I should not let you go with an Englishman."

"Miss Bessie wouldn't care to go with an Englishman!" Mr. Woodley declared with a faint asperity that was, perhaps, not unnatural in a young man, who, dressing in the manner that I have indicated and knowing a great deal, as I have said, about London, saw no reason for drawing these sharp distinctions. He agreed upon a day with Miss Bessie -- a day of that same week.

An ingenious mind might, perhaps, trace a connection between the young girl's allusion to her destitution of social privileges and a question she asked on the morrow as she sat with her sister at lunch.

"Don't you mean to write to -- to anyone?" said Bessie.

"I wrote this morning to Captain Littledale," Mrs. Westgate replied.

"But Mr. Woodley said that Captain Littledale had gone to India."

"He said he thought he had heard so; he knew nothing about it."

For a moment Bessie Alden said nothing more; then, at last, "And don't you intend to write to -- to Mr. Beaumont?" she inquired

"You mean to Lord Lambeth," said her sister.

"I said Mr. Beaumont because he was so good a friend of yours."

Mrs. Westgate looked at the young girl with sisterly candor. "I don't care two straws for Mr. Beaumont."

"You were certainly very nice to him."

"I am nice to everyone," said Mrs. Westgate simply.

"To everyone but me," rejoined Bessie, smiling.

Her sister continued to look at her; then, at last, "Are you in love with Lord Lambeth?" she asked.

The young girl stared a moment, and the question was apparently too humorous even to make her blush. "Not that I know of," she answered.

"Because if you are," Mrs. Westgate went on, "I shall certainly not send for him."

"That proves what I said," declared Bessie, smiling -- "that you are not nice to me."

"It would be a poor service, my dear child," said her sister.

"In what sense? There is nothing against Lord Lambeth that I know of."

Mrs. Westgate was silent a moment. "You *are* in love with him then?"

Bessie stared again; but this time she blushed a little. "Ah! if you won't be serious," she answered, "we will not mention him again."

For some moments Lord Lambeth was not mentioned again, and it was Mrs. Westgate who, at the end of this period, reverted to him. "Of course I will let him know we are here, because I think he would be hurt -- justly enough -- if we should go away without seeing him. It is fair to give him a chance to come and thank me for the kindness we showed him. But I don't want to seem eager."

"Neither do I," said Bessie with a little laugh.

"Though I confess," added her sister, "that I am curious to see how he will behave."

"He behaved very well at Newport."

"Newport is not London. At Newport he could do as he liked; but here it is another affair. He has to have an eye to consequences."

"If he had more freedom, then, at Newport," argued Bessie, "it is the more to his credit that he behaved well; and if he has to be so careful here, it is possible he will behave even better."

"Better -- better," repeated her sister. "My dear child, what is your point of view?"

"How do you mean -- my point of view?"

"Don't you care for Lord Lambeth -- a little?"

This time Bessie Alden was displeased; she slowly got up from the table, turning her face away from her sister. "You will oblige me by not talking so," she said.

Mrs. Westgate sat watching her for some moments as she moved slowly about the room and went and stood at the window. "I will write to him this afternoon," she said at last.

"Do as you please!" Bessie answered; and presently she turned round. "I am not afraid to say that I like Lord Lambeth. I like him very much."

"He is not clever," Mrs. Westgate declared.

"Well, there have been clever people whom I have disliked," said Bessie Alden; "so that I suppose I may like a stupid one. Besides, Lord Lambeth is not stupid."

"Not so stupid as he looks!" exclaimed her sister, smiling.

"If I were in love with Lord Lambeth, as you said just now, it would be bad policy on your part to abuse him."

"My dear child, don't give me lessons in policy!" cried Mrs. Westgate. "The policy I mean to follow is very deep."

The young girl began to walk about the room again; then she stopped before her sister. "I have never heard in the course of five minutes," she said, "so many hints and innuendoes. I wish you would tell me in plain English what you mean."

"I mean that you may be much annoyed."

"That is still only a hint," said Bessie.

Her sister looked at her, hesitating an instant. "It will be said of you that you have come after Lord Lambeth -- that you followed him."

Bessie Alden threw back her pretty head like a startled hind, and a look flashed into her face that made Mrs. Westgate rise from her chair. "Who says such things as that?" she demanded.

"People here."

"I don't believe it," said Bessie.

"You have a very convenient faculty of doubt. But my policy will be, as I say, very deep. I shall leave you to find out this kind of thing for yourself."

Bessie fixed her eyes upon her sister, and Mrs. Westgate thought for a moment there were tears in them. "Do they talk that way here?" she asked.

"You will see. I shall leave you alone."

"Don't leave me alone," said Bessie Alden. "Take me away."

"No; I want to see what you make of it," her sister continued.

"I don't understand."

"You will understand after Lord Lambeth has come," said Mrs. Westgate with a little laugh.

The two ladies had arranged that on this afternoon Willie Woodley should go with them to Hyde Park, where Bessie Alden expected to derive much entertainment from sitting on a little green chair, under the great trees, beside Rotten Row. The want of a suitable escort had hitherto rendered this pleasure inaccessible; but no escort now, for such an expedition, could have been more suitable than their devoted young countryman, whose mission in life, it might almost be said, was to find chairs for ladies, and who appeared on the stroke of half-past five with a white camellia in his buttonhole.

"I have written to Lord Lambeth, my dear," said Mr. Westgate to her sister, on coming into the room where Bessie Alden, drawing on her long gray gloves, was entertaining their visitor.

Bessie said nothing, but Willie Woodley exclaimed that his lordship was in town; he had seen his name in the *Morning Post*.

"Do you read the *Morning Post?*" asked Mrs. Westgate.

"Oh, yes; it's great fun," Willie Woodley affirmed.

"I want so to see it," said Bessie, "there is so much about it in Thackeray."

"I will send it to you every morning," said Willie Woodley.

He found them what Bessie Alden thought excellent places, under the great trees, beside the famous avenue whose humors had been made familiar to the young girl's childhood by the pictures in *Punch.* The day was bright and warm, and the crowd of riders and spectators, and the great procession of carriages, were proportionately dense and brilliant. The scene bore the stamp of the London Season at its height, and Bessie Alden found more entertainment in it than she was able to express to her companions. She sat silent, under her parasol, and her imagination, according to its wont, let itself loose into the great changing assemblage of striking and suggestive figures. They stirred up a host of old impressions and preconceptions, and she found herself fitting a history to this person and a theory to that, and making a place for them all in her little private museum of types. But if she said little, her sister on one side and Willie Woodley on the other expressed themselves in lively alternation.

"Look at that green dress with blue flounces," said Mrs. Westgate. "*Quelle toilette!*"

"That's the Marquis of Blackborough," said the young man -- "the one in the white coat. I heard him speak the other night in the House of Lords; it was something about ramrods; he called them 'wamwods.' He's an awful swell."

"Did you ever see anything like the way they are pinned back?" Mrs. Westgate resumed. "They never know where to stop."

"They do nothing but stop," said Willie Woodley. "It prevents them from walking. Here comes a great celebrity -- Lady Beatrice Bellevue. She's awfully fast; see what little steps she takes."

"Well, my dear," Mrs. Westgate pursued, "I hope you are getting some ideas for your *couturière?*"

"I am getting plenty of ideas," said Bessie, "but I don't know that my *couturière* would appreciate them."

Willie Woodley presently perceived a friend on horseback, who drove up beside the barrier of the Row and beckoned to him. He went forward, and the crowd of pedestrians closed about him, so that for some ten minutes he was hidden from sight. At last he reappeared, bringing a gentle man with him -- a gentleman whom Bessie at first supposed to be his friend dismounted. But at a second glance she found herself looking at Lord Lambeth, who was shaking hands with her sister.

"I found him over there," said Willie Woodley, "and I told him you were here!"

And then Lord Lambeth, touching his hat a little, shook hands with Bessie. "Fancy your being here!" he said. He was blushing and smiling; he looked very handsome, and he had a kind of splendor that he had not had in America. Bessie Alden's imagination, as we know, was just then in exercise; so that the tall young Englishman, as he stood there looking down at her, had the benefit of it. "He is handsomer and more splendid than anything I have ever seen," she said to herself. And then she remembered that he was a marquis, and she thought he looked like a marquis.

"I say, you know," he cried, "you ought to have let a man know you were here!"

"I wrote to you an hour ago," said Mrs. Westgate.

"Doesn't all the world know it?" asked Bessie, smiling.

"I assure you didn't know it!" cried Lord Lambeth "Upon my honor I hadn't heard of it. Ask Woodley now; -- had I, Woodley?"

"Well, I think you are rather a humbug," said Willie Woodley.

"You don't believe that -- do you, Miss Alden?" asked his lordship. "You don't believe I'm a humbug, eh?"

"No," said Bessie, "I don't."

"You are too tall to stand up, Lord Lambeth," Mrs. Westgate observed. "You are only tolerable when you sit down. Be so good as to get a chair."

He found a chair and placed it sidewise, close to the two ladies. "If I hadn't met Woodley I should never have found you," he went on. "Should I, Woodley?"

"Well I guess not," said the young American.

"Not even with my letter?" asked Mrs. Westgate.

"Ah, well, I haven't got your letter yet; I suppose I shall get it this evening. It was awfully kind of you to write."

"So I said to Bessie," observed Mrs. Westgate.

"Did she say so, Miss Alden?" Lord Lambeth inquired. "I daresay you have been here a month."

"We have been here three," said Mrs. Westgate.

"Have you been here three months?" the young man asked again of Bessie.

"It seems a long time," Bessie answered.

"I say, after that you had better not call me a humbug!" cried Lord Lambeth. "I have only been in town three weeks; but you must have been hiding away; I haven't seen you anywhere."

"Where should you have seen us -- where should we have gone?" asked Mrs. Westgate.

"You should have gone to Hurlingham," said Willie Woodley.

"No; let Lord Lambeth tell us," Mrs. Westgate insisted.

"There are plenty of places to go to," said Lord Lambeth; "each one stupider than the other. I mean people's houses; they send you cards."

"No one has sent us cards," said Bessie.

"We are very quiet," her sister declared. "We are here as travelers."

"We have been to Madame Tussaud's," Bessie pursued.

"Oh, I say!" cried Lord Lambeth.

"We thought we should find your image there," said Mrs. Westgate -- yours and Mr. Beaumont's."

"In the Chamber of Horrors?" laughed the young man.

"It did duty very well for a party," said Mrs. Westgate. "All the women were *décollétes*, and many of the figures looked as if they could speak if they tried."

"Upon my word," Lord Lambeth rejoined, "you see people at London parties that look as if they couldn't speak if they tried."

"Do you think Mr. Woodley could find us Mr. Beaumont?" asked Mrs. Westgate.

Lord Lambeth stared and looked round him. "I daresay he could. Don't you think you could find him, Woodley? Make a dive into the crowd."

"Thank you; I have had enough diving," said Willie Woodley. "I will wait till Mr. Beaumont comes to the surface."

"I will bring him to see you," said Lord Lambeth "where are you staying?"

"You will find the address in my letter -- Jones's Hotel."

"Oh, one of those places just out of Piccadilly? Beastly hole, isn't it?" Lord Lambeth inquired.

"I believe it's the best hotel in London," said Mrs. Westgate.

"But they give you awful rubbish to eat, don't they?" his lordship went on.

"Yes," said Mrs. Westgate.

"I always feel so sorry for the people that come up to town and go to live in those places," continued the young man. "They eat nothing but filth."

"Oh, I say!" cried Willie Woodley.

"Well, how do you like London, Miss Alden?" Lord Lambeth asked, unperturbed by this ejaculation.

"I think it's grand," said Bessie Alden.

"My sister likes it, in spite of the 'filth'!" Mrs. Westgate exclaimed.

"I hope you are going to stay a long time."

"As long as I can," said Bessie.

"And where is Mr. Westgate?" asked Lord Lambeth of this gentleman's wife.

"He's where he always is -- in that tiresome New York."

"He must be tremendously clever," said the young man.

"I suppose he is," said Mrs. Westgate.

Lord Lambeth sat for nearly an hour with his American friends; but it is not our purpose to relate their conversation in full. He addressed a great many remarks to Bessie Alden, and finally turned toward her altogether, while Willie Woodley entertained Mrs. Westgate. Bessie herself said very little; she was on her guard, thinking of what her sister had said to her at lunch. Little by little, however, she interested herself in Lord Lambeth again, as she had done at Newport; only it seemed to her that here he might become more interesting. He would be an unconscious part of the antiquity, the impressiveness, the picturesqueness, of England; and poor Bessie Alden, like many a Yankee maiden, was terribly at the mercy of picturesqueness.

"I have often wished I were at Newport again," said the young man. "Those days I spent at your sister's were awfully jolly."

"We enjoyed them very much; I hope your father is better."

"Oh, dear, yes. When I got to England, he was out grouse shooting. It was what you call in America a gigantic fraud. My mother had got nervous. My three weeks at Newport seemed like a happy dream."

"America certainly is very different from England," said Bessie.

"I hope you like England better, eh?" Lord Lambeth rejoined almost persuasively.

"No Englishman can ask that seriously of a person of another country."

Her companion looked at her for a moment. "You mean it's a matter of course?"

"If I were English," said Bessie, "it would certainly seem to me a matter of course that everyone should be a good patriot."

"Oh, dear, yes, patriotism is everything," said Lord Lambeth, not quite following, but very contented. "Now, what are you going to do here?"

"On Thursday I am going to the Tower."

"The Tower?"

"The Tower of London. Did you never hear of it?"

"Oh, yes, I have been there," said Lord Lambeth. "I was taken there by my governess when I was six years old. It's a rum idea, your going there."

"Do give me a few more rum ideas," said Bessie. "I want to see everything of that sort. I am going to Hampton Court, and to Windsor, and to the Dulwich Gallery."

Lord Lambeth seemed greatly amused. "I wonder you don't go to the Rosherville Gardens."

"Are they interesting?" asked Bessie.

"Oh, wonderful."

"Are they very old? That's all I care for," said Bessie.

"They are tremendously old; they are all falling to ruins."

"I think there is nothing so charming as an old ruinous garden," said the young girl. "We must certainly go there."

Lord Lambeth broke out into merriment. "I say, Woodley," he cried, "here's Miss Alden wants to go to the Rosherville Gardens!"

Willie Woodley looked a little blank; he was caught in the fact of ignorance of an apparently conspicuous feature of London life. But in a moment he turned it off. "Very well," he said, "I'll write for a permit."

Lord Lambeth's exhilaration increased. "Gad, I believe you Americans would go anywhere!" he cried.

"We wish to go to Parliament," said Bessie. "That's one of the first things."

"Oh, it would bore you to death!" cried the young man.

"We wish to hear you speak."

"I never speak -- except to young ladies," said Lord Lambeth, smiling.

Bessie Alden looked at him a while, smiling, too, in the shadow of her parasol. "You are very strange," she murmured. "I don't think I approve of you."

"Ah, now, don't be severe, Miss Alden," said Lord Lambeth, smiling still more. "Please don't be severe. I want you to like me -- awfully."

"To like you awfully? You must not laugh at me, then, when I make mistakes. I consider it my right -- as a freeborn American -- to make as many mistakes as I choose."

"Upon my word, I didn't laugh at you," said Lord Lambeth.

"And not only that," Bessie went on; "but I hold that all my mistakes shall be set down to my credit. You must think the better of me for them."

"I can't think better of you than I do," the young man declared.

Bessie Alden looked at him a moment again. "You certainly speak very well to young ladies. But why don't you address the House? -- isn't that what they call it?"

"Because I have nothing to say," said Lord Lambeth.

"Haven't you a great position?" asked Bessie Alden.

He looked a moment at the back of his glove. "I'll set that down," he said, "as one of your mistakes -- to your credit." And as if he disliked talking about his position, he changed the subject. "I wish you would let me go with you to the Tower, and to Hampton Court, and to all those other places."

"We shall be most happy," said Bessie.

"And of course I shall be delighted to show you the House of Lords -- some day that suits you. There are a lot of things I want to do for you. I want to make you have a good time. And I should like very much to present some of my friends to you, if it wouldn't bore you. Then it would be awfully kind of you to come down to Branches."

"We are much obliged to you, Lord Lambeth," said Bessie. "What is Branches?"

"It's a house in the country. I think you might like it."

Willie Woodley and Mrs. Westgate at this moment were sitting in silence, and the young man's ear caught these last words of Lord Lambeth's. "He's inviting Miss Bessie to one of his castles," he murmured to his companion.

Mrs. Westgate, foreseeing what she mentally called "complications," immediately got up; and the two ladies, taking leave of Lord Lambeth, returned, under Mr. Woodley's conduct, to Jones's Hotel.

Lord Lambeth came to see them on the morrow, bringing Percy Beaumont with him -- the latter having instantly declared his intention of neglecting none of the usual offices of civility. This declaration, however, when his kinsman informed him of the advent of their American friends, had been preceded by another remark.

"Here they are, then, and you are in for it."

"What am I in for?" demanded Lord Lambeth.

"I will let your mother give it a name. With all respect to whom," added Percy Beaumont, "I must decliné on this occasion to do any more police duty. Her Grace must look after you yourself."

"I will give her a chance," said her Grace's son, a trifle grimly. "I shall make her go and see them."

"She won't do it, my boy."

"We'll see if she doesn't," said Lord Lambeth.

But if Percy Beaumont took a somber view of the arrival of the two ladies at Jones's Hotel, he was sufficiently a man of the world to offer a smiling countenance. He fell in to animated conversation -- conversation, at least, that was animated on her side -- with Mrs. Westgate, while his companion made himself agreeable to the younger lady. Mrs. Westgate began confessing and protesting, declaring and expounding.

"I must say London is a great deal brighter and prettier just now than it was when I was here last -- in the month of November. There is evidently a great deal going on, and you seem to have a good many flowers. I have no doubt it is very charming for all you people, and that you amuse yourselves immensely. It is very good of you to let Bessie and me come and sit and look at you. I suppose you will think I am very satirical, but I must confess that that's the feeling I have in London."

"I am afraid I don't quite understand to what feeling you allude," said Percy Beaumont.

"The feeling that it's all very well for you English people. Everything is beautifully arranged for you."

"It seems to me it is very well for some Americans, sometimes," rejoined Beaumont.

"For some of them, yes -- if they like to be patronized. But I must say I don't like to be patronized. I may be very eccentric, and undisciplined, and outrageous, but I confess I never was fond of patronage. I like to associate with people on the same terms as I do in my own country; that's a peculiar taste that I have. But here people seem to expect something else -- Heaven knows what! I am afraid you will think I am very ungrateful, for I certainly have received a great deal of attention. The last time I was here, a lady sent me a message that I was at liberty to come and see her."

"Dear me! I hope you didn't go," observed Percy Beaumont.

"You are deliciously naive, I must say that for you!" Mrs. Westgate exclaimed. "It must be a great advantage to you here in London. I suppose that if I myself had a little more naïveté, I should enjoy it more. I should be content to sit on a chair in the park, and see the people pass, and be told that this is the Duchess of Suffolk, and that is the Lord Chamberlain, and that I must be thankful for the privilege of beholding them, I daresay it is very wicked and critical to me to ask for anything else. But I was always critical, and I freely confess to the sin of being fastidious. I am told there is some remarkably superior second-rate society provided here for strangers. *Merci*! I don't want any superior second-rate society. I want the society that I have been accustomed to."

"I hope you don't call Lambeth and me second rate," Beaumont interposed.

"Oh, I am accustomed to you," said Mrs. Westgate. "Do you know that you English sometimes make the most wonderful speeches? The first time I came to London I went out to dine -- as I told you, I have received a great deal of attention. After dinner, in the drawing room, I had some conversation with an old lady; I assure you I had. I forget what we talked about, but she presently said, in allusion to something we were discussing, 'Oh, you know, the aristocracy do so-and-so; but in one's own class of life it is very different.' In one's own class of life! What is a poor unprotected American woman to do in a country where she is liable to have that sort of thing said to her?"

"You seem to get hold of some very queer old ladies; I compliment you on your acquaintance!" Percy Beaumont exclaimed. "If you are trying to bring me to admit that London is an odious place, you'll not succeed. I'm extremely fond of it, and I think it the jolliest place in the world."

"*Pour vous autres.* I never said the contrary," Mrs. Westgate retorted. I make use of this expression, because both interlocutors had begun to raise their voices. Percy Beaumont naturally did not like to hear his country abused, and Mrs. Westgate, no less naturally, did not like a stubborn debater.

"Hallo!" said Lord Lambeth; "what are they up to now?" And he came away from the window, where he had been standing with Bessie Alden.

"I quite agree with a very clever countrywoman of mine," Mrs. Westgate continued with charming ardor, though with imperfect relevancy. She smiled at the two gentlemen for a moment with terrible brightness, as if to toss at their feet -- upon their native heath -- the gauntlet of defiance. "For me, there are only two social positions worth speaking of -- that of an American lady and that of the Emperor of Russia."

"And what do you do with the American gentlemen?" asked Lord Lambeth.

"She leaves them in America!" said Percy Beaumont.

On the departure of their visitors, Bessie Alden told her sister that Lord Lambeth would come the next day to go with them to the Tower, and that he had kindly offered to bring his "trap" and drive them thither. Mrs. Westgate listened in silence to this communication, and for some time afterward she said nothing. But at last, "If you had not requested me the other day not to mention it," she began, "there is something I should venture to ask you." Bessie frowned a little; her dark blue eyes were more dark than blue. But her sister went on. "As it is, I will take the risk. You are not in love with Lord Lambeth: I believe it, perfectly. Very good. But is there, by chance, any danger of your becoming so? It's a very simple question; don't take offense. I have a particular reason," said Mrs. Westgate, "for wanting to know."

Bessie Alden for some moments said nothing; she only looked displeased. "No; there is no danger," she answered at last, curtly.

"Then I should like to frighten them," declared Mrs. Westgate, clasping her jeweled hands.

"To frighten whom?"

"All these people; Lord Lambeth's family and friends."

"How should you frighten them?" asked the young girl.

"It wouldn't be I -- it would be you. It would frighten them to think that you should absorb his lordship's young affections."

Bessie Alden, with her clear eyes still overshadowed by her dark brows, continued to interrogate. "Why should that frighten them?"

Mrs. Westgate poised her answer with a smile before delivering it. "Because they think you are not good enough. You are a charming girl, beautiful and amiable, intelligent and clever, and as *bien-élevée* as it is possible to be; but you are not a fit match for Lord Lambeth."

Bessie Alden was decidedly disgusted. "Where do you get such extraordinary ideas?" she asked. "You have said some such strange things lately. My dear Kitty, where do you collect them?"

Kitty was evidently enamored of her idea. "Yes, it would put them on pins and needles, and it wouldn't hurt you. Mr. Beaumont is already most uneasy; I could soon see that."

The young girl meditated a moment. "Do you mean that they spy upon him -- that they interfere with him?"

"I don't know what power they have to interfere, but know that a British mama may worry her son's life out."

It has been intimated that, as regards certain disagreeable things, Bessie Alden had a fund of skepticism. She abstained on the present occasion from expressing disbelief, for she wished not to irritate her sister. But she said to herself that Kitty had been misinformed -- that this was a traveler's tale. Though she was a girl of a lively imagination, there could in the nature of things be, to her sense, no reality in the idea of her belonging to a vulgar category. What she said aloud was, "I must say that in that case I am very sorry for Lord Lambeth."

Mrs. Westgate, more and more exhilarated by her scheme, was smiling at her again. "If I could only believe it was safe!" she exclaimed. "When you begin to pity him, I, on my side, am afraid."

"Afraid of what?"

"Of your pitying him too much."

Bessie Alden turned away impatiently; but at the end of a minute she turned back. "What if I should pity him too much?" she asked.

Mrs. Westgate hereupon turned away, but after a moment's reflection she also faced her sister again. "It would come, after all, to the same thing," she said.

Lord Lambeth came the next day with his trap, and the two ladies, attended by Willie Woodley, placed themselves under his guidance, and were conveyed eastward, through some of the duskier portions of the metropolis, to the great turreted donjon which overlooks the London shipping. They all descended from their vehicle and entered the famous inclosure; and they secured the services of a venerable beefeater, who, though there were many other claimants for legendary information made a fine exclusive party of them and marched them through courts and corridors, through armories and prisons. He delivered his usual peripatetic discourse, and they stopped and stared, and peeped and stooped, according to the official admonitions. Bessie Alden asked the old man in the crimson doublet a great many questions; she thought it a most fascinating place. Lord Lambeth was in high good humor; he was constantly laughing; he enjoyed what he would have called the lark. Willie Woodley kept looking at the ceilings and tapping the walls with the knuckle of a pearl-gray glove; and Mrs. Westgate, asking at frequent intervals to be allowed to sit down and wait till they came back, was as frequently informed that they would never come back. To a great many of Bessie's questions -- chiefly on collateral points of English history -- the ancient warder was naturally unable to reply; whereupon she always appealed to Lord Lambeth. But his lordship was very ignorant. He declared that he knew nothing about that sort of thing, and he seemed greatly diverted at being treated as an authority.

"You can't expect everyone to know as much as you," he said.

"I should expect you to know a great deal more," declared Bessie Alden.

"Women always know more than men about names and dates and that sort of thing," Lord Lambeth rejoined. There was Lady Jane Grey we have just been hearing about, who went in for Latin and Greek and all the learning of her age."

"*You* have no right to be ignorant, at all events," said Bessie.

"Why haven't I as good a right as anyone else?"

"Because you have lived in the midst of all these things."

"What things do you mean? Axes, and blocks, and thumbscrews?"

"All these historical things. You belong to a historical family."

"Bessie is really too historical," said Mrs. Westgate catching a word of this dialogue.

"Yes, you are too historical," said Lord Lambeth, laughing, but thankful for a formula. "Upon my honor, you are too historical!"

He went with the ladies a couple of days later to Hampton Court, Willie Woodley being also of the party. The afternoon was charming, the famous horse chestnuts were in blossom, and Lord Lambeth, who quite entered into the spirit of the cockney excursionist, declared that it was a jolly old place. Bessie Alden was in ecstasies; she went about murmuring and exclaiming.

"It's too lovely," said the young girl; "it's too enchanting; it's too exactly what it ought to be!"

At Hampton Court the little flocks of visitors are not provided with an official bellwether, but are left to browse at discretion upon the local antiquities. It happened in this manner that, in default of another informant, Bessie Alden, who on doubtful questions was able to suggest a great many alternatives, found herself again applying for intellectual assistance to Lord Lambeth. But he again assured her that he was utterly helpless in such matters -- that his education had been sadly neglected.

"And I am sorry it makes you unhappy," he added in a moment.

"You are very disappointing, Lord Lambeth," she said.

"Ah, now don't say that," he cried. "That's the worst thing you could possibly say."

"No," she rejoined, "it is not so bad as to say that I had expected nothing of you."

"I don't know. Give me a notion of the sort of thing you expected."

"Well," said Bessie Alden, "that you would be more what I should like to be -- what I should try to be -- in your place."

"Ah, my place!" exclaimed Lord Lambeth. "You are always talking about my place!"

The young girl looked at him; he thought she colored a little; and for a moment she made no rejoinder.

"Does it strike you that I am always talking about your place?" she asked.

"I am sure you do it a great honor," he said, fearing he had been uncivil.

"I have often thought about it," she went on after a moment. "I have often thought about your being a hereditary legislator. A hereditary legislator ought to know a great many things."

"Not if he doesn't legislate."

"But you do legislate; it's absurd your saying you don't. You are very much looked up to here -- I am assured of that."

"I don't know that I ever noticed it."

"It is because you are used to it, then. You ought to fill the place."

"How do you mean to fill it?" asked Lord Lambeth.

"You ought to be very clever and brilliant, and to know almost everything."

Lord Lambeth looked at her a moment. "Shall I tell you something?" he asked. "A young man in my position, as you call it-----"

"I didn't invent the term," interposed Bessie Alden. "I have seen it in a great many books."

"Hang it! you are always at your books. A fellow in my position, then, does very well whatever he does. That's about what I mean to say."

"Well, if your own people are content with you," said Bessie Alden, laughing, "it is not for me to complain. But I shall always think that, properly, you should have been a great mind -- a great character."

"Ah, that's very theoretic," Lord Lambeth declared.

"Depend upon it, that's a Yankee prejudice."

"Happy the country," said Bessie Alden, "where even people's prejudices are so elevated!"

"Well, after all," observed Lord Lambeth, "I don't know that I am such a fool as you are trying to make me out."

"I said nothing so rude as that; but I must repeat that you are disappointing."

"My dear Miss Alden," exclaimed the young man, "I am the best fellow in the world!"

"Ah, if it were not for that!" said Bessie Alden with a smile.

Mrs. Westgate had a good many more friends in London than she pretended, and before long she had renewed acquaintance with most of them. Their hospitality was extreme, so that, one thing leading to another, she began, as the phrase is, to 'go out. Bessie Alden, in this way, saw something of what she found it a great satisfaction to call to herself English society. She went to balls and danced, she went to dinners and talked, she went to concerts and listened (at concerts Bessie always listened), she went to exhibitions and wondered. Her enjoyment was keen and her curiosity insatiable, and, grateful in general for all her opportunities, she especially prized the privilege of meeting certain celebrated persons -- authors and artists, philosophers and statesmen -- of whose renown she had been a humble and distant beholder and who now, as a part of the habitual furniture of London drawing rooms, struck her as stars fallen from the firmament and become palpable -- revealing also sometimes, on contact, qualities not to have been predicted of sidereal bodies. Bessie, who knew so many of her contemporaries by reputation, had a good many personal disappointments; but, on the other hand, she had innumerable satisfactions and enthusiasms, and she communicated the emotions of either class to a dear friend of her own sex, in Boston, with whom she was in voluminous correspondence. Some of her reflections, indeed, she attempted to impart to Lord Lambeth, who came almost every day to Jones's Hotel, and whom Mrs. Westgate admitted to be really devoted. Captain Littledale, it appeared, had gone to India; and of several others of Mrs. Westgate's ex-pensioners -- gentlemen who, as she said, had made, in New York, a clubhouse of her drawing room -- no tidings were to be obtained; but Lord Lambeth was certainly attentive enough to make up for the accidental absences, the short memories, all the other irregularities of everyone else. He drove them in the park, he took them to visit private collections of pictures, and, having a house of his own, invited them to dinner. Mrs. Westgate, following the fashion of many of her compatriots, caused herself and her sister to be presented at the English court by her diplomatic representative -- for it was in this manner that she alluded to the American minister to England, inquiring what on earth he was put there for, if not to make the proper arrangements for one's going to a Drawing Room.

Lord Lambeth declared that he hated Drawing Rooms, but he participated in the ceremony on the day on which the two ladies at Jones's Hotel repaired to Buckingham Palace in a remarkable coach which his lordship had sent to fetch them. He had on a gorgeous uniform, and Bessie Alden was particularly struck with his appearance -- especially when on her asking him, rather foolishly as she felt, if he were a loyal subject, he replied that he was a loyal subject to *her*. This declaration was emphasized by his dancing with her at a royal ball to·which the two ladies afterward went, and was not impaired by the fact that she thought he danced very ill. He seemed to her wonderfully kind; she asked herself, with growing vivacity, why he should be so kind. It was his disposition -- that seemed the natural answer. She had told her sister that she liked him very much, and now that she liked him more she wondered why. She liked him for his disposition; to this question as well that seemed the natural answer. When once the impressions of London life began to crowd thickly upon her, she completely forgot her sister's warning about the cynicism of public opinion. It had given her great pain at the moment, but there was no particular reason why she should remember it; it corresponded too little with any sensible reality; and it was disagreeable to Bessie to remember disagreeable things. So she was not haunted with the sense of a vulgar imputation. She was not in love with Lord Lambeth -- she assured herself of that. It will immediately be observed that when such assurances become necessary the state of a young lady's affections is already ambiguous; and, indeed, Bessie Alden made no attempt to dissimulate -- to herself, of course -- a certain tenderness that she felt for the young nobleman. She said to herself that she liked the type to which he belonged -- the simple, candid, manly, healthy English temperament. She spoke to herself of him as women speak of young men they like -- alluded to his bravery (which she had never in the least seen tested), to his honesty and gentlemanliness, and was not silent upon the subject of his good looks. She was perfectly conscious, moreover, that she liked to think of his more adventitious merits; that her imagination was excited and gratified by the sight of a handsome young man endowed with such large opportunities -- opportunities she hardly knew for what, but, as she supposed, for doing great things -- for setting an example, for exerting an influence, for conferring happiness, for encouraging the arts. She had a kind of ideal of conduct for a young man who should find himself in this magnificent position, and she tried to adapt it to Lord Lambeth's deportment, as you might attempt to fit a silhouette in cut paper upon a shadow projected upon a wall. But Bessie Alden's silhouette refused to coincide with his lordship's image, and this want of harmony sometimes vexed her more than she thought reasonable. When he was absent it was, of course, less striking; then he seemed to her a sufficiently graceful combination of high responsibilities and amiable qualities. But when he sat there within sight laughing and talking with his customary good humor and simplicity, she measured it more accurately, and she felt acutely that if Lord Lambeth's position was heroic, there was but little of the hero in the young man himself. Then her imagination wandered away from him -- very far away;

for it was an incontestable fact that at such moments he seemed distinctly dull. I am afraid that while Bessie's imagination was thus invidiously roaming, she cannot have been herself a very lively companion; but it may well have been that these occasional fits of indifference seemed to Lord Lambeth a part of the young girl's personal charm. It had been a part of this charm from the first that he felt that she judged him and measured him more freely and irresponsibly -- more at her ease and her leisure, as it were -- than several young ladies with whom he had been on the whole about as intimate. To feel this, and yet to feel that she also liked him, was very agreeable to Lord Lambeth. He fancied he had compassed that gratification so desirable to young men of title and fortune -- being liked for himself. It is true that a cynical counselor might have whispered to him, "Liked for yourself? Yes; but not so very much!" He had, at any rate, the constant hope of being liked more.

It may seem, perhaps, a trifle singular -- but it is nevertheless true -- that Bessie Alden, when he struck her as dull, devoted some time, on grounds of conscience, to trying to like him more. I say on grounds of conscience because she felt that he had been extremely "nice" to her sister, and because she reflected that it was no more than fair that she should think as well of him as he thought of her. This effort was possibly sometimes not so successful as it might have been, for the result of it was occasionally a vague irritation, which expressed itself in hostile criticism of several British institutions. Bessie Alden went to some entertainments at which she met Lord Lambeth; but she went to others at which his lordship was neither actually nor potentially present; and it was chiefly on these latter occasions that she encountered those literary and artistic celebrities of whom mention has been made. After a while she reduced the matter to a principle. If Lord Lambeth should appear anywhere, it was a symbol that there would be no poets and philosophers; and in consequence -- for it was almost a strict consequence -- she used to enumerate to the young man these objects of her admiration.

"You seem to be awfully fond of those sort of people," said Lord Lambeth one day, as if the idea had just occurred to him.

"They are the people in England I am most curious to see," Bessie Alden replied.

"I suppose that's because you have read so much," said Lord Lambeth gallantly.

"I have not read so much. It is because we think so much of them at home."

"Oh, I see," observed the young nobleman. "In Boston."

"Not only in Boston; everywhere," said Bessie. We hold them in great honor; they go to the best dinner parties."

"I daresay you are right. I can't say I know many of them."

"It's a pity you don't," Bessie Alden declared. "It would do you good."

"I daresay it would," said Lord Lambeth very humbly. "But I must say I don't like the looks of some of them."

"Neither do I -- of some of them. But there are all kinds, and many of them are charming."

"I have talked with two or three of them," the young man went on, "and I thought they had a kind of fawning manner.

"Why should they fawn?" Bessie Alden demanded

"I'm sure I don't know. Why, indeed?"

"Perhaps you only thought so," said Bessie.

"Well, of course," rejoined her companion, "that's a kind of thing that can t be proved."

"In America they don't fawn," said Bessie.

"Ah, well, then, they must be better company."

Bessie was silent a moment. "That is one of the things I don't like about England," she said; "your keeping the distinguished people apart."

"How do you mean apart?"

"Why, letting them come only to certain places. You never see them."

Lord Lambeth looked at her a moment. "What people do you mean?"

"The eminent people -- the authors and artists -- the clever people."

"Oh, there are other eminent people besides those," said Lord Lambeth.

"Well, you certainly keep them apart," repeated the young girl.

"And there are other clever people," added Lord Lambeth simply.

Bessie Alden looked at him, and she gave a light laugh. Not many," she said.

On another occasion -- on just after a dinner party -- she told him that there was something else in England she did not like.

"Oh, I say!" he cried, "haven't you abused us enough?"

"I have never abused you at all," said Bessie; "but I don't like your *precedence*."

"It isn't my precedence!" Lord Lambeth declared, laughing.

"Yes, it is yours -- just exactly yours; and I think it's odious," said Bessie.

"I never saw such a young lady for discussing things! Has someone had the impudence to go before you?" asked his lordship.

"It is not the going before me that I object to," said Bessie; "it is their thinking that they have a right to do it -- *a right that I recognize*."

"I never saw such a young lady as you are for not 'recognizing.' I have no doubt the thing is *beastly*, but it saves a lot of trouble."

"It makes a lot of trouble. It's horrid," said Bessie.

"But how would you have the first people go?" asked Lord Lambeth. "They can't go last."

"Whom do you mean by the first people?"

"Ah, if you mean to question first principles!" said Lord Lambeth.

"If those are your first principles, no wonder some of your arrangements are horrid," observed Bessie Alden with a very pretty ferocity. "I am a young girl, so of course I go last; but imagine what Kitty must feel on being informed that she is not at liberty to budge until certain other ladies have passed out."

"Oh, I say, she is not 'informed!'" cried Lord Lambeth. "No one would do such a thing as that."

"She is made to feel it," the young girl insisted -- "as if they were afraid she would make a rush for the door. No; you have a lovely country," said Bessie Alden, "but your precedence is horrid."

"I certainly shouldn't think your sister would like it," rejoined Lord Lambeth with even exaggerated gravity. But Bessie Alden could induce him to enter no formal protest against this repulsive custom, which he seemed to think an extreme convenience.

Percy Beaumont all this time had been a very much less frequent visitor at Jones's Hotel than his noble kinsman; he had, in fact, called but twice upon the two American ladies. Lord Lambeth, who often saw him, reproached him with his neglect and declared that, although Mrs. Westgate had said nothing about it, he was sure that she was secretly wounded by it. "She suffers too much to speak," said Lord Lambeth.

"That's all gammon," said Percy Beaumont; "there's a limit to what people can suffer!" And, though sending no apologies to Jones's Hotel, he undertook in a manner to explain his absence. "You are always there," he said, "and that's reason enough for my not going."

"I don't see why. There is enough for both of us."

"I don't care to be a witness of your -- your reckless passion," said Percy Beaumont.

Lord Lambeth looked at him with a cold eye and for a moment said nothing. "It's not so obvious as you might suppose," he rejoined dryly, "considering what a demonstrative beggar I am."

"I don't want to know anything about it -- nothing whatever," said Beaumont. "Your mother asks me everytime she sees me whether I believe you are really lost -- and Lady Pimlico does the same. I prefer to be able to answer that I know nothing about it -- that I never go there. I stay away for consistency's sake. As I said the other day, they must look after you themselves."

"You are devilish considerate," said Lord Lambeth. "They never question me."

"They are afraid of you. They are afraid of irritating you and making you worse. So they go to work very cautiously, and, somewhere or other, they get their information. They knew a great deal about you. They know that you have been with those ladies to the dome of St. Paul's and -- where was the other place? -- to the Thames Tunnel."

"If all their knowledge is as accurate as that, it must be very valuable," said Lord Lambeth.

"Well, at any rate, they know that you have been visiting the 'sights of the metropolis.' They think -- very naturally, as it seems to me -- that when you take to visiting the sights of the metropolis with a little American girl, there is serious cause for alarm." Lord Lambeth responded to this intimation by scornful laughter, and his companion continued, after a pause: "I said just now I didn't want to know anything about the affair; but I will confess that I am curious to learn whether you propose to marry Miss Bessie Alden."

On this point Lord Lambeth gave his interlocutor no immediate satisfaction; he was musing, with a frown. "By Jove," he said, "they go rather too far. They *shall* find me dangerous -- I promise them."

Percy Beaumont began to laugh. "You don't redeem your promises. You said the other day you would make your mother call."

Lord Lambeth continued to meditate. "I asked her to call," he said simply

"And she declined?"

"Yes; but she shall do it yet."

"Upon my word," said Percy Beaumont, "if she gets much more frightened I believe she will." Lord Lambeth looked at him, and he went on. "She will go to the girl herself."

"How do you mean she will go to her?"

"She will beg her off, or she will bribe her. She will take strong measures."

Lord Lambeth turned away in silence, and his companion watched him take twenty steps and then slowly return. "I have invited Mrs. Westgate and Miss Alden to Branches," he said, "and this evening I shall name a day."

"And shall you invite your mother and your sisters to meet them?"

"Explicitly!"

"That will set the duchess off," said Percy Beaumont. "I suspect she will come."

"She may do as she pleases."

Beaumont looked at Lord Lambeth. "You do really propose to marry the little sister, then?"

"I like the way you talk about it!" cried the young man. "She won't gobble me down; don't be afraid."

"She won't leave you on your knees," said Percy Beaumont. "What *is* the inducement!"

"You talk about proposing: wait till I *have* proposed," Lord Lambeth went on.

"That's right, my dear fellow; think about it," said Percy Beaumont.

"She's a charming girl," pursued his lordship.

"Of course she's a charming girl. I don't know a girl more charming, intrinsically. But there are other charming girls nearer home."

"I like her spirit," observed Lord Lambeth, almost as if he were trying to torment his cousin.

"What's the peculiarity of her spirit?"

"She's not afraid, and she says things out, and she thinks herself as good as anyone. She is the only girl I have ever seen that was not dying to marry me."

"How do you know that, if you haven't asked her?"

"I don't know how; but I know it."

"I am sure she asked me questions enough about your property and your titles," said Beaumont.

"She has asked me questions, too; no end of them," Lord Lambeth admitted. "But she asked for information, don't you know."

"Information? Aye, I'll warrant she wanted it. Depend upon it that she is dying to marry you just as much and just as little as all the rest of them."

"I shouldn't like her to refuse me -- I shouldn't like that."

"If the thing would be so disagreeable, then, both to you and to her, in Heaven's name leave it alone," said Percy Beaumont.

Mrs. Westgate, on her side, had plenty to say to her sister about the rarity of Mr. Beaumont's visits and the nonappearance of the Duchess of Bayswater. She professed, however, to derive more satisfaction from this latter circumstance than she could have done from the most lavish attentions on the part of this great lady. "It is most marked," she said -- "most marked. It is a delicious proof that we have made them miserable. The day we dined with Lord Lambeth I was really sorry for the poor fellow." It will have been gathered that the entertainment offered by Lord Lambeth to his American friends had not been graced by the presence of his anxious mother. He had invited several choice spirits to meet them; but the ladies of his immediate family were to Mrs. Westgate's sense -- a sense possibly morbidly acute -- conspicuous by their absence.

"I don't want to express myself in a manner that you dislike," said Bessie Alden; "but I don't know why you should have so many theories about Lord Lambeth's poor mother. You know a great many young men in New York without knowing their mothers."

Mrs. Westgate looked at her sister and then turned away. "My dear Bessie, you are superb!" she said.

"One thing is certain," the young girl continued. "If I believed I were a cause of annoyance -- however unwitting -- to Lord Lambeth's family, I should insist-----"

"Insist upon my leaving England," said Mrs. Westgate.

"No, not that I want to go to the National Gallery again; I want to see Stratford-on-Avon and Canterbury Cathedral. But I should insist upon his coming to see us no more."

"That would be very modest and very pretty of you; but you wouldn't do it now."

"Why do you say 'now'?" asked Bessie Alden. "Have I ceased to be modest?"

"You care for him too much. A month ago, when you said you didn't, I believe it was quite true. But at present, my dear child," said Mrs. Westgate, "you wouldn't find it quite so simple a matter never to see Lord Lambeth again. I have seen it coming on."

"You are mistaken," said Bessie. "You don't understand."

"My dear child, don't be perverse," rejoined her sister.

"I know him better, certainly, if you mean that," said Bessie. "And I like him very much. But I don't like him enough to make trouble for him with his family. However, I don't believe in that."

"I like the way you say 'however,'" Mrs. Westgate exclaimed. "Come; you would not marry him?"

"Oh, no," said the young girl.

Mrs. Westgate for a moment seemed vexed. "Why not, pray?" she demanded.

"Because I don't care to," said Bessie Alden.

The morning after Lord Lambeth had had, with Percy Beaumont, that exchange of ideas which has just been narrated, the ladies at Jones's Hotel received from his lordship a written invitation to pay their projected visit to Branches Castle on the following Tuesday. "I think I have made up a very pleasant party," the young nobleman said. "Several people whom you know, and my mother and sisters, who have so long been regrettably prevented from making your acquaintance." Bessie Alden lost no time in calling her sister's attention to the injustice she had done the Duchess of Bayswater, whose hostility was now proved to be a vain illusion.

"Wait till you see if she comes," said Mrs. Westgate. "And if she is to meet us at her son's house the obligation was all the greater for her to call upon us."

Bessie had not to wait long, and it appeared that Lord Lambeth's mother now accepted Mrs. Westgate's view of her duties. On the morrow, early in the afternoon, two cards were brought to the apartment of the American ladies -- one of them bearing the name of the Duchess of Bayswater and the other that of the Countess of Pimlico. Mrs. Westgate glanced at the clock. "It is not yet four," she said; "they have come early; they wish to see us. We will receive them." And she gave orders that her visitors should be admitted. A few moments later they were introduced, and there was a solemn exchange of amenities. The duchess was a large lady, with a fine fresh color the Countess of Pimlico was very pretty and elegant.

The duchess looked about her as she sat down -- looked not especially at Mrs. Westgate. "I daresay my son has told you that I have been wanting to come and see you," she observed.

"You are very kind," said Mrs. Westgate, vaguely -- her conscience not allowing her to assent to this proposition -- and, indeed, not permitting her to enunciate her own with any appreciable emphasis.

"He says you were so kind to him in America," said the duchess.

"We are very glad," Mrs. Westgate replied, "to have been able to make him a little more -- a little less -- a little more comfortable."

"I think he stayed at your house," remarked the Duchess of Bayswater, looking at Bessie Alden.

"A very short time," said Mrs. Westgate.

"Oh!" said the duchess; and she continued to look at Bessie, who was engaged in conversation with her daughter.

"Do you like London?" Lady Pimlico had asked of Bessie, after looking at her a good deal -- at her face and her hands, her dress and her hair.

"Very much indeed," said Bessie.

"Do you like this hotel?"

"It is very comfortable," said Bessie.

"Do you like stopping at hotels?" inquired Lady Pimlico after a pause.

"I am very fond of traveling," Bessie answered, "and I suppose hotels are a necessary part of it. But they are not the part I am fondest of."

"Oh, I hate traveling," said the Countess of Pimlico and transferred her attention to Mrs. Westgate.

"My son tells me you are going to Branches," the duchess presently resumed.

"Lord Lambeth has been so good as to ask us," said Mrs. Westgate, who perceived that her visitor had now begun to look a her, and who had her customary happy consciousness of a distinguished appearance. The only mitigation of her felicity on this point was that, having inspected her visitors own costume, she said to herself, "She won't know how well I am dressed!"

"He has asked me to go, but I am not sure I shall be able," murmured the duchess.

"He had offered us the p---the prospect of meeting you," said Mrs. Westgate.

"I hate the country at this season," responded the duchess.

Mrs. Westgate gave a little shrug. "I think it is pleasanter than London."

But the duchess's eyes were absent again; she was looking very fixedly at Bessie. In a moment she slowly rose, walked to a chair that stood empty at the young girl's right hand, and silently seated herself. As she was a majestic, voluminous woman, this little transaction had, inevitably, an air of somewhat impressive intention. It diffused a certain awkwardness, which Lady Pimlico, as a sympathetic daughter, perhaps desired to rectify in turning to Mrs. Westgate.

"I daresay you go out a great deal," she observed.

"No, very little. We are strangers, and we didn't come here for society."

"I see," said Lady Pimlico. "It's rather nice in town just now."

"It's charming," said Mrs. Westgate. "But we only go to see a few people -- whom we like."

"Of course one can't like everyone," said Lady Pimlico.

"It depends upon a one's society," Mrs. Westgate rejoined.

The Duchess meanwhile had addressed herself to Bessie. "My son tells me the young ladies in America are so clever."

"I am glad they made so good an impression on him," said Bessie, smiling.

The Duchess was not smiling; her large fresh face was very tranquil. "He is very susceptible," she said. He thinks everyone clever, and sometimes they are."

"Sometimes," Bessie assented, smiling still.

The duchess looked at her a little and then went on; "Lambeth is very susceptible, but he is very volatile, too."

"Volatile?" asked Bessie.

"He is very inconstant. It won't do to depend on him."

"Ah," said Bessie, "I don't recognize that description. We have depended on him greatly -- my sister and I -- and he has never disappointed us."

"He will disappoint you yet," said the duchess.

Bessie gave a little laugh, as if she were amused at the duchess's persistency. "I suppose it will depend on what we expect of him."

"The less you expect, the better," Lord Lambeth's mother declared.

"Well," said Bessie, "we expect nothing unreasonable."

The duchess for a moment was silent, though she appeared to have more to say. "Lambeth says he has seen so much of you," she presently began.

"He has been to see us very often; he has been very kind," said Bessie Alden.

"I daresay you are used to that. I am told there is a great deal of that in America."

"A great deal of kindness?" the young girl inquired, smiling.

"Is that what you call it? I know you have different expressions."

"We certainly don't always understand each other," said Mrs. Westgate, the termination of whose interview with Lady Pimlico allowed her to give her attention to their elder visitor.

"I am speaking of the young men calling so much upon the young ladies," the duchess explained.

"But surely in England," said Mrs. Westgate, "the young ladies don't call upon the young men?"

"Some of them do -- almost!" Lady Pimlico declared. "When the young men are a great *parti*."

"Bessie, you must make a note of that," said Mrs. Westgate. "My sister," she added, "is a model traveler. She writes down all the curious facts she hears in a little book she keeps for the purpose."

The duchess was a little flushed; she looked all about the room, while her daughter turned to Bessie. "My brother told us you were wonderfully clever," said Lady Pimlico.

"He should have said my sister," Bessie answered -- "when she says such things as that."

"Shall you be long at Branches?" the duchess asked abruptly, of the young girl.

"Lord Lambeth has asked us for three days," said Bessie.

"I shall go," the duchess declared, "and my daughter, too."

"That will be charming!" Bessie rejoined.

"Delightful!" murmured Mrs. Westgate.

"I shall expect to see a great deal of you," the duchess continued. "When I go to Branches I monopolize my son's guests."

"They must be most happy," said Mrs. Westgate very graciously.

"I want immensely to see it -- to see the castle," said Bessie to the duchess. "I have never seen one -- in England, at least; and you know we have none in America."

"Ah, you are fond of castles?" inquired her Grace.

"Immensely!" replied the young girl. "It has been the dream of my life to live in one."

The duchess looked at her a moment, as if she hardly knew how to take this assurance, which, from her Grace's point of view, was either very artless or very audacious. "Well," she said, rising, "I will show you Branches myself." And upon this the two great ladies took their departure.

"What did they mean by it?" asked Mrs. Westgate, when they were gone.

"They meant to be polite," said Bessie, "because we are going to meet them."

"It is too late to be polite," Mrs. Westgate replied almost grimly. "They meant to overawe us by their fine manners and their grandeur, and to make you *lâcher prise.*"

"*Lâcher prise?* What strange things you say!" murmured Bessie Alden.

"They meant to snub us, so that we shouldn't dare to go to Branches," Mrs. Westgate continued.

"On the contrary," said Bessie, "the duchess offered to show me the place herself."

"Yes, you may depend upon it she won't let you out of her sight. She will show you the place from morning till night."

"You have a theory for everything," said Bessie.

"And you apparently have none for anything."

"I saw no attempt to 'overawe' us," said the young girl. "Their manners were not fine."

"They were not even good!" Mrs. Westgate declared.

Bessie was silent a while, but in a few moments she observed that she had a very good theory. "They came to look at me," she said, as if this had been a very ingenious hypothesis. Mrs. Westgate did it justice; she greeted it with a smile and pronounced it most brilliant, while, in reality, she felt that the young girl's skepticism, or her charity, or, as she had sometimes called it appropriately her idealism, was proof against irony. Bessie, however, remained meditative all the rest of that day and well on into the morrow.

On the morrow, before lunch, Mrs. Westgate had occasion to go out for an hour, and left her sister writing a letter. When she came back she met Lord Lambeth at the door of the hotel, coming away. She thought he looked slightly embarrassed; he was certainly very grave. "I am sorry to have missed you. Won't you come back?" she asked.

"No," said the young man, "I can't. I have seen your sister. I can never come back." Then he looked at her a moment and took her hand. "Goodbye, Mrs. Westgate," he said. "You have been very kind to me." And with what she thought a strange, sad look in his handsome young face, he turned away.

She went in, and she found Bessie still writing her letter; that is, Mrs. Westgate perceived she was sitting at the table with the pen in her hand and not writing. "Lord Lambeth has been here," said the elder lady at last.

Then Bessie got up and showed her a pale, serious face. She bent this face upon her sister for some time, confessing silently and a little pleading. "I told him," she said at last, "that we could not go to Branches."

Mrs. Westgate displayed just a spark of irritation. "He might have waited," she said with a smile, "till one had seen the castle." Later, an hour afterward, she said, "Dear Bessie, I wish you might have accepted him."

"I couldn't," said Bessie gently.

"He is an excellent fellow," said Mrs. Westgate.

"I couldn't," Bessie repeated.

"If it is only," her sister added, "because those women will think that they succeeded -- that they paralyzed us!"

Bessie Alden turned away; but presently she added "They were interesting; I should have liked to see them again."

"So should I!" cried Mrs. Westgate significantly.

"And I should have liked to see the castle," said Bessie. "But now we must leave England," she added.

Her sister looked at her. "You will not wait to go to the National Gallery?"

"Not now."

"Nor to Canterbury Cathedral?"

Bessie reflected a moment. "We can stop there on our way to Paris," she said.

Lord Lambeth did not tell Percy Beaumont that the contingency he was not prepared at all to like had occurred; but Percy Beaumont, on hearing that the two ladies had left London, wondered with some intensity what had happened; wondered, that is, until the Duchess of Bayswater came a little to his assistance. The two ladies went to Paris, and Mrs. Westgate beguiled the journey to that city by repeating several times -- "That's what I regret; they will think they petrified us." But Bessie Alden seemed to regret nothing.

# On Being Crazy
## W. E. B. Du Bois

**W. E. B. Du Bois 1868-1963:** W. E. B. Du Bois was a leader of African-American protest in the United States. During the first half of the 1900's, the acclaimed historian and sociologist became a fierce opponent of racial discrimination. Historians, in fact, still refer to Du Bois' research on African-Americans in United States society.

William Edward Burghardt Du Bois was born in Great Barrington, Mass. He graduated from Fisk University in 1888. In 1895, he became the first African-American to receive a Ph.D. from Harvard University.

From 1897 to 1910, Du Bois taught history and economics at Atlanta University. He became a proponent for Pan-Africanism, the belief that all people of African descent should work together to conquer prejudice. He attended the First Pan African Conference in London in 1900. He later organized Pan-African conferences in Europe and the United States.

Du Bois strongly opposed the views of educator Booker T. Washington. Washington believed that Blacks could advance in society faster through hard work than through demands for equal rights. Du Bois was adamant that African-Americans must speak out constantly against discrimination. According to Du Bois the best way to defeat prejudice was for college educated African-Americans to lead the fight against it. His ideas are presented in his collection of essays, *The Souls of Black Folk* (1903). Other works include *Dark Princess* (1928), *Black Reconstruction in America* (1935) and *The Autobiography of W. E. B. Du Bois* (1968).

IT WAS ONE O'CLOCK and I was hungry. I walked into a restaurant, seated myself, and reached for the bill of fare. My table companion rose.

"Sir," said he, "do you wish to force your company on those who do not want you?"

No, said I, I wish to eat.

"Are you aware, sir, that this is social equality?"

Nothing of the sort, sir, it is hunger -- and I ate.

The day's work done, I sought the theatre. As I sank into my seat, the lady shrank and squirmed.

I beg pardon, I said.

"Do you enjoy being where you are not wanted?" she asked coldly.

Oh no, I said.

"Well you are not wanted here."

I was surprised. I fear you are mistaken. I said, I certainly want the music, and I like to think the music wants me to listen to it.

"Usher," said the lady, "this is social equality."

"No, madame," said the usher, "it is the second movement of Beethoven's Fifth Symphony."

After the theatre, I sought the hotel where I had sent my baggage. The clerk scowled.

"What do you want?"

Rest, I said.

"This is a white hotel," he said.

I looked around. Such a color scheme requires a great deal of cleaning, I said, but I don't know that I object.

"We object," said he.

Then why, I began, but he interrupted.

"We don't keep niggers," he said, "we don't want social equality."

Neither do I, I replied gently, I want a bed.

I walked thoughtfully to the train. I'll take a sleeper through Texas. I'm a little bit dissatisfied with this town.

"Can't sell you one."

I only want to hire it, said I, for a couple of nights.

"Can't sell you a sleeper in Texas," he maintained. "They consider that social equality."

I consider it barbarism, I said, and I think I'll walk.

Walking, I met another wayfarer, who immediately walked to the other side of the road, where it was muddy. I asked his reason.

"Niggers is dirty," he said.

So is mud, said I. Moreover, I am not as dirty as you -- yet.

"But you're a nigger, ain't you?" he asked.

My grandfather was so called.

"Well then!" he answered triumphantly.

Do you live in the South? I persisted, pleasantly.

"Sure," he growled, "and starve there."

I should think you and the Negroes should get together and vote out starvation.

"We don't let them vote."

We? Why not? I said in surprise.

"Niggers is too ignorant to vote."

But, I said, I am not so ignorant as you.

"But you're a nigger."

Yes. I'm certainly what you mean by that.

"Well then!" he returned with that curiously inconsequential note of triumph. "Moreover," he said. "I don't want my sister to marry a nigger."

I had not seen his sister, so I merely murmured, let her say no.

"By God, you shan't marry her, even if she said yes."

But -- but I don't want to marry her, I answered, a little perturbed at the personal turn.

"Why not!" he yelled, angrier than ever.

Because I'm already married and I rather like my wife.

"Is she a nigger?" he asked suspiciously.

Well, I said again, her grandmother was called that.

"Well then!" he shouted in that oddly illogical way.

I gave up.

Go on, I said, either you are crazy or I am.

"We both are," he said as he trotted along in the mud.

# Two Gentlemen Of Kentucky
## James Lane Allen

**James Lane Allen 1849-1925:** James Lane Allen was born in the bluegrass region of Kentucky which served as the setting for many of his stories. As a young man he taught Latin at local colleges in addition to writing fiction and literary criticism. In his late thirties he moved to New York and concentrated on his fiction. The most well-received of his novels was *The Choir Invisible* (1897).

James Lane Allen used his fiction to comment on World War I and the problems of urban America. He stirred the ire of religious fundamentalists with his defense of Darwinism in his novel, *The Reign of Law: A Tale of the Kentucky Hemp Fields* (1900). He is most often remembered, however, for the romance in his depictions of Kentucky. At at time when Realism was the predominant literary mode, Allen's work continued to be dinstinctly Romantic.

His works include *A Flute and Violin* (1891), *A Kentucky Cardinal* (1894), and the posthumously published *The Landmark.*

### THE WOODS ARE HUSHED

IT WAS NEAR the middle of the afternoon of an autumnal day, on the wide, grassy plateau of Central Kentucky.

The Eternal Power seemed to have quitted the universe and left all nature folded in the calm of the Eternal Peace. Around the pale-blue dome of the heavens a few pearl-colored clouds hung motionless, as though the wind had been withdrawn to other skies. Not a crimson leaf floated downward through the soft, silvery light that filled the atmosphere and created the sense of lonely, unimaginable spaces. This light overhung the far-rolling landscape of field and meadow and wood, crowning with faint radiance the remoter low-swelling hill-tops and deepening into dreamy half-shadows on their eastern slopes. Nearer, it fell in a white flake on an unstirred sheet of water which lay along the edge of a mass of sombre-hued woodland, and nearer still it touched to spring-like brilliancy a level, green meadow on the hither edge of the water, where a group of Durham cattle stood with reversed flanks near the gleaming trunks of some leafless sycamores. Still nearer, it caught the top of the brown foliage of a little bent oaktree and burned it into a silvery flame. It lit on the back and the wings of a crow flying heavily in the path of its rays, and made his blackness as white as the breast of a swan. In the immediate foreground, it sparkled in minute gleams along the stalks of the coarse, dead weeds that fell away from the legs and the flanks of a white horse, and slanted across the face of the rider and through the ends of his gray hair, which straggled from beneath his soft black hat.

The horse, old and patient and gentle, stood with low-stretched neck and closed eyes half asleep in the faint glow of the waning heat; and the rider, the sole human presence in all the field, sat looking across the silent autumnal landscape, sunk in reverie. Both horse and rider seemed but harmonious elements in the panorama of still-life, and completed the picture of a closing scene.

To the man it was a closing scene. From the rank, fallow field through which he had been riding he was now surveying, far the last time, the many features of a landscape that had been familiar to him from the beginning of memory. In the afternoon and the autumn of his age he was about to rend the last ties that bound him to his former life, and, like one who had survived his own destiny, turn his face towards a future that was void of everything he held significant or dear.

The Civil War had only the year before reached its ever-memorable close. From where he sat there was not a home in sight, as there was not one beyond the reach of his vision, but had felt its influence. Some of his neighbors had come home from its camps and prisons, aged or altered as though by half a lifetime of years. The bones of some lay whitening on its battle-fields. Families, reassembled around their hearth-stones, spoke in low tones unceasingly of defeat and victory, heroism and death. Suspicion and distrust and estrangement prevailed. Former friends met each other on the turnpikes without speaking; brothers avoided each other in the streets of the neighboring town. The rich had grown poor; the poor had become rich. Many of the latter were preparing to move West. The negroes were drifting blindly hither and thither, deserting the country and flocking to the towns. Even the once united church of his neighborhood was jarred by the unstrung and discordant spirit of the times. At affecting passages in the sermons men grew pale and set their teeth fiercely; women suddenly lowered their black veils and rocked to and fro in their pews; for it is always at the bar of Conscience and before the very altar of God that the human heart is most wrung by a sense of its losses and the memory of its wrongs. The war had divided the people of Kentucky as the false mother would have severed the child.

It had not left the old man unscathed. His younger brother had fallen early in the conflict, borne to the end of his brief warfare by his impetuous valor; his aged mother had sunk under the tidings of the death of her latest-born; his sister was estranged from him by his political differences with her husband; his old family servants, men and women, had left him, and grass and weeds had already grown over the door-steps of the shut, noiseless cabins. Nay, the whole vast social system of the old regime had fallen, and he was henceforth but a useless fragment of the ruins.

All at once his mind turned from the cracked and smoky mirror of the times and dwelt fondly upon the scenes of the past. The silent fields around him seemed again alive with the negroes, singing as they followed the ploughs down the corn-rows or swung the cradles through the bearded wheat. Again, in a frenzy of merriment, the strains of the old fiddles issued from crevices of cabin-doors to the rhythmic beat of hands and feet that shook the rafters and the roof. Now he was sitting on his porch, and one little negro was blacking his shoes, another leading his saddle-horse to the stiles, a third bringing his hat, and a fourth handing him a glass of ice-cold sangaree; or now he lay under the locust-trees in his yard, falling asleep in the drowsy heat of the summer afternoon, while one waved over him a bough of pungent walnut leaves, until he lost consciousness and by-and-by awoke to find that they both had fallen asleep side by side on the grass and that the abandoned fly-brush lay full across his face.

From where he sat also were seen slopes on which picnics were danced under the broad shade of maples and elms in June by those whom death and war had scattered like the transitory leaves that once had sheltered them. In this direction lay the district school-house where on Friday evenings there were wont to be speeches and debates; in that, lay the blacksmith's shop where of old he and his neighbors had met on horseback of Saturday afternoons to hear the news, get the mails, discuss elections, and pitch quoits. In the valley beyond stood the church at which all had assembled on calm Sunday mornings like the members of one united family. Along with these scenes went many a chastened reminiscence of bridal and funeral and simpler events that had made up the annals of his country life.

The reader will have a clearer insight into the character and past career of Colonel Romulus Fields by remembering that he represented a fair type of that social order which had existed in rank perfection over the blue-grass plains of Kentucky during the final decades of the old regime. Perhaps of all agriculturists in the United States the inhabitants of that region had spent the most nearly idyllic life, on account of the beauty of the climate, the richness of the land, the spacious comfort of their homes, the efficiency of their negroes, and the characteristic contentedness of their dispositions. Thus nature and history combined to make them a peculiar class, a cross between the aristocratic and the bucolic, being as simple as shepherds and as proud as kings, and not seldom exhibiting among both men and women types of character which were as remarkable for pure, tender, noble states of feeling as they were commonplace in powers and cultivation of mind.

It was upon this luxurious social growth that the war naturally fell as a killing frost, and upon no single specimen with more blighting power than upon Colonel Fields. For destiny had quarried and chiselled him, to serve as an ornament in the barbaric temple of human bondage. There *were* ornaments in that temple, and he was one. A slave-holder with Southern sympathies, a man educated not beyond the ideas of his genera-tion, convinced that slavery was an evil, yet seeing no present way of removing it, he had of all things been a model master. As such he had gone on record in Kentucky, and no doubt in á Higher Court; and as such his efforts had been put forth to secure the passage of many of those milder laws for which his State was distinguished. Often, in those dark days, his face, anxious and sad, was to be seen amid the throng that surrounded the blocks on which slaves were sold at auction; and more than one poor wretch he had bought to save him from separation from his family or from being sold into the Southern plantations -- afterwards riding far and near to find him a home on one of the neighboring farms.

But all those days were over. He had but to place the whole picture of the present beside the whole picture of the past to realize what the contrast meant for him.

At length he gathered the bridle reins from the neck of his old horse and turned his head homeward. As he rode slowly on, every spot gave up its memories. He dismounted when he came to the cattle and walked among them, stroking their soft flanks and feeling in the palm of his hand the rasp of their salt-loving tongues; on his sideboard at home was many a silver cup which told of premiums on cattle at the great fairs. It was in this very pond that as a boy he had learned to swim on a cherry rail. When he entered the woods, the sight of the walnut-trees and the hickory-nut trees, loaded on the topmost branches, gave him a sudden pang.

Beyond the woods he came upon the garden, which he had kept as his mother had left it -- an old-fashioned garden with an arbor in the centre, covered with Isabella grape-vines on one side and Catawba on the other; with walks branching thence in four directions, and along them beds of jump-up-johnnies, sweet-williams, daffodils, sweet-peas, larkspur, and thyme, flags and the sensitive-plant, celestial and maiden's-blush roses. He stopped and looked over the fence at the very spot where he had found his mother on the day when the news of the battle came.

She had been kneeling, trowel in hand, driving away vigorously at the loamy earth, and, as she saw him coming, had risen and turned towards him her face with the ancient pink bloom on her clear cheeks and the light of a pure, strong soul in her gentle eyes. Overcome by his emotions, he had blindly faltered out the words, "Mother, John was among the killed!" For a moment she had looked at him as though stunned by a blow. Then a violent flush had overspread her features, and then an ashen pallor; after which, with a sudden proud dilating of her form as though with joy, she had sunk down like the tenderest of her lily-stalks, cut from its root.

Beyond the garden he came to the empty cabin and the great wood-pile. At this hour it used to be a scene of hilarious activity -- the little negroes sitting perched in chattering groups on the topmost logs or playing leap-frog in the dust, while some picked up baskets of chips or dragged a back-log into the cabins.

At last he drew near the wooden stiles and saw the large house of which he was the solitary occupant. What darkened rooms and noiseless halls! What beds, all ready, that nobody now came to sleep in, and cushioned old chairs that nobody rocked! The house and the contents of its attic, presses, and drawers could have told much of the history of Kentucky from almost its beginning; for its foundations had been laid by his father near the beginning of the century, and through its doors had passed a long train of forms, from the veterans of the Revolution to the soldiers of the Civil War. Old coats hung up in closets; old dresses folded away in drawers; saddle-bags and buckskin-leggins; hunting-jackets, powder-horns, and militiamen hats; looms and knitting-needles; snuffboxes and reticules -- what a treasure-house of the past it was! And now the only thing that had the springs of life within its bosom was the great, sweet-voiced clock, whose faithful face had kept unchanged amid all the swift pageantry of changes.

He dismounted at the stiles and handed the reins to a gray-haired negro, who had hobbled up to receive them with a smile and a gesture of the deepest respect.

"Peter," he said, very simply, "I am going to sell the place and move to town. I can't live here any longer."

With these words he passed through the yard-gate, walked slowly up the broad pavement, and entered the house.

## MUSIC NO MORE

On the disappearing form of the colonel was fixed an ancient pair of eyes that looked out at him from behind a still more ancient pair of silver-rimmed spectacles with an expression of indescribable solicitude and love.

These eyes were set in the head of an old gentleman -- for such he was -- named Peter Cotton, who was the only one of the colonel's former slaves that had remained inseparable from his person and his altered fortunes. In early manhood Peter had been a wood chopper; but he had one day had his leg broken by the limb of a falling tree, and afterwards, out of consideration for his limp, had been made supervisor of the wood-pile, gardener, and a sort of nondescript servitor of his master's luxurious needs.

Nay, in larger and deeper characters must his history be writ, he having been, in days gone by, one of those ministers of the gospel whom conscientious Kentucky masters often urged to the exercise of spiritual functions in behalf of their benighted people. In course of preparation for this august work, Peter had learned to read and had come to possess a well-chosen library of three several volumes -- *Webster's Spelling-Book, The Pilgrim's Progress*, and the Bible. But even these unusual acquisitions he deemed not enough; for being touched with a spark of poetic fire from heaven, and fired by the African's fondness for all that is conspicuous in dress, he had conceived for himself the creation of a unique garment which should symbolize in perfection the claims and consolations of his apostolic office. This was nothing less than a sacred blue-jeans coat that he had had his old mistress make him, with very long and spacious tails, whereon, at his further direction, she embroidered sundry texts of Scripture which it pleased him to regard as the fit visible annunciations of his holy calling. And inasmuch as his mistress, who had had the coat woven on her own looms from the wool of her finest sheep, was, like other gentle-women of her time, rarely skilled in the accomplishments of the needle, and was moreover in full sympathy with the piety of his intent, she wrought of these passages a border enriched with such intricate curves, marvellous flourishes, and harmonious letterings, that Solomon never reflected the glory in which Peter was arrayed whenever he put it on. For after much prayer that the Almighty wisdom would aid his reason in the difficult task of selecting the most appropriate texts, Peter had chosen seven -- one for each day in the week -- with such tact, and no doubt heavenly guidance, that when braided together they did truly constitute an eloquent epitome of Christian duty, hope, and pleading.

From first to last they were as follows: "Woe is unto me if I preach not the gospel;" "Servants, be obedient to them that are your masters according to the flesh;" "Come unto me, all ye that labour and are heavy laden;" "Consider the lilies of the field, how they grow; they toil not, neither do they spin;" "Now abideth faith, hope, and charity, these three; but the greatest of these is charity;" "I would not have you to be ignorant, brethren, concerning them which are asleep;" "For as in Adam all die, even so in Christ shall all be made alive." This concatenation of texts Peter wished to have duly solemnized, and therefore, when the work was finished, he further requested his mistress to close the entire chain with the word "Amen," introduced in some suitable place.

But the only spot now left 'vacant was one of a few square inches, located just where the coat-tails hung over the end of Peters spine; so that when any one stood full in Peter's rear, he could but marvel at the sight of so solemn a word emblazoned in so unusual a locality.

Panoplied in this robe of righteousness, and with a worn leathern Bible in his hand, Peter used to go around of Sundays, and during the week, by night, preaching from cabin to cabin the gospel of his heavenly Master.

The angriest lightnings of the sultriest skies often played amid the darkness upon those sacred coat-tails and around that girdle of everlasting texts, as though the evil spirits of the air would fain have burned them and scattered their ashes on the roaring winds. The slow-sifting snows of winter whitened them as though to chill their spiritual fires; but winter and summer, year after year, in weariness of body, often in sore distress of mind, for miles along, this lonely road and for miles across that rugged way, Peter trudged on and on, withal perhaps as meek a spirit as ever grew foot-sore in the paths of its Master. Many a poor overburdened slave took fresh heart and strength from the sight of that celestial raiment; many a stubborn, rebellious spirit, whose flesh but lately quivered under the lash, was brought low by its humble teaching; many a worn-out old frame, racked with pain in its last illness, pressed a fevered lip to its hopeful hem;

and many a dying eye closed in death peacefully fixed on its immortal pledges.

When Peter started abroad, if a storm threatened, he carried an old cotton umbrella of immense size; and as the storm burst, he gathered the tails of his coat carefully up under his armpits that they might be kept dry. Or if caught by a tempest without his umbrella, he would take his coat off and roll it up inside out, leaving his body exposed to the fury of the elements. No care, however, could keep it from growing old and worn and faded; and when the slaves were set free and he was called upon by the interposition of Providence to lay it finally aside, it was covered by many a patch and stain as proofs of its devoted usage.

One after another the colonel's old servants, gathering their children about them, had left him, to begin their new life. He bade them all a kind good-bye, and into the palm of each silently pressed some gift that he knew would soon be needed. But no inducement could make Peter or Phillis, his wife, budge from their cabin. "Go, Peter! Go, Phillis!" the colonel had said time and again. "No one is happier that you are free than I am; and you can call on me for what you need to set you up in business." But Peter and Phillis asked to-stay with him. Then suddenly, several months before the time at which this sketch opens, Phillis had died, leaving the colonel and Peter as the only relics of that populous life which had once filled the house and the cabins. The colonel had succeeded in hiring a woman to do Phillis's work; but her presence was a strange note of discord in the old domestic harmony, and only saddened the recollections of its vanished peace.

Peter had a short, stout figure, dark-brown skin, smooth-shaven face, eyes round, deep-set and wide apart, and a short, stub nose which dipped suddenly into his head, making it easy for him to wear the silver-rimmed spectacles left him by his old mistress. A peculiar conformation of the muscles between the eyes and the nose gave him the quizzical expression of one who is about to sneeze, and this was heightened by a twinkle in the eyes which seemed caught from the shining of an inner sun upon his tranquil heart.

Sometimes, however, his face grew sad enough. It was sad on this afternoon while he watched the colonel walk slowly up the pavement, well overgrown with weeds, and enter the house, which the setting sun touched with the last radiance of the finished day.

## NEW LIFE

About two years after the close of the war, therefore, the colonel and Peter were to be found in Lexington, ready to turn over a new leaf in the volumes of their lives, which already had an old-fashioned binding, a somewhat musty odor, and but few unwritten leaves remaining.

After a long, dry summer you may have seen two gnarled old apple-trees, that stood with interlocked arms on the western slope of some quiet hill-side, make a melancholy show of blooming out again in the autumn of the year and dallying with the idle buds that mock their sapless branches. Much the same was the belated, fruitless efflorescence of the colonel and Peter.

The colonel had no business habits, no political ambition, no wish to grow richer. He was too old for society, and without near family ties. For some time he wandered through the streets like one lost -- sick with yearning for the fields and wood, for his cattle, for familiar faces. He haunted Cheapside and the courthouse square, where the farmers always assembled when they came to town; and if his eye lighted on one, he would button-hole him on the street-corner and lead him into a grocery and sit down for a quiet chat. Sometimes he would meet an aimless, melancholy wanderer like himself, and the two would go off and discuss over and over again their departed days; and several times he came unexpectedly upon some of his old servants who had fallen into bitter want, and who more than repaid him for the help he gave by contrasting the hardships of a life of freedom with the ease of their shackled years.

In the course of time, he could but observe that human life in the town was reshaping itself slowly and painfully, but with resolute energy. The colossal structure of slavery had fallen, scattering its ruins far and wide over the State; but out of the very debris was being taken the material to lay the deeper foundations of the new social edifice. Men and women as old as he were beginning life over ant trying to fit themselves for it by changing the whole attitude and habit of their minds -- by taking on a new heart and spirit. But when a great building falls, there is always some rubbish, and the colonel and others like him were part of this. Henceforth they possessed only an antiquarian sort of interest, like the stamped bricks of Nebuchadnezzar.

Nevertheless he made a show of doing something, and in a year or two opened on Cheapside a store for the sale of hardware and agricultural implements. He knew more about the latter than anything else; and, furthermore, he secretly felt that a business of this kind would enable him to establish in town a kind of head-quarters for the farmers. His account-books were to be kept on a system of twelve months' credit; and he resolved that if one of his customers couldn't pay then, it would make no difference.

Business began slowly. The farmers dropped in and found a good lounging-place. On county-court days, which were great market-days for the sale of sheep, horses, mules, and cattle in front of the colonel's door, they swarmed in from the hot sun and sat around on the counter and the ploughs and machines till the entrance was blocked to other customers.

When a customer did come in, the colonel, who was probably talking with some old acquaintance, would tell him just to look around and pick out what he wanted and the price would be all right. If one of those acquaintances asked for a pound of nails, the colonel would scoop up some ten pounds and say, "I reckon that's about a pound, Tom." He had never seen a pound of nails in his life; and if one had been weighed on his scales, he would have said the scales were wrong.

He had no great idea of commercial despatch. One morning a lady came in for some carpet-tacks, an article that he had forgotten to lay in. But he at once sent off an order for enough to have tacked a carpet pretty well over Kentucky; and when they came, two weeks later, he told Peter to take her up a dozen papers with his compliments. He had laid in, however, an ample and especially fine assortment of pocket-knives, for that instrument had always been to him one of gracious and very winning qualities Then when a friend dropped in he would say, "General, don't you need a new pocket-knife?" and, taking out one, would open all the blades and commend the metal and the handle. The "general" would inquire the price, and the colonel, having shut the blades, would hand it to him, saying in a careless, fond way, "I reckon I won't charge you anything for that." His mind could not come down to the low level of such ignoble barter, and he gave away the whole case of knives.

These were the pleasanter aspects of his business life which did not lack as well its tedium and crosses. Thus there were many dark stormy days when no one he cared to see came in; and he then became rather a pathetic figure, wandering absently around amid the symbols of his past activity, and stroking the ploughs, like dumb companions. Or he would stand at the door and look across at the old court-house, where he had seen many a slave sold and had listened to the great Kentucky orators.

But what hurt him most was the talk of the new farming and the abuse of the old which he was forced to hear; and he generally refused to handle the improved implements and mechanical devices by which labor and waste were to be saved.

Altogether he grew tired of "the thing," and sold out at the end of the year with a loss of over a thousand dollars, though he insisted he had done a good business.

As he was then seen much on the streets again and several times heard to make remarks in regard to the sidewalks, gutters, and crossings, when they happened to be in bad condition, the *Daily Press* one morning published a cart stating that if Colonel Romulus Fields would consent to make the race for mayor he would receive the support of many Democrats, adding a tribute to his virtues and his influential past. It touched the colonel, and he walked down-town with a rather commanding figure the next morning. But it pained him to see how many of his acquaintances returned his salutations very coldly; and just as he was passing the Northern Bank he met the young opposition candidate -- a little red-haired fellow, walking between two ladies, with a rose-bud in his button-hole -- who refused to speak at all, but made the ladies laugh by some remark he uttered as the colonel passed. The card had been inserted humorously, but he took it seriously; and when his friends found this out, they rallied round him. The day of election drew near. They told him he must buy votes. He said he wouldn't buy a vote to be mayor of the New Jerusalem. They told him he must "mix" and "treat." He refused. Foreseeing he had no chance, they besought him to withdraw. He said he would not. They told him he wouldn't poll twenty votes. He replied that *one* would satisfy him, provided it was neither begged nor bought. When his defeat was announced, he accepted it as another evidence that he had no part in the present -- no chance of redeeming his idleness.

A sense of this weighed heavily on him at times; but it is not likely that he realized how pitifully he was undergoing a moral shrinkage in consequence of mere disuse. Actually, extinction had set in with him long prior to dissolution, and he was dead years before his heart ceased beating. The very basic virtues on which had rested his once spacious and stately character were now but the mouldy corner-stones of a crumbling ruin.

It was a subtle evidence of deterioration in manliness that he had taken to dress. When he had lived in the country, he had never dressed up unless he came to town. When he had moved to town, he thought he must remain dressed up all the time; and this fact first fixed his attention on a matter which afterwards began to be loved for its own sake. Usually he wore a Derby hat, a black diagonal coat, gray trousers, and a white necktie. But the article of attire in which he took chief pleasure was hose; and the better to show the gay colors of these, he wore low-cut shoes of the finest calf-skin, turned up at the toes. Thus his feet kept pace with the present, however far his head may have lagged in the past; and it may be that this stream of fresh fashions, flowing perennially over his lower extremities like water about the roots of a tree, kept him from drying up altogether.

Peter always polished his shoes with too much blacking, perhaps thinking that the more the blacking the greater the proof of love. He wore his clothes about a season and a half -- having several suits -- and then passed them on to Peter, who, foreseeing the joy of such an inheritance, bought no new ones. In the act of transferring them the colonel made no comment until he came to the hose, from which he seemed unable to part without a final tribute of esteem, as: "These are fine, Peter;" or, "Peter, these are nearly as good as new." Thus Peter, too, was dragged through the whims of fashion. To have seen the colonel walking about his grounds and garden followed by Peter, just a year and a half behind in dress and a yard and a half behind in space, one might well have taken the rear figure for the colonel's double, slightly the worse for wear, somewhat shrunken, and cast into a heavy shadow.

Time hung so heavily on his hands at night that with a happy inspiration he added a dress suit to his wardrobe, and accepted the first invitation to an evening party.

He grew excited as the hour approached, and dressed in a great fidget for fear he should be too late.

"How do I look, Peter?" he inquired at length, surprised at his own appearance.

"Splendid, Marse Rom," replied Peter, bringing in the shoes with more blacking on them than ever before.

"I think," said the colonel, apologetically -- "I think I'd look better if I'd put a little powder on. I don't know what makes me so red in the face."

But his heart began to sink before he reached his hostess's, and he had a fearful sense of being the observed of all observers as he slipped through the hall and passed rapidly up to the gentlemen's room. He stayed there after the others had gone down, bewildered and lonely, dreading to go down himself. By-and-by the musicians struck up a waltz, and with a little cracked laugh at his own performance he cut a few shines of an unremembered pattern; but his ankles snapped audibly, and he suddenly stopped with the thought of what Peter would say if he should catch him at these antics. Then he boldly went down-stairs.

He had touched the new human life around him at various points: as he now stretched out his arms towards its society, for the first time he completely realized how far removed it was from him. Here he saw a younger generation -- the flowers of the new social order -- sprung from the very soil of fraternal battlefields, but blooming together as the emblems of oblivious peace. He saw fathers, who had fought madly on opposite sides, talking quietly in corners as they watched their children dancing, or heard them toasting their old generals and their campaigns over their champagne in the supper-room. He was glad of it; but it made him feel, at the same time, that, instead of treading the velvety floors, he ought to step up and take his place among the canvases of old-time portraits that looked down from the walls.

The dancing he had done had been not under the blinding glare of gaslight, but by the glimmer of tallow-dips and star-candles and the ruddy glow of cavernous firesides -- not to the accompaniment of an orchestra of wind-instruments and strings, but to a chorus of girls' sweet voices, as they trod simpler measures, or˜to the maddening sway of gray-haired negro fiddler standing on a chair in the chimney-corner. Still, it is significant to note that his saddest thought, long after leaving, was that his shirt bosom had not lain down smooth, but stuck out like a huge cracked egg-shell; and that when, in imitation of the others, he had laid his white silk handkerchief across his bosom inside his vest, it had slipped out during the evening, and had been found by him, on confronting a mirror, flapping over his stomach like a little white masonic apron.

"Did you have a nice time, Marse Rom?" inquired Peter, as they drove home through the darkness.

"Splendid time, Peter, splendid time," replied the colonel, nervously.

"Did you dance any, Marse Rom?"

"I didn't *dance*. Oh, I *could* have danced if I'd *wanted* to; but I didn't."

Peter helped the colonel out of the carriage with pitying gentleness when they reached home. It was the first and only party.

Peter also had been finding out that his occupation was gone.

Soon after moving to town, he had tendered his pastoral services to one of the fashionable churches of the city -- not because it was fashionable, but because it was made up of his brethren. In reply he was invited to preach a trial sermon, which he did with gracious unction.

It was a strange scene, as one calm Sunday morning he stood on the edge of the pulpit, dressed in a suit of the colonel's old clothes, with one hand in his trousers-pocket and his lame leg set a little forward at an angle familiar to those who know the statues of Henry Clay.

How self-possessed he seemed, yet with what a rush of memories did he pass his eyes slowly over that vast assemblage of his emancipated people! With what feelings must he have contrasted those silk hats, and walking-canes, and broadcloths; those gloves and satins, laces and feathers, jewelry and fans -- that whole many-colored panorama of life -- with the weary, sad, and sullen audiences that had often heard him of old under the forest trees or by the banks of some turbulent stream!

In a voice husky, but heard beyond the flirtation of the uttermost pew, he took his text: "Consider the lilies of the field, how they grow; they toil not, neither do they spin." From this he tried to preach a new sermon, suited to the newer day. But several times the thoughts of the past were too much for him, and he broke down with emotion.

The next day a grave committee waited on him and reported that the sense of the congregation was to call a colored gentleman from Louisville. Private objections to Peter were that he had a broken leg, wore Colonel Fields's second-hand clothes, which were too big for him, preached in the old-fashioned way, and lacked self-control and repose of manner.

Peter accepted his rebuff as sweetly as Socrates might have done. Humming the burden of an old hymn, he took his righteous coat from a nail in the wall and folded it away in a little brass-nailed deer-skin trunk, laying over it the spelling-book and the *Pilgrim's Progress,* which he had ceased to read. Thenceforth his relations to his people were never intimate, and even from the other servants of the colonel's household he stood apart. But the colonel took Peter's rejection greatly to heart, and the next morning gave him the new silk socks he had worn at the party. In paying his servants the colonel would sometimes say, "Peter, I reckon I'd better begin to pay you a salary; that's the style now." But Peter would turn off, saying he didn't "have no use fur no salary."

Thus both of them dropped more and more out of life, but as they did so drew more and more closely to each other. The colonel had bought a home on the edge of the town, with some ten acres of beautiful ground surrounding. A high osage-orange hedge shut it in, and forest trees, chiefly maples and elms, gave to the lawn and house abundant shade. Wild-grape vines, the Virginia-creeper, and the climbing-oak swung their long festoons from summit to summit, while honeysuckles, clematis, and the Mexican-vine clambered over arbors and trellises, or along the chipped stone of the low, old-fashioned house. Just outside the door of the colonel's bedroom slept an ancient, broken sundial.

The place seemed always in half-shadow, with hedgerows of box, clumps of dark holly, darker firs half a century old, and aged, crape-like cedars.

It was in the seclusion of this retreat, which looked almost like a wild bit of country set down on the edge of the town, that the colonel and Peter spent more of their time as they fell farther in the rear of onward events. There were no such flower-gardens in the city, and pretty much the whole town went thither for its flowers, preferring them to those that were to be had for a price at the nurseries.

There was, perhaps, a suggestion of pathetic humor in the fact that it should have called on the colonel and Peter, themselves so nearly defunct, to furnish the flowers for so many funerals; but, it is certain, almost weekly the two old gentlemen received this chastening admonition of their all-but-spent mortality. The colonel cultivated the rarest fruits also, and had under glass varieties that were not friendly to the climate; so that by means of the fruits and flowers there was established a pleasant social bond with many who otherwise would never have sought them out.

But others came for better reasons. To a few deep-seeing eyes the colonel and Peter were ruined landmarks on a fading historic landscape, and their devoted friendship was the last steady burning-down of that pure flame of love which can never again shine out in the future of the two races. Hence a softened charm invested the drowsy quietude of that shadowy paradise in which the old master without a slave and the old slave without a master still kept up a brave pantomime of their obsolete relations. No one ever saw in their intercourse ought but the finest courtesy, the most delicate consideration. The very tones of their voices in addressing each other were as good as sermons on gentleness, their antiquated playfulness as melodious as the babble of distant water. To be near them was to be exorcised of evil passions.

The sun of their day had indeed long since set; but like twin clouds lifted high and motionless into some far quarter of the gray twilight skies, they were still radiant with the glow of the invisible orb.

Henceforth the colonel's appearances in public were few and regular. He went to church on Sundays, where he sat on the edge of the choir in the centre of the building, and sang an ancient bass of his own improvisation to the older hymns, and glanced furtively around to see whether any one noticed that he could not sing the new ones. At the Sunday-school picnics the committee of arrangements allowed him to carve the mutton, and after dinner to swing the smallest children gently beneath the trees. He was seen on Commencement Day at Morrison Chapel, where he always gave his bouquet to the valedictorian. It was the speech of that young gentleman that always touched him, consisting as it did of farewells.

In the autumn he might sometimes be noticed sitting high up in the amphitheatre at the fair, a little blue around the nose, and looking absently over into the ring where the judges were grouped around the music-stand. Once he had strutted around as a judge himself, with a blue ribbon in his button-hole, while the band played "Sweet Alice, Ben Bolt," and "Gentle Annie." The ring seemed full of young men now, and no one even thought of offering him the privileges of the grounds. In his day the great feature of the exhibition had been cattle; now everything was turned into a horse show. He was always glad to get home again to Peter, his true yoke-fellow. For just as two old oxen -- one white and one black -- that have long toiled under the same yoke will, when turned out to graze at last in the widest pasture, come and put themselves horn to horn and flank to flank, so the colonel and Peter were never so happy as when ruminating side by side.

**NEW LOVE**

In their eventless life the slightest incident acquired the importance of a history. Thus, one day in June, Peter discovered a young couple lovemaking in the shrubbery, and with the deepest agitation reported the fact to the colonel.

Never before, probably, had the fluttering of the dear god's wings brought more dismay than to these ancient involuntary guardsmen of his hiding-place. The colonel was at first for breaking up what he considered a piece of underhand proceedings, but Peter reasoned stoutly that if the pair were driven out they would simply go to some other retreat; and without getting the approval of his conscience to this view, the colonel contented himself with merely repeating that they ought to go straight and tell the girl's parents. Those parents lived just across the street outside his grounds. The young lady he knew very well himself, having a few years before given her the privilege of making herself at home among his flowers. It certainly looked hard to drive her out now, just when she was making the best possible use of his kindness and her opportunity. Moreover, Peter walked down street and ascertained that the young fellow was an energetic farmer living a few miles from town, and son of one of the colonel's former friends; on both of which accounts the latter's heart went out to him. So when, a few days later, the colonel, followed by Peter, crept up breathlessly and peeped through the bushes at the pair strolling along the shady perfumed walks, and so plainly happy in that happiness which comes but once in a lifetime, they not only abandoned the idea of betraying the secret, but afterwards kept away from that part of the grounds, lest they should be an interruption.

"Peter," stammered the colonel, who had been trying to get the words out for three days, "do you suppose he has already -- *asked* her?"

"Some's pow'ful quick on de trigger, en some's mighty slow," replied Peter, neutrally. "En some," he added, exhaustively, "don't use de trigger 't all!"

"I always thought there had to be asking done by *somebody*," remarked the colonel a little vaguely.

"I nuver axed Phillis!" exclaimed Peter, with a certain air of triumph.

"Did Phillis ask *you*, Peter?" inquired the colonel, blushing and confidential.

"No, no, Marse Rom! I couldn't er stood dat from no 'oman!" replied Peter, laughing and shaking his head.

The colonel was sitting on the stone steps in front of the house, and Peter stood below, leaning against a Corinthian column, hat in hand, as he went on to tell his love-story.

"Hit all happ'n dis way, Marse Rom. We wuz gwine have pra'r-meetin', en I 'lowed to walk home wid Phillis en ax'er on de road. I been 'lowin' to ax 'er heap o' times befo', but I ain' jes nuver done so. So I says to myse'f, says I, 'I jes mek my sermon to-night kiner lead up to whut I gwine tell Phillis on de road home.' So I tuk my tex' from de *lef* tail o' my coat: 'De greates' o' dese is charity;' caze I knowed charity wuz same ez love. En all de time I wuz preachin' an' glorifyn' charity en identifyrn' charity wid love, I couldn' he'p thinkin' 'bout what I gwine say to Phillis on de road home. Dat mek me feel better; en de better I *feel*, de better I *preach,* so hit boun' to mek my *heahehs* feel better likewise -- Phillis 'mong um. So Phillis she jes sot dah listenin' en listenin' en lookin' like we wuz a'ready on de road home, till I got so wuked up in my feelin's I jes knowed de time wuz come. By-en-by, I had n' mo' 'n done preachin' en wuz lookin' roun' to git my Bible en my hat, 'fo' up popped dat big Charity Green, who been settin' 'longside o' Phillis en tekin' ev'y las' thing I said to *herse'f.* En she tuk hole o' my han' en squeeze it, en say she felt mos' like shoutin'. En 'fo' I knowed it, I jes see Phillis wrap 'er shawl roun' 'er head en tu'n 'er nose up at me right quick en flip out de dooh. De dogs howl mighty mou'nful when I walk home by myse'f *dat* night," added Peter, laughing to himself, "en I ain' preach dat sermon no mo' tell atter me en Phillis wuz married.

"Hit wuz long time," he continued, "'fo' Phillis come to heah me preach any mo'. But 'long 'bout de nex' fall we had big meetin', en heap mo' um j'ined. But Phillis, she ain't nuver j'ined yit. I preached mighty nigh all roun' my coat-tails till I say to myse'f, D' ain't but one tex' lef', en I jes got to fetch 'er wid dat! De tex' wuz on de *right* tail o' my coat: 'Come unto me, all ye dat labor en is heavy laden.' Hit wuz a ve'y momentous sermon, en all 'long I jes see Phillis wras'lin' wid 'erse'f, en I say, 'She got to come *dis* night, de Lohd he'pin' me.' En I had n' mo' 'n said de word, 'fo' she jes walked down en guv me 'er han'.

"Den we had de baptizin' in Elkhorn Creek, en de watter wuz deep en de curren' tol'ble swif'. Hit look to me like dere wuz five hundred uv um on de creek side. By-en-by I stood on de edge o' de watter, en Phillis she come down to let me baptize 'er. En me en 'er j'ined han's en waded out in the creek, mighty slow, caze Phillis didn' have no shot roun' de bottom uv 'er dress, en it kep' bobbin' on top de watter till I pushed it down. But by-en-by we got 'way out in de creek, en bof uv us wuz tremblin'. En I says to 'er ve'y kin'ly, 'When I put you un'er de watter, Phillis, you mus' try en hole yo'se'f stiff, so I can lif' you up easy.' But I hadn't mo' 'n jes got 'er laid back over de watter ready to souze 'er un'er when 'er feet flew up off de bottom uv de creek, en when I retched out to fetch 'er up, I stepped in a hole; en 'fo' I knowed it, we wuz flounderin' roun' in de watter, en de hymn dey was singin' on de bank sounded mighty confused-like. En Phillis she swallowed some watter, en all 't oncet she jes grap me right tight roun' de neck, en say mighty quick, says she, 'I gwine marry whoever gits me out'n dis yere watter!'

"En by-en-by, when me en 'er wuz walkin' up de bank o' de creek, drippin' all over, I says to 'er, says I:

"'Does you 'member what you said back yon'er in de watter, Phillis?'

"'I ain' out'n no watter yit,' says she, ve'y contemptuous.

"'When does you consider yo'se'f out'n de watter?' says I, ve'y humble.

"'When I git dese soakin' clo'es off'n my back,' says she.

"Hit wuz good dark when we got home, en atter a while I crope up to de dooh o' Phillis's cabin en put my eye down to de key-hole, en see Phillis jes settin' 'fo' dem blazin' walnut logs dressed up in 'er new red linsey dress, en 'er eyes shinin'. En I shuk so I 'mos' faint. Den I tap easy on de dooh, en say in a mighty tremblin' tone, says I:

"'Is you out'n de watter yit, Phillis?'

"'I got on dry dress,' says she.

"'Does you 'member what you said back yon'er in de watter, Phillis?' says I.

"'De latch-string on de outside de dooh,' says she, mighty sof'.

"En I walked in."

As Peter drew near the end of this reminiscence, his voice sank to a key of inimitable tenderness; and when it was ended he stood a few minutes, scraping the gravel with the toe of his boot, his head dropped forward. Then he added, huskily:

"Phillis been dead heap o' years now;" and turned away.

This recalling of the scenes of a time long gone by may have awakened in the breast of the colonel some gentle memory; for after Peter was gone he continued to sit a while in silent musing. Then getting up, he walked in the falling twilight across the yard and through the gardens until he came to a secluded spot in the most distant corner. There he stooped or rather knelt down and passed his hands, as though with mute benediction, over a little bed of old-fashioned China pinks. When he had moved in from the country he had brought nothing away from his mother's garden but these, and in all the years since no one had ever pulled them, as Peter well knew; for one day the colonel had said, with his face turned away:

"Let them have all the flowers they want; but leave the pinks."

He continued kneeling over them now, touching them softly with his fingers, as though they were the fragrant, never-changing symbols of voiceless communion with his past. Still it may have been only the early dew of the evening that glistened on them when he rose and slowly walked away, leaving the pale moonbeams to haunt the spot.

Certainly after this day he showed increasing concern in the young lovers who were holding clandestine meetings in his grounds.

"Peter," he would say, "why, if they love each other, don't they get married? Something may happen."

"I been spectin' some'n' to happ'n fur some time, ez dey been quar'lin' right smart lately," replied Peter, laughing.

Whether or not he was justified in this prediction, before the end of another week the colonel read a notice of their elopement and marriage; and several days later he came up from down-town and told Peter that everything had been forgiven the young pair, who had gone to house-keeping in the country. It gave him pleasure to think he had helped to perpetuate the race of blue-grass farmers.

## THE YEARNING PASSED AWAY

It was in the twilight of a late autumn day in the same year that nature gave the colonel the first direct intimation to prepare for the last summons. They had been passing along the garden walks, where a few pale flowers were trying to flourish up to the very winter's edge, and where the dry leaves had gathered unswept and rustled beneath their feet. All at once the colonel turned to Peter, who was a yard and a half behind, as usual, and said:

"Give me your arm, Peter, I feel tired;" and thus the two, for the first time in all their lifetime walking abreast, passed slowly on.

"Peter," said the colonel, gravely, a minute or two later, "we are like two dried-up stalks of fodder. I wonder the Lord lets us live any longer."

"I reck'n He's managin' to use us *some* way, or we wouldn' be heah," said Peter.

"Well, all I have to say is, that if He's using me, He can't be in much of a hurry for his work," replied the colonel.

"He uses snails, en I *know* we ain' ez slow ez *dem*," argued Peter, composedly.

"I don't know. I think a snail must have made more progress since the war than I have."

The idea of his uselessness seemed to weigh on him, for a little later he remarked, with a sort of mortified smile:

"Do you think, Peter, that we would pass for what they call representative men of the New South?"

"We done *had* ou' day, Marse Rom" replied Peter.

"We got to pass fur what we *wuz*. Mebbe de *Lohd's* got mo' use fur us yit 'n *people* has," he added, after a pause.

From this time on the colonel's strength gradually failed him; but it was not until the following spring that the end came.

A night or two before his death his mind wandered backward, after the familiar manner of the dying, and his delirious dreams showed the shifting, faded pictures that renewed themselves for the last time on his wasting memory. It must have been that he was once more amid the scenes of his active farm life, for his broken snatches of talk ran thus:

"Come, boys, get your cradles! Look where the sun is! You are late getting to work this morning. That is the finest field of wheat in the county. Be careful about the bundles! Make them the same size and tie them tight. That swath is too wide, and you don't hold your cradle right, Tom. . . .

"*Sell Peter! Sell Peter Cotton!* No sir! You might buy *me* some day and work *me* in your cotton-field; but as long as he's mine, you can't buy Peter, and you can't buy any of *my* negroes. . . .

"Boys! boys! If you don't work faster, you won't finish this field to-day. . . . You'd better go in the shade and rest now. The sun's very hot. Don't drink too much ice-water. There's a jug of whisky in the fence-corner. Give them a good dram around, and tell them to work slow till the sun gets lower.". . .

Once during the night a sweet smile played over his features as he repeated a few words that were part of an old rustic song and dance. Arranged, not as they came broken and incoherent from his lips, but as he once had sung them, they were as follows:

"O Sister Phoebe! How merry were we

When we sat under the juniper-tree,

The juniper-tree, heigho!

Put this hat on your head! Keep your head warm:

Take a sweet kiss! It will do you no harm,

Do you no harm, I know!"

After this he sank into a quieter sleep, but soon stirred with a look of intense pain.

"Helen! Helen!" he murmured. "Will you break your promise? Have you changed in your feelings towards me? I have brought you the pinks. Won't you take the pinks, Helen?"

Then he sighed as he added, "It wasn't her fault. If she had only known--"

Who was the Helen of that far-away time? Was this colonel's love-story?

But during all the night, whithersoever his mind wandered, at intervals it returned to the burden of a single strain -- the harvesting. Towards daybreak he took it up again for the last time:

"O boys, boys, *boys*! If you don't work faster you won't finish the field to-day. Look how low the sun is!. . . I am going to the house. They can't finish the field to-day. Let them do what they can, but don't let them work late. I want Peter to go to the house with me. Tell him to come on.". . .

In the faint gray of the morning, Peter, who had been watching by the bedside all night, stole out of the room, and going into the garden pulled a handful of pinks -- a thing he had never done before -- and, re-entering the colonel's bedroom, put them in a vase near his sleeping face. Soon afterwards the colonel opened his eyes and looked around him. At the foot of the bed stood Peter, and on one side sat the physician and a friend. The night-lamp burned low, and through the folds of the curtains came the white light of early day.

"Put out the lamp and open the curtains," he said, feebly. "It's day." When they had drawn the curtains aside, his eyes fell on the pinks, sweet and fresh with the dew on them. He stretched out his hand and touched them caressingly, and his eyes sought Peter's with a look of grateful understanding.

"I want to be alone with Peter for a while," he said, turning his face towards the others.

When they were left alone, it was some minutes before anything was said. Peter, not knowing what he did, but knowing what was coming, had gone to the window and hid himself behind the curtains, drawing them tightly around his form as though to shroud himself from sorrow.

At length the colonel said, "Come here!"

Peter, almost staggering forward, fell at the foot of the bed, and, clasping the colonel's feet with one arm, pressed his cheek against them.

"Come closer!"

Peter crept on his knees and buried his head on the colonel's thigh.

"Come up here -- *closer*;" and putting one arm around Peter's neck he laid the other hand softly on his head, and looked long and tenderly into his eyes. "I've got to leave you, Peter. Don't you feel sorry for me?"

"Oh, Marse Rom! cried Peter, hiding his face, his whole form shaken by sobs.

"Peter," added, the colonel with ineffable gentleness, "if I had served my Master as faithfully as you have served yours, I should not feel ashamed to stand in his presence."

"If my Marseter is ez mussiful to me ez you have been--"

"I have fixed things so that you will be comfortable after I am gone. When your time comes, I should like you to be laid close to me. We can take the long sleep together. Are you willing?"

"That's whar I want to be laid."

The colonel stretched out his hand to the vase, and taking the bunch of pinks, said very calmly:

"Leave these in my hand; I'll carry them with me." A moment more, and he added:

"If I shouldn't wake up any more, good-bye, Peter!"

"Good-bye, Marse Rom!"

And they shook hands a long time. After this the colonel lay back on the pillows. His soft, silvery hair contrasted strongly with his child-like, unspoiled, open face. To the day of his death, as is apt to be true of those who have lived pure lives but never married, he had a boyish strain in him -- a softness of nature, showing itself even now in the gentle expression of his mouth. His brown eyes had in them the same boyish look when, just as he was falling asleep, he scarcely opened them to say:

"Pray, Peter."

Peter, on his knees, and looking across the colonel's face towards the open door, through which the rays of the rising sun streamed in upon his hoary head, prayed, while the colonel fell asleep, adding a few words for himself now left alone.

Several hours later, memory led the colonel back again through the dim gate-way of the past and out of that gate-way his spirit finally took flight into the future.

Peter lingered a year. The place went to the colonel's sister, but he was allowed to remain in his quarters. With much thinking of the past, his mind fell into a lightness and a weakness. Sometimes he would be heard crooning the burden of old hymns, or sometimes seen sitting beside the old brass-nailed trunk, fumbling with the spelling-book and *The Pilgrim's Progress*. Often, too, he walked out to the cemetery on the edge of the town, and each time could hardly find the colonel's grave amid the multitude of the dead.

One gusty day in spring, the Scotch sexton, busy with the blades of blue-grass springing from the animated mould, saw his familiar figure standing motionless beside the colonel's resting-place. He had taken off his hat -- one of the colonel's last bequests -- and laid it on the colonel's head-stone. On his body he wore a strange coat of faded blue, patched and weather-stained, and so moth-eaten that parts of the curious tails had dropped entirely away. In one hand he held an open Bible, and on a much-soiled page he was pointing with his finger to the following words:

"I would not have you ignorant, brethren, concerning them which are asleep."

It would seem that, impelled by love and faith, and guided by his wandering reason, he had come forth to preach his last sermon on the immortality of the soul over the dust of his dead master.

The sexton led him home, and soon afterwards a friend, who had loved them both, laid him beside the colonel.

It was perhaps fitting that his winding-sheet should be the vestment in which, years agone, he had preached to his fellow-slaves in bondage; for if it so be that the dead of this planet shall come forth from their graves clad in the trappings of mortality, then Peter should arise on the Resurrection Day wearing his old jeans coat.

# Australia

Originally settled as a land for the exiled, Australia has, perhaps for this reason, developed a literature often preoccupied with questions of personal and national identity and conformity. Literary Australia is split between the city dwellers who find the countryside hostile and their rural neighbors who shun metropolitan life in favor of wild terrain and the romance of wilderness. Henry Lawson's "Send Round the Hat," full of cultural jargon and colloquialisms, expsoses the moral core beneath the coarse exterior of bush life.

## Send Round The Hat
### *Henry Lawson*

**Henry Lawson  1887-1922:**  Henry Lawson grew up in the Australian bush country. His father was a laborer. Though Lawson received only a few years of formal schooling, his mother read to her children and encouraged Henry, the eldest, to pursue his literary ambitions. Louise Lawson, in fact, has been credited with being the force behind Lawson's development as a literary artist. She read to her children and encouraged Henry, the eldest, to pursue his ambitions.

Lawson was influenced by such writers as Dickens, Harte, and Twain. Some of his characters are from the city, some are from the bush. He wrote, from within each character's experience, about the challenges of existence in a fledgling society.

Lawson was known first as a poet, until he published his first collection of stories, *Short Stories in Prose and Verse,* in 1894. This volume contained "The Drover's Wife," which received much attention and acclaim, though his writing began to decline following a bout with alcoholism and an attempted suicide.

*Now this is the creed from the Book of the Bush--*
*Should be simple and plain to aჟunce:*
*'If a man's in a hole you must pass round the hat--*
*Were he jail-bird or gentleman once.'*

'IS IT ANY harm to wake yer?'

It was about nine o'clock in the morning, and, though it was Sunday morning, it was no harm to wake me; but the shearer had mistaken me for a deaf jackeroo, who was staying at the shanty and was something like me, and had good-naturedly shouted almost at the top of his voice, and he woke the whole shanty. Anyway he woke three or four others who were sleeping on beds and stretchers, and one on a shakedown on the floor, in the same room. It had been a wet night, and the shanty was full of shearers from Big Billabong Shed which had cut-out the day before. My room-mates had been drinking and gambling overnight, and they swore luridly at the intruder for disturbing them.

He was six-foot-three or thereabout. He was loosely built, bony, sandy-complexioned and grey-eyed. He wore a good-humoured grin at most times, as I noticed later on; he was of a type of bushman that I always liked -- the sort that seem to get more good-natured the longer they grow, yet are hard-knuckled and would accommodate a man who wanted to fight, or thrash a bully in a good-natured way. The sort that like to carry somebody's baby round, and cut wood, carry water and do little things for overworked married bushwomen. He wore a saddle-tweed sac suit two sizes too small for him, and his face, neck, great hands and bony wrists were covered with sun-blotches and freckles.

'I hope I ain't disturbin' yer,' he shouted, as he bent over my bunk, 'but there's a cove----'

'You needn't shout!' I interrupted, 'I'm not deaf.'

'Oh -- I beg your pardon!' he shouted. 'I didn't know I was yellin'. I thought you was the deaf feller.'

'Oh, that's all right,' I said. 'What's the trouble?'

'Wait till them other chaps is done swearin' and I'll tell yer,' he said. He spoke with a quiet, good-natured drawl, with something of the nasal twang, but tone and drawl distinctly Australian -- altogether apart from that of the Americans.

'Oh, spit it out for Christ's sake, Long-un!' yelled One-eyed Bogan, who had been the worst swearer in a rough shed, and he fell back on his bunk as if his previous remarks had exhausted him.

'It's that there sick jackeroo that was pickin'-up at Big Billabong,' said the Giraffe. 'He had to knock off the first week, an' he's been here ever since. They're sendin' him away to the hospital in Sydney by the speeshall train. They're just goin' to take him up in the wagonette to the railway

station, an' I thought I might as well go round with the hat an' get him a
few bob. He's got a missus and kids in Sydney.'

'Yer always goin' round with yer gory hat!' growled Bogan. 'Yer'd
blanky well take it round in hell!'

'That's what he's doing, Bogan,' muttered Gentleman Once, on the
shakedown, with his face to the wall.

The hat was a genuine 'cabbage tree', one of the sort that 'last a
lifetime'. It was well coloured, almost black in fact with weather and age,
and it had a new strap round the base of the crown. I looked into it and
saw a dirty pound note and some silver. I dropped in half a crown, which
was more than I could spare, for I had only been a green hand at Big
Billabong.

'Thank yer!' he said. 'Now then, you fellers!'

'I wish you'd keep your hat on your head, and your money in your
pockets and your sympathy somewhere else,' growled Jack Moonlight as
he raised himself painfully on his elbow and felt under his pillow for two
half-crowns. 'Here,' he said, 'here's two half-casers. Chuck 'em in and let
me sleep for God's sake!'

Gentleman Once, the gambler, rolled round on his shakedown, bringing his good-looking, dissipated face from the wall. He had turned in in
his clothes and, with considerable exertion, he shoved his hand down into
the pocket of his trousers, which were a tight fit. He brought up a roll of
pound notes and could find no silver.

'Here,' he said to the Giraffe, ' I might as well lay a quid. I'll chance it
anyhow. Chuck it in.'

'You've got rats this mornin', Gentleman Once,' growled the Bogan.
'It ain't a blanky horse race.'

'P'r'aps I have,' said Gentleman Once, and he turned to the wall again
with his head on his arm.

'Now, Bogan, yer might as well chuck in somethin', said the Giraffe.

'What's the matter with the ---- jackeroo?' asked the Bogan, tugging
his trousers from under the mattress.

Moonlight said something in a low tone.

'The ---- he has!' said Bogan. 'Well, I pity the ----! Here, I'll chuck in
half a ---- quid!' and he dropped half a sovereign into the hat.

The fourth man, who was known to his face as 'Barcoo-Rot', and behind his back as 'The Mean Man', had been drinking all night, and not even Bogan's stump-splitting adjectives could rouse him. So Bogan got out of bed, and calling on us (as blanky female cattle) to witness what he was about to do, he rolled the drunkard over, prospected his pockets till he made up five shillings (or a 'caser' in bush language), and 'chucked' them into the hat.

And Barcoo-Rot is probably unconscious to this day that he was ever connected with an act of charity.

The Giraffe struck the deaf jackeroo in the next room. I heard the chaps cursing 'Long-'un' for waking them, and 'Deaf-'un' for being, as they thought at first, the indirect cause of the disturbance. I heard the Giraffe and his hat being condemned in other rooms and cursed along the veranda where more shearers were sleeping; and after a while I turned out.

The Giraffe was carefully fixing a mattress and pillows on the floor of a wagonette, and presently a man, who looked like a corpse, was carried out and lifted into the trap.

As the wagonette started, the shanty keeper -- a fat, soulless-looking man -- put his hand in his pocket and dropped a quid into the hat which was still going round, in the hands of the Giraffe's mate, little Teddy Thompson, who was as far below medium height as the Giraffe was above it.

The Giraffe took the horse's head and led him along on the most level parts of the road towards the railway station, and two or three chaps went along to help get the sick man into the train.

The shearing season was over in that district, but I got a job of house painting, which was my trade, at the Great Western Hotel (a two storey brick place), and I stayed in Bourke for a couple of months.

The Giraffe was a Victorian native from Bendigo. He was well known in Bourke and to many shearers who came through the great dry scrubs from hundreds of miles round. He was stakeholder, drunkard's banker, peacemaker where possible, referee or second to oblige the chaps when a fight was on, big brother or uncle to most of the children in town, final court of appeal when the youngsters had a dispute over a foot-race at the school picnic, referee at their fights, and he was the stranger's friend.

'The feller as knows can battle around for himself,' he'd say. 'But I always like to do what I can for a hard-up stranger cove. I was a green-hand jackeroo once meself, and I know what it is.'

'You're always bothering about other people, Giraffe,' said Tom Hall, the Shearers' Union Secretary, who was only a couple of inches shorter than the Giraffe. 'There's nothing in it, you can take it from me -- I ought to know.'

'Well, what's a feller to do?' said the Giraffe. 'I'm only hangin' round here till shearin' starts agen, an' a cove might as well be doin' something. Besides, it ain't as if I was like a cove that had old people or a wife an' kids to look after. I ain't got no responsibilities. A feller can't be doin' nothin'. Besides, I like to lend a helpin' hand when I can.'

'Well, all I've got to say,' said Tom, most of whose screw went in borrowed quids, etc.--'all I've got to say is that you'll get no thanks, and you might blanky well starve in the end.'

'There ain't no fear of me starvin' so long as I've got me hands about me; an' I ain't a cove as wants thanks,' said the Giraffe.

He was always helping someone or something. Now it was a bit of a 'darnce' that he was gettin' up for the girls; again it was Mrs. Smith, the woman whose husban' was drowned in the flood in the Bogan River lars' Crismas, or that there poor woman down by the Billagong -- her husban' cleared out and left her with a lot o' kids. Or Bill Something, the bullocky, who was run over by his own wagon, while he was drunk, and got his leg broke.

Toward the end of his spree One-eyed Bogan broke loose and smashed nearly all the windows of the Carriers' Arms, and next morning he was fined heavily at the police court. About dinner-time I encountered the Giraffe and his hat, with two half-crowns in it for a start.

'I'm sorry to trouble yer,' he said, 'but One-eyed Bogan carn't pay his fine, an' I thought we might fix it up for him. He ain't half a bad sort of feller when he ain't drinkin'. It's only when he gets too much booze in him.'

After shearing, the hat usually started round with the Giraffe's own dirty crumpled pound note in the bottom of it as a send-off, later on it was half a sovereign, and so on down to half a crown and a shilling, as he got short of stuff; till in the end he would borrow a 'few bob' -- which he always repaid after next shearing--'just to start the thing goin''.

There were several yarns about him and his hat. 'Twas said that the hat had belonged to his father, whom he resembled in every respect, and it had been going round for so many years that the crown was worn as thin as paper by the quids, half-quids, casers, half-casers, bobs and tanners or sprats -- to say nothing of the scrums -- that had been chucked into it in its time and shaken up.

They say that when a new governor visited Bourke the Giraffe happened to be standing on the platform close to the exit, grinning good-humouredly, and the local toady nudged him urgently and said in an awful whisper, 'Take off your hat! Why don't you take off your hat?'

'Why?' drawled the Giraffe; 'he ain't hard up, is he?'

And they fondly cherish an anecdote to the effect that, when the One-Man-One-Vote Bill was passed (or Payment of Members, or when the first Labour Party went in -- I forget on which occasion they said it was), the Giraffe was carried away by the general enthusiasm, got a few beers in him, 'chucked' a quid into his hat, and sent it round. The boys contributed by force of habit, and contributed largely, because of the victory and the beer. And when the hat came back to the Giraffe he stood holding it in front of him with both hands and stared blankly into it for a while. Then it dawned on him.

'Blowed if I haven't bin an' gone an' took up a bloomin' collection for meself!' he said.

He was almost a teetotaller, but he stood his shout in reason. He mostly drank ginger-beer.

'I ain't a feller that boozes, but I ain't got nothin' agen chaps enjoyin' themselves, so long as they don't go too far.'

It was common for a man on the spree to say to him:

'Here! here's five quid. Look after it for me, Giraffe, will yer, till I git off the booze.'

His real name was Bob Brothers, and his bush names, 'Long-'un', 'The Giraffe', 'Send-round-the-hat', 'Chuck-in-a-bob', and 'Ginger-ale'.

Some years before, camels and Afghan drivers had been imported to the Bourke district; the camels did very well in the dry country, they went right across country and carried everything from sardines to flooring boards. And the teamsters loved the Afghans nearly as much as Sydney furniture makers love the cheap Chinese in the same line. They loved 'em even as union shearers on strike love blacklegs brought up-country to take their places.

Now the Giraffe was a good, straight unionist, but in cases of sickness or trouble he was as apt to forget his unionism, as all bushmen are, at all times (and for all time), to forget their creed. So, one evening, the Giraffe blundered into the Carriers' Arms -- of all places in the world -- when it was full of teamsters; he had his hat in his hand and some small silver and coppers in it.

'I say, you fellers, there's a poor, sick Afghan in the camp down there along the----'

A big, brawny bullock driver took him firmly by the shoulders, or rather by the elbows, and ran him out before any damage was done. The Giraffe took it as he took most things, good-humouredly; but, about dusk, he was seen slipping down towards the Afghan camp with a billy of soup.

'I believe,' remarked Tom Hall, 'that when the Giraffe goes to heaven -- and he's the only one of us, as far as I can see, that has a ghost of a show -- I believe that when he goes to heaven, the first thing he'll do will be to take his infernal hat round amongst the angels -- getting up a collection for this damned world that he left behind.'

'Well, I don't think there's so much to his credit, after all,' said Jack Mitchell, shearer. 'You see, the Giraffe is ambitious; he likes public life, and that accounts for him shoving himself forward with his collections. As for bothering about people in trouble, that's only common curiosity; he's one of those chaps that are always shoving their nose into other people's troubles. And as for looking after sick men -- why! there's nothing the Giraffe likes better than pottering round a sick man, and watching him and studying him. He's awfully interested in sick men, and they're pretty scarce out here. I tell you there's nothing he likes better -- except, maybe, it's pottering round a corpse. I believe he'd ride forty miles to help and sympathize and potter round a funeral. The fact of the matter is that the Giraffe is only enjoying himself with other people's troubles -- that's all it is. It's only vulgar curiosity and selfishness. I set it down to his ignorance; the way he was brought up.'

A few days after the Afghan incident the Giraffe and his hat had a run of luck. A German, one of a party who were building a new wooden bridge over the Big Billabong, was helping unload some girders from a truck at the railway station, when a big log slipped on the skids and his leg was smashed badly. They carried him to the Carriers' Arms, which was the nearest hotel, and into a bedroom behind the bar, and sent for the doctor. The Giraffe was in evidence as usual.

'It vas not dat at all,' said German Charlie, when they asked him if he was in much pain. 'It vas not dat at all. I don't cares a damn for der bain;

but dis is der tird year -- und I vas going home dis year after der gontract -- und der contract yoost commence!'

That was the burden of his song all through, between his groans.

There were a good few chaps sitting quietly about the bar and veranda when the doctor arrived. The Giraffe was sitting at the end of the counter, on which he had laid his hat while he wiped his face, neck and forehead with a big speckled 'sweat-rag'. It was a very hot day.

The doctor, a good-hearted young Australian, was heard saying something. Then German Charlie, in a voice that rung with pain:

'Make dat leg right, doctor -- quick! Dis is der tird pluddy year -- und I must go home!'

The doctor asked him if he was in great pain.

'Neffer mind der pluddy bain, doctor! Neffer mind der pluddy bain! Dot vas nossing. Make dat leg well quick, doctor. Dis vas der last gontract, and I vas going home dis year.' Then the words jerked out of him by physical agony: 'Der girl vas vajting dree year, und -- by Got! I must go home.'

The publican -- Watty Braithwaite, known as 'Watty Broadweight' or, more familiarly, 'Watty Bothways' -- turned over the Giraffe's hat in a tired, bored sort of way, dropped a quid into it, and nodded resignedly at the Giraffe.

The Giraffe caught up the hint and the hat with alacrity. The hat went all round town, so to speak; and, as soon as his leg was firm enough not to come loose on the road, German Charlie went home.

It was well known that I contributed to the *Sydney Bulletin* and several other papers. The Giraffe's bump of reverence was very large, and swelled especially for sick men and poets. He treated me with much more respect than is due from a bushman to a man, and with an odd sort of extra gentleness, I sometimes fancied. But one day he rather surprised me.

'I'm sorry to trouble yer,' he said in a shamefaced way. 'I don't know as you go in for sportin', but One-eyed Bogan an' Barcoo-Rot is goin' to have a bit of a scrap down the Billybong this evenin', an'----'

'A bit of a what?' I asked.

'A bit of fight to a finish,' he said apologetically. 'An' the chaps is tryin' to finish up a fiver to put some life into the thing. There's bad blood between One-eyed Bogan and Barcoo-Rot, an' it won't do them any harm to have it out.'

It was a great fight, I remember. There must have been a couple of score blood-soaked handkerchiefs (or 'sweat-rags') buried in a hole on the field of battle, and the Giraffe was busy the rest of the evening helping to patch up the principals. Later on he took up a small collection for the loser, who happened to be Barcoo-Rot in spite of the advantage of an eye.

The Salvation Army lassie, who went round with the *War Cry*, nearly always sold the Giraffe three copies.

A new-chum parson, who wanted a subscription to build or enlarge a chapel, or something, sought the assistance of the Giraffe's influence with his mates.

'Well,' said the Giraffe, 'I ain't a churchgoer meself. I ain't what you might call a religious cove, but I'll be glad to do what I can to help yer. I don't suppose I can do much. I ain't been to church since I was a kiddy.'

The parson was shocked, but later on he learned to appreciate the Giraffe and his mates, and to love Australia for the bushman's sake, and it was he who told me the above anecdote.

The Giraffe helped fix some stalls for a Catholic church bazaar, and some of the chaps chaffed him about it in the union office.

'You'll be taking up a collection for a Joss-House down in the Chinamen's camp next,' said Tom Hall in conclusion.

'Well, I ain't got nothin' agen the Roming Carflics,' said the Giraffe. 'An' Father O'Donovan's a very decent sort of cove. He stuck up for the unions all right in the strike anyway.' ('He wouldn't be Irish if he wasn't,' someone commented.) 'I carried swags once for six months with a feller that was a Carflick, an' he was a very straight feller. And a girl I knowed turned Carflick to marry a chap that had got her into trouble, an' she was always jes' the same to me after as she was before. Besides, I like to help everything that's goin' on.'

Tom Hall and one or two others went out hurriedly to have a drink. But we all loved the Giraffe.

He was very innocent and very humorous, especially when he meant to be most serious and philosophical.

'Some of them bush girls is regular tomboys,' he said to me solemnly one day. 'Some of them is too cheeky altogether. I remember once I was stoppin' at a place -- they was sort of relations o' mine -- an' they put me to sleep in a room off the verander, where there was a glass door an' no blinds. An' the first mornin' the girls -- they was sort o' cousins o' mine --

they come gigglin' and foolin' round outside the door on the verander, an' kep' me in bed till nearly ten o'clock. I had to put me trowsis on under the bed-clothes in the end. But I got back on 'em the next night,' he reflected.

'How did you do that, Bob?' I asked.

'Why, I went to bed in me trowsis!'

One day I was on a plank, painting the ceiling of the bar of the Great Western Hotel. I was anxious to get the job finished. The work had been kept back most of the day by chaps handing up long beers to me, and drawing my attention to the alleged fact that I was putting on the paint wrong side out. I was slapping it all over the last few boards when--

'I'm very sorry to trouble yer; I always seem to be troublin' yer; but there's that there woman and them girls----'

I looked down -- about the first time I had looked down on him -- and there was the Giraffe, with his hat brim up on the plank and two half-crowns in it.

'Oh, that's all right, Bob,' I said, and I dropped in half a crown.

There were shearers in the bar, and presently there was some barrack-ing. It appeared that that there woman and them girls were strange women, in the local as well as the Biblical sense of the word, who had come from Sydney at the end of the shearing season, and had taken a cottage on the edge of the scrub on the outskirts of the town. There had been trouble this week in connexion with a row at their establishment, and they had been fined, warned off by the police, and turned out by their landlord.

'This is a bit too red-hot, Giraffe,' said one of the shearers. 'Them ----s made enough out of us coves. They've got plenty of stuff, don't you fret. Let 'em go to ----! I'm blanked if I give a sprat.'

'They ain't got their fares to Sydney,' said the Giraffe. 'An', what's more, the little 'un is sick, an' two of them has kids in Sydney.'

'How the ---- do you know?'

'Why, one of 'em come to me an' told me all about it.'

There was an involuntary guffaw.

'Look here, Bob,' said Billy Woods, the Rouse-about's Secretary, kindly. 'Don't you make a fool of yourself. You'll have all the chaps laughing at you. Those girls are only working you for all you're worth. I suppose one of 'em came crying and whining to you. Don't you bother about them. *You* don't know them; they can pump water at a moment's notice. You haven't had any experience with women yet, Bob.'

'She didn't come whinin' and cryin' to me' said the Giraffe, dropping his twanging drawl a little. 'She looked me straight in the face an' told me all about it.'

'I say, Giraffe,' said Box-o'-Tricks, 'what have you been doin'? You've bin down there on the nod. I'm surprised at yer, Giraffe.'

'An' he pretend to be so gory soft an' innocent too,' growled the Bogan. 'We know all about you, Giraffe.'

'Look here, Giraffe,' said Mitchell the shearer. 'I'd never have thought it of you. We all thought you were the only virgin youth west the river; I always thought you were a moral young man. You mustn't think that because your conscience is pricking you everyone else's is.'

'I ain't had anythin' to do with them,' said the Giraffe, drawling again. 'I ain't a cove that goes in for that sort of thing. But other chaps has, and I think they might as well help 'em out of their fix.'

'They're a rotten crowd,' said Billy Woods. 'You don't know them, Bob. Don't bother about them -- they're not worth it. Put your money in your pocket. You'll find a better use for it before next shearing.'

'Better shout, Giraffe,' said Box-o'-Tricks.

Now in spite of the Giraffe's softness he was the hardest man in Bourke to move when he'd decided on what he thought was 'the fair thing to do'. Another peculiarity of his was that on occasion, such for instance as 'sayin' a few words' at a strike meeting, he would straighten himself, drop the twang, and rope in his drawl, so to speak.

'Well, look here, you chaps,' he said now. 'I don't know anything about them women. I s'pose they're bad, but I don't suppose they're worse than men has made them. All I know is that there's four women turned out, without any stuff, and every woman in Bourke, an' the police, an' the law agen 'em. An' the fact that they is women is agenst 'em most of all. You don't expect 'em to hump their swags to Sydney! Why, only I ain't got the stuff I wouldn't trouble yer. I'd pay their fares meself. Look,' he said, lowering his voice, 'there they are now, an' one of the girls is cryin'. Don't let 'em see yer lookin'.'

I dropped softly from the plank and peeped out with the rest.

They stood by the fence on the opposite side of the street, a bit up towards the railway station, with their portmanteaux and bundles at their feet. One girl leant with her arms on the fence rail and her face buried in them, another was trying to comfort her. The third girl and the woman stood facing our way. The woman was good-looking; she had a hard face, but it might have been made hard. The third girl seemed half defiant, half inclined to cry. Presently she went to the other side of the girl who was crying on the fence and put her arm round her shoulder. The woman suddenly turned her back on us and stood looking away over the paddocks.

The hat went round. Billy Woods was first, then Box-o'-Tricks, and then Mitchell.

Billy contributed with eloquent silence. 'I was only jokin', Giraffe,' said Box-o'-Tricks, dredging his pockets for a couple of shillings. It was some time after the shearing, and most of the chaps were hard up.

'Ah, well,' sighed Mitchell. 'There's no help for it. If the Giraffe would take up a collection to import some decent girls to this God-forgotten hole there might be some sense in it. ... It's bad enough for the Giraffe to undermine our religious prejudices, and tempt us to take a morbid interest in sick chows and Afghans, and blacklegs and widows; but when he starts mixing us up with strange women it's time to buck.' And he prospected his pockets and contributed two shillings, some odd pennies, and a pinch of tobacco dust.

'I don't mind helping the girls, but I'm damned if I'll give a penny to help the old ----,' said Tom Hall.

'Well, she was a girl once herself,' drawled the Giraffe.

The Giraffe went round to the other pubs and to the union offices, and when he returned he seemed satisfied with the plate, but troubled about something else.

'I don't know what to do for them for to-night,' he said. 'None of the pubs or boardin'-houses will hear of them, an' there ain't no empty houses, an' the women is all agen 'em.'

'Not all,' said Alice, the big, handsome barmaid from Sydney. 'Come here, Bob.' She gave the Giraffe half a sovereign and a look for which some of us would have paid him ten pounds -- had we had the money, and had the look been transferable.

'Wait a minute, Bob,' she said, and she went in to speak to the landlord.

'There's an empty bedroom at the end of the store in the yard,' she said when she came back. 'They can camp there for to-night if they behave themselves. You'd better tell 'em Bob.'

'Thank yer, Alice,' said the Giraffe.

Next day, after work, the Giraffe and I drifted together and down by the river in the cool of the evening, and sat on the edge of the steep, drought-parched bank.

'I heard you saw your lady-friends off this morning, Bob,' I said, and was sorry I said it, even before he answered.

'Oh, they ain't no friends of mine,' he said. 'Only four poor devils of women. I thought they mightn't like to stand waitin' with the crowd on the platform, so I jest offered to get their tickets an' told 'em to wait round at the back of the station till the bell rung. ... An' what do yer think they did, Harry?' he went on, with an exasperatingly unintelligent grin. 'Why, they wanted to kiss me.'

'Did they?'

'Yes. An' they would have done it, too, if I hadn't been so long. ... Why, I'm blessed if they didn't kiss my hands.'

'You don't say so.'

'God's truth. Somehow I didn't like to go on the platform with them after that; besides they was cryin', and I can't stand women cryin'. But some of the chaps put them into an empty carriage.' He thought a moment. Then:

'There's some terrible good-hearted fellers in the world,' he reflected.

I thought so too.

'Bob,' I said, 'you're a single man. Why don't you get married and settle down?'

'Well,' he said, 'I ain't got no wife an' kids, that's a fact. But it ain't my fault.'

He may have been right about the wife. But I thought of the look that Alice had given him, and ----

'Girls seem to like me right enough,' he said, 'but it don' t go no further than that. The trouble is that I'm so long, and I always seem to get shook after little girls. At least there was one little girl in Bendigo that I was properly gone on.'

'And wouldn't she have you?'

'Well, it seems not.'

'Did you ask her?'

'Oh, yes, I asked her right enough.'

'Well, and what did she say?'

'She said it would be rediçilus for her to be seen trottin' alongside of a chimbley like me.'

'Perhaps she didn't mean that. There are any amount of little women who like tall men.'

'I thought of that too -- afterwards. P'r'aps she didn't mean it that way. I s'pose the fact of the matter was that she didn't cotton on to me, and wanted to let me down easy. She didn't want to hurt me feelin's, if yer understand -- she was a very good-hearted little girl. There's some terrible tall fellers where I come from, and I know two as married little girls.'

He seemed a hopeless case.

'Sometimes,' he said, ' sometimes I wish that I wasn't so blessed long.'

'There's that there deaf jackeroo,' he reflected presently. 'He's something in the same fix about girls as I am. He's too deaf and I'm too long.'

'How do you make that out?' I asked. 'He's got three girls, to my knowledge, and as for being deaf, why, he gasses more than any man in the town, and knows more of what's going on than old Mother Brindle the washerwoman.'

'Well, look at that now!' said the Giraffe slowly. 'Who'd have thought it? He never told me he had three girls, an' as for hearin' news, I always tell him anything that's goin' on that I think he doesn't catch. He told me his trouble was that whenever he went out with a girl people could hear what they was sayin' -- at least they could hear what she was sayin' to him, an' draw their own conclusions, he said. He said he went out one night with a girl, and some of the chaps foxed 'em an' heard her sayin' "don't" to him, an' put it all round town.'

'What did she say "don't" for?' I asked.

'He didn't tell me that, but I s'pose he was kissin' her or huggin' her or something.'

'Bob,' I said presently, 'didn't you try the little girl in Bendigo a second time?'

'No,' he said. 'What was the use? She was a good little girl, and I wasn't goin' to go botherin' her. I ain't the sort of cove that goes hangin' round where he isn't wanted. But somehow I couldn't stay about Bendigo after she gave me the hint, so I thought I'd come over an' have a knock round on this side for a year or two.'

'And you never wrote to her?'

'No. What was the use of goin' pesterin' her with letters? I know what trouble letters give me when I have to answer one. She'd have only had to tell me the straight truth in a letter an' it wouldn't have done me any good. But I've pretty well got over it by this time.'

A few days later I went to Sydney. The Giraffe was the last I shook hands with from the carriage window, and he slipped something in a piece of newspaper into my hand.

'I hope yer won't be offended,' he drawled, 'but some of the chaps thought you mightn't be too flush of stuff -- you've been shoutin' a good deal; so they put a quid or two together. They thought it might help yer to have a bit of a fly round in Sydney.'

I was back in Bourke before next shearing. On the evening of my arrival I ran against the Giraffe; he seemed strangely shaken over something, but he kept his hat on his head.

'Would yer mind takin' a stroll as fur as the Billerbong?' he said. 'I got something I'd like to tell yer.'

His big, brown, sunburnt hands trembled and shook as he took a letter from his pocket and opened it.

'I've just got a letter,' he said. 'A letter from that little girl at Bendigo. It seems it was all a mistake. I'd like you to read it. Somehow I feel as if I want to talk to a feller, and I'd rather talk to you than any of them other chaps.'

It was a good letter, from a big-hearted little girl. She had been breaking her heart for the great ass all these months. It seemed that he had left Bendigo without saying good-bye to her. 'Somehow I couldn't bring meself to it,' he said, when I taxed him with it. She had never been able to get his address until last week; then she got it from a Bourke man who had gone South. She called him 'an' awful long fool', which he was, without the slightest doubt, and she implored him to write, and come back to her.

'And will you go back, Bob?' I asked.

'My oath I'd take the train to-morrer only I ain't got the stuff. But I've got a stand in Big Billerbong shed an' I'll soon knock a few quid together.

I'll go back as soon as ever shearin's over. I'm goin' to write away to her to-night.'

The Giraffe was the 'ringer' of Big Billabong shed that season. His tallies averaged 120 a day. He only sent his hat round once during shearing, and it was noticed that he hesitated at first and only contributed half a crown. But then it was a case of a man being taken from the shed by the police for wife desertion.

'It's always that way,' commented Mitchell. 'Those soft, good-hearted fellows always end by getting hard and selfish. The world makes 'em so. It's the thought of the soft fools they've been that finds out sooner or later and makes 'em repent. Like as not the Giraffe will be the meanest man out-back before he's done.'

When Big Billabong cut out, and we got back to Bourke with our dusty swags and dirty cheques, I spoke to Tom Hall.

'Look here, Tom,' I said. 'That long fool, the Giraffe, has been breaking his heart for a little girl in Bendigo ever since he's been out-back, and she's been breaking her heart for him, and the ass didn't know it till he got a letter from her just before Big Billabong started. He's going to-morrow morning.'

That evening Tom stole the Giraffe's hat. 'I s'pose it'll turn up in the mornin',' said the Giraffe. 'I don't mind a lark,' he added, 'but it does seem a bit red-hot for the chaps to collar a cove's hat and a feller goin' away for good, p'r'aps, in the mornin'.'

Mitchell started the thing going with a quid.

'It's worth it,' he said, 'to get rid of him. We'll have some peace now. There won't be so many accidents or women in trouble when the Giraffe and his blessed hat are gone. Anyway, he's an eyesore in the town, and he's getting on my nerves for one. ... Come on, you sinners! Chuck 'em in; we're only taking quids and half-quids.'

About daylight next morning Tom Hall slipped into the Giraffe's room at the Carriers' Arms. The Giraffe was sleeping peacefully. Tom put the hat on a chair by his side. The collection had been a record one, and, besides the packet of money in the crown of the hat, there was a silver-mounted pipe with case -- the best that could be bought in Bourke, a gold brooch, and several trifles -- besides an ugly valentine of a long man in his shirt walking the room with a twin on each arm.

Tom was about to shake the Giraffe by the shoulder, when he noticed a great foot, with about half a yard of big-boned ankle and shank, sticking out at the bottom of the bed. The temptation was too Great. Tom took up the hair-brush, and, with the back of it, he gave a smart rap on the point of an ingrowing toe-nail, and slithered.

We heard the Giraffe swearing good-naturedly for a while, and then there was a pregnant silence. He was staring at the hat, we supposed.

We were all up at the station to see him off. It was rather a long wait. The Giraffe edged me up to the other end of the platform. He seemed overcome.

'There's -- there's some terrible good-hearted fellers in this world,' he said. 'You mustn't forget 'em, Harry, when you make a big name writin'. I'm -- well, I'm blessed if I don't feel as if I was jist goin' to blubber!'

I was glad he didn't. The Giraffe blubberin' would have been a spectacle. I steered him back to his friends.

'Ain't you going to kiss me, Bob?' said the Great Western's big, handsome barmaid, as the bell rang.

'Well, I don't mind kissin' you, Alice,' he said, wiping his mouth. 'But I'm goin' to be married, yer know.' And he kissed her fair on the mouth.

'There's nothin' like gettin' into practice,' he said, grinning round.

We thought he was improving wonderfully; but at the last moment something troubled him.

'Look here, you chaps,' he said hesitatingly, with his hand in his pocket, 'I don't know what I'm going to do with all this stuff. There's that there poor washerwoman that scalded her legs liftin' the boiler of cloths off the fire----'

We shoved him into the carriage. He hung -- about half of him -- out the window, wildly waving his hat till the train disappeared in the scrub.

And, as I sit here writing by lamplight at midday, in the midst of a great city of shallow social sham, of hopeless, squalid poverty, of ignorant selfishness, cultured or brutish, and of noble and heroic endeavour frowned down or callously neglected, I am almost aware of a burst of sunshine in the room, and a long form leaning over my chair, and --

'Excuse me for troublin' yer; I'm always troublin' yer; but there's that there poor woman . . .'

And I wish I could immortalize him!

# Italy

The foundation of the Italian literary canon rests on Dante Alighieri, Petrarch, and Giovanni Boccaccio, the exalted masters of the 14th century. This tradition, in the centuries following, has displayed a consciousness of beauty and form in the classical Greek and Latin sense. Themes of war and adventure appear as well, perhaps in attempt to define Italy's relationship as a nation to its colossal forerunner, ancient Rome. Leonardi Bruni, Galileo Galilei, and Gabriele d'Annunzio follow in this tradition, as does Antonio Fogazzaro, whose fiction appears in this volume.

Like Balzac's, Fogazzaro's cross symbolizes the pervasive importance of religion in his characters' lives. The story, set in a time when cholera consumed entire villages, offers more than a one-dimensional treatment of the peasant woman's cultural milieu, for, in that environment, Fogazzaro depicts the differences that occur between people of various social stations. The charitable piousness of the peasant, for example, is contrasted with the self-servitude of the countess.

# The Silver Crucifix
## Antonio Fogazzaro

**Antonio Fogazzaro 1842 - 1911:** Antonio Fogazzaro was born in Vicenza, and most of his life was spent there or at a summer home in Oria. He was greatly influenced by Giacomo Zanella who gave him a modern perspective on his religious beliefs. He thought of pursuing a musical career, but his parents disapproved and he eventually realized that his talent was insufficient. Instead he became active in public affairs and was made a Senator in 1900.

He began his literary career by writing poetry. In 1874 he published *Mirands*, a tragic romance in blank verse. He did not publish prose unitl 1881's novel *Malombra*. His spare plots often feature characters who suffer from unresolvable conflicts between weakness and idealism.

Other works include *A Little World of Former Time* (1895), *The Saint* (1905), and *Leila* (1910). He also published two collections of short stories, three short plays, and four volumes of essays and addresses.

"YOUR COFFEE, MILADY," said the maid.

The Countess did not reply. But altho the curtains were closed, her handsome young face could be dimly discerned on the white pillow. The maid, standing tray in hand at the foot of the bed, repeated more loudly:

"Your coffee, milady."

The Countess sat up, while she yawned, with eyes still unopened, "Let in some light."

Her maid went to the window without putting down the tray, and, in turning the handle of the shutters, managed to knock over the empty cup on its saucer.

"Keep quiet!" whispered the mistress in a tone of irritation. "What is the matter with you this morning? Don't you see you are waking the baby?"

And as a matter of fact the infant was now awake and crying in its crib. The lady turned toward the child's bed, and peremptorily called out "Hush!"

This silenced her offspring at once, excepting for a few faint moans.

"Now, then, I will have my coffee," commanded the Countess. "Have you seen your master yet? Why you are trembling all over! What is the matter with you?"

What, indeed, ailed the girl? Cup, saucer, sugar-bowl, and coffee-pot were rattling on the tray. "What is it?" repeated the Countess.

If the maid's face showed signs of alarm, no less was the mistress disturbed by doubts and fears.

"Nothing," replied the servant, still trembling.

The Countess hereupon seized her by the arm, shook it roughly, and exclaimed:

"Tell me!"

Meanwhile the pretty little head of a child of four was peering over the edge of the crib.

"It's a case," said the maid, half in tears, "it's a case of cholera."

Pale as death, the lady started up, and instinctively looked at her listening son. She jumped out of bed; by a single gesture she imposed silence on the girl, while motioning her to go into the next room. Then she darted to her child's crib.

The little fellow had begun to cry again, but his mother kissed and petted him, played and laughed with him until he forgot his woes, and stopped weeping. She pulled on her dressing-gown in great haste, and joined the servant, shutting the door behind her.

"Oh, my God, my God!" lamented the girl between her sobs, while the other woman too began to shed tears.

"Hush, for Heaven's sake! On no account must baby be frightened! What about this case -- where is it?"

"Here, milady! Rosa, the steward's wife. She was taken ill at midnight."

"Heavens! And now--?"

"She is dead. She died half an hour ago."

The baby was shrilly clamoring for his mother.

"Go," said the Countess; "go in and play with him. Keep him happy; do anything you like. Be quiet, darling!" she exclaimed. "I shall be back in a moment." Upon which she rushed to the Count's room.

The lady was blindly, insanely afraid of the cholera; nothing but her passion for her child could have been more intense than this feeling. At the first rumors of the epidemic she and her husband had fled the city, escaping to their splendid country seat -- her marriage portion -- in the hope that the disease would not spread thither. The place had been spared in 1836, and had even remained untouched in 1886. And now there it was, in the farmyard attached to the villa.

Disheveled and untidy, she flew into her husband's room. Before speaking she gave two violent tugs at the bellrope.

"Have you heard?" she said, with flaming eyes.

The Count, who was phlegmatically shaving his beard, turned round, inquiring, with the soapy brush in his hand: "What?"

"Don't you know about Rosa?"

"Oh, yes, I know," was his calm response.

If, in the first place, the Count had cherished some vague illusion that his wife was ignorant of Rosa's death, it now also seemed proper to reassure her by his cool demeanor. Instead, however, her ladyship's eyes shot fire, and her features were savage with anger.

"What!" she shouted, "you know and you can think of nothing better to do than shave? What sort of man are you -- what sort of father -- what sort of husband?"

"Good Lord!" cried the Count, throwing up his arms.

But before the poor man, soaped up to the eyes, and wrapped round with a towel, could add another word, in came the valet. Her ladyship commanded that not a peasant from the farmyard should be admitted to the house, and that no one should go thence to the farmyard. After this she gave orders for the coachman to be ready within an hour; he must harness to the landau the horses which his lordship would select.

"What are you going to do?" asked the latter, who had recovered himself meanwhile. "Nothing rash, I must insist."

"*Rash* -- how dare you say that? I am willing to be obedient to you in everything, but when it comes to a question of life and death -- my son's life, you understand -- then I will listen to no parley from any one. I wish to leave here at once. Order the horses, please."

The Count grew annoyed. How could matters have come to such a pass as this? Was there any propriety in running away after such a fashion? And then, what about business affairs? In two days, or one day, or maybe in twelve hours, he would be ready to start..But not before -- no. His wife, however, interrupted him violently: "Propriety, indeed, and business! For shame!"

"And clothes?" objected the husband. "We must certainly take some with us. You see, we shall really need more time."

The Countess made some contemptuous answer. She would see to it, she assured him, that the trunks were packed in an hour.

"But where do you expect to go?" persisted the Count.

"To the railway station, first of all, and then wherever you like. Now order the horse."

"I have had enough of this!" cried the other. "I'll give such orders as I choose! I'll let the business affairs go, and everything else! Your clothes, too! The sorrels," he added, enraged, to the domestic who was standing by impassively.

The Countess dressed and did her hair with the utmost speed, at moments clasping her hands in silent prayer, distributing commands, summoning servants from various parts of the house by frantic pulls at the bell. There was running up and down stairs, banging of doors, shouting, laughing, calling out of names, suppressed swearing. All the windows facing the fatal farmyard were immediately closed. Thus the cries of the unfortunate children who had lost their mother were shut out; besides a disagreeable odor of chlorin had penetrated into the villa, and even into the Countess's room, smothering the delicate Viennese perfume she habitually used.

"Heavens!" she exclaimed angrily, "now they are doing their best to ruin everything! Pack up quickly, and get those trunks locked! This frightful smell is enough to kill one! Don't they know that chlorin has no effect? They ought to burn the things. The steward will be dismissed if any thieving goes on."

"Some things are being burnt already, milady," observed one of the maids. "The doctor is having sheets, coverlid, and mattress burnt."

"That's not enough!" snapped the Countess.

Here the Count, shaved and dressed, entered his wife's apartment. He began talking to her aside.

"What shall we do with these servants? We can't take all of them with us."

"Anything you please. Send them away. Nothing will be safe in the house if they remain. I don't want them to get the cholera, and then fumigate the rooms with that vile chlorin, and perhaps burn up some of my best gowns. They have no respect whatever for their masters' property, and--"

Furious at having yielded, the Count now broke in with:

"A pretty state of things! As shame, I tell you, a scandal, to sneak off like this!"

"That's it!" retorted the woman "That's just how you men always are! To appear strong and courageous is more important to you than the life and safety of your family. You are afraid of becoming unpopular. Well, if you want to keep up your reputation, why don't you send for the mayor, and present him with a hundred lire for the cholera patients of the place?"

He thereupon suggested that he would stay at the villa alone, and that she should go with the child. Only he had not enough stability to carry out his own idea.

During this conversation the trunks were being filled. The little boy's playthings, his most expensive apparel, prayer-books, bathing-suits, jewelry, crested note-paper, furs, underlinen, many superfluous and few necessary articles were thrown in helter-skelter, and the lids closed down by sheer force. Then the Countess, followed by her spouse -- who made a great show of activity, but really accomplished nothing -- hurried through the whole house, opening drawers and cupboards, taking a last look into them, and locking them up with their own hands. The Count stated his opinion that it might be advisable to partake of some refreshment before commencing the journey.

"Yes, yes!" ironically said his consort, "we'll take some refreshment! I'll show you what to take!"

And she drew up her husband and all the servants, including those who were going home for a holiday, and dosed each one with ten drops of laudanum. Her son she regaled with some chocolates.

At last the landau stood before the door. Prior to actually departing, her ladyship, who was extremely pious, withdrew to the seclusion of her bedchamber for a final prayer. Kneeling at a chair, in her tight-fitting costume of white flannel, her black, eight-button gloves reaching to the elbows, and her gold and platinum bracelets, she raised her eyes devoutly to heaven -- under the overshadowing plume of her black velvet hat -- and murmured a feverish supplication. Not a word did she say to God about the poor wretches who had lost their mother; nor did she ask that the cholera might spare the humble workers chained to the rich soil which had given her this house, her jewels, clothes, Viennese perfume, her education, her dignity, her husband and child, her accommodating God. Neither did she ask anything for her own person. She, who already saw herself and her family smitten down with the dread disease on the journey, offered up no prayers excepting for her son. In fact, her lips simply muttered Paters and Aves and Glorias, while her mind was altogether with the child, thinking of the fearful fate which might befall him, of the danger to his health in this precipitate journey, of his possible loss of appetite, sleep, spirits, or color. Oh, if he could but be kept unconscious of any peril or pain assailing others!

Rapidly she crossed herself, donned a long, gray cloak, and shut a window that had remained open. Before the strong morning breeze clouds were chasing across the sky, the grass was bending on the lawn, and the tall poplars were swaying in the avenue leading to the villa. But the Countess, tho brought up on family traditions, had no thought for reminiscences of her youth belonging to this country estate. She merely closed the window and went downstairs.

The mayor was conversing with his lordship by the carriage door.

"Have you just come from there?" she asked the official, and, being informed that he had come from his home, she upbraided him for not having kept off the epidemic. He excused himself with polite smiles, to which the lady confusedly replied: "Never mind, then; never mind," as she hastened her child into the vehicle.

"Did you give him the money?" she whispered to her husband as soon as she was seated beside him. He made a sign in the affirmative.

"I should like to thank her ladyship, too," began the obsequious mayor, "for the generosity with which--"

"Oh, it was nothing -- nothing!" interrupted the Count, scarcely knowing what he said.

Established in the carriage, the Countess made a rapid survey of bags and boxes, coats, and shawls, umbrellas, and parasols. Her husband in the meantime turned round to see if all the luggage was in its place in the barouche, which had been fastened on behind to the landau. "But," he suddenly remarked, "what is the matter with that little boy?"

"Yes, who is that crying?" excitedly called out the Countess, leaning far out of the carriage.

"All ready! " exclaimed the peasant who had been assisting the servants with the luggage, and to whose side clung a small, ragged urchin. "Stop, can't you?" his father bade him, sharply, then repeating the words, "All ready!"

The Count, with his eye on the boy, plunged into one of his pockets. "Don't give way, my boy; you shall have a soldo all to yourself."

"Mother is ill," whined the lad sorrowfully; "mother has the cholera."

Up jumped the Countess. Her face livid and contorted, she brought down her folded sunshade across the coachman's back:

"Drive on!" she shrieked; "drive on -- quick!"

The menial whipped up the horses. They began to prance, and then went off at a gallop. The mayor barely had time to leap out of the way, and his lordship to fling out a handful of coppers, which scattered on the ground at the peasant's feet. He stood motionless -- while the boy continued weeping -- and stared after the flashing wheels of the carriage that rolled swiftly away, whirling up the dust.

"Damn those rich pigs!" he said.

Pretending not to hear, the mayor discreetly departed.

The peasant, a man of middle age and stature, pale, meager, evil-looking, and as rugged as his offspring, made the youngster pick up the coins. Then they went home together.

They inhabited, in the yard belonging to one of the Countess' farmhouses, a tumble-down, unplastered brick hovel, situated between a dunghill and a pigsty. Before the door gaped a dark ditch, from which issued an indescribable stench, and which was bridged by a single rough plank. Upon entering, one found one's self in a dingy, unpaved sort of cavern. There was no flooring, either wood or stone, but there was an irregular brick fireplace, and in front of it the ground had been depressed by poor wretches kneeling to cook their mess of cornmeal. A wooden stair -- three steps missing -- conducted to the room, foul with dirt and rubbish, where father, mother, and son were wont to pass the night in a single bed. Standing by this article of furniture, one might look down into the kitchen below through the broken boards. The bed occupied the only spot not soaked by the rain that dripped from the roof.

Crouching on the floor, her head leaning against the edge of the bed, sat the peasant's cholera-stricken wife. Altho but thirty, she looked old; at twenty she had been a blooming girl, and even now preserved remnants of mild beauty. At the first glance her husband understood; he swallowed an imprecation. The child, frightened by his mother's discolored face, kept in the doorway.

"For Christ's sake, send him away," she moaned feebly. "I have the cholera; send him away. Go to your aunt's, dear. Take him away, and send me the priest."

"I'll go," said the man to her; and to the boy, motioning toward the farmyard gate, "You go to your aunt's."

From the porch of the yard he fetched an armful of straw, carried it into the kitchen, and went upstairs to his wife, who by exerting all her strength had contrived to get on the bed.

"Listen," said the man, in accents of unusual tenderness; "I am sorry, but if you die in the bed it will have to be burnt. You understand, don't you? I have brought some straw into the kitchen -- a nice lot."

Too weak to answer, she made a mute signal of assent, and then a faint effort to rise from her couch. But the man took her up in his arms. By a gesture she begged him to reach first for a small silver crucifix hanging on the wall; she pressed it fervidly to her lips while her husband carried her down to the kitchen. Here he made her as comfortable as he could on the straw, before going for the priest.

And now she, too, this poor creature lying alone like a beast in a cage on the already infected straw -- she, too, before departing to an unknown world, began to pray. She prayed for the salvation of her soul, convinced that she was guilty of many sins, and tormented by her inability to remember them.

When the timid doctor, sent by the mayor, arrived, he asked in great fright whether there was any rum or marsala in the house. There was neither -- so he recommended hot bricks for her stomach, put up a notice of quarantine, and left her. The priest, who knew no fear, carelessly reeled off what he termed "the usual things," obscuring the divine message with words of his own. Nevertheless, tho benighted and ignorant, the dying woman derived comfort and serenity therefrom.

His task done, the priest went. Meanwhile the husband had put a few more handfuls of straw under her back, and lit the fire to heat the brick . His wife went on praying -- less for her child than for the man whom she had pardoned so often, and who was embarked on the road to perdition. Finally, kissing the cross, her mind turned to its giver. She had received it sixteen years back, at her confirmation, from the Countess, the mistress of the splendid manor where it was a joy to live and of the wretched hovel where it was a joy to die. At that time the Countess was a young girl, and had presented the silver crucifix to the laborer's daughter at the suggestion of her mother then mistress of the estate, a kind, gentle lady, long dead, but unforgotten by her humble tenants.

The dying woman acknowledged having thought ill of the new mistress, of having complained sometimes, so that *her* husband had cursed because, despite repeated petition, neither roof, nor flooring, nor staircase had ever been repaired, and because the window frames had not been filled with linen panes. Feeling truly penitent, in her heart she implored forgiveness of his lordship and her ladyship; and she besought the Holy Virgin to bless them both.

At the moment when her husband placed the scorching bricks on her stomach, a spasm ran through her body, and she gave up the ghost. The man flung some straw over her blackening face, wrenched the little cross out of her hand, stuffed it into his pocket with a scowl at its small value, mumbling some customary pious sentiment the while.

But he did not say, for she did not know, and we do not know, how much good this poor woman's crucifix had done, invoked and kissed by her on so many occasions. Still less can we tell how much benefit may yet spring from that charitable thought of an old lady, descending to an innocent child, and afterward reascending as a prayer from a pure heart to the Throne of Infinite Mercy.

The same evening the servants at the villa, who had been given leave of absence during the journey of the Count and Countess, got drunk in the drawing-room on rum and marsala.

# Sweden —————————————————————————————

Selma Lagerlof's "The Outlaws" portrays an aspect of the religious revivals that frequently occurred in late 19th-century Sweden. "The Outlaws" reveals the extent of the disruptive influence such a moral rebirth has on Tord's life and friendships. Known primarily for her novel, *Jerusalem*, Lagerlof endowed her short fiction as well with detailed character studies and evocative description of the country.

## The Outlaws
### *Selma Lagerlof*

**Selma Lagerlof 1858-1940:** Selma Lagerlof was next to youngest in a family of five children. Her family had been landed gentry since the seventeenth century but found their position slipping as economic difficulties forced them to sell their estate. Lagerlof wrote about her childhood and family in a series of three books *Marbacka* (1922), *Memories of My Childhood* (1930), and *The Diary of Selma Lagerlof* (1932).

Her education began at Marbacka with a governess. She was taught language, literature, music, and history. Unusually for a woman in her time, she was given the opportunity to attend a university. She graduated from the Higher Teacher's College for Women and, in 1885, she took a position as a teacher. In 1890, after receiving an award in a literary contest, she had the confidence to pursue a writing career. She took a leave of absence to complete her first novel, *Gosta Berling's Saga* (1891). It received negative criticism but she continued to write. Her short story collection *Invisible Links* (1893) was a success. In 1895, she received a travelling grant from King Oscar II and was able to tour Italy. It was there that she wrote her 1897 novel *The Miracles of Antichrist.* In 1907 she received an honorary doctoral degree from the University of Uppsala and in 1909 the Nobel Prize for Literature. In 1914 she became the first woman to be elected to the Swedish Academy. With her award money she was able to buy back the family estate, Marbacka, as well as the surrounding land.

A PEASANT HAD killed a monk and fled to the woods. He became an outlaw, upon whose head a price was set. In the forest he met another fugitive, a young fisherman from one of the outermost islands, who had been accused of the theft of a herring net. The two became companions, cut themselves a home in a cave, laid their nets together, cooked their food, made their arrows, and held watch one for the other. The peasant could never leave the forest. But the fisherman, whose crime was less serious, would now and then take upon his back the game they had killed, and would creep down to the more isolated houses on the outskirts of the village. In return for milk, butter, arrow-heads, and clothing he would sell his game, the black mountain cock, the moor hen, with her shining feathers, the toothsome doe, and the long-eared hare.

The cave which was their home cut down deep into a mountain-side. The entrance was guarded by wide slabs of stone and ragged thornbushes . High up on the hillside there stood a giant pine, and the chimney of the fireplace nestled among its coiled roots. Thus the smoke could draw up through the heavy hanging branches and fade unseen into the air. To reach their cave the men had to wade through the stream that sprang out from the hill slope. No pursuer thought of seeking their trail in this merry brooklet. At first they were hunted as wild animals are. The peasants of the district gathered to pursue them as if for a baiting of wolf or bear. The bowmen surrounded the wood while the spear carriers entered and left no thicket or ravine unsearched. The two outlaws cowered in their gloomy cave, panting in terror and listening breathlessly as the hunt passed on with noise and shouting over the mountain ranges.

For one long day the young fisherman lay motionless, but the murderer could stand it no longer and went out into the open where he could see his enemy. They discovered him and set after him, but this was far more to his liking than lying quiet in impotent terror. He fled before his pursuers, leaped the streams, slid down the precipices, climbed up perpendicular walls of rock. All his remarkable strength and skill awoke to energy under the spur of danger. His body became as elastic as a steel spring, his foot held firm, his hand grasped sure, his eye and ear were doubly sharp. He knew the meaning of every murmur in the foliage; he could understand the warning in an upturned stone.

When he had clambered up the side of a precipice he would stop to look down on his pursuers, greeting them with loud songs of scorn. When their spears sang above him in the air, he would catch them and hurl them back. As he crashed his way through tangled underbrush something within him seemed to sing a wild song of rejoicing. A gaunt, bare hilltop stretched itself through the forest, and all alone upon its crest there stood a towering pine. The red brown trunk was bare; in the thick grown boughs at the top a hawk's nest rocked in the breeze. So daring had the fugitive grown that on another day he climbed to the nest while his pursuers sought him in the woody slopes below. He sat there and twisted the necks of the young hawks as the hunt raged far beneath him. The old birds flew screaming about him in anger. They swooped past his face, they struck at his eyes with their beaks, beat at him with their powerful wings, and clawed great scratches in his weather-hardened skin. He battled with them laughing. He stood up in the rocking nest as he lunged at the birds with his knife, and he lost all thought of danger and pursuit in the joy of the battle. When recollection came again and he turned to look for his enemies, the hunt had gone off in another direction. Not one of the pursuers had thought of raising his eyes to the clouds to see the prey hanging there, doing schoolboy deeds of recklessness while his life hung in the balance. But the man trembled from head to foot when he saw that he was safe. He caught for a support with his shaking hands; he looked down giddily from the height to which he had climbed. Groaning in fear of a fall, afraid of the birds, afraid of the possibility of being seen, weakened through terror of everything and anything, he slid back down the tree trunk. He laid himself flat upon the earth and crawled over the loose stones until he reached the under-brush. There he hid among the tangled branches of the young pines, sinking down, weak and helpless, upon the soft moss. A single man might have captured him.

Tord was the name of the fisherman. He was but sixteen years old, but was strong and brave. He had now lived for a whole year in the wood.

The peasant's name was Berg, and they had called him "The Giant." He was handsome and well-built, the tallest and strongest man in the entire county. He was broad-shouldered and yet slender. His hands were delicate in shape, as if they had never known hard work; his hair was brown, his face soft-colored. When he had lived for some time in the forest his look of strength was awe-inspiring. His eyes grew piercing under bushy brows wrinkled by great muscles over the forehead. His lips were more firmly set than before, his face more haggard, with deepened hollows at the temples, and his strongly marked cheekbones stood out plainly. All the softer curves of his body disappeared, but the muscles grew strong as steel. His hair turned gray rapidly.

Tord had never seen any one so magnificent and so mighty before. In his imagination, his companion towered high as the forest, strong as the raging surf. He served him humbly, as he would have served a master; he revered him as he would have revered a god. It seemed quite natural that Tord should carry the hunting spear, that he should drag the game home, draw the water, and build the fire. Berg, the Giant, accepted all these services, but scarce threw the boy a friendly word. He looked upon him with contempt, as a common thief.

The outlaws did not live by pillage, but supported themselves by hunting and fishing. Had not Berg killed a holy man, the peasants would soon have tired of the pursuit and left them to themselves in the mountains. But they feared disaster for the villages if he who had laid hands upon a servant of God should go unpunished. When Tord took his game down into the valley they would offer him money and a pardon for himself if he would lead them to the cave of the Giant, that they might catch the latter in his sleep. But the boy refused, and if they followed him he would lead them astray until they gave up the pursuit.

Once Berg asked him whether the peasants had ever tried to persuade him to betrayal. When he learned what reward they had promised, he said scornfully that Tord was a fool not to accept such offers. Tord looked at him with something in his eyes that Berg, the Giant, had never seen before. No beautiful woman whom he had loved in the days of his youth had ever looked at him like that; not even in the eyes of his own children, or of his wife, had he seen such affection, "You are my God, the ruler I have chosen of my own free will." This was what the eyes said. "You may scorn me, or beat me, if you will, but I shall still remain faithful."

From this on Berg gave more heed to the boy and saw that he was brave in action but shy in speech. Death seemed to have no terrors for him. He would deliberately choose for his path the fresh-formed ice on the mountain pools, the treacherous surface of the morass in springtime. He seemed to delight in danger. It gave him some compensation for the wild ocean storms he could no longer go out to meet. He would tremble in the night darkness of the wood, however, and even by day the gloom of a thicket or a deeper shadow could frighten him. When Berg asked him about this he was silent in embarrassment.

Tord did not sleep in the bed by the hearth at the back of the cave, but every night, when Berg was asleep the boy would creep to the entrance and lie there on one of the broad stones. Berg discovered this, and although he guessed the reason, he asked the boy about it. Tord would not answer. To avoid further questions he slept in the bed for two nights, then returned to his post at the door.

One night, when a snow-storm raged in the tree-tops, piling up drifts even in the heart of the thickets, the flakes swirled into the cave of the outlaws. Tord, lying by the entrance, awoke in the morning to find himself wrapped in a blanket of melting snow. A day or two later he fell ill. Sharp pains pierced his lungs when he tried to draw breath. He endured the pain as long as his strength would stand it, but one evening, when he stooped to blow up the fire, he fell down and could not rise again. Berg came to his side and told him to lie in the warm bed. Tord groaned in agony, but could not move. Berg put his arm under the boy's body and carried him to the bed. He had a feeling while doing it as if he were touching a clammy snake; he had a taste in his mouth as if he had eaten unclean horseflesh, so repulsive was it to him to touch the person of this common thief. Berg covered the sick boy with his own warm bear-skin rug and gave him water. This was all he could do, but the illness was not dangerous, and Tord recovered quickly. But now that Berg had had to do his companion's work for a few days, and had had to care for him, they seemed to have come nearer to one another. Tord dared to speak to Berg sometimes, as they sat together by the fire cutting their arrows.

"You come of good people, Berg," Tord said one evening. "Your relatives are the richest peasants in the valley. The men of your name have served kings and fought in their castles."

"They have more often fought with the rebels and done damage to the king's property," answered Berg.

"Your forefathers held great banquets at Christmas time. And you held banquets, too, when you were at home in your house. Hundreds of men and women could find place on the benches in your great hall, the hall that was built in the days before St. Olaf came here to Viken for christening. Great silver urns were there, and mighty horns, filled with mead, went the rounds of your table."

Berg looked at the boy again. He sat on the edge of the bed with his head in his hands, pushing back the heavy tangled hair that hung over his eyes. His face had become pale and refined through his illness. His eyes still sparkled with fever. He smiled to himself at the pictures called up by his fancy -- pictures of the great hall and of the silver urns, of the richly clad guests, and of Berg, the Giant, lording it in the place of honor. The peasant knew that even in the days of his glory no one had ever looked at him with eyes so shining in admiration, so glowing in reverence as this boy did now, as he sat by the fire in his worn leather jacket. He was touched, and yet displeased. This common thief had no right to admire him.

"Were there no banquets in your home?" he asked.

Tord laughed: "Out there on the rocks where father and mother live? Father plunders the wrecks and mother is a witch. When the weather is stormy she rides out to meet the ships on a seal's back, and those who are washed overboard from the wrecks belong to her."

"What does she do with them?" asked Berg.

"Oh, a witch always needs corpses. She makes salves of them, or perhaps she eats them. On moonlit nights she sits out in the wildest surf and looks for the eyes and fingers of drowned children."

"That is horrible!" said Berg.

The boy answered with calm confidence: "It would be for others, but not for a witch. She can't help it."

This was an altogether new manner of looking at life for Berg. "Then thieves have to steal, as witches have to make magic?" he questioned sharply.

"Why, yes," answered the boy. "Every one has to do the thing he was born for." But a smile of sly cunning curled his lips, as he added: "There are thieves who have never stolen."

"What do you mean by that?" spoke Berg.

The boy still smiled his mysterious smile and seemed happy to have given his companion a riddle. "There are birds that do not fly; and there are thieves who have not stolen," he said..

Berg feigned stupidity, in order to trick the other's meaning: "How can any one be called a thief who has never stolen?" he said.

The boy's lips closed tight as if to hold back the words. "But if one has a father who steals--" he threw out after a short pause.

"A man may inherit house and money, but the name thief is given only to him who earns it."

Tord laughed gently. "But when one has a mother -- and that mother comes and cries, and begs one to take upon one's self the father's crime -- then one can laugh at the hangman and run away into the woods. A man may be outlawed for the sake of a fish net he has never seen."

Berg beat his fist upon the stone table, in great anger. Here this strong, beautiful boy had thrown away his whole life for another. Neither love, nor riches, nor the respect of his fellow men could ever be his again. The sordid care for food and clothing was all that remained to him in life. And this fool had let him, Berg, despise an innocent man. He scolded sternly, but Tord was not frightened any more than a sick child is frightened at the scolding of his anxious mother.

High up on one of the broad wooded hills there lay a black swampy lake. It was square in shape, and its banks were as straight, and their corners as sharp as if it had been the work of human hands. On three sides steep walls of rock rose up, with hardy mountain pines clinging to the stones, their roots as thick as a man's arm. At the surface of the lake, where the few strips of grass had been washed away, these naked roots twisted and coiled, rising out of the water like myriad snakes that had tried to escape from the waves, but had been turned to stone in their struggle. Or was it more like a mass of blackened skeletons of long-drowned giants which the lake was trying to throw off? The arms and legs were twisted in wild contortions, the long fingers grasped deep into the rocks, the mighty ribs formed arches that upheld ancient trees. But now and again these iron-hard arms, these steel fingers with which the climbing pines supported themselves, would loosen their hold, and then the strong north wind would hurl the tree from the ridge far out into the swamp. There it would lie, its crown burrowing deep in the muddy water. The fishes found good hiding places amid its twigs, while the roots rose up over the water like the arms of some hideous monster, giving the little lake a repulsive appearance.

The mountains sloped down on the fourth side of the little lake. A tiny rivulet foamed out here; but before the stream could find its path it twisted and turned among boulders and mounds of earth, forming a whole colony of islands, some of which scarce offered foothold, while others carried as many as twenty trees on their back.

Here, where the rocks were not high enough to shut out the sun, the lighter foliaged trees could grow. Here were the timid, gray-green alders, and the willows with their smooth leaves. Birches were here, as they always are wherever there is a chance to shut out the evergreens, and there were mountain ash and elder bushes, giving charm and fragrance to the place.

At the entrance to the lake there was a forest of rushes as high as a man's head, through which the sunlight fell as green upon the water as it falls on the moss in the true forest. There were little clearings among the reeds, little round ponds where the water lilies slumbered. The tall rushes looked down with gentle gravity upon these sensitive beauties, who closed their white leaves and their yellow hearts so quickly in their leather outer dress as soon as the sun withdrew his rays.

One sunny day the outlaws came to one of these little ponds to fish. They waded through the reeds to two high stones, and sat there throwing out their bait for the big, green, gleaming pike that slumbered just below the surface of the water. These men, whose life was now passed entirely among the mountains and the woods, had come to be as completely under the control of the powers of nature as were the plants or the animals. When the sun shone they were open-hearted and merry, at evening they became silent, and the night, which seemed to them so all-powerful, robbed them of their strength. And now the green light that fell through the reeds and drew out from the water stripes of gold, brown, and black-green, soothed them into a sort of magic mood. They were completely shut out from the outer world. The reeds swayed gently in the soft wind, the rushes murmured, and the long, ribbon-like leaves struck them lightly in the face. They sat on the gray stones in their gray leather garments, and the shaded tones of the leather melted into the shades of the stones. Each saw his comrade sitting opposite him as quietly as a stone statue. And among the reeds they saw giant fish swimming, gleaming and glittering in all colors of the rainbow. When the men threw out their lines and watched the rings on the water widen amid the reeds, it seemed to them that the motion grew and grew until they saw it was not they themselves alone that had occasioned it. A Nixie, half human, half fish, lay sleeping deep down in the water. She lay on her back, and the waves clung so closely to her body that the men had not seen her before. It was her breath that stirred the surface. But it did not seem to the watchers that there was anything strange in the fact that she lay there. And when she had disappeared in the next moment they did not know whether her appearance had been an illusion or not.

The green light pierced through their eyes into their brains like a mild intoxication. They saw visions among the reeds, visions which they would not tell even to each other. There was not much fishing done. The day was given up to dreams and visions.

A sound of oars came from among the reeds, and they started up out of their dreaming. In a few moments a heavy boat, hewn out of a tree trunk, came into sight, set in motion by oars not much broader than walking sticks. The oars were in the hands of a young girl who had been gathering water-lilies. She had long, dark-brown braids of hair, and great dark eyes, but she was strangely pale, a pallor that was not gray, but softly pink tinted. Her cheeks were no deeper in color than the rest of her face; her lips were scarce redder. She wore a bodice of white linen and a leather belt with a golden clasp. Her skirt was of blue with a broad red hem. She rowed past close by the outlaws without seeing them. They sat absolutely quiet, less from fear of discovery than from the desire to look at her undisturbed. When she had gone, the stone statues became men again and smiled:

"She was as white as the water-lilies," said one. "And her eyes were as dark as the water back there under the roots of the pines."

They were both so merry that they felt like laughing, like really laughing as they had never laughed in this swamp before, a laugh that would echo back from the wall of rock and loosen the roots of the pines.

"Did you think her beautiful?" asked the Giant.

"I do not know, she passed so quickly. Perhaps she was beautiful."

"You probably did not dare to look at her. Did you think she was the Nixie?"

And again they felt a strange desire to laugh.

While a child, Tord had once seen a drowned man. He had found the corpse on the beach in broad daylight, and it had not frightened him, but at night his dreams were terrifying. He had seemed to be looking out over an ocean, every wave of which threw a dead body at his feet. He saw all the rocks and islands covered with corpses of the drowned, the drowned that were dead and belonged to the sea, but that could move, and speak, and threaten him with their white, stiffened fingers.

And so it was again. The girl whom he had seen in the reeds appeared to him in his dreams. He met her again down at the bottom of the swamp lake, where the light was greener even than in the reeds, and there he had time enough to see that she was beautiful. He dreamed that he sat on one of the great pine roots in the midst of the lake while the tree rocked up and down, now under, now over the surface of the water. Then he saw her on one of the smallest islands. She stood under the red mountain ash and laughed at him. In his very last dream it had gone so far that she had kissed him. But then it was morning, and he heard Berg rising, but he kept his eyes stubbornly closed that he might continue to dream. When he did awake he was dazed and giddy from what he had seen during the night. He thought much more about the girl than he had done the day before. Toward evening it occurred to him to ask Berg if he knew her name.

Berg looked at him sharply. "It is better for you to know it at once," he said. "It was Unn. We are related to each other."

And then Tord knew that it was this pale maiden who was the cause of Berg's wild hunted life in forest and mountain. He tried to search his memory for what he had heard about her.

Unn was the daughter of a free peasant. Her mother was dead, and she ruled in her father's household. This was to her taste, for she was independent by nature, and had no inclination to give herself to any husband. Unn and Berg were cousins, and the rumor had long gone about that Berg liked better to sit with Unn and her maids than to work at home in his own house. One Christmas, when the great banquet was to be given in Berg's hall, his wife had invited a monk from Draksmark, who, she hoped, would show Berg how wrong it was that he should neglect her for another. Berg and others besides him hated this monk because of his appearance. He was very stout and absolutely white. The ring of hair around his bald head, the brows above his moist eyes, the color of his skin, of his hands, and of his garments, were all white. Many found him very repulsive to look at.

But the monk was fearless, and as he believed that his words would have greater weight if many heard them, he rose at the table before all the guests, and said: "Men call the cuckoo the vilest of birds because he brings up his young in the nest of others. But here sits a man who takes no care for his house and his children, and who seeks his pleasure with a strange woman. Him I will call the vilest of men." Unn rose in her place. "Berg, this is said to you and me," she cried. "Never have I been so shamed, but my father is not here to protect me." She turned to go, but Berg hurried after her. "Stay where you are," she said. "I do not wish to see you again." He stopped her in the corridor, and asked her what he should do that she might stay with him. Her eyes glowed as she answered that he himself should know best what he must do. Then Berg went into the hall again and slew the monk.

Berg and Tord thought on awhile with the same thoughts, then Berg said: "You should have seen her when the white monk fell. My wife drew the children about her and cursed Unn. She turned the faces of the children toward her, that they might always remember the woman for whose sake their father had become a murderer. But Unn stood there so quiet and so beautiful that the men who saw her trembled. She thanked me for the deed, and prayed me to flee to the woods at once. She told me never to become a robber, and to use my knife only in some cause equally just."

"Your deed had ennobled her," said Tord.

And again Berg found himself astonished at the same thing that had
before now surprised him in the boy. Tord was a heathen , or worse than
a heathen; he never condemned that which was wrong. He seemed to
know no sense of responsibility. What had to come, came. He knew of
God, of Christ, and the Saints, but he knew them only by name, as one
knows the names of the gods of other nations. The ghosts of the Scheeren
Islands were his gods. His mother, learned in magic, had taught him to
believe in the spirits of the dead. And then it was that Berg undertook a
task which was as foolish as if he had woven a rope for his own neck. He
opened the eyes of this ignorant boy to the power of God, the Lord of all
Justice, the avenger of wrong who condemned sinners to the pangs of hell
everlasting. And he taught him to love Christ and His Mother, and all the
saintly men and women who sit before the throne of God praying that His
anger may be turned away from sinners. He taught him all that mankind
has learned to do to soften the wrath of God. He told him of the long trains
of pilgrims journeying to the holy places; he told him of those who
scourged themselves in their remorse; and he told him of the pious monks
who flee the joys of this world.

The longer he spoke the paler grew the boy and the keener his attention
as his eyes widened at the visions. Berg would have stopped, but the
torrent of his own thoughts carried him away. Night sank down upon
them, the black forest night, where the scream of the owl shrills ghostly
through the stillness. God came so near to them that the brightness of His
throne dimmed the stars, and the angels of vengeance descended upon the
mountain heights. And below them in the flames of the underworld
fluttered up to the outer curve of the earth and licked greedily at this last
refuge of a race crushed by sin and woe.

Autumn came, and with it came storm. Tord went out alone into the
woods to tend the traps and snares, while Berg remained at home to mend
his clothes. The boy's path led him up a wooded height along which the
falling leaves danced in circles in the gust. Again and again the feeling
came to him that some one was walking behind him. He turned several
times, then went on again when he had seen that it was only the wind and
the leaves. He threatened the rustling circles with his fist, and kept on his
way. But he had not silenced the sounds of his vision. At first it was the
little dancing feet of elfin children; then it was the hissing of a great snake
moving up behind him. Beside the snake there came a wolf, a tall, gray
creature, waiting for the moment when the adder should strike at his feet
to spring upon his back. Tord hastened his steps, but the visions hastened

with him. When they seemed but two steps behind him, ready for the spring, he turned. There was nothing there, as he had known all the time. He sat down upon a stone to rest. The dried leaves played about his feet. The leaves of all the forest trees were there: the little yellow birch leaves, the red-tinged mountain ash leaves, the dried, black-brown foliage of the elm, the bright red aspen leaves, and the yellow-green fringes of the willows. Faded and crumpled, broken, and scarred, they were but little like the soft, tender shoots of green that had unrolled from the buds a few months ago.

"Ye are sinners," said the boy. "All of us are sinners. Nothing is pure in the eyes of God. Ye have already been shriveled up in the flame of His wrath."

Then he went on again, while the forest beneath him waved like a sea in storm, although it was still and calm on the path around him. But he heard something he had never heard before. The wood was full of voices. Now it was like a whispering, now a gentle plaint, now a loud threat, or a roaring curse. It laughed, and it moaned. It was as the voice of hundreds. This unknown something that threatened and excited, that whistled and hissed, a something that seemed to be, and yet was not, almost drove him mad. He shivered in deadly terror, as he had shivered before, the day that he lay on the floor of his cave, and heard his pursuers rage over him through the forest. He seemed to hear again the crashing of the branches, the heavy footsteps of the men, the clanking of their arms, and their wild, bloodthirsty shouts.

It was not alone the storm that roared about him. There was something else in it, something yet more terrible; there were voices he could not understand, sounds as of a strange speech. He had heard many a mightier storm than this roar through the rigging. But he had never heard the wind playing on a harp of so many strings. Every tree seemed to have its own voice, every ravine had another song, the loud echo from the rocky wall shouted back in its own voice. He knew all these tones, but there were other stranger noises with them. And it was these that awoke a storm of voices within his own brain.

He had always been afraid when alone in the darkness of the wood. He loved the open sea and the naked cliffs. Ghosts and spirits lurked here in the shadows of the trees.

Then suddenly he knew who was speaking to him in the storm. It was God, the Great Avenger, the Lord of all Justice. God pursued him because of his comrade. God demanded that he should give up the murderer of the monk to vengeance.

Tord began to speak aloud amid the storm. He told God what he wanted to do, but that he could not do it. He had wanted to speak to the Giant and to beg him make his peace with God. But he could not find the words; embarrassment tied his tongue. "When I learned that the world is ruled by a God of Justice," he cried, " I knew that he was a lost man. I have wept through the night for my friend. I know that God will find him, no matter where he may hide. But I could not speak to him; I could not find the words because of my love for him. Do not ask that I shall speak to him. Do not ask that the ocean shall rise to the height of the mountains."

He was silent again, and the deep voice of the storm, which he knew for God's voice, was silent also. There was a sudden pause in the wind, a burst of sunshine, a sound as of oars, and the gentle rustling of stiff reeds. These soft tones brought up the memory of Unn.

Then the storm began again, and he heard steps behind him, and a breathless panting. He did not dare to turn this time, or he knew that it was the white monk. He came from the banquet in Berg's great hall, covered with blood, and with an open ax cut in his forehead. And he whispered: " Betray him. Give him up, that you may have his soul."

Tord began to run. All this terror grew and grew in him, and he tried to flee from it. But as he ran he heard behind him the deep, mighty voice, which he knew was the voice of God. It was God himself pursuing him, demanding that he should give up the murderer. Berg's crime seemed more horrible to him than ever it had seemed before. A weaponless man had been murdered, a servant of God cut down by the steel. And the murderer still dared to live. He dared to enjoy the light of the sun and the fruits of the earth. Tord halted, clinched his fists, and shrieked a threat. Then, like a madman, he ran from the forest, the realm of terror, down into the valley.

When Tord entered the cave the outlaw sat upon the bench of stone, sewing. The fire gave but a pale light, and the work did not seem to progress satisfactorily. The boy's heart swelled in pity. This superb Giant seemed all at once so poor and so unhappy.

"What is the matter?" asked Berg. "Are you ill? Have you been afraid?"

Then for the first time Tord spoke of his fear. "It was so strange in the forest . I heard the voices of spirits and I saw ghosts. I saw white monks."

"Boy!"

"They sang to me all the way up the slope to the hilltop. I ran from them, but they ran after me, singing. Can I not lay the spirits? What have I to do with them? There are others to whom their appearance is more necessary."

"Are you crazy tonight, Tord?"

Tord spoke without knowing what words he was using. His shyness has left him all at once; speech seemed to flow from his lips. "They were white monks, as pale as corpses. And their clothes were spotted with blood. They draw their hoods down over their foreheads, but I can see the wound shining there. The great, yawning, red wound from the ax."

"Tord, " said the giant, pale and deeply grave, "the Saints alone know why you see wounds of ax thrusts. I slew the monk with a knife."

Tord stood before Berg trembling and wringing his hands. "They demand you of me. They would compel me to betray you."

"Who? The monks?"

"Yes, yes, the monks. They show me visions. They show me Unn. They show me the open, sunny ocean. They show me the camps of the fishermen, where there is dancing and merriment. I close my eyes, and yet I can see it all. 'Leave me,' I say to them. 'My friend has committed a murder, but he is not bad. Leave me alone, and I will talk to him, that he may repent and atone. He will see the wrong he has done, and he will make a pilgrimage to the Holy Grave.'"

"And what do the monks answer?" asked Berg. "They do not want to pardon me. They want to torture me and to burn me at the stake."

" 'Shall I betray my best friend?' I ask them. 'He is all that I have in the world. He saved me from the bear when its claws were already at my throat. We have suffered hunger and cold together. He covered me with his own garments while I was ill. I have brought him wood and water, I have watched over his sleep and led his enemies off the trail. Why should they think me a man who betrays his friend? My friend will go to the priest himself, and will confess to him, and then together we will seek absolution.'"

Berg listened gravely, his keen eyes searching in Tord's face. "Go to the priest yourself, and tell him the truth. You must go back again among mankind."

"What does it help if I go alone? The spirits of the dead follow me because of your sin. Do you not see how I tremble before you? You have lifted your hand against God himself. What crime is like unto yours? Why did you tell me about the just God? It is you yourself who compel me to betray you. Spare me this sin. Go to the priest yourself." He sank down on his knees before Berg.

The murderer laid his hand on his head and looked at him. He measured his sin by the terror of his comrade, and it grew and grew to monstrous size. He saw himself in conflict with the Will that rules the world. Remorse entered his heart.

"Woe unto me that I did what I did," he said. "And is not this miserable life, this life we lead here in terror, and in deprivation, is it not atonement enough? Have I not lost home and fortune? Have I not lost friends, and all the joys that make the life of a man? What more?"

As he heard him speak thus, Tord sprang up in wild terror. "You can repent!" he cried. "My words move your heart? Oh, come with me, come at once. Come, let us go while yet there is time."

Berg the Giant sprang up also. "You--did it----?"

"Yes, yes, yes. I have betrayed you. But come quickly. Come now, now that you can repent. We must escape. We will escape."

The murderer stooped to the ground where the battle-ax of his fathers lay at his feet. "Son of a thief," he hissed. "I trusted you--I loved you."

But when Tord saw him stoop for the ax, he knew that it was his own life that was in peril now. He tore his own ax from his girdle, and thrust at Berg before the latter could rise. The Giant fell headlong to the floor, the blood spurting out over the cave. Between the tangled masses of hair Tord saw the great, yawning, red wound of an ax thrust.

Then the peasants stormed into the cave. They praised his deed and told him that he should receive full pardon.

Tord looked down at his hands, as if he saw there the fetters that had drawn him on to kill the man he loved. Like the chains of the Fenris wolf, they were woven out of empty air. They were woven out of the green light amid the reeds, out of the play of shadows in the woods, out of the song of the storm, out of the rustling of the leaves, out of the magic vision of dreams. And he said aloud: "God is great."

He crouched beside the body, spoke amid his tears to the dead, and begged him to awake. The villagers made a litter of their spears, on which to carry the body of the free peasant to his home. The dead man aroused awe in their souls, they softened their voices in his presence. When they raised him on to the bier, Tord stood up, shook the hair from his eyes, and spoke in a voice that trembled:

"Tell Unn, for whose sake Berg the Giant became a murderer, that Tord the fisherman whose father plunders wrecks, and whose mother is a witch--tell her that Tord slew Berg because Berg had taught him that justice is the cornerstone of the world."

# France

Francois Rabelais, Pierre de Ronsard, and Michel Eyquem de Montaigne were the preeminent literary figures of 16th-century France. In subsequent centuries, much French literature has been inspired and influenced by writer-philosophers Voltaire and Rousseau. In the 20th century, French critics have produced one of the most influential bodies of literary criticism in world literature studies.

Balzac, though classified a Romantic, infuses his stories with a Realist's sense of detailed subject and setting. His fiction studies a range of character personalities and examines the effects of society's institutions upon the individual. "Mysterious Mansion" presents the earthly consequences of Madame Merret's inflexible adherence to a dogma, represented by her cross, that has been exaggerated from strong faith into superstition.

Katherine Mansfield's "An Indiscreet Journey," set in wartime France, is also included in this section. Herself a New Zealander, her story presents a finely wrought portrait of a segment of French society caught in the turmoil of war. The personal and political are combined in her protagonist, who, for a taste of whiskey, risks both her safety and social impropriety on a late-night excursion in the city.

# The Mysterious Mansion
### *Honore de Balzac*

**Honore de Balzac 1799-1850:** Balzac was born into a bourgeois family, and he alone added the "de" to his name. He was born in Tours, France, and his childhood was plagued with unhappiness both at home and at school. He attended grammar school at Tours and later a boarding school at Bendome, where he was an unsuccessful student but nevertheless a voracious reader. He studied law in Paris from 1816 to 1819, when he received his license. He soon abandoned law, however, to attend to his writerly ambitions. Balzac married Evelina Hanska, a friend of eighteen years, only a few months before his death.

Balzac began writing sensational novels to make his living, though he published these first works under a pseudonym. He often wrote more than sixteen hours a day for weeks at a time, keeping himself awake with coffee. During this time he accumulated many debts, which he often worsened by speculating on unsure business ventures.

His first success was the novel *Les Chouans* (1829). In the next twenty years he produced the massive collection of prose pieces titled *La Comedie Humaine*, a chronicle of French society that depicted in precise detail individuals of an exhaustive variety of classes and professions.

ABOUT A HUNDRED yards from the town of Vendôme, on the borders of the Loire, there is an old gray house, surmounted by very high gables, and so completely isolated that neither tanyard nor shabby hostelry, such as you may find at the entrance to all small towns, exists in its immediate neighborhood.

In front of this building, overlooking the river, is a garden, where the once well-trimmed box borders that used to define the walks now grow wild as they list. Several willows that spring from the Loire have grown as rapidly as the hedge that encloses it, and half conceal the house. The rich vegetation of those weeds that we call foul adorns the sloping shore. Fruit trees, neglected for the last ten years, no longer yield their harvest, and their shoots form coppices. The wall-fruit grows like hedges against the walls. Paths once graveled are overgrown with moss, but, to tell the truth, there is no trace of a path. From the height of the hill, to which cling the ruins of the old castle of the Dukes of Vendôme, the only spot whence the eye can plunge into this enclosure, it strikes you that, at a time not easy to determine, this plot of land was the delight of a country of gentleman, who cultivated roses and tulips and horticulture in general, and who was besides a lover of fine fruit. An arbor is still visible, or rather the debris of an arbor, where there is a table that time has not quite destroyed. The aspect of this garden of bygone days suggests the negative joys of peaceful, provincial life, as one might reconstruct the life of a worthy tradesman by reading the epitaph on his tombstone. As if to complete the sweetness and sadness of the ideas that possess one's soul, one of the walls displays a sun-dial decorated with the following commonplace Christian inscription: "Ultimam cogita!" The roof of this house is horribly dilapidated, the shutters are always closed, the balconies are covered with swallows' nests, the doors are perpetually shut, weeds have drawn green lines in the cracks of the flights of steps, the locks and bolts are rusty. Sun, moon, winter, summer, and snow have worn the paneling, warped the boards, gnawed the paint. The lugubrious silence which reigns there is only broken by birds, cats, martins, rats and mice, free to course to and fro, to fight and to eat each other. Everywhere an invisible hand has graven the word *mystery*.

Should your curiosity lead you to glance at this house from the side that points to the road, you would perceive a great door which the children of the place have riddled with holes. I afterward heard that this door had been closed for the last ten years. Through the holes broken by the boys you would have observed the perfect harmony that existed between the façades of both garden and courtyard. In both the same disorder prevails. Tufts of weed encircle the paving-stones. Enormous cracks furrow the walls, round whose blackened crests twine the thousand garlands of the pellitory. The steps are out of joint, the wire of the bell is rusted, the spouts are cracked. What fire from heaven has fallen here? What tribunal has decreed that salt should be strewn on this dwelling? Has God been blasphemed, has France been here betrayed? These are the questions we ask ourselves, but get no answer from the crawling things that haunt the place. The empty and deserted house is a gigantic enigma, of which the key is lost. In bygone times it was a small fief, and bears the name of the Grande Bretêche.

I inferred that I was not the only person to whom my good landlady had communicated the secret of which I was to be the sole recipient, and I prepared to listen.

"Sir," she said, "when the Emperor sent the Spanish prisoners of war and others here, the Government quartered on me a young Spaniard who had been sent to Vendôme on parole. Parole notwithstanding he went out every day to show himself to the sous-préfet. He was a Spanish grandee! Nothing less! His name ended in os and dia, something like Burgos de Férédia. I have his name on my books; you can read it if you like. Oh! but he was a handsome young man for a Spaniard; they are all said to be ugly. He was only five feet and a few inches high, but he was well-grown; he had small hands that he took such care of; ah! you should have seen! He had as many brushes for his hands as a woman for her whole dressing apparatus! He had thick black hair, a fiery eye, his skin was rather bronzed, but I liked the look of it. He wore the finest linen I have ever seen on any one, altho I have had princesses staying here, and, among others, General Bertrand, the Duke and Duchess d'Abrantès, Monsieur Decazes, and the King of Spain. He didn't eat much; but his manners were so polite, so amiable, that one could not owe him a grudge. Oh! I was very fond of him, altho he didn't open his lips four times in the day, and it was impossible to keep up a conversation with him. For if you spoke to him, he did not answer. It was a fad, a mania with them all, I heard say. He read his breviary like a priest, he went to Mass and to all the services regularly. Where did he sit? Two steps from the chapel of Madame de Merret. As he took his place there the first time he went to church, nobody suspected him of any intention in so doing. Besides, he never raised his eyes from his prayer-book, poor young man! After that, sir, in the evening he would walk on the mountains, among the castle ruins. It was the poor man's only amusement, it reminded him of his country. They say that Spain is all mountains! From the commencement of his imprisonment he stayed out late. I was anxious when I found that he did not come home before midnight; but we got accustomed to this fancy of his. He took the key of the door, and we left off sitting up for him. He lodged in a house of ours in the Rue des Casernes. After that, one of our stablemen told us that in the evening when he led the horses to the water, he thought he had seen the Spanish grandee swimming far down the river like a live fish. When he returned, I told him to take care of the rushes; he appeared vexed to have been seen in the water. At last, one day, or rather one morning, we did not find him in his room; he had not returned. After searching everywhere, I found some writing in the drawer of a table, where there were fifty gold pieces of Spain that are called doubloons and were worth about five thousand francs; and ten thousand francs' worth of diamonds in a small sealed box. The writing said, that in case he did not return, he left us the money and the diamonds, on condition of paying for Masses to thank God for his escape, and for his salvation. In those days my husband had not been taken from me; he hastened to seek him everywhere.

"And now for the strange part of the story. He brought home the Spaniard's clothes, that he had discovered under a big stone, in a sort of pilework by the river-side near the castle, nearly opposite to the Grande Bretêche. My husband had gone there so early that no one had seen him. After reading the letter, he burned the clothes, and according to Count Férédia's desire we declared that he had escaped. The sous-préfet sent all the gendarmerie in pursuit of him; but brust! they never caught him. Lepas believed that the Spaniard had drowned himself. I, sir, don't think so; I am more inclined to believe that he had something to do with the affair of Madame de Merret, seeing that Rosalie told me that the crucifix that her mistress thought so much of, that she had it buried with her, was of ebony and silver. Now in the beginning of his stay here, Monsieur de Férédia had one in ebony and silver, that I never saw him with later. Now, sir, don't you consider that I need have no scruples about the Spaniard's fifteen thousand francs, and that I have a right to them?"

"Certainly; but you haven't tried to question Rosalie?" I said.

"Oh, yes, indeed, sir; but to no purpose! the girl's like a wall. She knows something, but it is impossible to get her to talk."

After exchanging a few more words with me, my landlady left me a prey to vague and gloomy thoughts, to a romantic curiosity, and a religious terror not unlike the profound impression produced on us when by night, on entering a dark church, we perceive a faint light under high arches; a vague figure glides by -- the rustle of a robe or cassock is heard, and we shudder.

Suddenly the Grande Bretêche and its tall weeds, its barred windows, its rusty ironwork, its closed doors, its deserted apartments, appeared like a fantastic apparition before me. I essayed to penetrate the mysterious dwelling, and to find the knot of its dark story -- the drama that had killed three persons. In my eyes Rosalie became the most interesting person in Vendôme. As I studied her, I discovered the traces of secret care, despite the radiant health that shone in her plump countenance. There was in her the germ of remorse or hope; her attitude revealed a secret, like the attitude of a bigot who prays to excess, or of the infanticide who ever hears the last cry of her child. Yet her manners were rough and ingenuous -- her silly smile was not that of a criminal, and could you but have seen the great kerchief that encompassed her portly bust, framed and laced in by a lilac and blue cotton gown, you would have dubbed her innocent. No, I thought, I will not leave Vendôme without learning the history of the Grande Bretêche. To gain my ends I will strike up a friendship with Rosalie, if needs be.

"Rosalie," said I, one evening.

"Sir?"

"You are not married?"

She started slightly.

"Oh, I can find plenty of men, when the fancy takes me to be made miserable," she said, laughing.

She soon recovered from the effects of her emotion, for all women, from the great lady to the maid of the inn, possess a composure that is peculiar to them.

"You are too good-looking and well favored to be short of lovers. But tell me, Rosalie, why did you take service in an inn after leaving Madame de Merret? Did she leave you nothing to live on?"

"Oh, yes! But, sir, my place is the best in all Vendôme."

The reply was one of those that judges and lawyers would call evasive. Rosalie appeared to me to be situated in this romantic history like the square in the midst of a chessboard. She was at the heart of the truth and chief interest; she seemed to me to be bound in the very knot of it. The conquest of Rosalie was no longer to be an ordinary siege -- in this girl was centered the last chapter of a novel, therefore from this moment Rosalie became the object of my preference.

One morning I said to Rosalie: "Tell me all you know about Madame de Merret."

"Oh!" she replied in terror, "do not ask that of me, Monsieur Horace."

Her pretty face fell -- her clear, bright color faded -- and her eyes lost their innocent brightness.

"Well, then," she said, at last, "if you must have it so, I will tell you about it; but promise to keep my secret!" ˙

"Done! my dear girl, I must keep your secret with the honor of a thief, which is the most loyal in the world."

Were I to transcribe Rosalie's diffuse eloquence faithfully, an entire volume would scarcely contain it; so I shall abridge.

The room occupied by Madame de Merret at the Bretêche was on the ground floor. A little closet about four feet deep, built in the thickness of the wall, served as her wardrobe. Three months before the eventful evening of which I am about to speak, Madame de Merret had been so seriously indisposed that her husband had left her to herself in her own apartment, while he occupied another on the first floor. By one of those chances that it is impossible to foresee, he returned home from the club (where he was accustomed to read the papers and discuss politics with the inhabitants of the place) two hours later than usual. His wife supposed him to be at home, in bed and asleep. But the invasion of France had been the subject of a most animated discussion; the billiard-match had been exciting, he had lost forty francs, an enormous sum for Vendôme, where every one hoards, and where manners are restricted within the limits of a praiseworthy modesty, which perhaps is the source of the true happiness that no Parisian covets. For some time past Monsieur de Merret had been satisfied to ask Rosalie if his wife had gone to bed; and on her reply, which was always in the affirmative, had immediately gained his own room with the good temper engendered by habit and confidence. On entering his house, he took it into his head to go and tell his wife of his misadventure, perhaps by way of consolation. At dinner he found Madame de Merret most coquettishly attired. On his way to the club it had occurred to him that his wife was restored to health, and that her convalescence had added to her beauty. He was, as husbands are wont to be, somewhat slow in making this discovery. Instead of calling Rosalie, who was occupied just then in watching the cook and coachman play a difficult hand at brisque, Monsieur de Merret went to his wife's room by the light of a lantern that he deposited on the first step of the staircase. His unmistakable step resounded under the vaulted corridor. At the moment that the Count turned the handle of his wife's door, he fancied he could hear the door of the closet I spoke of close; but when he entered Madame de Merret was alone before the fireplace. The husband thought ingenuously that Rosalie was in the closet, yet a suspicion that jangled in his ear put him on his guard. He looked at his wife and saw in her eyes I know not what wild and hunted expression.

"You are very late," she said. Her habitually pure, sweet voice seemed changed to him.

Monsieur de Merret did not reply, for at that moment Rosalie entered. It was a thunderbolt for him. He strode about the room, passing from one window to the other, with mechanical motion and folded arms.

"Have you heard bad news, or are you unwell?" inquired his wife timidly, while Rosalie undressed her.

He kept silent.

"You can leave me," said Madame de Merret to her maid; "I will put my hair in curl papers myself." ˉ

From the expression of her husband's face she foresaw trouble, and wished to be alone with him. When Rosalie had gone, or was supposed to have gone (for she stayed in the corridor for a few minutes), Monsieur de Merret came and stood in front of his wife, and said coldly to her:

"Madame, there is someone in your closet!" She looked calmly at her husband and replied simply:

"No, sir."

This answer was heartrending to Monsieur de Merret; he did not believe in it. Yet his wife had never appeared to him purer or more saintly than at that moment. He rose to open the closet door; Madame de Merret took his hand, looked at him with an expression of melancholy, and said in a voice that betrayed singular emotion:

"If you find, no one there, remember this, all will be over between us!" The extraordinary dignity of his wife's manner restored the Count's profound esteem for her, and inspired him with one of those resolutions that only lack a vaster stage to become immortal.

"No," said he, "Josephine, I will not go there. In either case it would separate us forever. Hear me, I know how pure you are at heart, and that your life is a holy one. You would not commit a mortal sin to save your life."

At these words Madame de Merret turned a haggard gaze upon her husband.

"Here, take your crucifix," he added. "Swear to me before God that there is no one in there; I will believe you, I will never open that door."

Madame de Merret took the crucifix and said:

"I swear."

"Louder," said the husband, "and repeat 'I swear before God that there is no one in that closet.'"

She repeated the sentence calmly.

"That will do," said Monsieur de Merret, coldly.

After a moment of silence:

"I never saw this pretty toy before," he said, examining the ebony crucifix inlaid with silver, and most artistically chiseled.

"I found it at Duvivier's, who bought it of a Spanish monk when the prisoners passed through Vendôme last year."

"Ah!" said Monsieur de Merret, as he replaced the crucifix on the nail, and he rang. Rosalie did not keep him waiting. Monsieur de Merret went quickly to meet her, led her to the bay window that opened on to the garden and whispered to her:

"Listen! I know that Gorenflot wishes to marry you, poverty is the only drawback, and you told him that you would be his wife if he found the means to establish himself as a master mason. Well! go and fetch him, tell him to come here with his trowel and tools. Manage not to awaken any one in his house but himself; his fortune will be more than your desires. Above all, leave this room without babbling, otherwise--" He frowned. Rosalie went away, he recalled her.

"Here, take my latchkey," he said "Jean!" then cried Monsieur de Merret, in tones of thunder in the corridor. Jean, who was at the same time his coachman and his confidential servant, left his game of cards and came.

"Go to bed, all of you," said his master, signing to him to approach; and the Count added, under his breath: "When they are all asleep -- *asleep*, d'ye hear? -- you will come down and tell me." Monsieur de Merret, who had not lost sight of his wife all the time he was giving his orders, returned quietly to her at the fireside and began to tell her of the game of billiards and the talk of the club. When Rosalie returned she found Monsieur and Madame de Merret conversing very amicably.

The Count had lately had all the ceilings of his reception rooms on the ground floor repaired. Plaster of Paris is difficult to obtain in Vendôme; the carriage raises its price. The Count had therefore bought a good deal, being well aware that he could find plenty of purchasers for whatever might remain over. This circumstance inspired him with the design he was about to execute.

"Sir, Gorenflot has arrived," said Rosalie in low tones.

"Show him in," replied the Count in loud tones.

Madame de Merret turned rather pale when she saw the mason.

"Gorenflot," said her husband, "go and fetch bricks from the coach-house, and bring sufficient to wall up the door of this closet; you will use the plaster I have over to coat the wall with." Then calling Rosalie and the workman aside:

"Listen, Gorenflot," he said in an undertone "you will sleep here to-night. But to-morrow you will have a passport to a foreign country, to a town to which I will direct you. I shall give you six thousand francs for your journey. You will stay ten years in that town; if you do not like it, you may establish yourself in another, provided it be in the same country. You will pass through Paris, where you will await me. There I will insure you an additional six thousand francs by contract, which will be paid to you on your return, provided you have fulfilled the conditions of our bargain. This is the price for your absolute silence as to what you are about to do to-night. As to you, Rosalie, I will give you ten thousand francs on the day of your wedding, on condition of your marrying Gorenflot; but if you wish to marry, you must hold your tongues; or -- no dowry."

"Rosalie," said Madame de Merrit, "do my hair."

The husband walked calmly up an down, watching the door, the mason, and his wife, but without betraying any insulting doubts. Madame de Merret chose a moment when the workman was unloading bricks and her husband was at the other end of the room to say to Rosalie: "A thousand francs a year for you, my child, if you can tell Gorenflot to leave a chink at the bottom." Then out loud, she added coolly:

"Go and help him!"

Monsieur and Madame de Merret were silent all the time that Gorenflot took to brick up the door. This silence, on the part of the husband, who did not choose to furnish his wife with a pretext for saying things of a double meaning, had its purpose; on the part of Madame de Merret it was either pride or prudence. When the wall was about half-way up, the sly workman took advantage of a moment when the Count's back was turned, to strike a blow with his trowel in one of the glass panes of the closet door. This act informed Madame de Merret that Rosalie had spoken to Gorenflot.

All three then saw a man's face; it was dark and gloomy with black hair and eyes of flame. Before her husband turned, the poor woman had time to make a sign to the stranger that signified: Hope!

At four o'clock, toward dawn, for it was the month of September, the construction was finished. The mason was handed over to the care of Jean, and Monsieur de Merret went to bed in his wife's room.

On rising the following morning, he said carelessly:

"The deuce! I must go to the Mairie for the passport." He put his hat on his head, advanced three steps toward the door, altered his mind and took the crucifix.

His wife trembled for joy. "He is going to Duvivier," she thought. As soon as the Count had left, Madame de Merret rang for Rosalie; then in a terrible voice:

"The trowel, the trowel!" she cried, "and quick to work! I saw how Gorenflot did it; we shall have time to make a hole and to mend it again."

In the twinkling of an eye, Rosalie brought a sort of mattock to her mistress, who with unparalleled ardor set about demolishing the wall. She had already knocked out several bricks and was preparing to strike a more decisive blow when she perceived Monsieur de Merret behind her. She fainted.

"Lay Madame on her bed," said the Count coldly. He had foreseen what would happen in his absence and had set a trap for his wife; he had simply written to the mayor, and had sent for Duvivier. The jeweler arrived just as the room had been put in order.

"Duvivier," inquired the Count, "did you buy crucifixes of the Spaniards who passed through here?"

"No, sir."

"That will do, thank you," he said, looking at his wife like a tiger. "Jean," he added, "you will see that my meals are served in the Countess's room; she is ill, and I shall not leave her until she has recovered."

The cruel gentleman stayed with his wife for twenty days. In the beginning, when there were sounds in the walled closet, and Josephine attempted to implore his pity for the dying stranger, he replied, without permitting her to say a word:

"You have sworn on the cross that there is no one there."

*Translator Unknown*

# An Indiscreet Journey
## Katherine Mansfield

**Katherine Mansfield 1888-1923:** Katherine Mansfield (Katherine Middleton Murry, nee Kathleen Beauchamp) was born in Wellington, New Zealand. She was the third daughter of a family of five. Her earliest education was in a village school where the first acknowledgment of her literary talent was a prize for a composition on the subject "A Sea Voyage."

Mansfield attended Queen's College in England. She remained there for three years and edited the college magazine. In 1911 she began to write stories after she trained as a violoncellist. Her first volume of short stories, *In a German Pension* (1911), received little attention but the stories in *Bliss* (1920) and *The Garden Party* (1922) established her as a literary force and revealed a Chekovian influence in her work. Other volumes of her short stories include *The Dove's Nest* (1923) and *Something Childish* (1924). After an unhappy first marriage, she married John Middleton Murry, an editor, in 1918. She died at age thirty-five from tuberculosis. Murry edited her poems, her letters, and a collection of her unfinished writing.

SHE IS LIKE St. Anne. Yes, the concierge is the image of St. Anne, with that black cloth over her head, the wisps of grey hair hanging, and the tiny smoking lamp in her hand. Really very beautiful, I thought, smiling at St. Anne, who said severely: "Six o'clock. You have only just got time. There is a bowl of milk on the writing table." I jumped out of my pyjamas and into a basin of cold water like any English lady in any French novel. The concierge, persuaded that I was on my way to prison cells and deaths by bayonets, opened the shutters and the cold clear light came through. A little steamer hooted on the river; a cart with two horses at a gallop flung past. The rapid swirling water; the tall black trees on the far side, grouped together like negroes conversing. Sinister, very, I thought, as I buttoned on my age-old Burberry. (That Burberry was very significant. It did not belong to me. I had borrowed it from a friend. My eye lighted upon it hanging in her little dark hall. The very thing! The perfect and adequate disguise -- an old Burberry. Lions have been faced in a Burberry. Ladies have been rescued from open boats in mountainous seas wrapped in nothing else. An old Burberry seems to me the sign and the token of the undisputed venerable traveller, I decided, leaving my purple pegtop with the real seal collar and cuffs in exchange.)

"You will never get there," said the concierge, watching me turn up the collar. "Never! Never!" I ran down the echoing stairs -- strange they sounded, like a piano flicked by à sleepy housemaid -- and on to the Quai. "Why so fast, *ma mignonne?*" said a lovely little boy in coloured socks, dancing in front of the electric lotus buds that curve over the entrance to the Metro. Alas! there was not even time to blow him a kiss. When I arrived at the big station I had only four minutes to spare, and the platform entrance was crowded and packed with soldiers, their yellow papers in one hand and big untidy bundles. The Commissaire of Police stood on one side, a Nameless Official on the other. Will he let me pass? Will he? He was an old man with a fat swollen face covered with big warts. Horn-rimmed spectacles squatted on his nose. Trembling, I made an effort. I conjured up my sweetest early-morning smile and handed it with the papers. But the delicate thing fluttered against the horn spectacles and fell. Nevertheless, he let me pass, and I ran, ran in and out among the soldiers and up the high steps into the yellow-painted carriage.

"Does one go direct to X?" I asked the collector who dug at my ticket with a pair of forceps and handed it back again. "No, Mademoiselle, you must change at X.Y.Z."

"At---?"

"X.Y.Z."

Again I had not heard. "At what time do we arrive there if you please?"

"One o'clock." But that was no good to me. I hadn't a watch. Oh, well -- later.

Ah! the train had begun to move. The train was on my side. It swung out of the station, and soon we were passing the vegetable gardens, passing the tall blind houses to let, passing the servants beating carpets. Up already and walking in the fields, rosy from the rivers and the red-fringed pools, the sun lighted upon the swinging train and stroked my muff and told me to take off that Burberry. I was not alone in the carriage. An old woman sat opposite, her skirt turned back over her knees, a bonnet of black lace on her head. In her fat hands, adorned with a wedding and two mourning rings, she held a letter. Slowly, slowly she sipped a sentence, and then looked up and out of the window, her lips trembling a little, and then another sentence, and again the old face turned to the light, tasting it . . . Two soldiers leaned out of the window, their heads nearly touching -- one of them was whistling, the other had his coat fastened with some rusty safety-pins. And now there were soldiers everywhere working on the railway line, leaning against trucks or standing hands on hips, eyes fixed on the train as though they expected at least one camera at every window. And now we were passing big wooden sheds like rigged-up dancing halls or seaside pavilions, each flying a flag. In and out of them walked the Red Cross men; the wounded sat against the walls sunning themselves. At all the bridges, the crossings, the stations, a *petit soldat*, all boots and bayonet. Forlorn and desolate he looked, -- like a little comic picture waiting for the joke to be written underneath. Is there really such a thing as war? Are all these laughing voices really going to the war? These dark woods lighted so mysteriously by the white stems of the birch and the ash -- these watery fields with the big birds flying over -- these rivers green and blue in the light -- have battles been fought in places like these?

What beautiful cemeteries we are passing! They flash gay in the sun. They seem to be full of corn-flowers and poppies and daisies. How can there be so many flowers at this time of the year? But they are not flowers at all. They are bunches of ribbons tied on to the soldiers' graves.

I glanced up and caught the old woman's eye. She smiled and folded the letter. "It is from my son -- the first we have had since October. I am taking it to my daughter-in-law."

" . . .?"

"Yes, very good," said the old woman, shaking down her skirt and putting her arm through the handle of her basket. "He wants me to send him some handkerchiefs and a piece of stout string."

What is the name of the station where I have to change? Perhaps I shall never know. I got up and leaned my arms across the window rail, my feet crossed. One cheek burned as in infancy on the way to the sea-side. When the war is over I shall have a barge and drift along these rivers with a white cat and a pot of mignonette to bear me company.

Down the side of the hill filed the troops, winking red and blue in the light. Far away, but plainly to be seen, some more flew by on bicycles. But really, *ma France adorée*, this uniform is ridiculous. Your soldiers are stamped upon your bosom like bright irreverent transfers.

The train slowed down, stopped . . . Everybody was getting out except me. A big boy, his sabots tied to his back with a piece of string, the inside of his tin wine cup stained a lovely impossible pink, looked very friendly. Does one change here perhaps for X? Another whose képi had come out of a wet paper cracker swung my suit-case to earth. What darlings soldiers are! "Merci bien, Monsieur, vous êtes tout à fait aimable . . ." "Not this way," said a bayonet. "Nor this," said another. So I followed the crowd. "Your passport, Mademoiselle ". . ." "*We, Sir Edward Grey* . . ." I ran through the muddy square and into the buffet.

A green room with a stove jutting out and tables on each side. On the counter, beautiful with coloured bottles, a woman leans, her breasts in her folded arms. Through an open door I can see a kitchen, and the cook in a white coat breaking eggs into a bowl and tossing the shells into a corner. The blue and red coats of the men who are eating hang upon the walls. Their short swords and belts are piled upon chairs. Heavens! what a noise. The sunny air seemed all broken up and trembling with it. A little boy, very pale, swung from table to table, taking the orders, and poured me out a glass of purple coffee. *Sssh*, came from the eggs. They were in a pan. The woman rushed from behind the counter and began to help the boy. *Toute de suite, tout' suite!* she chirruped to the loud impatient voices. There came a clatter of plates and the pop-pop of corks being drawn.

Suddenly in the doorway I saw someone with a pail of fish -- brown speckled fish, like the fish one sees in a glass case, swimming through forests of beautiful pressed sea-weed. He was an old man in a tattered jacket, standing humbly, waiting for someone to attend to him. A thin beard fell over his chest, his eyes under the tufted eyebrows were bent on the pail he carried. He looked as though he had escaped from some holy picture, and was entreating the soldiers' pardon for being there at all . . .

But what could I have done? I could not arrive at X with two fishes hanging on a straw; and I am sure it is a penal offence in France to throw fish out of railway-carriage windows. I thought, miserably climbing into a smaller, shabbier train. Perhaps I might have taken them to -- *ah, mon Dieu* -- I had forgotten the name of my uncle and aunt again! Buffard, Buffon -- what was it? Again I read the unfamiliar letter in the familiar handwriting.

"My dear niece,

"Now that the weather is more settled, your uncle and I would be charmed if you would pay us a little visit. Telegraph me when you are coming. I shall meet you outside the station if I am free. Otherwise our good friend, Madame Grinçon, who lives in the toll-house by the bridge, *juste en face de le gare*, will conduct you to our home. *Je vous embrasse bien tendrement*, JULIE BOIFFARD."

A visiting card was enclosed: *M. Paul Boiffard.*

Boiffard -- of course that was the name. *Ma tante Julie et mon oncle Paul* -- suddenly they were there with me, more real, more solid than any relations I had ever known. I saw *tante Julie* bridling, with the soup-tureen in her hands, and *oncle Paul* sitting at the table, with a red and white napkin tied round his neck. Boiffard -- Boiffard -- I must remember the name. Supposing the Commissaire Militaire should ask me who the relations were I was going to and I muddled the name -- Oh, how fatal! Buffard -- no, Boiffard. And then for the first time, folding Aunt Julie's letter, I saw scrawled in a corner of the empty back page: *Venez vite, vite.* Strange impulsive woman! My heart began to beat . . .

"Ah, we are not far off now," said the lady opposite. "You are going to X, Mademoiselle?"

"Oui, Madame."

"I also . . . You have been there before?"

"No, Madame. This is the first time."

"Really, it is a strange time for a visit."

I smiled faintly, and tried to keep my eyes off her hat. She was quite an ordinary little woman, but she wore a black velvet toque, with an incredibly surprised looking sea-gull camped on the very top of it. Its round eyes, fixed on me so inquiringly, were almost too much to bear. I had a dreadful impulse to shoo it away, or to lean forward and inform her of its presence. . . .

"*Excusez-moi, madame,* but perhaps you have not remarked there is an *espéce de sea-gull couché sur votre chapeau.*"

Could the bird be there on purpose? I must not laugh. . . . I must not laugh. Had she ever looked at herself in a glass with that bird on her head?

"It is very difficult to get into X at present, to pass the station," she said, and she shook her head with the sea-gull at me. "Ah, such an affair. One must sign one's name and state one's business."

"Really, is it as bad as all that?"

"But naturally. You see the whole place is in the hands of the military, and" -- she shrugged -- "they have to be strict. Many people do not get beyond the station at all. They arrive. They are put in the waiting-room, and there they remain."

Did I or did I not detect in her voice a strange, insulting relish?

"I suppose such strictness is absolutely necessary," I said coldly, stroking my muff.

"Necessary," she cried. "I should think so. Why, *mademoiselle*, you cannot imagine what it would be like otherwise! You know what women are like about soldiers" -- she raised a final hand -- "mad, completely mad. But --" and she gave a little laugh of triumph -- "they could not get into X. *Mon Dieu*, no! There is no question about that."

"I don't suppose they even try," said I.

"Don't you?" said the sea-gull.

Madame said nothing for a moment. "Of course the authorities are very hard on the men. It means instant imprisonment, and then -- off to the firing-line without a word."

"What are *you* going to X for?" said the sea-gull. "What on earth are *you* doing here?"

"Are you making a long stay in X, *mademoiselle*?"

She had won, she had won. I was terrified. A lamp-post swam past the train with the fatal name upon it. I could hardly breathe -- the train had stopped. I smiled gaily at Madame and danced down the steps to the platform. . . .

It was a hot little room completely furnished with two colonels seated at two tables. They were large grey-whiskered men with a touch of burnt red on their cheeks. Sumptuous and omnipotent they looked. One smoked what ladies love to call a heavy Egyptian cigarette, with a long creamy ash, the other toyed with a gilded pen. Their heads rolled on their tight collars, like big overripe fruits. I had a terrible feeling, as I handed my passport and ticket, that a soldier would step forward and tell me to kneel. I would have knelt without question.

What's this?" said God I., querulously. He did not like my passport at all. The very sight of it seemed to annoy him. He waved a dissenting hand at it, with a "*Non, je ne peux pas manger ça*" air.

"But it won't do. It won't do at all, you know. Look, -- read for yourself," and he glanced with extreme distaste at my photograph, and then with even greater distaste his pebble eyes looked at me.

"Of course the photograph is deplorable," I said, scarcely breathing with terror, "but it has been viséd and viséd."

He raised his big bulk and went over to God II.

"Courage!" I said to my muff and held it firmly, "Courage!"

God II. held up a finger to me, and I produced Aunt Julie's letter and her card. But he did not seem to feel the slightest interest in her. He stamped my passport idly, scribbled a word on my ticket, and I was on the platform again.

"That way -- you pass out that way."

Terribly pale, with a faint smile on his lips, his hand at salute, stood the little corporal. I gave no sign, I am sure I gave no sign. He stepped behind me.

"And then follow me as though you do not see me," I heard him half whisper, half sing.

How fast he went, through the slippery mud towards a bridge. He had a postman's bag on his back, a paper parcel and the *Matin* in his hand. We seemed to dodge through a maze of policemen, and I could not keep up at all with the little corporal who began to whistle. From the toll-house "our good friend, Madame Grinçon," her hands wrapped in a shawl, watched our coming, and against the toll-house there leaned a tiny faded cab. *Montez vite, vite!* said the little corporal, hurling my suitcase, the postman's bag, the paper parcel and the *Matin* on to the floor.

"A-ie! A-ie! Do not be so mad. Do not ride yourself. You will be seen," wailed "our good friend, Madame Grinçon."

"Ah, je m'en f . . ." said the little corporal.

The driver jerked into activity. He lashed the bony horse and away we flew, both doors, which were the complete sides of the cab, flapping and banging.

"Bon jour, mon amie."

"Bon jour, mon ami."

And then we swooped down and clutched at the banging doors. They would not keep shut. They were fools of doors.

"Lean back, let me do it!" I cried. "Policemen are as thick as violets everywhere."

At the barracks the horse reared up and stopped. A crowd of laughing faces blotted the window.

"Prends ça, mon vieux," said the little corporal, handing the paper parcel.

"It's all right," called someone.

We waved, we were off again. By a river, down a strange white street, with little houses on either side, gay in the late sunlight.

"Jump out as soon as he stops again. The door will be open. Run straight inside. I will follow. The man is already paid. I know you will like the house. It is quite white. And the room is white, too, and the people are--"

"White as snow."

We looked at each other. We began to laugh. "Now," said the little corporal.

Out I flew and in at the door. There stood, presumably, my aunt Julie. There in the background hovered, I supposed, my uncle Paul.

"Bon jour, madame!" "Bon jour, monsieur!"

"It is all right, you are safe," said my aunt Julie. Heavens, how I loved her! And she opened the door of the white room and shut it upon us. Down went the suit-case, the postman's bag, the *Matin*. I threw my passport up into the air, and the little corporal caught it.

What an extraordinary thing. We had been there to lunch and to dinner each day; but now in the dusk and alone I could not find it. I clop-clopped in my borrowed *sabots* through the greasy mud, right to the end of the village, and there was not a sign of it. I could not even remember what it looked like, or if there was a name painted on the outside, or any bottles or tables showing at the window. Already the village houses were sealed for the night behind big wooden shutters. Strange and mysterious they looked in the ragged drifting light and thin rain, like a company of beggars perched on the hill-side, their bosoms full of rich unlawful gold. There was nobody about but the soldiers. A group of wounded stood under a lamp-post, petting a mangy, shivering dog. Up the street came four big boys singing:

Dodo, mon homme, fais vit' dodo . . .

and swung off down the hill to their sheds behind the railway station. They seemed to take the last breath of the day with the them. I began to walk slowly back.

"It must have been one of these houses. I remember it stood far back from the road -- and there were no steps, not even a porch -- one seemed to walk right through the window." And then quite suddenly the waiting-boy came out of just such a place. He saw me and grinned cheerfully, and began to whistle through his teeth.

"Bon soir, mon petit."

"Bon soir, madame." And he followed me up the cafe to our special table, right at the far end by the window, and marked by a bunch of violets that I had left in a glass there yesterday.

"You are two?" asked the waiting-boy, flicking the table with a red and white cloth. His long swinging steps echoed over the bare floor. He disappeared into the kitchen and came back to light the lamp that hung from the ceiling under a spreading shade, like a hay-maker's hat. Warm light shone on the empty place that was really a barn, set out with dilapidated tables and chairs. Into the middle of the room a black stove jutted. At one side of it there was a table with a row of bottles on it, behind which Madame sat and took the money and made entries in a red book. Opposite her desk a door led into the kitchen. The walls were covered with a creamy paper patterned all over with green and swollen trees -- hundreds and hundreds of trees reared their mushroom heads to the ceiling. I began to wonder who had chosen the paper and why. Did Madame think it was beautiful, or that it was a gay and lovely thing to eat one's dinner at all seasons in the middle of a forest. . . . On either side of the clock there hung a picture: one, a young gentleman in black tights wooing a pear-shaped lady in yellow over the back of a garden seat, *Premier Rencontre*; two, the black and yellow in amorous confusion, *Triomphe d'Amour*.

The clock ticked to a soothing lilt, *C'est ça, c'est ça*. In the kitchen the waiting-boy was washing up. I heard the ghostly clatter of the dishes.

And years passed. Perhaps the war is long since over -- there is no village outside at all -- the streets are quiet under the grass. I have an idea this is the sort of thing one will do on the very last day of all -- sit in an empty café and listen to a clock ticking until--

Madame came through the kitchen door, nodded to me and took her seat behind the table, her plump hands folded on the red book. *Ping* went the door. A handful of soldiers came in, took off their coats and began to play cards, chaffing and poking fun at the pretty waiting-boy, who threw up his little round head, rubbed his thick fringe out of his eyes and cheeked them back in his broken voice. Sometimes his voice boomed up from his throat, deep and harsh, and then in the middle of a sentence it broke and scattered in a funny squeaking. He seemed to enjoy it himself.

You would not have been surprised if he had walked into the kitchen on his hands and brought back your dinner turning a catherine-wheel.

*Ping* went the door again. Two more men came in. They sat at the table nearest Madame, and she leaned to them with a bird-like movement, her head on one side. Oh, they had a grievance! The Lieutenant was a fool -- nosing about -- springing out at them -- and they'd only been sewing on buttons. Yes, that was all -- sewing on buttons, and up comes this young spark. "Now then, what are you up to?" They mimicked the idiotic voice. Madame drew down her mouth, nodding sympathy. The waiting-boy served them with glasses. He took a bottle of some orange-coloured stuff and put it on the table-edge. A shout from the card-players made him turn sharply, and crash! over went the bottle, spilling on the table, the floor -- smash! to tinkling atoms. An amazed silence. Through it the drip-drip of the wine from the table on to the floor. It looked very strange dropping so slowly, as though the table were crying. Then there came a roar from the card-players. "You'll catch it, my lad! That's the style! Now you've done it! . . . Sept, huit, neuf." They started playing again. The waiting-boy never said a word. He stood, his head bent, his hands spread out, and then he knelt and gathered up the glass, piece by piece, and soaked the wine up with a cloth. Only when Madame cried cheerfully, "You wait until *he* finds out," did he raise his head.

"He can't say anything, if I pay for it," he muttered, his face jerking, and he marched off into the kitchen with the soaking cloth.

"*Il pleure de colère*," said Madame delightedly, patting her hair with her plump hands.

The café slowly filled. It grew very warm. Blue smoke mounted from the tables and hung about the haymaker's hat in misty wreaths. There was a suffocating smell of onion soup and boots and damp cloth. In the din the door sounded again. It opened to let in a weed of a fellow, who stood with his back against it, one hand shading his eyes.

"Hullo! you've got the bandage off?"

"How does it feel, *mon vieux*?"

"Let's have a look at them."

But he made no reply. He shrugged and walked unsteadily to a table, sat down and leant against the wall. Slowly his hand fell. In his white face his eyes showed, pink as a rabbit's. They brimmed and spilled, brimmed and spilled. He dragged a white cloth out of his pocket and wiped them.

"It's the smoke," said someone. "It's the smoke tickles them up for you."

His comrades watched him a bit, watched his eyes fill again, again brim over. The water ran down his face, off his chin on to the table. He rubbed the place with his coat-sleeve, and then, as though forgetful, went on rubbing, rubbing with his hand across the table, staring in front of him. And then he started shaking his head to the movement of his hand. He gave a loud strange groan and dragged out the cloth again.

"*Huit, neuf, dix,*" said the card-players.

"*P'tit*, some more bread."

"Two coffees."

"*Un Picon!*"

The waiting-boy, quite recovered, but with scarlet cheeks, ran to and fro. A tremendous quarrel flared up among the card-players, raged for two minutes, and died in flickering laughter. "Ooof!" groaned the man with the eyes, rocking and mopping. But nobody paid any attention to him except Madame. She made a little grimace at her two soldiers.

"*Mais vous savez, c'est un peu dégoûtant, ça,*" she said severely.

"*Ah, oui, Madame,*" answered the soldiers, watching her bent head and pretty hands, as she arranged for the hundredth time a frill of lace on her lifted bosom.

"*V'là monsieur!*" cawed the waiting-boy over his shoulder to me. For some silly reason I pretended not to hear, and I leaned over the table smelling the violets, until the little corporal's hand closed over mine.

"Shall we have *un peu de charcuterie* to begin with?" he asked tenderly.

"In England," said the blue-eyed soldier, "you drink whiskey with your meals. *N'est-ce pas, mademoiselle*? A little glass of whiskey neat before eating. Whiskey and soda with your *bifteks*, and after, more whiskey with hot water and lemon."

"Is it true, that? " asked his great friend who sat opposite, a big red-faced chap with a black beard and large moist eyes and hair that looked as though it had been cut with a sewing-machine.

"Well, not quite true," said I.

"*Si, si,*" cried the blue-eyed soldier. " I ought to know. I'm in business. English travellers come to my place, and it's always the same thing."

"Bah, I can't stand whiskey," said the little corporal. "It's too disgusting the morning after. Do you remember, *ma fille*, the whiskey in that little bar at Montmartre?"

"*Souvenir tendre*," sighed Blackbeard, putting two fingers in the breast of his coat and letting his head fall. He was very drunk.

"But I know something that you've never tasted," said the blue-eyed soldier pointing a finger at me; "something really good." *Cluck* he went with his tongue. "*É-patant!* And the curious thing is that you'd hardly know it from whiskey except that it's" -- he felt with his hand for the word -- "finer, sweeter perhaps, not so sharp, and it leaves you feeling gay as a rabbit next morning."

"What is it called?"

"Mirabelle!" He rolled the word round his mouth, under his tongue. "Ah-ha, that's the stuff."

"I could eat another mushroom," said Blackbeard. "I would like another mushroom very much. I am sure I could eat another mushroom if Mademoiselle gave it to me out of her hand."

"You ought to try it," said the blue-eyed soldier, leaning both hands on the table and speaking so seriously that I began to wonder how much more sober he was than Blackbeard. "You ought to try it, and to-night. I would like you to tell me if you don't think it's like whiskey."

"Perhaps they've got it here," said the little corporal, and he called the waiting-boy. "P'tit!"

"*Non, monsieur*," said the boy, who never stopped smiling. He served us with dessert plates painted with blue parrots and horned beetles.

"What is the name for this in English?" said Blackbeard, pointing. I told him "Parrot."

"*Ah, mon Dieu!* . . . Pair-rot . . ." He put his arms round his plate. "I love you, *ma petit* pair-rot. You are sweet, you are blonde, you are English. You do not know the difference between whiskey and mirabelle."

The little corporal and I looked at each other, laughing. He squeezed up his eyes when he laughed, so that you saw nothing but the long curly lashes.

"Well, I know a place where they do keep it," said the blue-eyed soldier. "*Café des Amis*. We'll go there -- I'll pay -- I'll pay for the whole lot of us." His gesture embraced thousands of pounds.

But with a loud whirring noise the clock on the wall struck half-past eight; and no soldier is allowed in a cafe after eight o'clock at night.

"It is fast," said the blue-eyed soldier. The little corporal's watch said the same. So did the immense turnip that Blackbeard produced, and carefully deposited on the head of one of the horned beetles.

"Ah, well, we'll take the risk," said the blue-eyed soldier, and he thrust his arms into his immense cardboard coat. "It's worth it," he said. "It's worth it. You just wait."

Outside, stars shone between wispy clouds, and the moon fluttered like a candle flame over a pointed spire. The shadows of the dark plume-like trees waved on the white houses. Not a soul to be seen. No sound to be heard but the *Hsh! Hsh!* of a faraway train, like a big beast shuffling in its sleep.

"You are cold," whispered the little corporal. "You are cold, *ma fille.*"

"No, really not."

"But you are trembling."

"Yes, but I'm not cold."

"What are the women like in England?" asked Blackbeard. "After the war is over I shall go to England. I shall find a little English woman and marry her -- and her pair-rot." He gave a loud choking laugh.

"Fool!" said the blue-eyed soldier, shaking him; and he leant over to me. "It is only after the second glass that you really taste it," he whispered. "The second little glass and then -- ah! -- then you know."

*Café des Amis* gleamed in the moonlight. We glanced quickly up and down the road. We ran up the four wooden steps, and opened the ringing glass door into a low room lighted with a hanging lamp, where about ten people were dining. They were seated on two benches at a narrow table.

"Soldiers!" screamed a woman, leaping up from behind a white soup-tureen -- a scrag of a woman in a black shawl. "Soldiers! At this hour! Look at that clock, look at it." And she pointed to the clock with the dripping ladle.

"It's fast," said the blue-eyed soldier. It's fast, madame. And don't make so much noise, I beg of you. We will drink and we will go."

"Will you?" she cried, running round the table and planting herself in front of us. "That's just what you won't do. Coming into an honest woman's house this hour of the night -- making a scene -- getting the police after you. Ah, no! Ah, no. It's a disgrace, that's what it is."

"Sh!" said the little corporal, holding up his hand. Dead silence. In the silence we heard steps passing.

"The police," whispered Blackbeard, winking at a pretty girl with rings in her ears, who smiled back at him, saucy. "Sh!"

The faces lifted, listening. "How beautiful they are!" I thought.

"They are like a family party having supper in the New Testament. . ." "The steps died away.

"Serve you very well right if you had been caught," scolded the angry woman. "I'm sorry on your account that the police didn't come. You deserve it -- you deserve it."

"A little glass of mirabelle and we will go," persisted the blue-eyed soldier.

Still scolding and muttering she took four glasses from the cupboard and a big bottle. "But you're not going to drink in here. Don't you believe it." The little corporal ran into the kitchen. "Not there! Not there! Idiot!" she cried. "Can't you see there's a window there, and a wall opposite where the police come every evening to . . ."

"Sh!" Another scare.

"You are mad and you will end in prison, -- all four of you," said the woman. She flounced out of the room. We tiptoed after her into a dark smelling scullery, full of pans of greasy water, of salad leaves and meat-bones.

"There now," she said, putting down the glasses. "Drink and go!"

"Ah, at last!" The blue-eyed soldier's happy voice trickled through the dark. "What do you think? Isn't it just as I said? Hasn't it got a taste of excellent -- *ex-cellent* whiskey?"

# Ireland

Like other world literatures, the literature of Ireland has often used aged cultural legends and myths as catalysts in the development of modern writing. Irish writers of the 1880's, however, set out to develop a blend of Romanticism and Realism, the fantastic and the possible, the melancholy and the ironic or satirical, that would mark their work as distinctly Irish. They attempted to derive from their common experience and folklore a voice distinguishable from that of other literature written in the English language. William Butler Yeats, James Joyce, and Samuel Beckett are but three of the many figures who emerged from this heritage onto the world scene.

George Moore's story "Home Sickness," the tale of a man returning to Ireland after more than a decade abroad, explores the mutability of memory and contrasts "the modern restlessness and cold energy" of his adopted America with the "primitive" submissiveness to authority exhibited by the villagers of the Irish countryside.

## Home Sickness
### George Moore

George Moore 1852-1933: George Moore, born in Ireland, lived in Paris and studied at various art schools. He was greatly influenced by Turgenev, Zola, Flaubert, and other 19th-century French Realists. Moore published his successful first novel, *A Modern Lover,* in 1883. *A Mummer's Wife* (1885), with its portrayal of a woman's struggle with alcohol, introduced Naturalism into the Victorian novel. Moore's most famous novel, though, is *Esther Waters* (1894) in which he relates the hardships endured by a young religious woman. Around 1900, Moore returned to Ireland and associated with William Butler Yeats, George Russell, and other figures of the Irish Renaissance. His other works include the novels *Confessions of a Young Man* (1888), *Evelyn Innes* (1898), *Sister Teresa* (1901); and the volumes of short stories *Celibates* (1895) and *The Untilled Field* (1903).

HE TOLD THE doctor he was due in the bar-room at eight o'clock in the morning; the bar-room was in a slum in the Bowery; and he had only been able to keep himself in health by getting up at five o'clock and going for long walks in the Central Park.

'A sea voyage is what you want,' said the doctor. 'Why not go to Ireland for two or three months? You will come back a new man.'

'I'd like to see Ireland again.'

And he began to wonder how the people at home were getting on. The doctor was right. He thanked him, and three weeks afterwards he landed in Cork.

As he sat in the railway carriage he recalled his native village -- he could see it and its lake, and then the fields one by one, and the roads. He could see a large piece of rocky land -- some three or four hundred acres of headland stretching out into the winding lake. Upon this headland the peasantry had been given permission to build their cabins by former owners of the Georgian house standing on the pleasant green hill. The present owners considered the village a disgrace, but the villagers paid high rents for their plots of ground, and all the manual labour that the Big House required came from the village: the gardeners, the stable helpers, the house and the kitchen maids.

Bryden had been thirteen years in America, and when the train stopped at his station, he looked round to see if there were any changes in it. It was just the same blue limestone station-house as it was thirteen years ago. The platform and the sheds were the same, and there were five miles of road from the station to Duncannon. The sea voyage had done him good, but five miles were too far for him today; the last time he had walked the road, he had walked it in an hour and half, carrying a heavy bundle on a stick.

He was sorry he did not feel strong enough for the walk, the evening was fine, and he would meet many people coming home from the fair, some of whom he had known in his youth, and they would tell him where he could get a clean lodging. But the carman would be able to tell him that; he called the car that was waiting at the station, and soon he was answering questions about America. But he wanted to hear of those who were still living in the old country, and after hearing the stories of many people he had forgotten, he heard that Mike Scully, who had been away in a situation for many years as a coachman in the King's County, had come back and built a fine house with a concrete floor. Now there was a good loft in Mike Scully's house, and Mike would be pleased to take in a lodger.

Bryden remembered that Mike had been in a situation at the Big House; he had intended to be a jockey, but had suddenly shot up into a fine tall man, and had had to become a coachman instead. Bryden tried to recall the face, but he could only remember a straight nose, and a somewhat dusky complexion. Mike was one of the heroes of his child-hood, and now his youth floated before him, and he caught glimpses of himself, something that was more than a phantom and less than a reality. Suddenly his reverie was broken: the carman pointed with his whip, and Bryden saw a tall, finely built, middle-aged man coming through the gates, and the driver said:

'There's Mike Scully.'

Mike had forgotten Bryden even more completely than Bryden had forgotten him, and many aunts and uncles were mentioned before he began to understand.

'You've grown into a fine man, James,' he said, looking at Bryden's great width of chest. 'But you are thin in the cheeks, and you're very sallow in the cheeks too.'

'I haven't been very well lately -- that is one of the reasons I have come back; but I want to see you all again.'

Bryden paid the carman, wished him 'God-speed', and he and Mike divided the luggage between them, Mike carrying the bag and Bryden the bundle, and they walked round the lake, for the townland was at the back of the demesne; and while they walked, James proposed to pay Mike ten shillings a week for his board and lodging.

He remembered the woods thick and well-forested; now they were windworn, the drains were choked, and the bridge leading across the lake inlet was falling away. Their way led between long fields where herds of cattle were grazing; the road was broken -- Bryden wondered how the villagers drove their carts over it, and Mike told him that the landlord could not keep it in repair, and he would not allow it to be kept in repair out of the rates, for then it would be a public road, and he did not think there should be a public road through his property.

At the end of many fields they came to the village, and it looked a desolate place, even on this fine evening, and Bryden remarked that the county did not seem to be as much lived in as it used to be. It was at once strange and familiar to see chickens in the kitchen; and, wishing to re-knit himself to the old habits, he begged of Mrs. Scully not to drive them out, saying he did not mind them. Mike told his wife that Bryden was born in Duncannon, and when she heard Bryden's name she gave him her hand, after wiping it on her apron, saying he was heartily welcome, only she was afraid he would not care to sleep in a loft.

'Why wouldn't I sleep in a loft, a dry loft! You're thinking a good deal of America over here,' said he, 'but I reckon it isn't all you think it. Here you work when you like and you sit down when you like; but when you have had a touch of blood-poisoning as I had, and when you have seen young people walking with a stick, you think that there is something to be said for old Ireland.'

'Now won't you be taking a sup of milk? You'll be wanting a drink after travelling,' said Mrs. Scully.

And when he had drunk the milk Mike asked him if he would like to go inside or if he would like to go for a walk.

'Maybe it is sitting down you would like to be.'

And they went into the cabin, and started to talk about the wages a man could get in America, and the long hours of work.

And after Bryden had told Mike everything about America that he thought of interest, he asked Mike about Ireland. But Mike did not seem to be able to tell him much that was of interest. They were all very poor -- poorer, perhaps, than when he left them.

'I don't think anyone except myself has a five pound note to his name.'

Bryden hoped he felt sufficiently sorry for Mike. But after all Mike's life and prospects mattered little to him. He had come back in search of health; and he felt better already; the milk had done him good, and the bacon and cabbage in the pot sent forth a savoury odour. The Scullys were very kind, they pressed him to make a good meal; a few weeks of country air and food, they said, would give him back the health he had lost in the Bowery; and when Bryden said he was longing for a smoke, Mike said there was no better sign than that. During his long illness he had never wanted to smoke, and he was a confirmed smoker.

It was comfortable to sit by the mild peat fire watching the smoke of their pipes drifting up the chimney, and all Bryden wanted was to be let alone; he did not want to hear of anyone's misfortunes, but about nine o'clock a number of villagers came in, and their appearance was depressing. Bryden remembered one or two of them -- he used to know them very well when he was a boy; their talk was as depressing as their appearance, and he could feel no interest whatever in them . He was not moved when he heard that Higgins the stone-mason was dead; he was not affected

when he heard that Mary Kelly, who used to go to do the laundry at the
Big House, had married; he was only interested when he heard she had
gone to America. No, he had not met her there; America is a big place.
Then one of the peasants asked him if he remembered Patsy Carabine,
who used to do the gardening at the Big House. Yes, he remembered Patsy
well. Patsy was in the poor-house. He had not been able to do any work
on account of his arm; his house had fallen in; he had given up his holding
and gone into the poor-house. All this was very sad, and to avoid hearing
any further unpleasantness, Bryden began to tell them about America.
And they sat round listening to him; but all the talking was on his side; he
wearied of it; and looking round the group he recognized a ragged
hunchback with grey hair; twenty years ago he was a young hunchback,
and, turning to him, Bryden asked him if he were doing well with his five
acres.

'Ah, not much. This has been a bad season. The potatoes failed; they
were watery -- there is no diet in them.'

These peasants were all agreed that they could make nothing out of
their farms. Their regret was that they had not gone to America when they
were young; and after striving to take an interest in the fact that O'Connor
had lost a mare and foal worth forty pounds Bryden began to wish himself
back in the slum. When they left the house he wondered if every evening
would be like the present one. Mike piled fresh sods on the fire, and he
hoped it would show enough light in the loft for Bryden to undress
himself by.

The cackling of some geese in the road kept him awake, and the
loneliness of the country seemed to penetrate to his bones, and to freeze
the marrow in them. There was a bat in the loft -- a dog howled in the
distance -- and then he drew the clothes over his head. Never had he been
so unhappy, and the sound of Mike breathing by his wife's side in the
kitchen added to his nervous terror. Then he dozed a little; and lying on
his back he dreamed he was awake, and the men he had seen sitting round
the fireside that evening seemed to him like spectres come out of some
unknown region of morass and reedy tarn. He stretched out his hands for
his clothes, determined to fly from this house, but remembering the lonely
road that led to the station he fell back on his pillow. The geese still
cackled, but he was too tired to be kept awake any longer. He seemed to
have been asleep only a few minutes when he heard Mike calling him.
Mike had come half-way up the ladder and was telling him that breakfast
was ready. 'What kind of breakfast will he give me?' Bryden asked

himself as he pulled on his clothes. There were tea and hot griddle cakes for breakfast, and there were fresh eggs; there was sunlight in the kitchen, and he liked to hear Mike tell of the work he was going to do in the fields. Mike rented a farm of about fifteen acres, at least ten of it was grass; he grew an acre of potatoes and some corn, and some turnips for his sheep. He had a nice bit of meadow, and he took down his scythe, and as he put the whetstone in his belt Bryden noticed a second scythe, and he asked Mike if he should go down with him and help him to finish the field.

'You haven't done any mowing this many a year; I don't think you'd be of much help. You'd better go for a walk by the lake, but you may come in the afternoon if you like and help to turn the grass over.'

Bryden was afraid he would find the lake shore very lonely, but the magic of returning health is sufficient distraction for the convalescent, and the morning passed agreeably. The weather was still and sunny. He could hear the ducks in the reeds. The days dreamed themselves away, and it became his habit to go to the lake every morning. One morning he met the landlord, and they walked together, talking of the country , of what it had been, and the ruin it was slipping into. James Bryden told him that ill health had brought him back to Ireland; and the landlord lent him his boat, and Bryden rowed about the islands, and resting upon his oars he looked at the old castles, and remembered the prehistoric raiders that the landlord had told him about. He came across the stones to which the lake dwellers had tied their boats, and these signs of ancient Ireland were pleasing to Bryden in his present mood.

As well as the great lake there was a smaller lake in the bog where the villagers cut their turf. This lake was famous for its pike, and the landlord allowed Bryden to fish there, and one evening when he was looking for a frog with which to bait his line he met Margaret Dirken driving home the cows for the milking. Margaret was the herdsman's daughter, and she lived in a cottage near the Big House; but she came up to the village whenever there was a dance, and Bryden had found himself opposite to her in the reels. But until this evening he had had little opportunity of speaking to her, and he was glad to speak to someone, for the evening was lonely, and they stood talking together.

'You're getting your health again,' she said. 'You'll soon be leaving us.'

'I'm in no hurry.'

'You're grand people over there; I hear a man is paid four dollars a day for his work.'

'And how much,' said James, 'has he to pay for his food and for his clothes?'

Her cheeks were bright and her teeth small, white, and beautifully even; and a woman's soul looked at Bryden out of her soft Irish eyes. He was troubled and turned aside, and catching sight of a frog looking at him out of a tuft of grass he said--

'I have been looking for a frog to put upon my pike line.'

The frog jumped right and left, and nearly escaped in some bushes, but he caught it and returned with it in his hand.

'It is just the kind of frog a pike will like,' he said. 'Look at its great white belly and its bright yellow back.'

And without more ado he pushed the wire to which the hook was fastened through the frog's fresh body, and dragging it through the mouth he passed the hooks through the hind legs and tied the line to the end of the wire.

'I think,' said Margaret, 'I must be looking after my cows; it's time I got them home.'

'Won't you come down to the lake while I set my line?'

She thought for a moment and said:

'No I'll see you from here.'

He went down to the reedy tarn, and at his approach several snipe got up, and they flew above his head uttering sharp cries. His fishing-rod was a long hazel stick, and he threw the frog as far as he could into the lake. In doing this he roused some wild ducks; a mallard and two ducks got up, and they flew toward the larger lake. Margaret watched them; they flew in a line with an old castle; and they had not disappeared from view when Bryden came toward her, and he and she drove the cows home together that evening.

They had not met very often when she said, 'James, you had better not come here so often calling to me.'

'Don't you wish me to come?'

'Yes, I wish you to come well enough, but keeping company is not the custom of the country, and I don't want to be talked about.'

'Are you afraid the priest would speak against us from the altar?'

'He has spoken against keeping company, but it is not so much what the priest says, for there is no harm in talking.'

'But if you are going to be married there is no harm in walking out together.'

'Well, not so much, but marriages are made differently in these parts; there is not much courting here.'

And next day it was known in the village that James was going to marry Margaret Dirken.

His desire to excel the boys in dancing had caused a stir of gaiety in the parish, and for some time past there had been dancing in every house where there was a floor fit to dance upon; and if the cottages had no money to pay for a barrel of beer, James Bryden, who had money, sent him a barrel, so that Margaret might get her dance. She told him that they sometimes crossed over into another parish where the priest was not so averse to dancing, and James wondered. And next morning at Mass he wondered at their simple fervour. Some of them held their hands above their head as they prayed, and all this was very new and very old to James Bryden. But the obedience of these people to their priest surprised him. When he was a lad they had not been so obedient, or he had forgotten their obedience; and he listened in mixed anger and wonderment to the priest, who was scolding his parishioners, speaking to them by name, saying that he had heard there was dancing going on in their homes. Worse than that, he said he had seen boys and girls loitering about the roads, and the talk that went on was one of a kind -- love. He said that newspapers containing love stories were finding their way into the people's houses, stories about love, in which there was nothing elevating or ennobling. The people listened, accepting the priest's opinion without question. And their submission was pathetic. It was the submission of a primitive people clinging to religious authority, and Bryden contrasted the weakness and incompetence of the people about him with the modern restlessness and cold energy of the people he had left behind him.

One evening, as they were dancing, a knock came to the door, and the piper stopped playing, and the dancers whispered:

'Someone has told on us; it is the priest.'

And the awe-stricken villagers crowded round the cottage fire, afraid to open the door. But the priest said that if they did not open the door he would put his shoulder to it and force it open. Bryden went towards the door, saying he would allow no one to threaten him, priest or no priest, but Margaret caught his arm and told him that if he said anything to the priest, the priest would speak against them from the altar, and they would be shunned by the neighbours. It was Mike Scully who went to the door and let the priest in, and he came in saying they were dancing their souls into hell.

'I've heard of your goings on,' he said -- 'of your beer-drinking and dancing. I will not have it in my parish. If you want that sort of thing you had better go to America.'

'If that is intended for me, sir, I will go back tomorrow. Margaret can follow.'

'It isn't the dancing, it's the drinking I'm opposed to,' said the priest, turning to Bryden.

'Well, no one has drunk too much, sir,' said Bryden.

'But you'll sit here drinking all night,' and the priest's eyes went toward the corner where the women had gathered, and Bryden felt that the priest looked on the women as more dangerous than the porter. 'It's after midnight,' he said, taking out his watch. .

By Bryden's watch it was only half-past eleven, and while they were arguing about the time Mr. Scully offered Bryden's umbrella to the priest, for in his hurry to stop the dancing the priest had gone out without his; and, as if to show Bryden that he bore him no ill will, the priest accepted the loan of the umbrella, for he was thinking of the big marriage fee that Bryden would pay him.

'I shall be badly off for the umbrella tomorrow,' Bryden said, as soon as the priest was out of the house. He was going with his father-in-law to a fair. His father-in-law was learning him how to buy and sell cattle. And his father-in-law was saying that the country was mending, and that a man might become rich in Ireland if he only had a little capital. Bryden had the capital, and Margaret had an uncle on the other side of the lake who would leave her all he had, that would be fifty pounds, and never in the village of Duncannon had a young couple begun life with so much prospect of success as would James Bryden and Margaret Dirken.

Some time after Christmas was spoken of as the best time for the marriage; James Bryden said that he would not be able to get his money out of America before the spring. The delay seemed to vex him, and he seemed anxious to be married, until one day he received a letter from America, from a man who had served in the bar with him. This friend wrote to ask Bryden if he were coming back. The letter was no more than a passing wish to see Bryden again. Yet Bryden stood looking at it, and everyone wondered what could be in the letter. It seemed momentous, and they hardly believed him when he said it was from a friend who wanted to know if his health were better. He tried to forget the letter, and he looked at the worn fields, divided by walls of loose stones, and a great longing came upon him.

The smell of the Bowery slum had come across the Atlantic, and had found him out in this western headland; and one night he awoke from a dream in which he was hurling some drunken customer through the open doors into the darkness. He had seen his friend in his white duck jacket throwing drink from glass into glass amid the din of voices and strange accents; he had heard the clang of money as it was swept into the till, and his sense sickened for the bar-room. But how should he tell Margaret Dirken that he could not marry her? She had built her life upon this marriage. He could not tell her that he would not marry her ... yet he must go. He felt as if he were being hunted; the thought that he must tell Margaret that he could not marry her hunted him day after day as a weasel hunts a rabbit. Again and again he went to meet her with the intention of telling her that he did not love her, that their lives were not for one another, that it had all been a mistake, and that happily he had found out it was a mistake soon enough. But Margaret, as if she guessed what he was about to speak of, threw her arms about him and begged him to say he loved her, and that they would be married at once. He agreed that he loved her, and that they would be married at once. But he had not left her many minutes before the feeling came upon him that he could not marry her -- that he must go away. The smell of the bar-room hunted him down. Was it for the sake of the money that he might make there that he wished to go back? No, it was not the money. What then? His eyes fell on the bleak country, on the little fields divided by bleak walls; he remembered the pathetic ignorance of the people, and it was these things that he could not endure. It was the priest who came to forbid the dancing. Yes, it was the priest. As he stood looking at the line of the hills the bar-room seemed by him. He heard the politicians, and the excitement of politics was in his blood again. He must go away from this place -- he must get back to the bar-room. Looking up, he saw the scanty orchard, and he hated the spare road that led to the village, and he hated the little hill at the top of which the village began, and he hated more than all other places the house where he was to live with Margaret Dirken -- if he married her. He could see it from where he stood -- by the edge of the lake, with twenty acres of pasture land about it, for the landlord had given up part of his demesne land to them.

He caught sight of Margaret, and he called her to come through the stile.

'I have just had a letter from America.'

'About the money?' she said.

'Yes, about the money. But I shall have to go over there.'

He stood looking at her, seeking for words; and she guessed from his embarrassment that he would say to her that he must go to America before they were married.

'Do you mean, James, you will have to go at once?'

'Yes,' he said, 'at once. But I shall come back in time to be married in August. It will only mean delaying our marriage a month.'

They walked on a little way talking, and every step he took James felt that he was a step nearer the Bowery slum. And when they came to the gate Bryden said:

'I must hasten or I shall miss the train.'

'But,' she said, 'you are not going now -- you are not going today?'

'Yes, this morning. It is seven miles. I shall have to hurry not to miss the train.'

And then she asked him if he would ever come back.

'Yes,' he said, 'I am coming back.'

'If you are coming back, James, why not let me go with you?'

'You could not walk fast enough. We should miss the train.'

'One moment, James. Don't make me suffer; tell me the truth. You are not coming back. Your clothes -- where shall I send them?'

He hurried away, hoping he would come back. He tried to think that he liked the country he was leaving, that it would be better to have a farmhouse and live there with Margaret Dirken than to serve drinks behind a counter in the Bowery. He did not think he was telling her a lie when he said he was coming back. Her offer to forward his clothes touched his heart, and at the end of the road he stood and asked himself if he should go back to her. He would miss the train if he waited another minute, and he ran on. And he would have missed the train if he had not met a car. Once he was on the car he felt himself safe -- the country was already behind him. The train and the boat at Cork were mere formulae; he was already in America.

The moment he landed he felt the thrill of home that he had not found in his native village, and he wondered how it was that the smell of the bar seemed more natural than the smell of fields, and the roar of crowds more welcome than the silence of the lake's edge. He offered up a thanksgiving for his escape, and entered into negotiations for the purchase of the bar-room.

He took a wife, she bore him sons and daughters, the bar-room prospered, property came and went; he grew old, his wife died, he retired from business, and reached the age when a man begins to feel there are not many years in front of him, and that all he has had to do in life has been done. His children married, lonesomeness began to creep about him in the evening and when he looked into the fire-light, a vague, tender reverie floated up, and Margaret's soft eyes and name vivified the dusk. His wife and children passed out of mind, and it seemed to him that a memory was the only real thing he possessed, and the desire to see Margaret again grew intense. But she was an old woman, she had married, maybe she was dead. Well, he would like to be buried in the village where he was born.

There is an unchanging, silent life within every man that none knows but himself, and his unchanging, silent life was his memory of Margaret Dirken. The bar-room was forgotten and all that concerned it and the things he saw most clearly were the green hill-side, and the bog lake and the rushes about it, and the greater lake in the distance, and behind it the blue line of wandering hills.

# Scotland

Scottish literature, too, developed its combination of the poetic, the anecdotal, and careful study of character from traditional legendary tales. Some acclaimed Scottish prose writers include Sir Walter Scott, Robert Louis Stevenson, and R.B. Cunninghame Graham. The narrator of Graham's story "Miss Christian Jean" views two paintings of the Irish countryside, finding in this art the beauty he feels has been banished from his life by the chores of modern existence. Here the reader is presented with an examination of what Graham saw as the modern Scottish sensibility's relationship to art, nature, and tradition.

## Miss Christian Jean
### R. B. Cunninghame Graham

**R. B. Cunninghame Graham   1852 - 1936:** Robert Bontine Cunninghame Graham was born to William Cunninghame Grahame Bontine of Ardoch, near Cardoss in Dunbartonshire, and Gartmore, near the Lake of Menteith in West Perthshire, and of the Hon. Anne Elizabeth, the fourth daughter of Admiral the Hon. Charles Elphinstone Fleeming of Cumbernauld, Lanarkshire, and the sister of the the 14th Baron Elphinstone. He was educated at Harrow. In 1879 he married Gabriela, the daughter of Don Francisco Jose de la Balmondiere. They were married for twenty-seven years, until Gabriela's death in 1906.

Graham combined his literary talents with his passion for travel and interest in socialist politics. For his attuned sense of literary verisimilitude and appropriately figurative language he has been called the Scottish Maupassant. His works include *Notes on the District of Menteith* (1895); *Aurora, la Cujini, a Realistic Sketch in Seveille* (1898); *The Ipane* (1899); *His People* (1906); *Scottish Stories* (1914). Bernard Shaw's Moroccan play *Captian Brassbound's Conversion* is based on Graham's *Mogreb-el-Acksa, a Journey in Morocco* (1898).

TWO PICTURES HANG upon my study wall, faded and woolly, but well stippled up, the outlines of the hills just indicated with a fine reed pen, showing the water, coloured saffron; deepening to pink in the deep shadows of the lake. Although one picture is a sunset and the other done as it would seem at sunrise, they show a country which even yet is undefiled by any human step.

So accurately is the dark brown tree set in position on the border of the fleecy lake, one feels an artist, superior to mere Nature, has been about the task. The castle, on the mountain top in one of the two masterpieces, is at the bottom of the hill in its compeer, and in the two a clear blue sky throws a deep shadow over the unruffled water, on which float boats with tall white sails, progressing without wind.

Still, with their frames, which are but fricassees of gingerbread well gilt, to me they say a something all the art of all the masters leaves unsaid.

A masterpiece speaks of imagination in its maker; but those pale blue-grey hills and salmon-coloured pinkish lakes, castles which never could have been inhabited, boats sailing in a calm, and trees that seem to rustle without breeze, set me reflecting upon things gone by, and upon places of which I was once part, places which still ungratefully live on, whilst that of me which lived in them is dead.

A long low Georgian room, in which the pictures hung, with its high mantelpiece, its smell of damp and Indian curiosities, and window looking out on the sunk garden underneath the terraces, the sides of which were honeycombed by rabbits, rises in my view, making me wonder in what substance of the body or the mind they have been stamped.

How few such rooms remain, and how few houses such as that, to which the dark and dampish chamber, with its three outside walls, and deep-cut mouldings on the windows and the doors, was library. We called it 'book-room', in the Scottish way, although the books were few and mostly had belonged to a dead uncle who had bought them all in India, and on their yellowing leaves were stains of insects from the East, and now and then a grass or flower from Hyderabad or Kolapur (as pencilled notes upon the margin said), transported children to a land so gorgeous that the like of it was never seen on earth. These books were all well chosen, and such as men read fifty years ago -- Macaulay's *Essays*, with the *Penny Cyclopaedia*, Hume, Smollett, Captain Cook, the *Life of Dost Mohammed*, Elphinstone's *Cabul Mission*, with Burckhardt's *Travels*, enthralling Mungo Park, and others of the kind that at hill stations in the rains, or in the plains during the summer, must have passed many an hour of boredom and of heat away for their dead purchaser. The rest were books of heraldry and matters of the kind together with a set of Lever and of Dickens, with plates by Cruikshank or by Hablot Brown. One in particular set forth a man upon a horse, with a red fluttering cloak streaming out in the wind, galloping in the midst of buffaloes with a long knife between his teeth. But books and furniture and Indian curiosities, with the high

Adam chimney-piece and portraits of the favourite hounds and horses of three generations, were, as it were, keyed up to the two water-colours, one of which hung up above a cabinet sunk far into the wall and glazed, the other over a low double door, deep as an embrasure.

All through the house the smell of damp, of kingwood furniture, and roses dried in bowls, blended and formed a scent which I shall smell as long as life endures. This may, of course, have been mere fancy; but often in old houses some picture or some piece of furniture appears to give the keynote to the rest. But it seemed evident to me that, in some strange mysterious way, the pictures, outstanding in their badness, had stamped themselves upon the house more than the Reynoldses and Raeburns on the walls, though they were pictures of my ancestors, and the two water-colours represented no known landscape upon earth. They entered into my ideas so strongly (though they were unobtrusive in themselves) that, looking from the window-seat in the deep bay of the sunk window in the dining-room, across the terraces, over the sea of laurels, beyond the rushy 'park', and out upon the moss and the low lumpy hills that ran down to the distant lake, almost divided into two by a peninsula set with dark pine trees and with planes, the landscape seemed unfinished and lacking interest without the castles and the chrome-laden skies of the twin masterpieces.

It may be, too, that the unnatural 'landscape caused me to form unnatural views of life, finding things interesting and people worthy of remark whom others found quite commonplace, merely upon their own account, and not from the surroundings of their lives. So everyone connected with the house of the two works of art became mixed up somehow with them in a mysterious way, as well as things inanimate and trees, the vegetation and the white mist which half the year hung over moss and woods, shrouding the hills and everything in its unearthly folds, making them strange and half unreal, as is a landscape in a dream.

Perhaps the fact that the house stood just at the point where Lowlands end and the great jumble of the Highland hills begins, and that the people were compounded of both simples, Saxon and Celtic mixed in equal parts, gave them and all the place an interest such as clings to borderlands the whole world over, for even fifty years ago one talked of 'up above the pass' as of a land distinct from where we lived. Down from those regions wandered men speaking a strange tongue, shaggy, and smelling of a mixture of raw wool and peat smoke, whose dogs obeyed them in a way in which no dog of any man quite civilized, broken to railways and refreshment-rooms, obeys his master's call. The bond of union may have been that both slept out in the wet dew, huddling together in the morning round the fire for warmth, or something else, the half-possession of some sense that we have lost, by means of which, all unknown to themselves, the drover and his dog communicated. Communion, very likely, is the word, the old communion of all living things, the lost connexion between man and all the other animals, which modern life destroys.

But, be that as it may, the men and dogs seemed natives, and we who lived amongst the mosses and the hills seemed strangers, by lack of something or by excess of something else, according to your view.

The herds of ponies that the men drove before them on the road fell naturally into the scheme of Nature; sorrels and yellow chestnuts, creams and duns, they blended with the scrubbing woods and made no blot upon the shaggy hills. Instinctively they took the long-forgotten fords, crossing below the bridges, and standing knee-deep in the stream, the water dripping from the ropy tails and burdock-knotted manes. The herds of kyloes too have gone, which looked like animals of some race older than our own. The men who drove them, with their rough clothes of coarse grey wool, their hazel crooks, and plaids about their shoulders, whether the wind blew keenly or midges teased in August, all have disappeared. Their little camps upon the selvedge of the roads are all forgotten, although I know them still, by the bright grass that grows upon the ashes of the fires. Or have they gone, and are the hills brown, lumpy, heather-clad, and jewelled after rain by myriad streams, merely illusions; and is it really that I myself have gone, and they live on, deep down in the recesses of some fairy hill of which I am not free?

Men, too, like my friend Wallace of Gartchorrachan, have disappeared, and I am not quite sure if we should bless the Lord on that account. All through Menteith, and right 'across the hill' as far as Callander and Doune, he was well known, and always styled Laird Wallace, for though our custom is to call men by the title of their lands, thus making them *adsripti glebae* to the very soul, the word Gartchorrachan stuck in our throats, although we readily twist and distort the Gaelic place-names in our talk just as the Spaniards mutilate the Arab words, smoothing their corners and their angles out in the strong current of their speech.

Dressed in grey tweed with bits of buckskin let into the shoulders of his coat, for no one ever saw him leave his house without a gun, he was about the age that farmers in the north seem to be born at -- that is, for years he had been grey, but yet was vigorous, wore spectacles, and his thick curly hair was matted like the wool upon a ram, whilst from his ears and nostrils grew thick tufts of bristles, just as a growth of twigs springs from the trunk of an old oak tree, where it has got a wound.

His house was like himself, old, grey, and rambling and smelt of gun oil, beeswax, and of camphor, for he was versed in entomology, and always had a case of specimens, at which he laboured with a glass stuck in his eye reminding me of Cyclops or of Polyphemus, or of an ogre in a story-book. Botany and conchology, and generally those sciences which when pursued without a method soon become trifling and a pastime, were his joys, and he had cabinets in which the specimens reposed under a heavy coat of dust, but duly ticketed each with its Latin name.

He spoke good English as a general rule, and when unmoved, as was the custom with the people of his class and upbringing, but often used broad Scotch, which he employed after the fashion of a shield against the world, half in a joking way and half against the sin of self-revealment which we shun as the plague, passing our lives like pebbles in a brook, which rub against each other for an age, and yet remain apart.

In early life, he had contracted what he called a 'local liassong', the fruit of which had been a daughter whom he had educated, and who lived with him, half as his daughter, half as housekeeper. Her father loved her critically, and when she not infrequently swept china on the floor as she passed through the drawing-room (just as tapir walks about a wood, breaking down all the saplings in its path), he would screw up one eye, and looking at her say, 'That's what you get from breeding from a cart-mare, the filly's sure to throw back to the dam.'

Withal he was a gentleman, having been in the army and travelled in his youth, but had not got much more by his experience than the raw youth of whom his father said, 'Aye, Willie's been to Rome and back again, and a' he's learnt is but to cast his sark aince every day.' But still he was a kindly man, the prey of anyone who had a specious story, the providence of all lame horses and of dogs quite useless for any kind of sport, all which he bought at prices far above the value of the most favoured members of their race.

His inner nature always seemed to be just struggling forth almost against his will, mastering his rough exterior, just as in pibrochs, after the skirling of the pipes has died away, a tender melody breaks out, fitful and plaintive, speaking of islands lost in misty seas, of things forgotten and misunderstood, of the faint, swishing noise of heather in the rain moved by the breeze at night, and which through minor modulations and fantastic trills ends in a wild lament for some Fingalian hero, like the wind sighing through the pines.

Nothing was more congenial to his humour than to unpack his recollections of the past, seated before the fire, an oily black cigar which he chewed almost like a quid between his teeth, and with a glass of whisky by his side.

After expatiating upon the excellences of his lame, jibbing chestnut mare, that he had bought at Falkirk Tryst from a quite honest dealer, but which had gone mysteriously so lame that even whisky for his groom had no effect in curing her, he usually used to lament upon the changes which the course of time had brought about. All was grief to him, as it is really to all of us, if we all knew it, that some particular landmark of his life had disappeared. No one spoke Gaelic nowadays, although he never in his life had known a word of it. The use of 'weepers' and crape hat-bands by the country-folk on Sunday was quite discontinued, and no one took their collie dogs to church. Coffins were now no longer carried shoulder-high across the hills from lonely upland straths, as he remembered to have seen them in this youth. Did not some funeral party in his childhood, taking a short cut on a frozen loch, fall through and perish to a man? -- a circumstance he naturally deplored, but still regretted, as men of older generations may have regretted highwaymen, as they sat safely by their fire. Although he never fished, he was quite certain no one now alive could busk a fly as well as a departed worthy of his youth, one Dan-a-Haltie, or make a withy basket or those osier loops which formerly were stuck between the 'divots' in a dry stone dike, projecting outwards like a torpedo netting, to stop sheep jumping from a field. Words such as *flauchtered feal* and *laroch* were hardly understood, shepherds read newspapers as they lay out upon the hill, the Shorter Catechism had been miserably abridged, and the old fir-tree by the Shannochill was blasted at the top.

All these complaints he uttered philosophically, not in a plaintive way, but as a man who, at his birth, had entered as it were into a covenant with life just as it was, which he for his part had faithfully observed, but was deceived by fate.

Then when he had relieved his mind he used to laugh and, puffing out the smoke of his thick black cigar, which hung about the tufts which sprung out of his nostrils, just as the mist hangs dank about a bog, he would remark, 'I'm haverin',' as if he was afraid of having to explain himself to something in his mind. On these occasions, I used to let him sit a little, and usually, he would begin again, after a look to see if I had noticed the gag he suddenly had put upon himself, and then start off again. 'Ye mind my aunt, Miss Christian Jean?' I did, eating her sweetmeats in my youth, and trembling at her frown.

'Ye never heard me tell how it was I kisted her,' he said, and then again fell into contemplation, and once again began. 'My aunt, Miss Christian Jean, was a survival of the fittest -- aye, ye know I am in some things quite opposed to Darwin, the survival of the potter's wheel in the Fijis and several other things . . . aye, haverin' again . . . or the most unfitted to survive.

'She was a gentlewoman . . . yes, yes, the very word is now half ludicrous, ye need not smile . . . lady is a poor substitute. Tall, dark, and masculine, and with a down upon her upper lip that many a cornet of dragoons, for there were cornets in those days, might well have envied, she was a sort of providence, jealous and swift in chastisement, but yet a providence to all the younger members of her race who came across her path.

'I see her now, her and her maid, old Katherine Sinclair, a tall, gaunt Highland woman, who might easily have walked straight from the pages of *Rob Roy*, an her old butler, Robert Cameron, grey and red-faced, and dressed eternally in a black suit, all stained with snuff, a pawky sort of chiel, religious and still with the spirit of revolt against all dogmatism which modern life and cheap and stereotyped instruction has quite stamped out today. My aunt kept order in her house, that is as far as others were concerned. Each day she read her chapter, in what she styled the Book, not taking over heed how she selected it, so that the chapter once was duly read. It happened sometimes that when she came into the room where, as my cousin Andrew used to say -- ye mind that he was drowned in one of those Green's ships, fell from aloft whilst they were reefing topsails in a dark night somewhere about the Cape.

'I've heard him say he could come down the weather-leach of a topsail, just like a monkey, by the bolt ropes. ... Where was I, eh? Aye, I mind, he used to say that my aunt's prayers reminded him of service in a ship, with all hands mustered; so as I said, my aunt would sometimes open up the Book and come upon a chapter full of names, and how some one begat another body, and sometimes upon things perfectly awesome for a maiden lady to read aloud, for 'twas all one to her.

'Then the old butler would put his hand up to his mouth and whisper, "Mem, Miss Christian, Mem, ye're wandered," and she would close the book, or start again upon another chapter and maybe twice as long.

'My aunt and her two satellites kept such good order, that a visitor from England, seeing her neat and white-capped maids file in and take their seats facing the men-servants, expressed her pleasure at the well-ordered, comely worship, and received the answer, "Yes, my dear, ye see at family prayers we have the separation of the sexes, but I understand when they meet afterwards at the stair foot, the kissing beats the cracking of a whip."

'Poor Aunt Christian, I used to shiver at her nod, and well remember when a youth how she would flyte me when I pinched the maids, and say, "Laddie, I canna' have you making the girls squeal like Highland ponies; it is not decent, and decency comes after morality, sometimes, I think, before it, for it can be attained, whereas the other is a counsel of perfection set up on high, but well out of our reach."

'A pretty moralizer was my poor aunt, almost a heathen in her theory, guided by what she said were natural laws, and yet a Puritan in practice, whereas I always was a theoretic Puritan, but shaped my life exclusively by natural laws, as they appear to me.

'Let ministers just haver as they will, one line of conduct is not possible for nephews and for aunts. Take David, now, the man after the Lord's own heart, and ask yourself what would have happened if his aunt . . . aye, aye, I'm wandered from my tale . . . I ken I'm wandering.

'Well, well, it seemed as if my aunt might have gone on for ever, getting a little dryer and her face more peakit, as the years went by and her old friends dropped off and left her all alone. That's what it is, ye see; it's got to come, although it seems impossible whilst we sit talking here and drinking -- that is, I drinking and you listening to me talk. One wintry day I was just sitting wiping the cee-spring of a gun, and looking out upon the avenue, when through the wreaths, I saw a boy on a bit yellow pony beast come trotting through the snow.

'It was before the days of telegrams, and I jaloused that there was something special, or no one would have sent the laddie out on such a day, with the snow drifted half a yard upon the ground, the trees all white with cranreuch like the sugar on a cake, and the first frost keen enough to split a pudding stone and grind it into sand.

'I sent the laddie to the kitchen fire, and ripped the envelope, whilst the bit pony rooted round for grass and walked upon the reins. The letter told me that my aunt had had a fit, was signed by "Robert Cameron, butler", and was all daubed with snuff, and in a postcript I was asked to hurry, for the time was short, and to come straight across the hill as the low road was blocked by the snow drifting and nobody could pass. I harnessed up my mare -- not the bit blooded chestnut I drive now' -- this was the way in which he spoke of the lame cripple which had conveyed him to my house -- 'but a stout sort of Highland mouse-coloured beastie that I had, rather short backit, a little hammerheaded, and with the hair upon the fetlocks like a Clydesdale. ... Maun, I think ye dinna' often see such sort of beasts the now.' I mentally thanked God for it, and he again launched out in his tale.

'An awful drive, I'm tellin' ye! I hadna' got above Auchyle -- ye mind, at the old bridge just where yon English tourist coupit his creels, and gaed to heaven, maybe last summer -- when I saw I had a job. The snow balled in the mare's feet as big as cabbages, and made her stotter in her gait, just like a drunken curler ettlin' to walk upon a rink. I had to take her by the head till we got on the flat ground, up about Rusky. Man, it was arctic and the little loch lay like a sheet of glass that had been breathed upon, with dead bulrushes and reeds all sticking through the ice! The island in the loch seemed like a blob of white, and the old tower (I dinna' richtly mind, if, at one time, it belonged to some of your own folk) loomed up like Stirling Castle or like Doune in the keen frosty air. The little firwood on the east side of the old change-house -- that one they called Wright, or some such name, once keepit -- was full of roe, all sheltering like cows, so cold and starved they scarcely steered when I passed by and gave a shout to warm my lungs and hearten up the mare; and a cock capercailzie, moping and miserable, sat on a fir-tree like a barn-door fowl. I ploutered on just to where there used to be a gate across the road, where ye see Uamh Var and the great shoulder of Ben Ledi stretching up out by the pass of Leny and the old chapel of St. Bryde. It was fair awesome; I did not rightly know the landscape with the familiar features blotted out. I very nearly got myself wandered just in the straight about the Gart, for all the dikes were sunk beneath the snow, and the hedge-tops peeped up like box in an old cabbage-garden. At last I reached the avenue, the mare fair taigled, and the ice hanging from her fetlocks and her mane and wagging to and fro. The evergreens were, so to speak, a-wash, and looked like beds of parsley or of greens, and underneath the trees the squirrels' footsteps in the snow seemed those of some strange birds, where they had melted and then frozen on the ground. Across the sky a crow or two flew slowly, flapping their wings as if the joint oil had been frozen in their bones and cawing sullenly.

'On the high steps which led up to the door the butler met me, and as he took my coat, said, "Laird ye are welcome; your poor dear auntie's going. Hech, sirs, 'twill be an awfu' nicht for the poor leddy to be fleein' naked through the air towards the judgement seat. Will ye tak' speerits or a dish o' tea after your coldsome drive, or will I tak' ye straight in to your aunt? I'm feared she willna' know you. But His will be done, though I could wish He micht hae held His hand a little longer; but we must not repine. I've just been readin' out to her from the old Book, ye ken, passin' the time awa' and waitin' for the end."

'All day my aunt lay dozing, half-conscious and half-stupefied, and all the day the butler, sitting by the bed, read psalms and chapters, to which she sometimes seemed to pay attention, and at others lay so still we thought that she was dead. Now and again he stopped his reading, and peering at his mistress with his spectacles pushed up, wiped off the tears that trickled down his face with his red handkerchief, and, as if doubting he were reading to the living or the dead, said, "Nod yer heid, Miss Christian," which she did feebly, and he, satisfied she understood, mumbled on piously in a thick undertone.

'Just about morning she passed away quite quietly, the maids and her butler standing round the bed, they crying silently, and he snorting in his red pocket-handkerchief, with the tears running down his face. The gaunt old Highland waiting-woman raised a high wail which echoed through the cold and silent house, causing the dogs to bark and the old parrot scream, and the butler stottered from the room, muttering that he would go and see if tea was ready, closing the door behind him with his foot, as if he feared the figure on the bed would scold him, as she had often done during her life, if it slammed to and made a noise.

'All the week through it snowed, and my aunt's house was dismal, smelling of cheese and honey, yellow soap, of jam, of grease burnt in the fire, and with the dogs and cats uncared for rambling about and sleeping on the chairs. The cold was penetrating, and I wandered up and down the stairs quite aimlessly, feeling like Alexander Selkirk in the melancholy house, which seemed an island cut off from the world by a white sea of snow. None of Aunt Christian's friends or relatives could come, as all the roads were blocked; even her coffin was not sent till a few hours before the funeral, the cart that brought it stalling in the snow, and the black-coated undertaker's men carrying it shoulder-high through the thick wreaths upon the avenue.

'The servants would not have a stranger touch the corpse, and the old butler and myself kisted my aunt, lifting her body from the bed between the two of us. A week had passed and she looked black and shrunken, and as I lifted her, the chill from the cold flesh struck me with horror, and welled into the bones. I could not kiss her as she lay like a mummy in the kist, for the shrunk face with the white clothes about the chin was not the same Aunt Christian's whom I had loved and before whom I trembled for so many years, but changed somehow and horrible to see.

'The butler did, looking at me, as I thought, half-reproachfully as I stood silently, not once crying but half stupefied, and then as she lay shrunken and brown on the white satin lining of the kist, we stood and looked at one another, just as we had been partners in a crime, till they began to hammer down the lid. A drearsome sound it makes. One feels the nails are sticking in the flesh, and every time ye hear it, it affects ye more than the last time, the same as an earthquake, as I mind I heard a traveller say one day in Edinburgh. What the old butler did, I do not mind; but I just dandered out into the garden, and washed my hands in snow, now that I felt a skunner at my poor Aunt Christian's flesh, but somehow I had to do it, for ye ken 'twas the first time.'

Laird Wallace stopped just as a horse props suddenly when he is fresh and changes feet, then breaking into Scotch, said: 'I have talked enough. That's how I kisted my Aunt Christian Jean, puir leddy, a sair job it was, and dreich. ... Thank ye, nae soddy, I'll tak' a drop of Lagavoulin.' Then lighting a cigar, he said, 'Ring for my dog-cart, please,' and when it came he clambered to the seat, and pointing to his spavined mare, said, 'Man a gran' beast clean thoroughbred, fit to run for her life' (and this to me who knew her); then bidding me good-night, drew his whip smartly on her scraggy flank, and vanished through the trees.

# England

English literature's Victorian Period, 1837 to 1901, was the great age of the novel. The increase in practice of and attention to prose writing in this period produced the forms that continue to characterize modern English literature. The works were ostensibly realistic, heavy in plot, and crowded with characters. Notable Victorian literary figures and their works include William Makepeace Thackeray, *Vanity Fair* (1848), Emily Bronte, *Wuthering Heights* (1847), George Eliot, *Silas Marner* (1861), and Charles Dickens, the prolific novelist whose works include *A Tale of Two Cities* and *Great Expectations*.

Rudyard Kipling is an important short story writer of this period. Born in Bombay, India, then under English control, Kipling spent his childhood there, but was educated mainly in England. He did, however, return to India upon the completion of his education to pursue a career in journalism. He composed verse and wrote stories and dramatic pieces, all incorporating detailed descriptions of Indian life. It was during his journalistic career that Kipling wrote the *Departmental Ditties* of 1886. The satire of this work attacked both corrupt members of the British service and those naysayers in England who took a bitterly cynical view of the British civil services stationed in India.

Similarly, "The Mark of the Beast" satirizes the British settlers' backward ignorance of Indian culture. Caddish Fleete, uneducated in Indian religious folklore, and not interested in modifying his boorish behavior in any case, offends the Indian monkey-god Hanuman. The ensuing events suggest Fleete has been cursed for his offense. More significantly, they portray, in a satirical mode, the consequences of persisting within a culturally ignorant model of behavior.

Often pushed to the margins of literary fiction, but no less capable of offering cultural commentary than other genres, is science fiction. H. G. Wells is credited with ushering science fiction into the modern age in terms of content and style. "The Plattner Story" explores the possibilities of time, a fourth dimension. Wells constructs a tangibility for this dimension by placing his protagonist, Plattner, on this ethereal plane. Plattner experiences time more slowly than inhabitants of the physical dimensions, and he encounters beings whom he suspects may in fact be guardians, or "Watchers," who have expired from earthly life.

# The Plattner Story
## *H. G. Wells*

**H. G. Wells 1866-1946:** Herbert George Wells was born into the lower middle class and was the son of a maid and a gardener. He felt the stigmata placed upon his humble origin by the social rigidity of Victorianism. He was apprenticed to a draper at the age of fourteen, and with the aid of grants he was eventually able to attend the University of London. He taught biology until 1893, when he began in earnest his career as a writer. He became friends with Henry James despite their differing social stations. James was the more urbane and aesthetic of the two, but Wells' intelligence and visible talents permitted him to move among this social class so foreign to that of his beginnings.

H. G. Wells is best known for his science fiction, but he was also a dedicated social thinker who wanted to remove all vestiges of Victorian social, moral, and religious attititudes from 20th-century life. His works include *The Time Machine* (1895), *The Wonderful Visit* (1895), *The Invisible Man* (1897), and *The War of the Worlds* (1898).

WHETHER THE STORY of Gottfried Plattner is to be credited or not, is a pretty question in the value of evidence. On the one hand, we have seven witnesses - to be perfectly exact, we have six and a half pairs of eyes, and one undeniable fact; and on the other we have - what is it? - prejudice, common sense, the inertia of opinion. Never were there seven more honest-seeming witnesses; never was there a more undeniable fact than the inversion of Gottfried Plattner's anatomical structure, and - never was there a more preposterous story than the one they have to tell! The most preposterous part of the story is the worthy Gottfried's contribution (for I count him as one of the seven). Heaven forbid that I should be led into giving countenance to superstition by a passion for impartiality, and so come to share the fate of Eusapia's patrons! Frankly, I believe there is something crooked about this business of Gottfried Plattner, but what that crooked factor is, I will admit as frankly, I do not know. I have been surprised at the credit accorded to the story in the most unexpected and authoritative quarters. The fairest way to the reader, however, will be for me to tell it without further comment.

Gottfried Plattner is, in spite of his name, a free-born Englishman. His father was an Alsatian, who came to England in the sixties, married a respectable English girl of unexceptional antecedents, and died, after a wholesome and uneventful life (devoted, I understand, chiefly to the laying of parquet flooring), in 1887. Gottfried's age is seven-and-twenty. He is, by virtue of his heritage of three languages, Modern Languages Master in a small private school in the South of England. To the casual observer he is singularly like any other Modern Languages Master in any other small private school. His costume is neither very costly nor very fashionable, but, on the other hand, it is not markedly cheap or shabby; his complexion, like his height and his bearing, is inconspicuous. You would notice perhaps that, like the majority of people, his face was not absolutely symmetrical, his right eye a little larger than the left, and his jaw a trifle heavier on the right side. If you, as an ordinary careless person, were to bare his chest and feel his heart beating, you would probably find it quite like the heart of anyone else. But here you and the trained observer would part company. If you found his heart quite ordinary, the trained observer would find it quite otherwise. And once the thing was pointed out to you, you too would perceive the peculiarity easily enough. It is that Gottfried's heart beats on the right side of his body.

Now that is not the only singularity of Gottfried's structure, although it is the only one that would appeal to the untrained mind. Careful sounding of Gottfried's internal arrangements, by a well-known surgeon, seems to point to the fact that all the other unsymmetrical parts of his body are similarly misplaced. The right lobe of his liver is on the left side, the left on his right; while his lungs, too, are similarly contraposed. What is still more singular, unless Gottfried is a consummate actor we must believe that his right hand has recently become his left. Since the occurrences we are about to consider (as impartially as possible), he has found the utmost difficulty in writing except from right to left across the paper with his left hand. He cannot throw with his right hand, he is perplexed at meal times between knife and fork, and his ideas of the rule of the road - he is a cyclist - are still a dangerous confusion. And there is not a scrap of evidence to show that before these occurrences Gottfried was at all left-handed.

There is yet another wonderful fact in this preposterous business. Gottfried produces three photographs of himself. You have him at the age of five or six, thrusting fat legs at you from under a plaid frock, and scowling. In that photograph his left eye is a little larger than his right, and his jaw is a trifle heavier on the left side. This is the reverse of his present living conditions. The photograph of Gottfried at fourteen seems to contradict these facts, but that is because it is one of those cheap 'Gem' photographs that were then in vogue, taken direct upon metal, and therefore reversing things just as a looking-glass would. The third photograph represents him at one-and-twenty, and confirms the record of the others. There seems here evidence of the strongest confirmatory character that Gottfried has exchanged his left side for his right. Yet how a human being can be so changed, short of a fantastic and pointless miracle, it is exceedingly hard to suggest.

In one way, of course, these facts might be explicable on the supposition that Plattner has undertaken an elaborate mystification on the strength of his heart's displacement. Photographs may be fudged, and left-handedness imitated. But the character of the man does not lend itself to any such theory. He is quiet, practical, unobtrusive, and thoroughly sane from the Nordau standpoint. He likes beer and smokes moderately, takes walking exercise daily, and has a healthily high estimate of the value of his teaching. He has a good but untrained tenor voice, and takes a pleasure in singing airs of a popular and cheerful character. He is fond, but not morbidly fond, of reading - chiefly fiction pervaded with a vaguely pious optimism - sleeps well, and rarely dreams. He is, in fact, the very last person to evolve a fantastic fable. Indeed, so far from forcing this story upon the world, he has been singularly reticent on the matter. He meets inquiries with a certain engaging - bashfulness is almost the word, that disarms the most suspicious. He seems genuinely ashamed that anything so unusual has occurred to him.

It is to be regretted that Plattner's aversion to the idea of postmortem dissection may postpone, perhaps for ever, the positive proof that his entire body has had its left and right sides transposed. Upon that fact mainly the credibility of his story hangs. There is no way of taking a man and moving him about *in space*, as ordinary people understand space, that will result in our changing his sides. Whatever you do, his right is still his right, his left his left. You can do that with a perfectly thin and flat thing, of course. If you were to cut a figure out of paper, any figure with a right and left side, you could change its sides simply by lifting it up and turning it over. But with a solid it is different. Mathematical theorists tell us that the only way in which the right and left sides of a solid body can be changed is by taking that body clean out of space as we know it - taking it out of ordinary existence, that is - and turning it somewhere outside space. This is a little abstruse, no doubt, but anyone with a slight knowledge of mathematical theory will assure the reader of its truth. To put the thing in technical language, the curious inversion of Plattner's right and left sides is proof that he has moved out of our space into what is called the Fourth Dimension, and that he has returned again to our world. Unless we choose to consider ourselves the victims of an elaborate and motiveless fabrication, we are almost bound to believe that this has occurred.

So much for the tangible facts. We come now to the account of the phenomena that attended his temporary disappearance from the world. It appears that in the Sussexville Proprietary School, Plattner not only discharged the duties of Modern Languages Master, but also taught chemistry, commercial geography, bookkeeping, shorthand, drawing, and any other additional subject to which the changing fancies of the boys' parents might direct attention. He knew little or nothing of these various subjects, but in secondary as distinguished from Board or elementary schools, knowledge in the teacher is, very properly, by no means so necessary as high moral character and gentlemanly tone. In chemistry he was particularly deficient, knowing, he says, nothing beyond the Three Gases (whatever the three gases may be). As, however, his pupils began by knowing nothing, and derived all their information from him, this caused him (or anyone) but little inconvenience for several terms. Then a little boy named Whibble joined the school, who had been educated, it seems, by some mischievous relative into an inquiring habit of mind. This little boy followed Plattner's lessons with marked and sustained interest, and in order to exhibit his zeal on the subject, brought at various times substances for Plattner to analyse. Plattner, flattered by this evidence of his power to awaken interest and trusting to the boy's ignorance, analysed these and even made general statements as to their composition. Indeed he was so far stimulated by his pupil as to obtain a work upon analytical chemistry, and study it during his supervision of the evening's preparation. He was surprised to find chemistry quite an interesting subject.

So far the story is absolutely commonplace. But now the greenish powder comes upon the scene. The source of that greenish powder seems, unfortunately, lost. Master Whibble tells a tortuous story of finding it done up in a packet in a disused limekiln near the Downs. It would have been an excellent thing for Plattner, and possibly for Master Whibble's family, if a match could have been applied to that powder there and then. The young gentleman certainly did not bring it to school in a packet, but in a common eight-ounce graduated medicine bottle, plugged with masticated newspaper. He gave it to Plattner at the end of the afternoon school. Four boys had been detained after school prayers in order to complete some neglected tasks, and Plattner was supervising these in the small

classroom in which the chemical teaching was conducted. The appliances
for the practical teaching of chemistry in the Sussexville Proprietary
School, as in most private schools in this country, are characterized by a
severe simplicity. They are kept in a cupboard standing in a recess and
having about the same capacity as a common travelling trunk. Plattner,
being bored with his passive superintendence, seems to have welcomed
the intervention of Whibble with his green powder as an agreeable
diversion, and, unlocking this cupboard, proceeded at once with his
analytical experiments. Whibble sat, luckily for himself, at a safe distance, regarding him. The four malefactors, feigning a profound absorption in their work, watched him furtively with the keenest interest. For
even within the limits of the Three Gases, Plattner's practical chemistry
was, I understand, temerarious.

They are practically unanimous in their account of Plattner's proceedings. He poured a little of the green powder into a test-tube and tried the
substance with water, hydrochloric acid, nitric acid, and sulphuric acid in
succession. Getting no result, he emptied out a little heap - nearly half the
bottleful, in fact - upon a slate and tried a match. He held the medicine
bottle in his left hand. The stuff began to smoke and melt, and then -
exploded with deafening violence and a blinding flash.

The five boys, seeing the flash and being prepared for catastrophes,
ducked below their desks, and were none of them seriously hurt. The
window was blown out into the playground, and the blackboard on its
easel was upset. The slate was smashed to atoms. Some plaster fell from
the ceiling. No other damage was done to the school edifice or appliances,
and the boys at first, seeing nothing of Plattner, fancied he was knocked
down and lying out of their sight below the desks. They jumped out of
their places to go to his assistance, and were amazed to find the space
empty. Being still confused by the sudden violence of the report, they
hurried to the open door, under the impression that he must have been
hurt, and have rushed out of the room. But Carson, the foremost, nearly
collided in the doorway with the principal, Mr Lidgett.

Mr Lidgett is a corpulent, excitable man with one eye. The boys
describe him as stumbling into the room mouthing some of those tem-
pered expletives irritable schoolmasters accustom themselves to use - lest
worse befall. 'Wretched mumchancer!' he said. 'Where's Mr Plattner?'
The boys are agreed on the very words. ('Wobbler', 'snivelling puppy',
and 'mumchancer' are, it seems, among the ordinary small change of Mr
Lidgett's scholastic commerce.)

Where's Mr Plattner? That was a question that was to be repeated many times in the next few days. It really seemed as though that frantic hyperbole, 'blown to atoms', had for once realized itself. There was not a visible particle of Plattner to be seen; not a drop of blood nor a stitch of clothing to be found. Apparently he had been blown clean out of existence and left not a wrack behind. Not so much as would cover a sixpenny piece, to quote a proverbial expression! The evidence of his absolute disappearance, as a consequence of that explosion, is indubitable.

It is not necessary to enlarge here upon the commotion excited in the Sussexville Proprietary School, and in Sussexville and elsewhere, by this event. It is quite possible, indeed, that some of the readers of these pages may recall the hearing of some remote and dying version of that excitement during the last summer holidays. Lidgett, it would seem, did everything in his power to suppress and minimize the story. He instituted a penalty of twenty-five lines for any mention of Plattner's name among the boys, and stated in the schoolroom that he was clearly aware of his assistant's whereabouts. He was afraid, he explains, that the possibility of an explosion happening, in spite of the elaborate precautions taken to minimize the practical teaching of chemistry, might injure the reputation of the school; and so might any mysterious quality of Plattner's departure. Indeed, he did everything in his power to make the occurrence seem as ordinary as possible. In particular, he cross-examined the five eye-witnesses of the occurrence so searchingly that they began to doubt the plain evidence of their senses. But, in spite of these efforts, the tale, in a magnified and distorted state, made a nine days' wonder in the district, and several parents withdrew their sons on colourable pretexts. Not the least remarkable point in the matter is the fact that a large number of people in the neighbourhood dreamed singularly vivid dreams of Plattner during the period of excitement before his return, and that these dreams had a curious uniformity. In almost all of them Plattner was seen, sometimes singly, sometimes in company, wandering about through a coruscating iridescence. In all cases his face was pale and distressed, and in some he gesticulated towards the dreamer. One or two of the boys, evidently under the influence of nightmare, fancied that Plattner approached them with remarkable swiftness, and seemed to look closely into their very eyes. Others fled with Plattner from the pursuit of vague and extraordinary creatures of a globular shape. But all these fancies were forgotten in inquiries and speculations when on the Wednesday next but one after the Monday of the explosion, Plattner returned.

# 330 H.G. Wells

The circumstances of his return were as singular as those of his departure. So far as Mr Lidgett's somewhat choleric outline can be filled in from Plattner's hesitating statements, it would appear that on Wednesday evening, towards the hour of sunset, the former gentleman, having dismissed evening preparation, was engaged in his garden, picking and eating strawberries, a fruit of which he is inordinately fond. It is a large old-fashioned garden, secured from observation, fortunately, by a high and ivy-covered red-brick wall. Just as he was stooping over a particularly prolific plant, there was a flash in the air and a heavy thud, and before he could look round, some heavy body struck him violently from behind. He was pitched forward, crushing the strawberries he held in his hand, and with such force that his silk hat - Mr Lidgett adheres to the older ideas of scholastic costume - was driven violently down upon his forehead, and almost over one eye. This heavy missile, which slid over him sideways and collapsed into a sitting posture among the strawberry plants, proved to be our long-lost Mr Gottfried Plattner, in an extremely dishevelled condition. He was collarless and hatless, his linen was dirty, and there was blood upon his hands. Mr Lidgett was so indignant and surprised that he remained on all-fours, and with his hat jammed down on his eye, while he expostulated vehemently with Plattner for his disrespectful and unaccountable conduct.

This scarcely idyllic scene completes what I may call the exterior version of the Plattner story - its exoteric aspect. It is quite unnecessary to enter here into all the details of his dismissal by Mr Lidgett. Such details, with the full names and dates and references, will be found in the larger report of these occurrences that was laid before the Society for the Investigation of Abnormal Phenomena. The singular transposition of Plattner's right and left sides was scarcely observed for the first day or so, and then first in connexion with his disposition to write from right to left across the blackboard. He concealed rather than ostended this curious confirmatory circumstance, as he considered it would unfavourably affect his prospects in a new situation. The displacement of his heart was discovered some months after, when he was having a tooth extracted under anaesthetics. He then, very unwillingly, allowed a cursory surgical examination to be made of himself, with a view to a brief account in the *Journal of Anatomy*. That exhausts the statement of the material facts; and we may now go on to consider Plattner's account of the matter.

But first let us clearly differentiate between the preceding portion of this story and what is to follow. All I have told thus far is established by such evidence as even a criminal lawyer would approve. Every one of the witnesses is still alive; the reader, if he have the leisure, may hunt out the lads tomorrow, or even brave the terrors of the redoubtable Lidgett, and cross-examine and trap and test to his heart's content; Gottfried Plattner, himself, and his twisted heart and his three photographs are producible. It may be taken as proved that he did disappear for nine days as the consequence of an explosion; that he returned almost as violently, under circumstances in their nature annoying to Mr Lidgett, whatever the details of those circumstances may be; and that he returned inverted, just as a reflection returns from a mirror. From the last fact, as I have already stated, it follows almost inevitably that Plattner, during those nine days, must have been in some state of existence altogether out of space. The evidence of these statements is, indeed, far stronger than that upon which most murderers are hanged. But for his own particular account of where he had been, with its confused explanations and well-nigh self-contradictory details, we have only Mr Gottfried Plattner's word. I do not wish to discredit that, but I must point out - what so many writers upon obscure psychic phenomena fail to do - that we are passing here from the practically undeniable to that kind of matter which any reasonable man is entitled to believe or reject as he thinks proper. The previous statements render it plausible; its discordance with common experience tilts it towards the incredible. I would prefer not to sway the beam of the reader's judgement either way, but simply to tell the story as Plattner told it to me.

He gave me his narrative, I may state, at my house at Chislehurst; and so soon as he had left me that evening, I went into my study and wrote down everything as I remembered it. Subsequently he was good enough to read over a type-written copy, so that its substantial correctness is undeniable.

He states that at the moment of the explosion he distinctly thought he was killed. He felt lifted off his feet and driven forcibly backward. It is a curious fact for psychologists that he thought clearly during his backward flight, and wondered whether he should hit the chemistry cupboard or the blackboard easel. His heels struck ground, and he staggered and fell heavily into a sitting position on something soft and firm. For a moment the concussion stunned him. He became aware at once of a vivid scent of singed hair, and he seemed to hear the voice of Lidgett asking for him. You will understand that for a time his mind was greatly confused.

At first he was distinctly under the impression that he was still in the classroom. He perceived quite distinctly the surprise of the boys and the entry of Mr Lidgett. He is quite positive upon that score. He did not hear their remarks, but that he ascribed to the deafening effect of the experiment. Things about him seemed curiously dark and faint, but his mind explained that on the obvious but mistaken idea that the explosion had engendered a huge volume of dark smoke. Through the dimness the figures of Lidgett and the boys moved, as faint and silent as ghosts. Plattner's face still tingled with the stinging heat of the flash. He was, he says, 'all muddled'. His first definite thoughts seem to have been of his personal safety. He thought he was perhaps blinded and deafened. He felt his limbs and face in gingerly manner. Then his perceptions grew clearer, and he was astonished to miss the old familiar desks and other school-room furniture about him. Only dim, uncertain, grey shapes stood in the place of these. Then came a thing that made him shout aloud, and awoke his stunned faculties to instant activity. *Two of the boys, gesticulating, walked one after the other clean through him!* Neither manifested the slightest consciousness of his presence. It is difficult to imagine the sensation he felt. They came against him, he says, with no more force than a wisp of mist.

Plattner's first thought after that was that he was dead. Having been brought up with thoroughly sound views in these matters, however, he was a little surprised to find his body still about him. His second conclusion was that he was not dead, but that the others were: that the explosion had destroyed the Sussexville Proprietary School and every soul in it except himself. But that, too, was scarcely satisfactory. He was thrown back upon astonished observation.

Everything about him was extraordinarily dark: at first it seemed to have an altogether ebony blackness. Overhead was a black firmament. The only touch of light in the scene was a faint greenish glow at the edge of the sky in one direction, which threw into prominence a horizon of undulating black hills. This, I say, was his impression at first. As his eyes grew accustomed to the darkness, he began to distinguish a faint quality of differentiating greenish colour in the circumambient night. Against this background the furniture and occupants of the classroom, it seems, stood out like phosphorescent spectres, faint and impalpable. He extended his hand, and thrust it without an effort through the wall of the room by the fireplace.

He describes himself as making a strenuous effort to attract attention. He shouted to Lidgett, and tried to seize the boys as they went to and fro. He only desisted from these attempts when Mrs Lidgett, whom he as an

Assistant Master naturally disliked, entered the room. He says the sensation of being in the world, and yet not part of it, was an extraordinarily
disagreeable one. He compared his feelings, not inaptly, to those of a cat
watching a mouse through a window. Whenever he made a motion to
communicate with the dim, familiar world about him, he found an invisible, incomprehensible barrier preventing intercourse.

He then turned his attention to his solid environment. He found the
medicine bottle still unbroken in his hand, with the remainder of the green
powder therein. He put this in his pocket, and began to feel about him.
Apparently, he was sitting on a boulder of rock covered with a velvety
moss. The dark country about him he was unable to see, the faint, misty
picture of the schoolroom blotting it out, but he had a feeling (due
perhaps to a cold wind) that he was near the crest of a hill, and that a steep
valley fell away beneath his feet. The green glow along the edge of the sky
seemed to be growing in extent and intensity. He stood up, rubbing his
eyes.

It would seem that he made a few steps, going steeply downhill, and
then stumbled, nearly fell, and sat down again upon a jagged mass of rock
to watch the dawn. He became aware that the world about him was
absolutely silent. It was as still as it was dark, and though there was a cold
wind blowing up the hill-face, the rustle of grass, the sighing of the
boughs that should have accompanied it, were absent. He could hear,
therefore, if he could not see, that the hillside upon which he stood was
rocky and desolate. The green grew brighter every moment, and as it did
so a faint, transparent blood-red mingled with, but did not mitigate, the
blackness of the sky overhead and the rocky desolations about him.
Having regard to what follows, I am inclined to think that that redness
may have been an optical effect due to contrast. Something black fluttered
momentarily against the livid yellow-green of the lower sky, and then the
thin and penetrating voice of a bell rose out of the black gulf below him.
An oppressive expectation grew with the growing light.

It is probable that an hour or more elapsed while he sat there, the
strange green light growing brighter every moment, and spreading slowly,
in flamboyant fingers, upward towards the zenith. As it grew, the spectral
vision of *our* world became relatively or absolutely fainter. Probably both,
for the time must have been about that of our earthly sunset. So far as his
vision of our world went, Plattner, by his few steps downhill, had passed
through the floor of the classroom, and was now, it seemed, sitting in
mid-air in the larger schoolroom downstairs. He saw the boarders dis-

tinctly, but much more faintly than he had seen Lidgett. They were preparing their evening tasks, and he noticed with interest that several were cheating with their Euclid riders by means of a crib, a complication whose existence he had hitherto never suspected. As the time passed they faded steadily, as steadily as the light of the green dawn increased.

Looking down into the valley, he saw that the light had crept far down its rocky sides, and that the profound blackness of the abyss was now broken by a minute green glow, like the light of a glow-worm. And almost immediately the limb of a huge heavenly body of blazing green rose over the basaltic undulations of the distant hills, and the monstrous hill masses about him came out gaunt and desolate, in green light and deep, ruddy black shadows. He became aware of a vast number of ball-shaped objects drifting as thistledown drifts over the high ground. There were none of these nearer to him than the opposite side of the gorge. The bell below twanged quicker and quicker, with something like impatient insistence, and several lights moved hither and thither. The boys at work at their desks were now almost imperceptibly faint.

This extinction of our world, when the green sun of this other universe rose, is a curious point upon which Plattner insists. During the Other-World night it is difficult to move about, on account of the vividness with which the things of this world are visible. It becomes a riddle to explain why, if this is the case, we in this world catch no glimpse of the Other-World. It is due, perhaps, to the comparatively vivid illumination of this world of ours. Plattner describes the midday of the Other-World, at its brightest, as not being nearly so bright as this world at full moon, while its night is profoundly black. Consequently, the amount of light, even in an ordinary dark room, is sufficient to render the things of the Other-World invisible, on the same principle that faint phosphorescence is only visible in the profoundest darkness. I have tried, since he told me his story, to see something of the Other-World by sitting for a long space in a photographer's darkroom at night. I have certainly seen indistinctly the form of greenish slopes and rocks, but only, I must admit, very indistinctly indeed. The reader may possibly be more successful. Plattner tells me that since his return he has seen and recognized places in the Other-World in his dreams, but this is probably due to his memory of these scenes. It seems quite possible that people with unusually keen eyesight may occasionally catch a glimpse of this strange Other-World about us.

However, this is a digression. As the green sun rose, a long street of black buildings became perceptible though only darkly and indistinctly, in the gorge, and, after some hesitation, Plattner began to clamber down the precipitous descent towards them. The descent was long and exceedingly tedious, being so not only by the extraordinary steepness, but also by reason of the looseness of the boulders with which the whole face of the hill was strewn. The noise of his descent - now and then his heels struck fire from the rocks - seemed now the only sound in the universe, for the beating of the bell had ceased. As he drew nearer he perceived that the various edifices had a singular resemblance to tombs and mausoleums and monuments, saving only that they were all uniformly black instead of being white as most sepulchres are. And then he saw, crowding out of the largest building, very much as people disperse from church, a number of pallid, rounded, pale-green figures. These scattered in several directions about the broad street of the place, some going through side alleys and reappearing upon the steepness of the hill, others entering some of the small black buildings which lined the way.

At the sight of these things drifting up towards him, Plattner stopped, staring. They were not walking, they were indeed limbless; and they had the appearance of human heads beneath which a tadpolelike body swung. He was too astonished at their strangeness, too full indeed of strangeness, to be seriously alarmed by them. They drove towards him, in front of the chill wind that was blowing uphill, much as soap-bubbles drive before a draught. And as he looked at the nearest of those approaching, he saw it was indeed a human head, albeit with singularly large eyes, and wearing such an expression of distress and anguish as he had never seen before upon mortal countenance. He was surprised to find that it did not turn to regard him, but seemed to be watching and following some unseen moving thing. For a moment he was puzzled, and then it occurred to him that this creature was watching with its enormous eyes something that was happening in the world he had just left. Nearer it came, and nearer, and he was too astonished to cry out. It made a very faint fretting sound as it came close to him. Then it struck his face with a gentle pat - its touch was very cold - and drove past him, and upward towards the crest of the hill.

An extraordinary conviction flashed across Plattner's mind that this head had a strong likeness to Lidgett. Then he turned his attention to the other heads that were now swarming thickly up the hillside. None made the slightest sign of recognition. One or two, indeed, came close to his head and almost followed the example of the first, but he dodged convulsively out of the way. Upon most of them he saw the same expression of unavailing regret that he had seen upon the first, and heard the same faint sounds of wretchedness from them. One or two wept, and one rolling swiftly uphill wore an expression of diabolical rage. But others were cold, and several had a look of gratified interest in their eyes. One, at least, was almost in an ecstasy of happiness. Plattner does not remember that he recognized any more likenesses in those he saw at this time.

For several hours, perhaps, Plattner watched these strange things dispersing themselves over the hills, and not till long after they had ceased to issue from the clustering black buildings in the gorge did he resume his downward climb. The darkness about him increased so much that he had a difficulty in stepping true. Overhead the sky was now a bright pale green. He felt neither hunger nor thirst. Later, when he did, he found a chilly stream running down the centre of the gorge, and the rare moss upon the boulders, when he tried it at last in desperation, was good to eat.

He groped about among the tombs that ran down the gorge, seeking vaguely for some clue to these inexplicable things. After a long time he came to the entrance of the big mausoleumlike building from which the heads had issued. In this he found a group of green lights burning upon a kind of basaltic altar, and a bell-rope from a belfry overhead hanging down into the centre of the place. Round the wall ran a lettering of fire in a character unknown to him. While he was still wondering at the purport of these things, he heard the receding tramp of heavy feet echoing far down the street. He ran out into the darkness again, but he could see nothing. He had a mind to pull the bell-rope, and finally decided to follow the footsteps. But although he ran far, he never overtook them; and his shouting was of no avail. The gorge seemed to extend an interminable distance. It was as dark as earthly starlight throughout its length, while the ghastly green day lay along the upper edge of its precipices. There were none of the heads, now, below. They were all, it seemed, busily occupied along the upper slopes. Looking up, he saw them drifting hither and thither, some hovering stationary, some flying swiftly through the air. It reminded him, he said, of 'big snowflakes'; only these were black and pale green.

In pursuing the firm, undeviating footsteps that he never overtook, in groping into new regions of this endless devil's dyke, in clambering up and down the pitiless heights, in wandering about the summits, and in watching the drifting faces, Plattner states that he spent the better part of seven or eight days. He did not keep count, he says. Though once or twice he found eyes watching him, he had word with no living soul. He slept among the rocks on the hillside. In the gorge things earthly were invisible, because, from the earthly standpoint, it was far underground. On the altitudes, so soon as the earthly day began, the world became visible to him. He found himself sometimes stumbling over the dark green rocks, or arresting himself on a precipitous brink, while all about him the green branches of the Sussexville lanes were swaying; or, again, he seemed to be walking through the Sussexville streets, or watching unseen the private business of some household. And then it was he discovered that to almost every human being in our world there pertained some of these drifting heads; that everyone in the world is watched intermittently by these helpless disembodiments.

What are they - these Watchers of the Living? Plattner never learned. But two that presently found and followed him were like his childhood's memory of his father and mother. Now and then other faces turned their eyes upon him; eyes like those of dead people who had swayed him, or injured him, or helped him in his youth and manhood. Whenever they looked at him, Plattner was overcome with a strange sense of responsibility. To his mother he ventured to speak; but she made no answer. She looked sadly, steadfastly, and tenderly - a little reproachfully, too, it seemed - into his eyes.

He simply tells this story: he does not endeavour to explain. We are left to surmise who these Watchers of the Living may be, or, if they are indeed the Dead, why they should so closely and passionately watch a world they have left for ever. It may be - indeed to my mind it seems just - that, when our life has closed, when evil or good is no longer a choice for us, we may still have to witness the working out of the train of consequences we have laid. If human souls continue after death, then surely human interests continue after death. But that is merely my own guess at the meaning of the things seen. Plattner offers no interpretation, for none was given him. It is well the reader should understand this clearly. Day after day, with his head reeling, he wandered about this green-lit world outside the world, weary and, towards the end, weak and hungry. By day - by our earthly day, that is - the ghostly vision of the old familiar scenery of Sussexville, all about him, irked and worried him. He could not see where to put his feet, and ever and again with a chilly touch one of these Watching Souls would come against his face. And after dark the multitudes of these Watchers about him, and their intent distress, confused his mind beyond describing. A great longing to return to the earthly life that was so near and yet so remote consumed him. The unearthliness of things about him produced a positively painful mental distress. He was worried beyond describing by his own particular followers. He would shout at them to desist from staring at him, scold at them, hurry away from them. They were always mute and intent. Run as he might over the uneven ground, they followed his destinies.

On the ninth day, towards evening, Plattner heard the invisible footsteps approaching, far away down the gorge. He was then wandering over the broad crest of the same hill upon which he had fallen in his entry into this strange Other-World of his. He turned to hurry down into the gorge, feeling his way hastily, and was arrested by the sight of the thing that was happening in a room in a back street near the school. Both of the people in the room he knew by sight. The windows were open, the blinds up, and the setting sun shone clearly into it, so that it came out quite brightly at first, a vivid oblong of room, lying like a magic-lantern picture upon the black landscape and the vivid green dawn. In addition to the sunlight, a candle had just been lit in the room.

On the bed lay a lank man, his ghastly white face terrible upon the tumbled pillow. His clenched hands were raised above his head. A little table beside the bed carried a few medicine bottles, some toast and water, and an empty glass. Every now and then the lank man's lips fell apart, to indicate a word he could not articulate. But the woman did not notice that he wanted anything, because she was busy turning out papers from an old-fashioned bureau in the opposite corner of the room. At first the picture was very vivid indeed, but as the green dawn behind it grew brighter and brighter, so it became fainter and more and more transparent.

As the echoing footsteps paced nearer and nearer, those footsteps that sound so loud in that Other-World and come so silently in this, Plattner perceived about him a great multitude of dim faces gathering together out of the darkness and watching the two people in the room. Never before had he seen so many of the Watchers of the Living. A multitude had eyes only for the sufferer in the room, another multitude, in infinite anguish, watched the woman as she hunted with greedy eyes for something she could not find. They crowded about Plattner, they came across his sight and buffeted his face, the noise of their unavailing regrets was all about him. He saw clearly only now and then. At other times the pictures quivered dimly, through the veil of green reflections upon their movements. In the room it must have been very still, and Plattner says the candle flame streamed up into a perfectly vertical line of smoke, but in his ears each footfall and its echoes beat like a clap of thunder. And the faces! Two more particularly, near the woman's; one a woman's also, white and clear-featured, a face which might have once been cold and hard but which was now softened by the touch of a wisdom strange to earth. The other might have been the woman's father. Both were evidently absorbed in the contemplation of some act of hateful meanness, so it seemed, which they could no longer guard against and prevent. Behind were others, teachers it may be who had taught ill, friends whose influence had failed. And over the man, too - a multitude, but none that seemed to be parents or teachers! Faces that might once have been coarse, now purged to strength by sorrow! And in the forefront one face, a girlish one, neither angry nor remorseful but merely patient and weary, and, as it seemed to Plattner, waiting for relief. His powers of description failed him at the memory of this multitude of ghastly countenances. They gathered on the stroke of the bell. He saw them all in the space of a second. It would seem that he was so worked upon by his excitement that quite involuntarily his restless fingers took the bottle of green powder out of his pocket and held it before him. But he does not remember that.

Abruptly the footsteps ceased. He waited for the next and there was silence, and then suddenly, cutting through the unexpected stillness like a keen, thin blade, came the first stroke of the bell. At that the multitudinous faces swayed to and fro, and a louder crying began all about him. The woman did not hear; she was burning something now in the candle flame. At the second stroke everything grew dim, and a breath of wind, icy cold, blew through the host of watchers. They swirled about him like an eddy of dead leaves in the spring, and at the third stroke something was extended through them to the bed. You have heard of a beam of light. This was like a beam of darkness, and looking again at it, Plattner saw that it was a shadowy arm and hand.

The green sun was now topping the black desolations of the horizon, and the vision of the room was very faint. Plattner could see that the white of the bed struggled, and was convulsed; and that the woman looked round her over her shoulder at it, startled.

The cloud of watchers lifted high like a puff of green dust before the wind, and swept swiftly downward towards the temple in the gorge. Then suddenly Plattner understood the meaning of the shadowy black arm that stretched across his shoulder and clutched its prey. He did not dare turn his head to see the Shadow behind the arm. With a violent effort, and covering his eyes, he set himself to run, made perhaps twenty strides, then slipped on a boulder and fell. He fell forward on his hands; and the bottle smashed and exploded as he touched the ground.

In another moment he found himself, stunned and bleeding, sitting face to face with Lidgett in the old walled garden behind the school.

There the story of Plattner's experiences ends. I have resisted, I believe successfully, the natural disposition of a writer of fiction to dress up incidents of this sort. I have told the thing as far as possible in the order in which Plattner told it to me. I have carefully avoided any attempt at style, effect, or construction. It would have been easy, for instance, to have worked the scene of the death-bed into a kind of plot in which Plattner might have been involved. But quite apart from the objectionableness of falsifying a most extraordinary true story, such trite devices would spoil, to my mind, the peculiar effect of this dark world, with its livid green illuminations and its drifting Watchers of the Living, which, unseen and unapproachable to us, is yet lying all about us.

It remains to add, that a death did actually occur in Vincent Terrace, just beyond the school garden, and, so far as can be proved, at the moment of Plattner's return. Deceased was a rate-collector and insurance agent. His widow, who was much younger than himself, married last month a Mr Whymper, a veterinary surgeon of Allbeeding. As the portion of this story given here has in various forms circulated orally in Sussexville, she has consented to my use of her name, on condition that I make it distinctly known that she emphatically contradicts every detail of Plattner's account of her husband's last moments. She burnt no will, she says, although Plattner never accused her of doing so; her husband made but one will, and that just after their marriage. Certainly, from a man who had never seen it, Plattner's account of the furniture of the room was curiously accurate.

One other thing, even at the risk of an irksome repetition, I must insist upon lest I seem to favour the credulous superstitious view. Plattner's absence from the world for nine days is, I think, proved. But that does not prove his story. It is quite conceivable that even outside space hallucinations may be possible. That, at least, the reader must bear distinctly in mind.

# The Mark Of The Beast
## Rudyard Kipling

**Rudyard Kipling   1865 - 1936:** Kipling wrote both verse and prose that won popular acclaim. He also won acceptance in literary and academic circles when he received the Nobel Prize for Literature and several honorary degrees. Kipling wrote such well-known works as *Kim* and *The Jungle Book* which make up only a small portion of the writing produced during his prolific career.

Kipling was born in India but was educated at the United Services College in England where he began to write actively. He contributed to the school paper and did in fact become a journalist upon his eventual return to India.

He experienced the social forces of industrialism and imperialism throughout his periods of world travel and service in the army. These appear in various forms in his fiction, which was not immediately accepted by publishers in America and England because his settings were deemed too exotic. The themes of his work also often ran counter to the sensibilities of his time. He portrayed rough characters and used language that was often less than genteel. The initial rejection of his subject matter, however, did not discourage his literary efforts.

EAST OF SUEZ, some hold, the direct control of Providence ceases; Man being there handed over to the power of the Gods and Devils of Asia, and the Church of England Providence only exercising an occasional and modified supervision in the case of Englishmen.

This theory accounts for some of the more unnecessary horrors of life in India: it may be stretched to explain my story.

My friend Strickland of the Police, who knows as much of natives of India as is good for any man, can bear witness to the facts of the case. Dumoise, our doctor, also saw what Strickland and I saw. The inference which he drew from the evidence was entirely incorrect. He is dead now; he died in a rather curious manner, which has been elsewhere described.

When Fleete came to India he owned a little money and some land in the Himalayas, near a place called Dharmsala. Both properties had been left him by an uncle, and he came out to finance them. He was a big, heavy, genial, and inoffensive man. His knowledge of natives was, of course, limited, and he complained of the difficulties of the language.

He rode in from his place in the hills to spend New Year in the station, and he stayed with Strickland. On New Year's Eve there was a big dinner at the club, and the night was excusably wet. When men foregather from the uttermost ends of the Empire, they have a right to be riotous. The Frontier had sent down a contingent o' Catch-'em-Alive-O's who had not seen twenty white faces for a year, and were used to ride fifteen miles to dinner at the next Fort at the risk of a Khyberee bullet where their drinks should lie. They profited by their new security, for they tried to play pool with a curled-up hedge-hog found in the garden, and one of them carried the marker round the room in his teeth. Half a dozen planters had come in from the south and were talking-"horse" to the Biggest Liar in Asia, who was trying to cap all their stories at once. Everybody was there, and there was a general closing up of ranks and taking stock of our losses in dead or disabled that had fallen during the past year. It was a very wet night, and I remember that we sang "Auld Lang Syne" with our feet in the Polo Championship Cup, and our heads among the stars, and swore that we were all dear friends. Then some of us went away and annexed Burma, and some tried to open up the Soudan and were opened up by Fuzzies in that cruel scrub outside Suakim, and some found stars and medals, and some were married, which was bad, and some did other things which were worse, and the others of us stayed in our chains and strove to make money on insufficient experiences.

Fleete began the night with sherry and bitters, drank champagne steadily up to dessert, then raw, rasping Capri with all the strength of whiskey, took Benedictine with his coffee, four or five whiskies and sodas to improve his pool strokes, beer and bones at half-past two, winding up with old brandy. Consequently, when he came out, at half past three in the morning, into fourteen degrees of frost, he was very angry with his horse for coughing, and tried to leap-frog into the saddle. The horse broke away and went to his stables; so Strickland and I formed a Guard of Dishonor to take Fleete home.

Our road lay through the bazaar, close to a little temple of Hanuman, the Monkey-god, who is a leading divinity worthy of respect. All gods have good points, just as have all priests. Personally, I attach much importance to Hanuman, and am kind to his people -- the great grey apes of the hills. One never knows when one may want a friend.

There was a light in the temple, and as we passed, we could hear voices of men chanting hymns. In a native temple, the priests rise at all hours of the night to do honor to their god. Before we could stop him, Fleete dashed up the steps, patted two priests on the back, and was gravely grinding the ashes of his cigar-butt into the forehead of the red, stone image of Hanuman. Strickland tried to drag him out, but he sat down and said solemnly:

"Shee that? 'Mark of the B-- beasht! *I* made it. Ishn't it fine?"

In half a minute the temple was alive and noisy, and Strickland, who knew what came of polluting gods, said that things might occur. He, by virtue of his official position, long residence in the country, and weakness for going among the natives, was known to the priests and he felt unhappy. Fleete sat on the ground and refused to move. He said that "good old Hanuman" made a very soft pillow.

Then, without any warning, a Silver Man came out of a recess behind the image of the god. He was perfectly naked in that bitter, bitter cold, and his body shone like frosted silver, for he was what the Bible calls "a leper as white as snow." Also he lad no face, because he was a leper of some years' standing, and his disease was heavy upon him. We two stooped to haul Fleete up, and the temple was filling and filling with folk who seemed to spring from the earth, when the Silver Man ran in under our arms, making a noise exactly like the mewing of an otter, caught Fleete round the body and dropped his head on Fleete's breast before we could wrench him away. Then he retired to a corner and sat mewing while the crowd blocked all the doors.

The priests were very angry until the Silver Man touched Fleete. That nuzzling seemed to sober them.

At the end of a few minutes' silence one of the priests came to Strickland and said, in perfect English, "Take your friend away. He has done with Hanuman, but Hanuman has not done with him." The crowd gave room and we carried Fleete into the road.

Strickland was very angry. He said that we might all three have been knifed, and that Fleete should thank his stars that he had escaped without injury.

Fleete thanked no one. He said that he wanted to go to bed. He was gorgeously drunk.

We moved on. Strickland silent and wrathful, until Fleete was taken with violent shivering fits and sweating. He said that the smells of the bazaar were overpowering, and he wondered why slaughter-houses were permitted so near English residences. "Can't you smell the blood?" said Fleete.

We put him to bed at last, just as the dawn was breaking, and Strickland invited me to have another whisky and soda. While we were drinking he talked of the trouble in the temple, and admitted that it baffled him completely. Strickland hates being mystified by natives, because his business in life is to overmatch them with their own weapons. He has not yet succeeded in doing this, but in fifteen or twenty years he will have made some small progress.

"They should have mauled us," he said, "instead of mewing at us. I wonder what they meant. I don't like it one little bit."

I said that the Managing Committee of the temple would in all probability bring a criminal action against us for insulting their religion. There was a section of the Indian Penal Code which exactly met Fleete's offence. Strickland said he only hoped and prayed that they would do this. Before I left I looked into Fleete's room, and saw him lying on his right side, scratching his left breast. Then I went to bed cold, depressed, and unhappy, at seven o'clock in the morning.

At one o'clock I rode over to Strickland's house to inquire after Fleete's head. I imagined that it would be a sore one. Fleete was breakfasting and seemed unwell. His temper was gone, for he was abusing the cook for not supplying him with an underdone chop. A man who can eat raw meat after a wet night is a curiosity. I told Fleete this and he laughed.

"You breed queer mosquitoes in these parts," he said. "I've been bitten to pieces, but only in one place."

"Let's have a look at the bite," said Strickland. "It may have gone down since this morning."

While the chops were being cooked, Fleete opened his shirt and showed us, just over his left breast, a mark, the perfect double of the black rosettes -- the five or six irregular blotches arranged in a circle -- on a leopard's hide. Strickland looked and said, "It was only pink this morning. It's grown black now."

Fleete ran to a glass.

"By Jove!" he said, "this is nasty. What is it?"

We could not answer. Here the chops came in, all red and juicy, and Fleete bolted three in a most offensive manner. He ate on his right grinders only, and threw his head over his right shoulder as he snapped the meat. When he had finished, it struck him that he had been behaving strangely, for he said, apologetically, "I don't think I ever felt so hungry in my life. I've bolted like an ostrich."

After breakfast Strickland said to me, "Don't go. Stay here, and stay for the night."

Seeing that my house was not three miles from Strickland's, this request was absurd. But Strickland insisted, and was going to say something when Fleete interrupted by declaring in a shame-faced way that he felt hungry again. Strickland sent a man to my house to fetch over my bedding and a horse, and we three went down to Strickland's stables to pass the hours until it was time to go out for a ride. The man who has a weakness for horses never wearies of inspecting them; and when two men are killing time in this way they gather knowledge and lies the one from the other.

There were five horses in the stables, and I shall never forget the scene as we tried to look them over. They seemed to have gone mad. They reared and screamed and nearly tore up their pickets; they sweated and shivered and lathered and were distraught with fear. Strickland's horses used to know him as well as his dogs; which made the matter more curious. We left the stable for fear of the brutes throwing themselves in their panic. Then Strickland turned back and called me. The horses were still frightened, but they let us "gentle" and make much of them, and put their heads in our bosoms.

"They aren't afraid of us," said Strickland. "D' you know, I'd give three months' pay if Outrage here could talk."

But Outrage was dumb, and could only cuddle up to his master and blow out his nostrils, as is the custom of horses when they wish to explain things but can't. Fleete came up when we were in the stalls, and as soon as the horses saw him, their fright broke out afresh. It was all that we could do to escape from the place unkicked. Strickland said, "They don't seem to love you, Fleete."

"Nonsense," said Fleete; "my mare will follow me like a dog." He went to her; she was in a loose-box; but as he slipped the bars she plunged, knocked him down, and broke away into the garden. I laughed, but Strickland was not amused. He took his moustache in both fists and pulled at it till it nearly came out. Fleete, instead of going off to chase his property, yawned, saying that he felt sleepy. He went to the house to lie down, which was a foolish way of spending New Year's Day.

Strickland sat with me in the stables and asked if I had noticed anything peculiar in Fleete's manner. I said that he ate his food like a beast; but that this might have been the result of living alone in the hills out of the reach of society as refined and elevating as ours for instance. Strickland was not amused. I do not think that he listened to me, for his next sentence referred to the mark on Fleete's breast, and I said that it might have been caused by blister-flies, or that it was possibly a birthmark newly born and now visible for the first time. We both agreed that it was unpleasant to look at, and Strickland found occasion to say that I was a fool.

"I can't tell you what I think now," said he, "because you would call me a madman; but you must stay with me for the next few days, if you can. I want you to watch Fleete, but don't tell me what you think till I have made up my mind."

"But I am dining out to-night," I said.

"So am I," said Strickland, "and so is Fleete. At least if he doesn't change his mind."

We walked about the garden smoking, but saying nothing -- because we were friends, and talking spoils good tobacco -- till our pipes were out. Then we went to wake up Fleete. He was wide awake and fidgeting about his room.

"I say, I want some more chops," he said. "Can I get them?"

We laughed and said, "Go and change. The ponies will be round in a minute."

"All right," said Fleete. "I'll go when I get the chops -- underdone ones, mind."

He seemed to be quite in earnest. It was four o'clock, and we had had breakfast at one; still, for a long time, he demanded those underdone chops. Then he changed into riding clothes and went out into the veranda. His pony -- the mare had not been caught -- would not let him come near. All three horses were unmanageable -- mad with fear -- and finally Fleete said that he would stay at home and get something to eat. Strickland and I rode out wondering. As we passed the temple of Hanuman, the Silver Man came out and mewed at us.

"He is not one of the regular priests of the temple," said Strickland. "I think I should peculiarly like to lay my hands on him."

There was no spring in our gallop on the race-course that evening. The horses were stale, and moved as though they had been ridden out.

"The fright after breakfast has been too much for them," said Strickland.

That was the only remark he made through the remainder of the ride. Once or twice I think he swore to himself; but that did not count.

We came back in the dark at seven o'clock, and saw that there were no lights in the bungalow. "Careless ruffians my servants are!" said Strickland.

My horse reared at something on the carriage drive, and Fleete stood up under its nose.

"What are you doing, grovelling about the garden?" said Strickland.

But both horses bolted and nearly threw us. We dismounted by the stables and returned to Fleete, who was on his hands and knees under the orange-bushes.

"What the devil's wrong with you?" said Strickland.

"Nothing, nothing in the world," said Fleete, speaking very quickly and thickly. "I've been gardening -- botanizing you know. The smell of the earth is delightful. I think I'm going for a walk -- a long walk -- all night."

Then I saw that there was something excessively out of order somewhere, and I said to Strickland, "I am not dining out."

"Bless you!" said Strickland. "Here, Fleete, get up. You'll catch fever there. Come in to dinner and let's have the lamps lit. We'll all dine at home."

Fleete stood up unwillingly, and said, "No lamps--no lamps. It's much nicer here. Let's dine outside and have some more chops--lots of 'em and underdone -- bloody ones with gristle."

Now a December evening in Northern India is bitterly cold, and Fleete's suggestion was that of a maniac.

"Come in," said Strickland, sternly. "Come in at once."

Fleete came, and when the lamps were brought, we saw that he was literally plastered with dirt from head to foot. He must have been rolling in the garden. He shrank from the light and went to his room. His eyes were horrible to look at. There was a green light behind them, not in them, if you understand, and the man's lower lip hung down.

Strickland said, "There is going to be trouble--big trouble--to-night. Don't you change your riding-things."

We waited and waited for Fleete's re-appearance, and ordered dinner in the meantime. We could hear him moving about his own room, but there was no light there. Presently from the room came the long-drawn howl of a wolf.

People write and talk lightly of blood running cold and hair standing up and things of that kind. Both sensations are too horrible to be trifled with. My heart stopped as though a knife had been driven through it, and Strickland turned as white as the table-cloth.

The howl was repeated, and was answered by another howl far across the fields.

That set the gilded roof on the horror. Strickland dashed into Fleet's room. I followed, and we saw Fleete getting out of the window. He made beast-noises in the back of his throat. He could not answer us when we shouted at him. He spat.

I don't quite remember what followed, but I think that Strickland must have stunned him with the long boot-jack or else I should never have been able to sit on his chest. Fleete could not speak, he could only snarl, and his snarls were those of a wolf, not of a man. The human spirit must have been giving way all day and have died out with the twilight. We were dealing with a beast that had once been Fleete.

The affair was beyond any human and rational experience. I tried to say "Hydrophobia," but the word wouldn't come, because I knew that I was lying.

We bound this beast with leather thongs of the punkah-rope, and tied its thumbs and big toes together, and gagged it with a shoe-horn, which makes a very efficient gag if you know how to arrange it. Then we carried it into the dining-room, and sent a man to Dumoise, the doctor, telling him to come over at once. After we had despatched the messenger and were drawing breath, Strickland said, "It's no good. This isn't any doctor's work." I, also, knew that he spoke the truth.

The beast's head was free, and it threw it about from side to side. Any one entering the room would have believed that we were curing a wolf's pelt. That was the most loathsome accessory of all.

Strickland sat with his chin in the heel of his fist, watching the beast as it wriggled on the ground, but saying nothing. The shirt had been torn open in the scuffle and showed the black rosette mark on the left breast. It stood out like a blister.

In the silence of the watching we heard something without mewing like a she-otter. We both rose to our feet, and, I answer for myself, not Strickland, felt sick--actually and physically sick. We told each other, as did the men in Pinafore, that it was the cat.

Dumoise arrived, and I never saw a little man so unprofessionally shocked. He said that it was a heart-rending case of hydrophobia, and that nothing could be done. At least any palliative measures would only prolong the agony. The beast was foaming at the mouth. Fleete, as we told Dumoise, had been bitten by dogs once or twice. Any man who keeps half a dozen terriers must expect a nip now and again. Dumoise could offer no help. He could only certify that Fleete was dying of hydrophobia. The beast was then howling, for it had managed to spit out the shoe-horn. Dumoise said that he would be ready to certify to the cause of death, and that the end was certain. He was a good little man, and he offered to remain with us; but Strickland refused the kindness. He did not wish to poison Dumoise's New Year. He would only ask him not to give the real cause of Fleete's death to the public.

So Dumoise left, deeply agitated; and as soon as the noise of the cart wheels had died away, Strickland told me, in a whisper, his suspicions. They were so wildly improbable that he dared not say them out aloud; and I, who entertained all Strickland's beliefs, was so ashamed of owning to them that I pretended to disbelieve.

"Even if the Silver Man had bewitched Fleete for polluting the image of Hanuman, the punishment could not have fallen so quickly."

As I was whispering this the cry outside the house rose again, and the beast fell into a fresh paroxysm of struggling till we were afraid that the thongs that held it would give way.

"Watch!" said Strickland. "If this happens six times I shall take the law into my own hands. I order you to help me."

He went into his room and came out in a few minutes with the barrels of an old shot-gun, a piece of fishing-line, some thick cord, and his heavy wooden bedstead. I reported that the convulsions had followed the cry by two seconds in each case, and the beast seemed perceptibly weaker.

Strickland muttered, "But he can't take away the life! He can't take away the life!"

I said, though I knew that I was arguing against myself, "It may be a cat. It must be a cat. If the Silver Man is responsible, why does he dare to come here?"

Strickland arranged the wood on the hearth, put the gun-barrels into the glow of the fire, spread the twine on the table and broke a walking stick in two. There was one yard of fishing line, gut, lapped with wire, such as is used for *mahseer-fishing*, and he tied the two ends together in a loop.

Then he said, "How can we catch him? He must be taken alive and unhurt."

I said that we must trust in Providence, and go out softly with polo-sticks into the shrubbery at the front of the house. The man or animal that made the cry was evidently moving round the house as regularly as a night-watchman. We could wait in the bushes till he came by and knock him over.

Strickland accepted this suggestion, and we slipped out from a bathroom window into the front veranda and then across the carriage drive into the bushes. In the moonlight we could see the leper coming round the corner of the house. He was perfectly naked, and from time to time mewed and stopped to dance with his shadow. It was an unattractive sight, and thinking of poor Fleete, brought to such degradation by so foul a creature, I put away all my doubts and resolved to help Strickland from the heated gun-barrels to the loop of twine--from the loins to the head and back again--with all tortures that might be needful.

The leper halted in the front porch for a moment and we jumped out on him with the sticks. He was wonderfully strong, and we were afraid that he might escape or be fatally injured before we caught him. We had an idea that lepers were frail creatures, but this proved to be incorrect. Strickland knocked his legs from under him and I put my foot on his neck. He mewed hideously, and even through my riding-boots I could feel that his flesh was not the flesh of a clean man.

He struck at us with his hand and feet-stumps. We looped the lash of a dog-whip round him, under the armpits, and dragged him backward into the hall and so into the dining-room where the beast lay. There we tied him with trunkstraps. He made no attempt to escape, but mewed.

When we confronted him with the beast the scene was beyond description. The beast doubled backward into a bow as though he had been poisoned with strychnine, and moaned in the most pitiable fashion. Several other things happened also, but they cannot be put down here.

"I think I was right," said Strickland. "Now we will ask him to cure this case."

But the leper only mewed. Strickland wrapped a towel round his hand and took the gun-barrels out of the fire. I put the half of the broken walking stick through the loop of the fishing-line and buckled the leper comfortably to Strickland's bedstead. I understood then how men and women and little children can endure to see awitch burned alive; for the beast was moaning on the floor, and though the Silver Man had no face, you could see horrible feelings passing through the slab that took its place, exactly as waves of heat play across red-hot iron--gun-barrels for instance.

Strickland shaded his eyes with his hands for a moment and we got to work. This part is not to be printed.

The dawn was beginning to break when the leper spoke. His mewings had not been satisfactory up to that point. The beast had fainted from exhaustion and the house was very still. We unstrapped the leper and told him to take away the evil spirit. He crawled to the beast and laid his hand upon the left breast. That was all. Then he fell face down and whined, drawing in his breath as he did so.

We watched the face of the beast, and saw the soul of Fleet coming back into the eyes. Then a sweat broke out on the forehead and the eyes -- they were human eyes -- closed. We waited for an hour but Fleete still slept. We carried him to his room and bade the leper go, giving him the bedstead, and the sheet on the bedstead to cover his nakedness, the gloves and the towels with which we had touched him, and the whip that had been hooked round his body. He put the sheet about him and went out into the early morning without speaking or mewing.

Strickland wiped his face and sat down. A night-gong, far away in the city, made seven o'clock.

"Exactly four-and-twenty hours!" said Strickland. "And I've done enough to ensure my dismissal from the service, besides permanent quarters in a lunatic asylum. Do you believe that we are awake?"

The red-hot gun-barrel had fallen on the floor and was singeing the carpet. The smell was entirely real.

That morning at eleven we two together went to wake up Fleete. We looked and saw that the black leopard-rosette on his chest had disappeared. He was very drowsy and tired, but as soon as he saw us, he said, "Oh! Confound you fellows. Happy New Year to you. Never mix your liquors. I'm nearly dead."

"Thanks for your kindness, but you're over time," said Strickland. "To-day is the morning of the second. You've slept the clock round with a vengeance."

The door opened, and little Dumoise put his head in. He had come on foot, and fancied that we were laying out Fleete.

"I've brought a nurse," said Dumoise. "I suppose that she can come in for...what is necessary."

"By all means," said Fleete, cheerily, sitting up in bed. "Bring on your nurses."

Dumoise was dumb. Strickland led him out and explained that there must have been a mistake in the diagnosis. Dumoise remained dumb and left the house hastily. He considered that his professional reputation had been injured, and was inclined to make a personal matter of the recovery. Strickland went out too. When he came back, he said that he had been to call on the Temple of Hanuman to offer redress for the pollution of the god, and had been solemnly assured that no white man had ever touched the idol and that he was an incarnation of all the virtues laboring under a delusion. "What do you think?" said Strickland.

"I said, "'There are more things....'"

But Strickland hates that quotation. He says that I have worn it threadbare.

One other curious thing happened which frightened me as much as anything in all the night's work. When Fleete was dressed he came into the dining-room and sniffed. He had a quaint trick of moving his nose when he sniffed. "Horrid doggy smell, here," said he. "You should really keep those terriers of yours in better order. Try sulphur, Strick."

But Strickland did not answer. He caught hold of the back of a chair, and, without warning, went into an amazing fit of hysterics. It is terrible to see a strong man overtaken with hysteria. Then it struck me that we had fought with Fleete's soul with the Silver Man in that room, and had disgraced ourselves as Englishmen forever, and I laughed and gasped and gurgled just as shamefully as Strickland, while Fleete thought that we had both gone mad. We never told him what we had done.

Some years later, when Strickland had married and was a church-going member of society for his wife's sake, we reviewed the incident dispassionately,s and Strickland suggested that I should put it before the public.

I cannot myself see that this step is likely to clear up the mystery; because, in the first place, no one will believe a rather unpleasant story, and, in the second, it is well known to every right-minded man that the gods of the heathen are stone and brass, and any attempt to deal with them otherwise is justly condemned.

# Index to Volumes I - IX

*A cumulative index to authors and stories*

# 366   The World's Best Short Stories